AMY S. KWEI

A CONCUBINE FOR THE FAMILY

A FAMILY SAGA IN CHINA

ISBN: 0981549918
ISBN 13: 9780981549910

Contents

Acknowledgment

I want to thank my two grandmothers, whose exemplary lives of virtuous living, in times of war and Diaspora, inspired this book. Thanks also to my mother's nursemaid, the many aunts and helpers in the house who told stories while they made dumplings or sat in sewing circles. They enriched my life.

I owe my undying gratitude to my husband Tom, (who will not receive a concubine from me) for his unfailing support — technical and emotional — in all the years of preparing for this book. Many thanks go to Dalia Geffen, Judith Neuman, Jane Rosenman, Cathy O'Connell, Sandra Chen, Marie Cantlon, Anna Fang, Sue Tatem, Zhou Xiofen, The Taconic Writers, The Tuesday Morning Writers, and the Aspen Tuesday evening writers. They offered constructive criticisms, encouragement and good fellowship. I specially appreciate the support of the Aspen Writers' Foundation.

Thanks also to Jonathan D. Spence, whose many books on China, especially The Search for Modern China, and The Chan's Great Continent, Edmund Clubb, Twentieth Century China, Hallett Abend's My Life in China (1926—1941), C.P. Fitzgerald's China—A Short Cultural History, and John King Fairbank's The United States and China, for much of the historical background. I owe my understanding on Chinese herbs and acupuncture to my friends, relatives and Alexander Macdonald and his book Acupuncture—From Ancient Art to Modern Medicine.

Author's Note

Language can be a window to the mind and heart of a culture. Unfortunately, translations do not always convey a people's zest and vibrancy. The Chinese often speak in metaphors, and their manner of expression reflects the vivid landscape of their culture. In order to retain the picturesque quality of the language, I have used many expressions literally. For instance, when a mother calls her child "my heart-and-liver," it is clear how precious the child is to her.

For thousands of years, countries surrounding China have borrowed from Chinese culture. On a visit to Kyoto, the cultural capital of Japan, one will see the finest examples of these: Chinese architecture, dwarf tree designs, bronze and porcelain ware, paintings on silk, calligraphy, origami and other features. The national costume of the Korean ladies today is in the style of fourteenth-century Chinese fashion. Whenever a meal is served in a Southeast Asian country, one will taste soy sauce, eat with chopsticks, and sample Chinese culinary touches. Cognizant of their great influence, the Chinese have fostered an ancient pride that is far more enduring than the twentieth century concepts of nationalism and patriotism. Many Chinese know that before the advent of the Westerners, they were never described as "primitive" or "underdeveloped." In fact, for millenniums, neighboring cultures in Asia recognized the "Middle Kingdom" as the center of the civilized world.

As a result of this perceived cultural supremacy, the Chinese language reflects an aristocratic pride. A person deprived of the old culture, whether Occidental or Oriental in origin, is considered a "barbarian." When the barbarians became terrifying, they were called "foreign devils." The "East Ocean Devils" were the Japanese; Westerners were the "West Ocean Devils."

Readers should keep in mind that the place of a Chinese in society is very much tied to his family. The word "individual" has connotations of selfishness and secretiveness. The word "independence" literally translates to "alone standing." To the Chinese, "one" is an unlucky number.

Chinese do not call each other by name except when addressing children, servants and others of lesser station. Relational address delineates their position in the family clan: e.g. "jei jei" for older sister, "dee dee" for younger brother, "jeo jeo" for mother's younger brother, "soo soo" for father's younger brother. Relationships are specified even to the point of identifying whether they are of paternal or maternal origin. Even when two people are not related, a relational appellation is added. Therefore, Peony calls Iris, "Iris-jei." It is also polite for husband and wife to address each other as brother and sister. Righteous Virtue calls Purple Jade, "Jade-mei." To avoid confusion, only the appellations for brothers and sisters are used in the book.

The author translated all the Chinese poems and songs. Some relational addresses, commonly used idiomatic expressions, popular philosophies, salient historical events, names, and places referred to in the story are clarified in the glossary.

I was born a blue-hearted baby. As a sickly child, I was given the gift of reading and listening. This novel is a fictional account based upon family history. The characters and their experiences are composites, drawn from stories I have heard. They are not intended to represent real people or events.

Since most of the story is set in 1937, I have rendered the Chinese names in the Wade-Giles system familiar at the time. The Pinyin system is used only for some famous people and a few places, such as Hangzhou and Beijing that have become popular tourist attractions on recent maps.

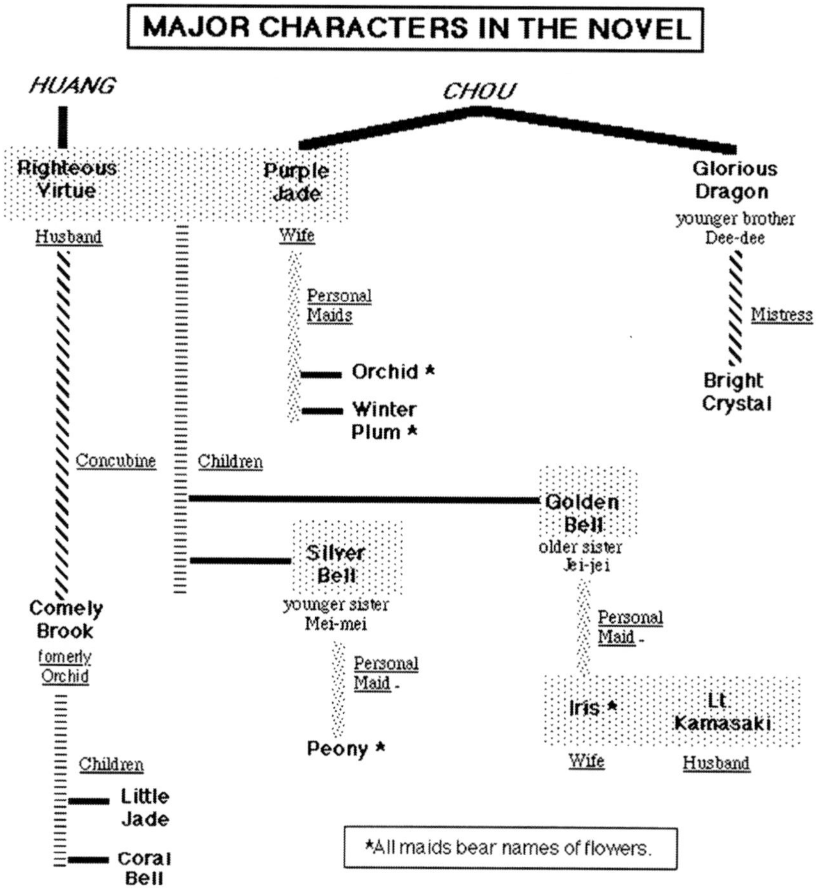
MAJOR CHARACTERS IN THE NOVEL
HUANG
CHOU
Righteous Virtue
Purple Jade
Glorious Dragon
younger brother
Dee-dee
Husband
Wife
Personal Maids
Mistress
Orchid *
Winter Plum *
Bright Crystal
Concubine
Children
Golden Bell
older sister
Jei-jei
Silver Bell
younger sister
Mei-mei
Comely Brook
fomerly Orchid
Personal Maid -
Personal Maid -
Iris *
Lt. Kamasaki
Peony *
Wife
Husband
Children
Little Jade
Coral Bell
*All maids bear names of flowers.

BOOK ONE

A Concubine for the Family

Chapter 1

Hangzhou, 1937

IT WAS EIGHT in the morning. A gentle breeze rustled the bamboo grove outside Purple Jade's window like ten thousand fans waving moist air into the room.

Rain is coming.

Purple Jade, lying on her rosewood four-poster bed, turned in the dark alcove to face the light. She waited for her personal maid.

Orchid came in carrying a basin of warm water and laid it beside her mistress's footstool. "Morning peace, *Tai-tai*."

"Orchid, have you eaten your morning rice?"

"Yes, *Tai-tai*." Orchid touched her mouth, deciding not to mention the uproar in the kitchen where all the servants were discussing the drowning of a girl in the river. To announce bad news first thing in the morning would mean bad luck for the rest of the day.

She pushed aside the embroidered silk panels hanging from the intricately carved wooden valence edging the canopy. With her other hand she led her mistress out of the enclosure.

Purple Jade leaned heavily on Orchid's arm as her foot, wrapped in silk bindings and stockings, touched the ground. She wobbled unsteadily toward her rosewood armchair.

A washcloth, a towel and a porcelain soap dish were assembled on the bedside table. Purple Jade sat expectantly as Orchid moved the basin of water closer. Her sure hands slipped off Purple Jade's silk night tunic and laid it on the bed. Lines of concentration etched Orchid's round, dewy face. She dipped the washcloth in the basin and lathered it. Then she gently rubbed her mistress's face, chest, breasts and armpits. She tackled each task like an artist and handled the details with care. The rustle of leaves outside the window accompanied the swish of bathwater as Orchid rinsed her mistress's supple upper body three times. At thirty-nine, Purple Jade's creamy skin was still unblemished. Her flesh shone like a silken chemise. Orchid did not seem to notice the sensual gleam. She had served her mistress since she was five years old and performed the same task for almost eighteen years. Orchid's experienced fingers dried Purple Jade with the towel and then dressed her in a fresh silk undershirt. She was now ready to wash her mistress's lower body.

The early morning light cast somber shadows on the walls. Purple Jade saw herself reflected in the mirror and turned away. Her inbred modesty forbade her to gaze at her naked and still sinuous torso, but she took note of her sagging breasts. She lowered her eyes. Her lips lifted to smile, and for one instant she beamed with pleasure at Orchid's gentle message and the clean, fresh feel of soft silk.

Purple Jade tilted her head toward the ceiling, examining the shifting shadows, while her maid helped her to stand. Orchid washed her hips, her legs and her private parts. She repeated the rinsing and drying routines and finally helped her mistress into fresh undergarments. She directed her mistress to sit, and then handed her her embroidery. She left to fetch hot water.

Although Orchid was not quite five feet tall, her big feet made a soft putt-putt sound as she walked in again with a pitcher of hot water. Carefully, she set it down. She emptied the bathwater outside the window, and refilled the basin from the pitcher.

Without a word, Orchid knelt to remove Purple Jade's silk socks and unwind the yards of silk bindings. A musty stench filled her nostrils and her nose twitched in spite of the familiar smell. Purple Jade's club-like feet were arched and small. The last two toes on each foot had been bent under the soles and the toe bones crushed when Purple Jade was only three years old.

Orchid placed the feet in the basin and Purple Jade sighed with relief.

"Sorry this is taking so long, *Tai-tai*. Everyone in the kitchen is talking about a body found in the river."

"The river brings such horrors!" Purple Jade's arched brows pulled her long eyes into dark pools of anxiety, distorting her oval face.

"Do you think the East Ocean Devils are killing people upstream?" Orchid asked.

"No, they have not occupied the land there." Purple Jade answered in a flat tone.

Anxiety about war hung like a shroud over Purple Jade. She was proud the Chinese had repelled several Japanese attacks on Shanghai but was still alarmed by reports of the enemy extending their control from Manchuria to the neighboring provinces and using local slave labor to cultivate opium on all the arable land. The dribble of news about cheap opium flooding all corners of China set her insides quivering. Now, even the poorest rickshaw puller could afford a smoke to soothe his aching muscles. She had warned her household staff to avoid the drug or to risk dismissal. Good news would not come. This drowned girl felt like the harbinger of more devastation. She took a deep breath. She must concentrate on her family affairs, and her words must sound casual. She proceeded to talk about her old pains — her bound feet.

"Ah, last night you left the bandages so loose, my feet felt like lost ships tossing in the ocean."

Orchid added more hot water to the bath. "Are your feet hurting you again? *Tai-tai*, in a few months you'll get used to the looser binding."

"No one calls them golden lilies anymore. Now they are only tiny feet, and worse than your big feet."

Orchid looked at her mistress; her round eyes glistened. She quickly lowered them. It would not do for her mistress to know that she pitied her. Gently, she massaged Purple Jade's feet.

"Li *tai-tai* told me that after soaking and loosening her bindings, she could wear the modern high-heeled shoes!" Purple Jade said. "I don't know how she can tolerate the pain."

"Today, I'll have to leave the bindings very loose and try to bring out one toe from under your feet." Orchid carefully lifted one bent toe.

"Better leave them alone. The last time you tried, I was up all night with the pain." Their eyes met in a shared memory. Long ago Purple Jade had told Orchid that when she was two, her mother had wept while ordering her nursemaid to bind her feet. She did not dare to leave Purple Jade's feet unbound. In a family of their stature, it would be a disgrace to bring up a daughter with big feet — as if the family had to prepare her for menial labor.

"Yes, it is cruel," Orchid said, as if she, too, remembered the pain. She rubbed her mistress's feet in the hot water.

"At first, it didn't hurt much," Purple Jade continued. "Of course, she wound the bandages a little bit tighter each day to get me accustomed to it." Purple Jade rambled on as if she were telling Orchid the story for the very first time. "Later, when I was three, they brought in a professional foot binder and she broke the bones and bent the last two little toes under my feet. I screamed and cried every night."

Orchid knew the next step was to force the heels under the instep to meet the toes.

Purple Jade moaned, reliving the torture. "I became delirious. My mother and my nursemaid stayed up night after night weeping with me. Finally, they could no longer stand to see me suffer. They loosened the bandages somewhat, so that at least my ankles and heels were not completely deformed." She grimaced. "There is never a day when I am not in pain."

Orchid looked at the clublike feet in her hands and smelled again the odor of compressed flesh. Her hands shook, and she massaged Purple Jade's feet more vigorously.

"My mother berated herself and the nursemaid for allowing my feet to grow almost six inches long, instead of the ideal three-inches." Purple Jade clutched her embroidery to her heart. "Father took pity on me, and promised Mother that my dowry would be so handsome that any smart family would overlook my oversized feet!"

"Yes, I remember old master Chou was always kind and thoughtful." Orchid could not express her outrage and disgust. *Why did they impose such suffering in a home that had never known hunger and cold?*

"We were supposed to be seductive, stir up men's desires with our undulating lily walk.' Who could imagine things would change so . . . Now big feet are in fashion, and I have to suffer again to straighten my feet."

Orchid nodded. She said, "I wonder what does stir men's desires?"

Purple Jade blushed. Restraint and reciprocal affection dominated her relationship with her husband after seventeen years of marriage. She shifted in her seat, too embarrassed to answer. She had long accepted her bound feet as her fate. She had buried her anger, tolerated indignities, and accepted her deformity; now they were barriers to a modern life in which she had no desire to participate. She returned to her embroidery and began stitching; her hand looked like a small bird pecking at the cloth.

Orchid had often noticed how her mistress's and the lord's eyes gleamed and their cheeks flushed after a game of chess. Another time, she had noticed the lord's trembling hands as he bade his wife good night. Her mistress had never spoken of desire, so it must be something that was not talked about. She pressed and squeezed her mistress's feet. "No one should have to suffer like this just to please men."

Purple Jade stirred to attention. This uneducated girl had voiced a truth she herself did not dare contemplate. She looked into her maid's unusually large round eyes. *Ah, those cow eyes have seen my sorrow.*

"Orchid, you're almost twenty-three. Soon I must find you a husband."

"*Tai-tai*, you've been like a mother to me. I don't wish to leave your side." She continued to manipulate her mistress's feet. Remembering the fiery eyes of the male servants in the house, she trembled.

"Because you're like a daughter to me, I must find you the right husband. Ah, how will I manage without you?"

"Then I shall stay." Orchid added more hot water to the footbath.

Orchid went behind her mistress and loosened her chignon. Thick and dark long hair tumbled loose. Orchid began combing. "Aiya, here are two more white hairs!"

"Don't fuss about hiding them. Pull them out!" Purple Jade winced as Orchid yanked the hairs out. *I'm already thirty-nine. My two daughters were difficult births, and still we have no sons. Who will carry on the Huang family name and perform the necessary ancestral rites?*

A son would mean the continuation of the family. Her half-brother, Chou Glorious Dragon, was the savior of her maiden family—the Chous. Her father took a concubine, who gave birth to Glorious Dragon when Purple Jade was thirteen years old. She had been an only child for a long time. Her father had educated her as if she were a son, but the Chou family could not maintain its social standing without a boy in the family. Now she managed the Chou silk factory books and supervised the Chou family homestead next door, and her brother lived in Shanghai and managed the business there. Though Dragon consulted her on all aspects of Chou family welfare, she directed everything in his name. She shivered. *Who else would want to take business advice from a woman with bound-feet? And now, with only two daughters, who would save the Huang family?*

"Dragon is always so busy with his own pleasures in Shanghai," she said aloud. "I hope he will come to check on our Hangzhou factory today." Totally immersed now in her household concerns, and feeling refreshed from her morning routine, she felt she had walked out from a fog into a shaft of sunlight.

"*Tai-tai*, the water must be getting cold." Orchid finished setting the chignon and quickly brought out fresh bindings. She dried her mistress's feet and loosely bound each foot.

Without another word, she knelt and put on her mistress's tiny silk brocade shoes. She had embroidered their plum blossoms. Since a maid could embroider only under poor light when the day's work was done, it would never equal the fine stitching of a lady. It was a great honor that her mistress had accepted the new shoes at the New Year and begun wearing them.

Orchid dressed Purple Jade in a dark silk skirt and a blue and silver brocade jacket.

"Orchid, tell Golden Bell and Silver Bell we must go boating on the West Lake when the weather clears."

The cleansing rite completed in the dim comfort of her mistress's bedroom, Orchid smiled and proceeded to tidy up the room.

Chapter 2

"SILVER BELL, WHAT are you doing?" Golden Bell pointed a manicured finger at her sister.

Silver Bell was swinging her legs over the riverbank behind their house, whittling down a piece of bamboo. Dirt and wood chips speckled her clothes, and tousled pigtails framed her round cheeks. Mischief glinted in her long, narrow eyes as she glanced up at her sister.

"Ouch!" Silver Bell sucked her finger and wiped it on her jacket. She held up the bamboo. "I made a flute." She blew on it. A shrill sound pierced the morning air. "Maybe only a whistle? For Father's birthday."

"Oh, make up your mind!"

Silver Bell's cotton play clothes were a shabby contrast to her sister's green brocade jacket and dark silk trousers. Golden Bell's long braids were coiled behind her ears and short bangs fringed her forehead.

A thin vapor shrouded the river that flowed into West Lake. A pleasure boat glided past a twisted pine, clumps of bamboo, and willow trees lining the banks of the opposite shore. Behind the greenery, a footpath led uphill toward the distant monastery of Tiger Run Spring. Low clouds veiled the wooden pillars of the temple. Only the pinnacles of the incredible roofs floated above the drifting haze.

"Oh *Mei-mei*, you are a mess!" Golden Bell stamped her foot; her elegant suit shimmered. "Look at you! You are nearly ten, but you're worse than a naughty boy! Where is Peony?"

"Just because you are six years older, you think you can boss Peony and me around." Silver Bell rose and led her sister around a bend in the river where a young girl of thirteen was pulling a basket from the water.

"Oh look, look, *Jei-jei*, Peony picked up so many snails and crabs — a few shrimp too!"

"Peony, what are you doing? You are going to smell like the fish market!" Golden Bell covered her nose and glared at the maid.

"Morning peace, elder-young-mistress. I'm checking on the catch." Peony bowed. She was as disheveled as Silver Bell. "Second young-mistress didn't finish her morning rice. She wanted me to come and feed it to the fish." Peony emptied the catch into a bucket. "Cook says we must catch lots of shrimp for your father's birthday banquet."

"That's right, *Jei-jei*." Silver Bell straightened her shoulders. "I asked Peony to come here for Father's shrimp."

Golden Bell ignored her. "Peony, go clean yourself. It is almost seven thirty. We'll have to pay our morning respect to our parents soon. Before that, I want you to go to the servants' quarters. The chauffeur has a package for me."

"Peony is my maid. You have Iris."

"I don't mind. I'll go!" Peony called out. The chauffeur had been hired from Shanghai. All the servants wanted to learn his city ways. She quickly lowered the basket back into the water.

As their eyes followed the basket, they noticed something floating toward them. Silver Bell screamed. In spite of themselves, they stared.

It was the body of a young woman. Long strands of dark hair slithered, snake-like, in the water around her white and bloated face. Her lips were creased in a grimace; fish eyes bulged up at the sisters.

Silver Bell continued to shriek.

"Don't look, *Mei-mei*, don't look," said Golden Bell, pulling her away. Bodies were found in the river every year, but this was the first time they had seen one.

Silver Bell buried her head in her sister's jacket. "Who is she? . . . Who . . ."

"I don't know." Golden Bell's voice trembled. She hugged her sister and mumbled to herself as much as to the little girl, "Let's be calm; we must keep calm."

"Are the Japanese attacking Shanghai again?" Silver Bell whispered.

"I don't know." Her sister squeezed her closer. "The body could not have come from Shanghai, because the river does not flow from there."

Peony stood riveted and ashen-faced. Finally, she averted her eyes. "Young mistresses, we'd better go home." She turned and ran.

Golden Bell pulled her sister away. "Peony, wait! Wait for us."

Peony slowed to a walk. Clutching her cloth jacket over her heart, she beat her chest, chanting: "Oh-me-to-fo, send her soul to the Jade Emperor. Don't allow her to haunt me . . . please oh-me-to-fo, oh-me-to-fo."

Silver Bell wiped her sweaty brow and stared, open-mouthed, at Peony and her sister.

"You can't go running into the house like this," said Golden Bell. "You'll get a whipping if you awaken *M-ma* with such horrible news. Go get the gardener. Ask him to" — Golden Bell swallowed hard — "to fish the body out."

"I'll go." Peony ran.

"Wait, Peony! After you've told the gardener, go to the chauffeur — get my package; bring it to my room. I'm taking

Silver Bell there." Golden Bell waved her hand to dismiss her. "Come, *Mei-mei*, I'll ask Iris to wash you."

"Why can't you ask Iris to get your package?" Silver Bell asked.

"*M-ma* promised Iris a thrashing the next time she bothered the chauffeur again."

"Why?"

"Chauffeur bragged about the many fashionable foreigners in Shanghai. Their days begin in the late afternoon. After dressing in fancy gowns and tuxedos, they enjoy their dinners with free-flowing wine, songs, dance and maybe also opium. The parties last until the wee hours of the morning. He told Iris there was no place on earth that offers such freedom and pleasure."

"*M-ma* wouldn't like that. But aren't the foreigners afraid of the Japanese bombs?"

"Chauffeur said the Japanese fired only into the Chinese sections and left the International Concessions in peace. Many foreigners love to come out of their nightclubs dressed in their evening fineries to watch the bombs fall on Chaipei and enjoy the fireworks from the burning buildings." Golden Bell winced, even though she was secretly intrigued by the glamour and excitements.

Silver Bell kicked a pebble away. She sensed something was wrong with the fancy people but could not understand the full implications of what they were doing.

"Anyway, lots of other interesting people come to Shanghai. Miss Tyler told me George Bernard Shaw, the famous author, had visited Shanghai," she added. "Remember last December, the king of England abdicated to marry a Mrs. Simpson? Chauffeur said she also came to Shanghai to sample the gaiety."

Silver Bell had no interest in the famous people. "I wonder why the girl drowned?" she began again. "That light blue gown . . . don't they wear them in the missionary school?"

"You can't tell . . . when she is like that. Why would a girl from the missionary school . . ."

"Let's go wake up Father!"

"No. Pretend we never went near the river."

"Why should we lie? Can't we go and tell him?"

Golden Bell grabbed her sister's arm. "You're going to get us all into trouble. Weren't you supposed to be studying your classics?"

Silver Bell did not respond. She followed like a maid tailing her young mistress. They had climbed from the riverbank, passing the higher ground of their back garden. Now they mounted the seven brick steps that led to the main buildings. The rooms of the house were built around a series of landscaped courtyards. The arrangement of the buildings was the same in each square of open space. The girls passed the moon-gate leading to their parents' compound. The south-facing center hall was used for entertaining intimate friends. A suite of rooms abutting the hall belonged to their father, and on the opposite side, directly across from their father's suite, were their mother's quarters. On sunny days, the roof and trees cast crisp shadows in the brilliant golden light of the open courtyards, visible from every room.

As they neared their parents' compound, they could hear the bump and scrape of furniture, and Orchid sweeping her bedroom behind their mother's private sitting area with a bamboo broom.

"*M-ma* must already know what's happened."

"Ssh . . ." Golden Bell put a finger to her lips. "Not so loud! Orchid tells *M-ma* everything."

"Orchid can't hear. She's working."

"Maybe not. *M-ma* says she never needs to summon other servants into the inner court because Orchid cleans every corner," Golden Bell whispered. "Please don't tell *M-ma* what we saw by the river."

"Why?"

"You know *M-ma* wants us to study in the morning. There are too many servants in the house wasting mouth water." She held her sister's hand. "The chauffeur will bring me new magazines of American movie stars. You may look at them if you behave."

"All right, I won't tell if you'll teach me the English words in your magazines." Silver Bell brushed a stray hair from her eyes, leaving a black smudge across her forehead.

"Oh, look at you — you're messier than ever!" Golden Bell shook her upturned hands in exasperation. "*M-ma* won't let you study English because she wants to bring you up like a proper Chinese lady. Instead, you are turning into a wild animal."

"*M-ma* says Father is bringing you up like the son they don't have, but you're really a fussy old woman!"

"Ssh . . . I'm thinking."

They passed another moon gate as they crossed from their parents' courtyard into their own compound. The same arrangement of buildings surrounded their square courtyard — a center hall, and on two sides flanking the hall rooms for the girls and their maids.

In her room, Golden Bell whispered their morning trauma to Iris, her eighteen-year-old maid, and ordered a wash for Silver Bell.

"Perhaps Miss Tyler knows this girl!" Silver Bell said.

"Perhaps." Golden Bell trudged into the schoolroom where Miss Tyler, the American missionary, had come daily for the past five years to teach Golden Bell English and science. "Please, don't talk about it anymore." Golden Bell sank down by her desk, and buried her head in her arms. She would have to find out more about what happened later on.

Silver Bell picked up an old American magazine and looked at the pictures, waiting for Iris to wash her.

When Iris came in with the warm water, Silver Bell scurried to her sister. "*Jei-jei*, come and watch Iris wash me."

Iris scrubbed off the smudge on Silver Bell's forehead. She tried to distract the girls: "It feels so warm today. Did you notice any leaves on the mulberry tree when you passed the back garden?" She helped Silver Bell out of her play clothes.

"No, I think the tree is still bare," answered Silver Bell.

"I hope the silkworm eggs don't hatch. They will have nothing to eat." Iris instructed Silver Bell to wash her hands before helping her into a peach-colored silk jacket and brown trousers.

"It's only the second month — too early in the year," Golden Bell added.

Iris handed her a copy of Life magazine. "Remember this New Year's special issue? You liked the spring fashions of the Western year 1937."

Silver Bell peered over her sister's shoulder. "The West Ocean Devils are so strange! Look at that woman — her shoulders and arms are all bare. I wonder what's holding up her dress?"

"I don't know. I'll ask Miss Tyler." Golden Bell tried to close the magazine.

Silver Bell forced it open with her index finger. "Look at all that bloated white flesh. Doesn't it remind you of that . . . that corpse?"

Iris snatched the magazine away. "We're not to speak of this anymore."

Peony rushed in and gave Golden Bell her package, buzzing: "Iris, we saw . . ."

"I know," Iris pressed a finger over her closed lips. "I heard everything when I fetched your young mistress's warm water. Peony, get me the wood-shaving water from Silver Bell's room. I am doing her hair today. You'd better go and clean yourself." Iris's lips quivered as she spoke, but her voice was firm. "You'd better hurry. It is almost time for the young mistresses to pay their morning respects to their parents."

Chapter 3

PURPLE JADE fidgeted. New worries were nagging at her. The dread of war was her constant companion, and this tragedy near her home added to her apprehension. For a long while she sat, fretting. She tapped her fingers on the desk to calm herself.

Finally, she decided to recalculate her priorities. Her husband would have to handle the details of the drowning. She hoped things would become clearer in a few days. In the meantime, she must carry on her household duties. She dipped her sable-hair brush into a small porcelain cup full of water and shook a few droplets onto the inkstone. She placed the brush on the edge of the stone. Every morning, she checked the accountant's report of her household's expenses, and wrote out her instructions for the kitchen staff. Today she would meet with Lao Wang the accountant, and make plans for her husband's birthday feast. The courts of the house must be prepared for days of celebratory activities: mahjong, games of chance, chess, pantomime, magic shows, music played on the Chinese mandolins — pi-pa, the two string violin — erhu and the bamboo flute. A troupe of Shanghai opera singers should perform every night, she thought. The band that played in the Tai Wha Restaurant was exceptionally good; perhaps they could be hired as strolling minstrels. Lao Wang probably had more ideas about other troupes of singers, comics, jugglers and dancers they could engage. Now she must compile the guest list.

"Morning peace, *M-ma*." Her daughters bowed, and their personal maids followed.

"Morning peace, girls. Have you eaten your morning rice?"

"Oh, *M-ma*, let me grind the ink for you." Silver Bell ran to the desk. She picked up the ink stick and rubbed it around and around in the water on the inkstone. "*M-ma*, did you hear what they found in the river?"

"Of course! Orchid said the kitchen was in an uproar when she went to fetch my hot water this morning." She composed herself as her voice turned metallic. "This shouldn't be your concern. Who told you so early in the morning?"

Golden Bell glared at her sister. She brushed a finger over her compressed lips. "Oh, *M-ma*, everyone knows because there are so many servants in the house!"

"*Tai-tai*." Iris addressed the mistress of the house but gave Golden Bell a conspiratorial look. "The weather is so warm today, do you think the silkworm eggs will hatch?"

"They'd better not." Golden Bell had caught on immediately. "I don't think any mulberry leaves are out yet."

"Orchid," Purple Jade responded, "go fetch the sheets of silkworm eggs from the workroom and place them on the rafters of the cold house. That should keep them cool until the mulberry leaves are out."

Every winter, large chunks of ice were hauled into a thatched hut north of the kitchen, where they remained through August.

"*M-ma*, oh, *M-ma* . . ." Silver Bell tugged on her mother's sleeve. "I want to help Orchid. I promise I won't climb. Peony will climb to the rafters for Orchid." She splattered ink onto her hand.

"Aiya, my little heart-and-liver." Purple Jade grabbed her daughter's hand. "You are so careless. Orchid, fetch me some fresh water." She noticed the cut on her daughter's finger. "Where did your young mistress get that nasty cut?" she asked Peony.

"Uh, uh . . ." Peony twisted the corner of her cotton tunic. "Young mistress was making a bamboo whistle by the back garden."

"Why weren't you studying the Three Character Book I assigned you?"

Silver Bell felt her cheeks burn. Golden Bell hastened to comment: "*M-ma*, you really must send Silver Bell to the school room. She's running wild like an animal."

"I suppose you've been studying the Five Classics and the Four Books all morning?" her mother responded with a side-long glance. "You know I don't like your Western learning in the school room. Your father promised to tutor you in the classics. When did you have your last lesson?"

"Last Wednesday, I think. He's been so busy in the council."

Orchid brought in a basin of water and placed it on the rosewood night table. She then took out her mistress's box of Chinese medicines. Purple Jade always took an interest in the ancient arts of acupuncture and herbal medicines. Everyone in the household went to her for their ailments: headaches, menstrual cramps, muscle strains, stomachaches and various cuts and bruises. Leaning on Orchid, Purple Jade wobbled over and took out some alcohol to rinse Silver Bell's finger.

"Ouch, ouch! It hurts!"

"A Western education may be useful in the West, but it is courting disaster to have a Western mind and a Chinese body! Who would marry such a girl?" Purple Jade lapsed into her usual complaint.

"Miss Tyler is not married," Golden Bell said. "She doesn't need approval from any man!"

"But you're Chinese!" She rubbed Silver Bell's finger with more alcohol.

"Ouch!"

"Never forget who you are. We have no sons! Your first duty is toward your family. If no one wants to marry you and take our name . . ." The thought was too repugnant; she took a deep breath. "Without an heir, who will burn incense and make monthly offerings before our ancestral tablets at home and in our village temple? This family will be the laughing-stock of the whole region. Hai, the West Ocean barbarians are so strange." Purple Jade looked up from the basin to collect her thoughts. "When I first met your Miss Tai . . . Tai . . ." She could not pronounce the name.

"Tai-lar!" Orchid offered.

"Oh yes, Tai-Lar, 'Spicy-Too-Hot!'" Purple Jade smiled as she translated Miss Tyler's name into Chinese. Everyone laughed except Golden Bell.

"Your Miss Spicy-Too-Hot was such a frightful sight. With that red curly hair, blue eyes and enormous nose, she looked like the devil herself!"

"Oh *M-ma*, Miss Tyler is so kind! She has taught Iris at no extra charge," Golden Bell said.

"Iris is good company for you." Purple Jade wiped Silver Bell's hand. She turned toward Iris. "Don't let your fancy education turn your head. There are plenty of sing-song girls who know English and are working in the Shanghai bars."

Orchid brought a clean strip of silk, and Purple Jade wrapped it around her daughter's finger.

"Orchid, take Peony and her mistress to fetch the silkworm eggs. Make sure you don't go out the back door!" She wagged a finger at the two maids and Silver Bell.

As Purple Jade wobbled back to her writing table, Iris hurried to her side. Purple Jade leaned on Iris's arm, saying:

"I must admit, your Miss Spicy-Too-Hot is rather gracious for a West Ocean barbarian. She spoke Chinese to me very properly, though she had to think of the east and west before she said anything."

The sight of her mother toddling with the help of a maid always made Golden Bell want to turn away, but she did not. She wanted to say Westerners were not cruel. They would never bind women's feet. She sensed that would be going for her mother's jugular. She swallowed and cleared her throat. "I've learned so much from her, *M-ma*," she said. "Please invite her to Father's birthday party."

"I suppose there is no harm in that." Her mother nodded. "It will please your father. I have used all my influence to keep you at home, away from that missionary school. Imagine, a daughter from this book-fragrant family going to school with orphans, children of peasants and common shopkeepers!"

The ink was running dry. Purple Jade dribbled a few more drops of water onto the inkstone. While her right hand rubbed the ink stick against the stone, her left hand held the wide cuff of her jacket away. Although women in the big cities were wearing silk stockings and *cheongsams* — the sleek, shapely, ankle-length sheaths with daring side slits — Purple Jade dressed her daughters and herself in the fashions of traditional, comfortable elegance.

Golden Bell saw an opportunity to bring up a new topic. "Oh, *M-ma*, have you prepared a present for Father yet? His birthday is only three months away!"

"Not really. I have some ideas." Her mother picked up the brush again and mixed the thick, pasty ink. At last she began her guest list: the Huang family relatives, the Chous (her relatives), members and associates of the legislative council, the friends and classmates of her husband from his Shanghai student days at St. John's University.

"Some will come from far away, from Beijing," she said. "They will need housing in the family compound and elsewhere in town.' She made a mark to remind herself to speak to her husband and the accountant about housing.

"*M-ma*." Golden Bell edged close to her mother's desk. "May I go into town to buy a fountain pen for Father? It is so much easier than writing with brush and inkstone."

"Aiya, is that what your Miss Spicy-Too-Hot is teaching you?" Her mother laid down her brush. "The virtue of writing lies in the art and the thought. What does convenience have to do with it? Write a Chinese poem for your father. It will mean more to him than anything you can buy!"

"Oh, *M-ma*, you never want anyone to have any fun." Golden Bell stamped her foot. "You don't understand anything!" She fled. She was afraid more hurtful words would escape her lips.

In the back garden, clusters of whispering servants gathered around the master of the house. They consulted with the gardener and the accountant about the body from the river. What should they do about its interment? Was she an orphan from the missionary school? They must start the inquiry.

"The river brings another body," an elderly servant hissed. "The old Huang household in town never sees such horrors."

"People don't kill when they're not starving," another whispered.

"Must be a suicide!"

Others shuffled their feet, dragging on their cigarettes. Ripples of smoke and murmuring voices rose amongst them.

Huang Righteous Virtue was five feet eight inches tall, though he looked much taller because of his erect bearing and lanky build. He stood at least half a head taller than the men around him. He wore an ankle-length silk gown in a straight cut, with side slits reaching above his knees. The blue gown had a soft, high mandarin collar set off by cream-colored cuffs and trousers. His hair was graying near the temples. It softened the effect of his dense dark brows and sharp flashing eyes.

It was rumored that when Righteous Virtue returned to his ancestral home after his graduation from St. John's University in Shanghai, he refused to accept Chou Purple Jade — the bride his father had selected. To induce his compliance, his father had given him permission to establish a household of his own. This was a radical departure from tradition. Purple Jade's father offered him land beside a causeway of West Lake, and Righteous Virtue began his marriage building their house of three courts; it adjoined the large Chou family garden.

When Orchid, Silver Bell and Peony emerged from the workroom, the master saw them. "What are you doing here, Silver Bell?"

"Morning peace, Father. We're taking the silkworm eggs to the cold house." Silver Bell held up the sheets.

"Go to it quickly!" Her father frowned and waved her on with a sweep of his wide sleeve. "Tell your mother not to worry; everything is under control."

Silver Bell and Peony left. Orchid trailed behind them hoping to glean some information. She felt a sharp tug at her tunic. The chauffeur, Ah Lee, was beside her. He smiled and reached for her hand. "Follow me!"

Orchid blushed. She withdrew her hand and hugged her sides. She decided to follow Ah Lee at a respectable distance.

The chauffeur had learned to drive from his European master in Shanghai. He stood almost six feet tall. While the other male servants wore dark, Chinese-style cotton jackets and baggy pants, Ah Lee donned a Western chauffeur's uniform of crisp black wool. With a cigarette on his lips, he was the cynosure of the servants' quarters.

Orchid remained beyond his reach. Ah Lee had found out that Orchid had come from a family of itinerant beggars. When she was only five years old, Purple Jade happened to see her gnawing on a tree trunk and bought her. When Purple Jade married, Orchid came into the Huang household as part of her dowry. The mistress of the house had taught her embroidery, reading, writing and all the fine manners of a lady. Ah Lee admired her unassuming grace. He found her slim figure, her unusually large round eyes, and glowing cheeks most alluring.

Ah Lee led Orchid out the back door toward the bamboo groves. No breeze stirred the leaves. The eerie stillness heightened Orchid's anxiety. News of the dead girl must have driven away all the pleasure boats in the area. The river flowed like a graphite sheet. The morning mist over the water had thickened. It blurred all perspective of depth.

Orchid felt her chest tighten and her breath grow short when they approached. The body lay in a tangle of fishing nets that the servants had used to bring her ashore.

No one had thought to close the drowned girl's eyes. Orchid stifled a scream. She ran to the other side of the bamboo grove, hid her face and cried. Before she knew it, Ah Lee had wrapped his arms around her and turned her toward him. He held her with one arm, murmuring words of comfort and whispering endearments. His other hand slipped under her tunic and sought her breasts. Orchid wore a tight undervest, buttoned in front. The chauffeur fumbled with the buttons but they would not yield. He heaved with frustration and gave up on the vest.

Ah Lee's hand felt big and warm against Orchid's spine. His caresses spread strange sensations into all the secret places she had long ignored. The excitement was so intense she could hardly breathe. This was the first time she had been held by a man. Her heart raced, thumping against her ribs. She felt a strange tickling in her inner chest wall. A giddy warmth arose from her womb, flooding her breasts; it reached her face, and flushed her cheeks.

Her trembling further excited Ah Lee. He squeezed her breasts and leaned deep into her face. He kissed her eyes; his tongue worked all over her cheeks, playing in her mouth. He pushed his hips into her body. Squeezing Orchid ever closer, he circled one leg around her slim figure. He started to pull the drawstrings on Orchid's trousers and cursed when he couldn't untangle the knot with one hand.

Orchid smelled his hot breath. Being so much shorter, she was tucked under Ah Lee's sweaty armpit. His wool clothes reeked of perspiration and cigarette smoke. Something deep inside her balked. She awakened as if from a trance, and her whole body stiffened. She could not move her arms or legs. In her mind's eye she saw the dark slimy eyes of the dead girl. The roving tongue in her mouth filled her with nausea. Her stomach churned; vomit surged up her throat and gushed over both of them. She jerked away.

Ah Lee blanched. He spat, cursed and pushed her away. "You country bumpkin! A swine! No one in Shanghai would be so disgusting!"

Orchid felt faint and ashamed. She wailed and sat trembling on the ground.

They heard people coming. Ah Lee cursed more loudly. He ran and wiped his clothes with bamboo leaves. He fled to the servants' quarters through another back door.

Orchid's face felt hot. She squeezed herself into the thick of the bamboo grove. Hidden among the tall canes, she watched as several men untangled the corpse from the fishing net.

A susurrus of dismay rustled through the group.

"The chauffeur said the West Ocean Devils do not condone suicide," pronounced a gruff voice.

"Strange that this girl is wearing the missionary school uniform."

"The East Ocean Devils getting near?"

"The Japanese already bombed Shanghai. We drove them away!"

"They rape and kill women who don't give in!"

"They're not in Shanghai; they're still far north — in Manchuria, I think."

They closed the dead girl's eyes, and covered her with an old cloth. Placing her on a stretcher, they carried her toward the servants' door.

Alone once more, Orchid brushed off her soiled tunic. She had learned her propriety from being the hands and feet of Purple Jade. The chauffeur made her feel trampled and unclean. She wished she could tell her mistress about Ah Lee, but she knew she must not. After all, she was only a servant. Why had she allowed herself to be led out the back door? The chauffeur could deny everything, or worse, accuse her of seducing him. Surely tongues would wag then.

Orchid stole back to her room to wash and change. The main courts of the house were deserted. The housemaids who usually dusted the rosewood furniture and swept the courtyards in the morning were absent. Everyone had retreated to the kitchen and the servants' quarters to gossip about the corpse. Orchid resolved never to look at the chauffeur again.

Chapter 4

GOLDEN BELL'S SHOUT "You don't understand anything!" rang in Purple Jade's ears. When did her daughter learn to shout at her mother? Did Miss Tyler encourage her daughter to "have fun" and be audacious? When had she become so defiant? She rubbed her temple and pushed all thoughts of recrimination away. It was time to meet this Miss Spicy-Too-Hot and learn some of the foreign magic. Yes, she would invite Miss Tyler to the birthday party.

Purple Jade refreshed her ink. More than one hundred guests would be arriving. She must compile a list of groceries to start the preparations:

10 catties of red beans
20 catties of sweet rice
7 dozen duck's eggs
10 catties of salt
1 slaughtered pig for smoking.

"That will keep the kitchen busy for a few days," she said to herself. Her voice came out low, with unexpected cracks in it. Her throat and skin often felt dry. Did that point to the end of her menstrual years? *That would be a merciful relief*, she thought.

"Orchid." No reply. She cleared her throat. She remembered the silkworm eggs. She sighed and leaned back to raise one foot and then the other onto the opposite knee, rubbing them. "Orchid gives me arms and legs. I'm useless without her. Curse my feet," she mumbled. She did not insist on bound feet for her children. Yet, despite her example of virtuous living, Golden Bell had become rude and brazen.

Purple Jade thought of a Po Chu-i poem she had read the night before:

Fluttering birds welcome the green foliage;
Scaly fish frolic in the new weeds.
But summer did not stir my heart;
I remain like a withered straw . . .

"I could write a poem for my lord's birthday," she said to herself. She knew the gift her husband really needed was an heir. But she was almost forty. The only verse that came to mind brought tears into her eyes.

The spring greens turn dark.
Where is the summer lark?

The ink felt dry, and in any case, she was not in the mood for writing. She washed her brush, covered her inkstone. Yes, her daughter was right. It would be easier to write with a fountain pen. Still, within the settled comforts of her household, she felt challenged by her daughter's fascination with this intrusive foreign world. She took out her book of poems.

While Purple Jade fingered the pages, her mind wandered. Golden Bell had once shown her a color photograph from one of Miss Tyler's magazines. It was the scene of a snow-capped, bell-shaped mountain reflected in a shimmering aqua-blue lake. The limpid water rendered the stones and branches on the bottom visible, and the image of the mountain floated on the surface ripples. The light blue sky with streaks of pinkish orange clouds added magic to the placid scene. She felt the urge to morph into a bird and fly onto the stately pine tree that stood on one side of the craggy red mountain. An unfamiliar anxiety flooded her mind. She had always thought of the wilderness as something unruly and forbidding — somehow it related to her free-floating fear of war. This picture of serene beauty, however, had set her heart fluttering with a strange vitality. She had been inordinately proud of West Lake in her backyard, but the water was dark and pleasure boats frequented the lake. Now something inside her was stirring. A poem by her favorite poet, Tu Fu, about random pleasure crossed her mind:

Young mulberry leaves come forth for the picking.
Tender and soft new wheat runs along the river.
When spring has turned into summer,
how much hope is left in life?
Good wine is sweeter than honey. Do not let it pass.

While growing up, Purple Jade's bound feet had been her shackles. Yet, even with these physical limitations, she had found vicarious pleasures in the rambunctious life of her half-brother, Chou Glorious Dragon. She watched him run, climb, and play shuttlecock, but as a girl it was her special privilege to fine-tune the simple acts of daily living.

She had acquired her seemingly casual grace with careful discipline. Like the refined ladies of old, she had learned to discern whether the water in a cup of tea came from mountain snow or from spring water. The clarity of pale green tea symbolized purity; its aroma inspired lofty thoughts; the subtle taste, the gentle fragrance, instilled delicate sensibility. Despite her physical confinement, she had learned to be content.

Then she remembered her betrothal to Huang Righteous Virtue, the scion of a large landowning family and an ardent follower of Dr. Sun Yat-sen. Her parents told her that like many college students of his generation, he was disillusioned with the corrupt Manchu monarchy. After graduation, he continued his clandestine activities and helped to establish the Republican government. When they finally married, Righteous Virtue was thirty-three years old. She was twenty-two — old for a marriageable girl of her time. She was in awe of his patriotism.

Now Righteous Virtue had come into his full inheritance. He had built schools and a hospital, and his generosity had become legendary. People admired his modern education, and he was elected to the local legislative council with support from the gentry. Purple Jade had always been impressed by his quiet confidence and thought of him as the ideal Chinese gentleman — erudite, tolerant of human frailties, and correct in his behavior to ancestors, friends, and family.

Purple Jade's thoughts drifted to her present concerns again, and she groaned. In spite of her close supervision of her family and part of the Chou family silk business, she found it difficult to concentrate when the country was in turmoil. She still felt outraged that the Westerners had carved up prime real estate in the major cities into concessions where foreigners could enjoy extraterritorial rights and privileges. Japan had occupied Manchuria for some time now, but China remained weak because the Chinese Communists, Nationalists, Fascists, Socialists and other ideologues never ceased to squabble for control. Her husband had told her something important was happening in Xian. The Japanese had killed Marshal Zhang Hsueh-liang's father in Manchuria. Now, the young marshal wanted revenge to fulfill his filial duty. He kidnapped Generalissimo Chiang Kai-shek in Xian and forced him to unite with the Communists to fight Japan. Purple Jade's heart warmed at the thought of civilized Confucian gentlemen, Marshal Zhang, the generalissimo, Chou En-lai, about to unite and set an example of virtuous living. They would become national heroes. Would that mean war with Japan and chaos for the country? She wiped the thought from her mind. Like everyone else, she hoped for peace but also wanted China to remain Chinese. The thoughts brought on the usual fog of apprehension. It seemed to infuse the air she was breathing.

Silver Bell entered with Peony. She carried a copy of the Three Character Book. "*M-ma*, Father said everything will be all right."

"Where is Orchid?"

No one answered.

"Well, Peony, go fetch us some tea. Silver Bell, we'll start our lesson."

"Oh *M-ma*, there is so much going on! Can we skip a day?"

"No, Silver Bell. Now repeat after me."

Purple Jade recited aloud:

"Origin of man
Is always kind."

Her daughter repeated but her eyes roamed the room.

Soon, Peony returned with a tea service on a tray. Orchid followed with lowered eyes. Peony was serving tea when suddenly Orchid tipped the basin of water on the night table.

"What's wrong Orchid?" Purple Jade faced her. "That is not like you."

"*Tai-tai*, I am sorry . . . I went out the back door and saw the corpse," Orchid blurted out. "They said the girl was from the mission school."

"Oh no! Who is she?" Purple Jade looked straight into Orchid's frightened eyes. She sounded more firm and brave than she felt.

"No one knows yet."

"Have you heard any opposition to the students of . . . of the missionary school?" Purple Jade paused when she remembered her own opposition.

"Oh, there is the usual wasting of mouth water!" Orchid answered.

"I heard the girls are taught not to bring the rice bowl to their mouths," Peony volunteered.

"They are also forbidden to slurp their soup!" Orchid mopped up the spilled water. "They learn silly things in that school, but some girls put on airs!"

"The Western customs are strange, but these are not provocations." Purple Jade frowned. "There must be some personal reason."

"The lord sent a message into town. Some family will come to claim the body soon." Orchid gave the floor a vigorous scrub. When she stood up, she felt better.

"Orchid, take this grocery list to the accountant." Purple Jade thrust out the paper. Her firm order was given in a voice just loud enough to summon the authority of her class and breeding; she wanted no more speculation about the body. "Don't go out the back door again. All the freedom and fancy learning did not bring this girl any peace!" She glared at her daughter.

"Golden Bell said it is fun to learn how the electric light works!"

"Hai," her mother said with a sigh. "Western learning favors the practical, but it doesn't build character. It is your father's fault. He is too fascinated by Western toys."

Purple Jade stopped sipping her tea, remembering all the novelties her husband had brought into the house. Seven years earlier, Righteous Virtue had installed electric lights; two years later, he added "self-coming water" to the schoolroom and the kitchen; last year, he bought a new "gas car."

"That Shanghai chauffeur he hired," Purple Jade shook her head. "He's causing such an uproar among the servants!"

She put down her teacup. The Dragon Well tea did not taste right. She dabbed her mouth with her handkerchief. It tasted as if it had been brewed with river water taken from the muddy shore. Water from the center of the river was clearer, although nothing could equal the clean, crisp taste of water from Tiger Run Spring. The Dragon Well tea of her household was always brewed from Tiger Run Spring water. The servants were delinquent. She must look into this.

"Peony said the chauffeur is really interesting. Imagine, he said he isn't afraid of any foreign devil." Silver Bell brought her mother back from her private thoughts.

"Are you afraid of the foreign devils, Silver Bell?" Her mother smiled. A few laugh lines appeared at the corners of her eyes, but her cheeks were still gleaming and taut.

"No. Sometimes I go by the schoolroom to watch Miss Tyler. She doesn't scare me. But the chauffeur says that in Shanghai men and women openly hug and kiss each other! The barbarians know no shame."

"That is exactly how I feel, my little heart-and-liver." She took her daughter's hand. "And that is one reason you are not going to the schoolroom."

"Will *jei-jei* also hug and kiss when she goes to Shanghai?"

"Golden Bell is not going to Shanghai." Her mother dropped the hand. "Now, are you ready to recite your lesson?"

"No *M-ma*, it's too hard to memorize things I don't understand!"

"It is good discipline to memorize. You'll understand when you're older." Her mother opened the book. "These passages are relevant to what we were talking about. The first couplet says man is always born good and kind.

Origin of man,
Is always kind.

"The second couplet says while nature will stay true, bad habits will corrupt man and bring him far from his original goodness.

Nature brings close
Habit channels away.

"So the third couplet concludes that if a child is not properly taught, his good nature will change.

If not taught
Nature will change.

Now, do you think you can memorize these few couplets?"

"I'll try. But I wish I could learn about the electric lights instead."

"Hai, what's a mother to do?" she moaned. In her mind, she knew perfectly well how her daughters felt — as if a fluttering bird from that foreign picture had flown inside them.

Silver Bell smiled. "*M-ma*, have you thought of a birthday present for Father?"

"I am embroidering this vest for him." She shifted in her seat. "Except for our chess games, he isn't interested in anything I do anymore." Her eyes narrowed as she reached for her embroidery. She did not mean to confide her innermost fears to her young daughter.

"Father is a book-fragrant gentleman. You always said he never indulges in sleeping with the willows and lying with the flowers." Silver Bell tilted her head to peer into her mother's face.

"Yes, he is too noble." Purple Jade shuddered at the thought of an unfaithful husband. "He deserves a better wife. All the wind-and-water men chose the best date and time for our marriage, yet we have no sons."

"Would Father take a concubine?"

Purple Jade paused. Giving her husband a concubine — this would be the traditional way to ensure an heir. The thought sent her heart thumping. Somehow, her silk thread became tangled. She laid down her embroidery and looked for her scissors. "No, my little heart-and-liver, your father is too Westernized. If you do not go near the schoolroom but study your classics instead, I will find you a husband someday who is willing to take our name. Then no male relative would dare claim to be a master of this house."

"But Father says I must go to the school room, after I turn ten next winter."

Purple Jade stared into the empty space ahead. Fingering the mangled threads, she asked: "If you should become Westernized, who will marry you and serve as our heir?"
Silver Bell was not listening. "*M-ma*, I'll try to memorize the couplets!" She touched her mother's back and ran off.

Chapter 5

"MORNING PEACE, JADE-*jei*." Glorious Dragon entered his sister's sitting room. He was five-feet-ten. In his gray wool suit he looked like an Oxford student on a foreign holiday.

"Morning peace, Dragon, but it is already past ten o'clock. Were you up last night checking the company books I sent you?" Turning to her maid, she ordered: "Orchid, bring us tea."

"I don't want tea." Glorious Dragon motioned Orchid to stay and started pacing. "Everyone knows I'm here to check on our family business, but I don't need to look at the books." He stared at the ground. "I'm here to ask for your help. It's a worthy adventure."

"What do you mean?" Purple Jade frowned. "What are you up to now?"

"You know how Father used to call his nephew Yu Wei a depraved brat? Well, now he is addicted to opium and has so much gambling debt . . ."

"He's had to sell his mansion in town." Purple Jade finished her brother's sentence. "He's a disgrace to the Chou family."

"Exactly!" Dragon stabbed the air with his hand; his voice rose in anger. "General Chin Bar-tau has turned it into an elite opium den — now called the Prosperous Dream."

"The same General Chin who's in the secret police, and is one of Generalissimo Chiang Kai-shek's bodyguards?"

"That's him! We must do something before the Chous lose more face."

"I'll speak to my lord and see what he can do."

"I wouldn't ask him and put him in danger. General Chin has connections to the underworld, and he's so powerful politically you'll jeopardize your husband's career and maybe even his life!"

"Yes, you're right." Purple Jade shuddered, twisting her handkerchief. Her rapid heartbeat seemed to have become a bird twittering inside her. She asked, "What can anyone do?"

"I have a plan." He winked. His eyes were a near copy of his half-sister's. "I plan to go in there and create some disturbance."

"What kind of disturbance? What good would that do?" Her brother — the bright swath in her life — had always supplied challenges and diversions. Now she felt like a bird perched on that pine next to the bell-shaped mountain, ready to dive into the clear water.

"You know the smokers are all lethargic and prefer a quiet place. Maybe if I picked a fight and caused an uproar, people would shun the place."

"Oh no! You're going to get both the Huangs and the Chous into trouble." Purple Jade slammed the handkerchief onto her lap.

"I'm not in town too often. If I put on a mustache, some glasses and a Chinese robe, no one will recognize me." Glorious Dragon shrugged, but his eyes were sparkling. "I think a female companion might divert attention from me."

"How are you to pick a fight with people who loll around as if they're half dead? They won't fight back!"

"I'm not sure." Her brother paced away. "I'll just take a look and improvise something. Maybe I'll tip over some furniture, pretend I'm drunk or I've gone crazy. I promise you. I'll return safely. No one will know I'm involved."

"Such bold plans." Purple Jade snickered. She tried hard to silence the twittering bird. "I'm sure you'll have no trouble starting a disturbance, but how are you going to escape?"

"I'll slip away in the confusion."

"Don't get us involved!"

"Haven't you always blamed the foreigners for bringing opium into our country?"

"Yes, they did!"

"So why would you allow opium in our town?"

"Oh." Purple Jade fidgeted with her handkerchief, ruminating on the consequences if she should get involved. But the fluttering bird inside her seemed ready to take flight. She tried in vain to hold it back. "I know my lord will berate me for being too permissive with you. I have never refused you anything. But an opium den in town is truly obnoxious." Her face turned red and she could almost feel the shaft of sunlight shining over that snow-capped Bell Mountain. Oh, she could almost taste the sweet wine of freedom. "What can we do?" she asked finally.

"Be brave and help me!"

"I'm not sure if I can help. You said you need a female companion?"

"Yes."

Her heart was pounding like a drum, but she could feel the sunlight warming that crystalline lake. She furrowed her brow and mumbled, "You're determined to do this?"

"Yes, I'll do it with or without your help."

It was so seldom that Purple Jade could do anything important outside her home. She would love to practice medicine, but who would want to train a female? Now her brother had asked for help. Maybe she could supply the

For the rest of the day, Orchid practiced walking on high-heeled shoes in the privacy of her mistress's bedroom. She pretended she was in the back of the car and learned to take off her cotton jacket and trousers and slip on the *cheongsam*. Purple Jade helped her apply makeup and pile her hair into a chignon .

Glorious Dragon did not tell his sister that he had already visited Prosperous Dream two days earlier. He found out that by four o'clock, the lunchtime crowd had departed but the evening patrons hadn't yet arrived. In fact, the service personnel would have their evening meal at five and only a few malingerers would remain in the opium pavilion. The sickeningly sweet smell of opium smoke, mingled with the sour stench of perspiration sent him rushing out into the sunlight, reeling with nausea. To regain his composure, he took a stroll and found a cache of fireworks stashed just outside a corner of the opium pavilion, ready for the opening celebration on Saturday.

When Glorious Dragon arrived the next afternoon to take his sister and her maid for a drive, no one suspected anything. Once inside the car, Purple Jade drew the curtains closed around the back seat. Despite her practice sessions, Orchid trembled so much that Purple Jade had to help assemble her disguise.

"You'll do just fine. Remember how families and fortunes are destroyed by the drug." Purple Jade applied Orchid's makeup and tried to keep her hands steady. She repeated the same instructions she had given the day before: "You don't have to say anything. Just serve the opium the way they served my father when he was alive."

"Yes, I'll try my best, *Tai-tai*," Orchid answered. She had heard enough about the evils of opium, but she had never entered an opium den. She was intrigued, but also edgy. Her mistress had guided her all her life, and now her blind trust tempered her anxiety and excitement.

Glorious Dragon drove into a quiet lane to take off his suit jacket. He slipped on a Chinese robe and put on a jaunty hat, glasses and a mustache.

"Oh you look like a stranger." Purple Jade laughed nervously.

They parked behind the Silver Palace. When they saw that no one was around, Glorious Dragon helped Orchid out of the car. Crouched behind the front seat, Purple Jade watched her brother adopt a splayed walk while Orchid clung to his arm. Orchid walked with mincing steps, which gave her a seductive sway.

Purple Jade's legs felt sore and she was twisted into an uncomfortable position, but she did not feel the usual pain in her feet. If she weren't a cripple, would she have taken Orchid's place in this plot? Yes, she might have. Her outrage at the presence of an opium den in town overshadowed her usual concerns with propriety and decorum. She perspired. She felt restless and young again. She shifted in the cramped space, fiddled with her handkerchief and imagined herself swimming in the aqua lake. She peeked out the window. Everything was quiet. Should she tap on the horn if she saw something suspicious? "Oh please, please don't let anyone find out about our role," she prayed to Kwan Ying Buddha.

Glorious Dragon led Orchid into the parlor. As expected, the proprietor greeted them as he would any prosperous couple ready to forego dinner for the pipe — and so addicted that they need not be watched. Orchid, in her fancy clothes, passed as a prostitute. Her shaky steps amply demonstrated that she was in dire need of a fix and would lapse into oblivion after just a few puffs. Reassured, the proprietor left for his evening meal.

The smokers lolled on their rosewood beds and sucked on their pipes. The opium lamps lit the artificially darkened den like fireflies, fluttering with each draw of the smokers. Glorious Dragon and Orchid walked by several wasted figures hunched over the miniature hurricane lamps. Some stared up at them with vacant eyes. Saliva dribbled from their gaping mouths, revealing smoke-stained teeth. The addicts would not have recognized their own mothers.

Several serving girls hovered over the reclining bodies. Some twirled a thin stick in a jar of opium paste, shaping it into a pellet. After turning and warming the brown blob over a small dusty lamp, they placed the pellet into the pipe's porcelain bowl, inverting it over a glowing fire to burn the opium. The smoker sucked on the pipe and exhaled; thin wisps of fumes curled around his mouth and nostrils. Then he leaned into his pipe, and slowly and steadily he inhaled again. The little flame winked eerily in the darkness.

Glorious Dragon chose a bed near the entrance for a quick getaway. After picking out the pipes and opium, he motioned the serving girl to leave them alone.

Orchid began to twirl the opium paste. The atmosphere of lazy inattention stirred Glorious Dragon to action. With a sleight of hand, he pulled out strings of firecrackers from his robe and lit the long fuse lines. He hurled them toward the corner draperies where the fireworks were stacked outside the window. He threw his opium lamp after the firecrackers, adding fuel to the sparks.

Firecrackers banged, immediately followed by screams and shouts. Fire crept up the draperies and burst into flaming columns that consumed the wooden beams overhead.

Everyone, even those who looked comatose, struggled to reach the door. Some hobbled, some crawled on their hands and knees, and many had to be carried to safety.

Once outside, Glorious Dragon avoided looking into the frightened eyes surrounding him. More loud bursts followed. The burning building ignited the fireworks outside, which looked anemic under the afternoon sky. The roar of flames sent everyone coughing and scrambling. The staff and other shouting men gathered to help. They flailed their arms in frustration. Their buckets of water could not contain the fire. Crowds gathered across the street; all eyes were riveted on the fiery display. Glorious Dragon and Orchid slipped into their car unnoticed.

Purple Jade peeked through her curtains and mumbled her "oh-me-to-fu" to her Kwan Yin Buddha.

"Oh, Dragon, you didn't tell me you would burn this place!" Purple Jade gasped as soon as her brother came near. "People can get killed!"

"They're half dead anyway!" Glorious Dragon scrunched down in the front seat and removed his disguise.

"The service people — they'll be hurt!" As if handling a medical emergency, Purple Jade rapidly creamed Orchid's face and scrubbed away her makeup. "And I helped you!"

"There weren't too many people inside," her brother muttered.

"Some addicts were so debilitated, they couldn't even groan," Orchid said in an excited whisper. "I saw some serving girls drag out the limp ones." Her whole body shook, but she now looked like her normal self with a flushed face.

With trembling hands, Purple Jade helped her maid put on her old cotton suit. She combed her hair and braided it into pigtails. "Orchid, why didn't you stop him? Why did you let him do this?"

"I didn't know what happened. I was twirling the paste, and Master Dragon was so fast . . ." She started to cry.

"Hush, hush." Glorious Dragon put on his suit jacket. He checked himself in the rear-view mirror and found the reflection acceptable. "Orchid, are you ready? We should slip out of the car and pretend we meant to go to the restaurant, but stopped to watch the fire."

The steel in his voice calmed the women, and they obeyed. They joined the crowd of spectators. All eyes were on the fire.

Orchid wrapped her arms around her middle to still her jittery stomach.

"Lucky the mansion is in a large garden, and the fire cannot spread," someone said.

"Poor cousin Yu Wei; his mansion is destroyed." Purple Jade felt strangely exhilarated.

"He sold his mansion. Remember?" Dragon sneered.

"Oh yes, it's now Prosperous Dream." Purple Jade grabbed Orchid's arm and leaned on her. Orchid felt reassurance from the familiar grip, and both women grew calm.

"Not so prosperous for General Chin anymore, eh?" Glorious Dragon whispered.

"Oh . . ." The women felt dazed.

A tiny hand tugged on Purple Jade's jacket. It was a little girl of about ten. "Please," she said in a pleading voice. "What am I to do?" The innocent but overly rouged face stunned Purple Jade. The child wore a slinky *cheongsam*, with exaggerated slits going all the way up her thighs. It was obvious that the girl worked at the opium den. Many dens combined opium with prostitution, but Purple Jade had assumed the prostitutes would be nubile young women, not children.

"What's your name?" Purple Jade bent down to take the child's hand and tried to still her wobbly voice.

"Little Six," the girl replied. "Will they send me back in there?"

"No." Purple Jade suppressed a gasp. "No one will miss you there. Where is your home?"

"In the mountains somewhere. A man took me and brought me to Hangzhou two years ago." She sobbed.

Purple Jade draped her black silk wrap over the child and edged her away from the crowd. She hustled all of them into the car. "Dragon *dee*, stop gawking at the fire. Drive us home!"

"How are we to hide the child? You know the underworld controls all the opium dens." Glorious Dragon scowled.

"We'll sneak her into the house and tell people we picked up this beggar girl outside the restaurant because we need a new scullery maid," Purple Jade replied.

Dragon started the car. Once they were on their way, Glorious Dragon instructed: "Little Six, no one must know you worked for the opium den or you'll be sent back. You can tell people your parents left your home in the mountains because of poor harvests. They passed through Hangzhou and somehow left you behind."

"I never , ever want to be sent back! I will die before I tell anyone!" Little Six cried.

Purple Jade creamed the child's face and scrubbed it. "I'll teach you to read." She held the child close.

Chapter 6

ORCHID'S FINGERS TREMBLED as she scrubbed away the smoky smell from Little Six's skin before dressing the child in Silver Bell's old play clothes. She would tell the kitchen staff that her mistress had found Little Six begging on the street, shouting, "No Baba, No Mama." As she transformed Little Six into an ordinary child, she mumbled her thanks to the kind Buddha. Orchid could not remember how she herself was brought into this book-fragrant family who would never sell her. One day her kind mistress would arrange a suitable marriage and she would continue her life of service to her husband and his family. Yes, she would never suffer the same fate as Little Six.

She could see her mistress was distressed; she resolved to never mention this to anyone. She knew she would be rewarded for her discretion. Since she was usually in her mistress's quarters attending to her chores, no one in the household had suspected her afternoon activities.

Purple Jade feigned a headache and excused herself from dinner. Still jittery from the day's adventure, she could not understand why she had behaved that way. She could not believe that she, who had spent all her life facilitating a steady and orderly household, would participate in such a reckless act. Was she attempting to ward off her war fears? To ease her turmoil, she recited over and over again Tu Fu's Quatrain:

The beautiful late sun colored the hills and streams,
Spring breezes gathered fragrance from flowers and grasses,
Swallows flew over hazy mudflats in teams,
Ducks mated and slept on the warm sand in the passes.

These were the familiar scenes around her home. She must concentrate on them and never, ever again dream of flying to the bell-shaped mountains and transparent lake.

Before he took the night train back to Shanghai, Glorious Dragon went to his sister's room to bid her farewell.

"Brother-in-law Virtue told me no one was killed in the fire this afternoon."

"Good. Ssh . . . not so loud." Purple Jade mustered all her self-control to keep her voice steady. "Casualties?"

"A few, but they'll recover. I told Virtue we saw the fire, but we must forget everything else." He stared at Orchid until she nodded and lowered her head.

Purple Jade felt uncomfortable that her afternoon adventure could never be mentioned again. Still, that was the only prudent strategy. She had determined to banish any reckless behavior from her family life. She would expel the twittering bird inside her. For now, she must rally all her reserves and act normally so that Orchid would not be rattled.

Glorious Dragon seemed to have forgotten his actions of the afternoon. He said: "The company books show you've added more than a dozen small silkworm farmers, so you'll be sending well over two thousand skeins of raw silk to our Shanghai factory this year."

Purple Jade nodded.

"Virtue-*ko* said you provided small loans, so the farmers' wives can buy silkworm eggs and breed the worms. What a clever idea!"

"Yes, my lord thought it was a good idea." It was her habit to attribute any important decision she made to her husband. She also recognized that her brother was providing an opportunity for distraction.

"But Lao Wang told me he brought in almost one hundred farm women for you to interview. What did you ask them?"

"Oh, I asked them what they did every day." Purple Jade was pleased that her brother recognized her initiative. She had prepared for this accounting for a long time. "Many women were surprised to be asked. They were impulsive and had no strict routine for their days, and their work depended upon their enthusiasm of the moment. I rejected them outright."

"So you chose those who were organized and disciplined?"

"Yes, but I also wanted resourceful women." Purple Jade knew that her brother also needed to distract himself from their conspiracy, and in any case he was always interested in practical details. "I asked how they might supply the mulberry leaves. I was surprised that many had no idea where they could gather the leaves or how much money they'd need to buy them."

"And still you were able to find more than a dozen women who had adequate supplies?"

"Yes. They all have relatives who own trees with enough leaves to spare. Two women are related to our gardener, so I won't be surprised if they get a good supply from our garden." She laughed. "All the women will be able to repay some of our loans when we buy their first crop of cocoons."

"Ah, what would I do without your Hangzhou supplies?" He took a sip of tea and opened his briefcase. "Here is a sample of the new Thai silk."

"I love the iridescent color. Do you think your factories can produce the same?"

"I'm sure we can, if we spend some time analyzing it. However, I think I'll just sell the Thais my extra raw silk for now."

"That sounds like a good beginning." She stopped. She still didn't feel right, but somehow this calm business conversation had steadied her nerves and she could see Orchid looking more relaxed while standing in the corner, waiting to prepare her mistress for bed.

"How is Little Six?" Dragon asked.

"The cook's granddaughter died last year, so he is happy to take Little Six under his wings and teach her to read!"

"The dragon slew an enemy, and you did a good deed today," her brother whispered. "You must always remind yourself of that."

"Yes." Purple Jade nodded. "Nothing will ever be mentioned outside this room. You have my word on it."

Glorious Dragon bade his sister good night and left to catch his train.

In 1937, Shanghai had many miles of trolley lines, and crowds of human conveyers too. Hawkers scurried past. They carried yoked panniers of nuts and fruits, buckets of steaming hot bean-curd custard and live chickens squawking in baskets. Rickshaw pullers cursed and grunted; impatient bicycles and pedicabs rattled their tiny bells; motorists leaned into their horns; and buses ground and grated through the jumble of human traffic and rumbling streetcars. Chou Glorious Dragon thought Shanghai was a beautiful city.

On this sunny Saturday afternoon, he lunched with his mistress Bright Crystal in her villa on Avenue Joffre.

"Tonight's dinner party will start late because General Chin will be coming back from Hangzhou. Remember? I told you he will be cutting the ribbon for his new opium den, Prosperous Dream," said Bright Crystal.

"Yes, one party after another with your General Chin!" Glorious Dragon puckered his lips and pushed away his lunch. He didn't tell Crystal what had happened. "He is a busy man."

She detected his note of sarcasm. "So what's the matter with your food? You hardly touched anything."

"I think I smelled something bad." He made a face. "Maybe it is my sour stomach."

"Would you like to join me for an afternoon nap?"

"You need your beauty rest. I'll go for a walk."

"Remember to order the wine for tonight."

Once outside, Dragon hopped on the nearest trolley. He needed fresh air — a walk along the Bund. He was only twenty-six and in excellent health, but waves of disgust and agitation made him sweat in the cool breeze. Yesterday he was wound up and in full control. Today, he needed distractions.

The trolley clanked down street after street flanked by unbroken rows of three-and-four-story apartment buildings. In the Chinese sections, laundry fluttered on bamboo poles jutting from the upper floors; restaurants, wedged into slots on the ground floor, flew red pennants proclaiming their specials; fortune-teller stalls dangled wind chimes; gold signs on red billboards advertised jewelry. The jumbled cloths in the fabric stores spilled out into the street; customers stopped by to finger the lustrous silks and complain about the itchy foreign wools. Jugglers were performing on the sidewalk and Dragon craned his neck to catch the act. Indeed, he was a juggler himself. So far, he had been able to keep all his balls in the air. A gong summoned all to form a circle and watch monkeys doing tricks and putting on masks to impersonate ancient heroes. Yes, he was also wearing a mask. His bravado and charm masked his anger at his predicament — the woman he loved could not be his. He took a deep breath. The air was thick with the aromas of incense shops; the scent of teakwood from the coffin-maker mingled with that of roasting chestnuts and savory meats from the peddlers. Beggars buttonholed passersby. They tangled with craftsmen repairing shoes or mending porcelain with rivets. The festive bustle in the streets restored Glorious Dragon's spirits like a military reveille.

Up one street and down the next the trolley danced along the tracks, passing movie houses and shops in the French Concession. Blond mannequins in exaggerated shoulder pads and glassy blue eyes stared out the windows. Paramount, the city's biggest nightclub stood solid and sedate in the bright sunlight. The image of Little Six in her *cheongsam* came to Dragon's mind. Yes, he had done something right; he had saved a child. He smiled.

Still a nameless agony deep inside refused to let go of him. To distract himself, Glorious Dragon tried concentrating on Western fashions and the quiet glamour of the international restaurants and retail shops. Their shiny brass lanterns, sparkling plate glass and uniformed doormen contrasted with the array of Chinese shops on adjoining avenues. The sight of a black suited member of the Green Gang patrolling the street made him sweat. They were allied with General Chin.

Whenever Glorious Dragon thought of his association with Bright Crystal, he grinned to think of the scandal, gossip and envy he had stirred up in Hangzhou. The family had sent him to Shanghai to attend St. John's University, but his heart was not in formal learning. He dropped out of school, much to the chagrin of his father. His mother had died giving birth to him, so he had no maternal protection. But thanks to the pacifying counsel of Purple Jade, he was given a position in the family-owned silk factory. It was hardly a sinecure. In five short years not only did his natural acumen for business make him the director of the Chou family's silk enterprises but he also functioned as a comprador between the Westerners and the silk trade council. His success provided jobs for all the Chou cousins. Though he was the youngest, he was proud to be the head of the whole Chou clan. Indeed, he felt he could overcome all obstacles.

Ever since foreigners had arrived to trade in China they depended on compradors to explain their barbarian business ways to the Chinese. While the foreigners masked their ignorance with hauteur, the smooth compradors became fabulously rich, carrying themselves with the urbane self-confidence of multinational sophisticates. Five years earlier, Glorious Dragon had aspired to this role, but his English was poor. He had enrolled in an intensive English-language course. There, by pure serendipity, he met Bright Crystal. With her help, he became fluent in English within eight months. He was ready now to broaden his trade beyond the silk industry. But he was also "swatting a fly on the tiger's head" — he shared General Chin's mistress and tried to destroy his opium dens.

Chin was a member of Generalissimo Chiang Kai-shek's entourage. His wife and concubines lived in Nanking, the nation's capital. But his business interests reached all over the country. He bought a red brick villa for Bright Crystal in Shanghai's French Concession to facilitate his transactions in China's largest city. Bright Crystal lived as a socialite of independent means — a situation far more acceptable to the foreigners who wanted to do business in Shanghai.

To add respectability to her household, Bright Crystal called Glorious Dragon her *Tang-ko*. Everyone knew that a *Tang-ko*, an elder cousin from the father's side, was almost as close as a full brother. Therefore, it was taboo to marry a *Tang* cousin. Marriages among *Piao* cousins were common, because *Piao* indicated the mother's side — a distant relation. As a *Tang-ko*, Glorious Dragon often played host in Bright Crystal's house and extended his hospitality.

Glorious Dragon hated General Chin and his stranglehold on Crystal's life. He and Bright Crystal joked about their clever deception, but anxiety always clouded their passionate love. Out of sheer outrage, he wanted to shout and punch everyone associated with the general. He chuckled to himself when he remembered the fireworks outside Prosperous Dream. Yes, he had hit the general where it mattered — his pocketbook. There were many factions in the underworld. It would be natural for the general to suspect foul play from a competitor. People could not possibly link him to the fire. No one would suspect him even if he had been seen there. He was with his sister — a woman with a reputation for righteousness. Everyone knew her to be a whetstone, ever ready to sharpen a sword in defense of virtuous living. He smiled at his cleverness.

He stepped off the streetcar near the esplanade on the Bund of the International Settlement area that operated as a British port. Concrete and steel buildings housing the Hong Kong and Shanghai Bank, the Cathay Hotel and the Customs House with its clock tower dominated the Bund. A cool breeze from the Hwangpo River soothed him. Pale young sycamore leaves fluttered over the paved promenade. He strolled under the trees and lit a cigarette. Lingering on the walkway, he watched the river traffic. All manner of watercraft plied the waterway at his feet: sampans festooned with laundry and larger boats loading and unloading rice, vegetables, and furniture. Coolies squatted to smoke and food vendors clustered around the wharves. Farther out, the masts of large junks contrasted with the sturdy funnels and cables of ocean liners, warships flying flags of many nations and cargo ships anchored in deeper water. His own life was a mirror of this harbor. He straddled the East and the West — the nobility of his sister's household and the duplicity and adventures of his life here. Feeling calmer, he remembered he could not tarry. He must be on his way to order the finest Kaoliang — potent whiskey made of sorghum. Prominent persons from the Chinese and European business communities would be attending Bright Crystal's party that evening.

Glorious Dragon walked briskly to the wine shop. He tasted and selected the liquor for delivery to Avenue Joffre. On his way to his bachelor apartment on Seymour Road, the scent of frying bean curd wafted through the air and hit his nostril. He ordered a string. The vendor's sweaty face grinned with pleasure as he fished out three cubes of golden crispy bean-cakes from the pot of boiling oil. With the fried bean-cakes nesting in the wire-basket ladle in one hand, he threaded a straw through the cakes with the other. He laid down the ladle, brushed red chili pepper sauce over the cakes, and served the bean-cakes dangling them over a piece of brown paper.

Walking and eating the hot cakes from the straw, Glorious Dragon cupped his chin with a handkerchief. The crunchy, spicy fried skin of the bean curd tingled in his mouth; the warm, soft texture of the interior soothed it.

"Ah, the earthy joys of street food!" he exclaimed out loud. The vendor nodded and laughed. "Ha, ha, ha!" Dragon walked away thinking of the glistening crystal and silverware of the Western table and mumbled, "My West Ocean friends would be aghast to learn of my activities yesterday!"

Chapter 7

BRIGHT CRYSTAL'S HOUSE on Avenue Joffre glittered with festive lights. "My Blue Heaven" played softly on the record player in the living room. It could have been a house in Hollywood but for the aroma of Chinese cooking — soy sauce, ginger and garlic, five-spice and sesame oil — wafting through the cool evening air.

Shanghai had developed and consumed energy like a hungry lion. Dragon wanted to take advantage of the city's needs and bring in more generators. At a time of looming war and confusion, he hoped to diversify his family fortunes rather than concentrate on the silk trade.

In the late afternoon, Glorious Dragon played tennis with Messrs. Peter Wilson and George Dunning, the new representatives of Babson and Westcott, a British engineering company. He knew that these Englishmen must be cultivated with the utmost care, because no one had the money to buy generators.

As the men stepped out of their shower stalls after the games, giggling young servant girls greeted them with warm towels. After drying and powdering the men, the girls led them to silk-covered massage tables. The masseuses proceeded to give them a soothing rubdown in scented oils. A more vigorous massage of each muscle followed, from the scalp all the way down to the toes. Initially the Englishmen were surprised and embarrassed, but soon, as the kinks and knots in their arms and legs disappeared in blissful warmth, their tensions and suspicions evaporated. They dozed for half an hour. "That Dragon fellow is a most sporting chap." They agreed.

Afterward, the threesome relaxed on the stone patio. They sipped their whiskey and nibbled on Russian caviar, Chinese fried peanuts, and Japanese seaweed crackers.

"Shanghai is now one of the great metropolises of the world," Glorious Dragon said. "As you can see, we'll need more electric-generating power. Tonight I'll introduce you to several directors of the Shanghai Power and Light Company. They're interested in your generators, but you must convince your company or government to supply the loans."

Red Chinese lanterns danced among the trees, and the shifting shadows on the broad lawns made Wilson and Dunning feel they had arrived in paradise. The gloom of England, on the verge of another war, seemed very far away.

Glorious Dragon understood their mood. The Englishmen had no interest in discussing China's dread of yet more foreign political interference. He had to remain positive. "Of course, being a poor country, we can accept loans only on the most favorable terms. We'll discuss the details in my office tomorrow. Your company will prosper and you'll become great humanitarians for helping us develop."

"Yes, Mr. Chou, we'll be most happy to help." Wilson spoke for both of them. "You have our word!"

The Englishmen appreciated hearing this fine fellow speak humbly, like the most courteous of Chinamen. These would be very risky loans. Japan might invade China, but Shanghai would still need power. If the English company would not supply the loans, the Chinese could persuade American bankers to finance the deal. Yes, the English were ready to grease whatever wheels were necessary to sell generators to the Chinese. With the increase in business, perhaps they could get themselves transferred to the Orient, where they would be treated like kings. Such complicated arrangements would be time-consuming, but this Dragon chap seemed to know how to take care of a fellow. They agreed to meet at ten-thirty the next morning.

Like Glorious Dragon, Bright Crystal had lost her mother in infancy. Since her father was a cook for a foreign family, she had grown up in a foreigner's home. She had a small straight nose and an infectious smile that made the most of her beguiling dimples. As a child, she played freely with her master's two young boys. When the boys were old enough to attend boarding schools in England, she capitalized on her childhood English to become a hostess in the Cathay Hotel on the Bund. With her hair elegantly bobbed, and her judicious use of makeup and scent, she radiated cosmopolitan charm. Although her manners were reserved and her eyes modestly hooded, she had a habit of throwing back her head whenever she laughed. She soon won General Chin Bartau's patronage.

Bright Crystal's father now supervised her famous kitchen. No one except Glorious Dragon knew the identity of the rotund master chef. Bright Crystal was fully aware that the foreigners expected a genuine Chinese meal in her house. Her father also knew that the Westerners could not tolerate the raucous gaiety and unusual flavors of a true Chinese banquet. He made sure that the shrimp had been shelled and the fish deboned and sautéed without any heavy seasonings that could offend stomachs accustomed to bland food. Chicken and other meats were cut into large chunks so that clumsy fingers could handle them with chopsticks. There would be no slurping and sucking of bones before the foreigners.

A twelve-course banquet awaited them all. Two round tables were set for ten guests each. The guests included a White Russian, two Eurasian gentlemen from the Shanghai Power and Light Company, a man representing the Silk Council, Eugene Ma, and a flour tycoon who arrived with a movie starlet and two aides. General Chin brought his usual entourage of government officials along with an American reporter, a Mr. Archie Strong.

Strong was short and pear-shaped. Round lines dominated his profile. His large eyes bored into everything — a glance from those blue eyes made one feel exposed. General Chin introduced Bright Crystal: "My niece is giving this dinner party for her friends in Shanghai industry and commerce. I thought it might be interesting for you to write home about the leading citizens of our biggest city."

"My assignment is to report on the Xian incident." Mr. Strong smiled. He raked his coppery brown hair with his fingers. "Do you think the generalissimo will ever release Marshal Zhang Hsueh-liang?"

"I read your report last week." Wilson sipped his wine. "Is it all true?"

Everyone knew the headlines dominating the newspapers: Generalissimo Chiang Kai-shek went to Xian to confer with Marshal Zhang on his sixth campaign against the Communists. Zhang kidnapped him and forced him to unite with the Communists to fight Japan. Then Zhang followed the generalissimo to Nanking and was placed under house arrest.

"The whole incident is incomprehensible to us," Dunning joined in. "It is as if Neville Chamberlain had kidnapped Churchill, followed Churchill home and allowed himself to be put under house arrest!"

General Chin signaled the serving girl to pour more Kaoliang. "Marshal Zhang is a loyal, sympathetic friend of our anti-Japanese cause. The generalissimo would be a poor host if Zhang were sent home before his time." He laughed. "Now, let's enjoy our dinner."

Archie Strong knew Chin was trying to distract him. He thought Marshal Zhang a fool for accepting only a verbal agreement from the generalissimo. "We in the West are so baffled by this whole Xian incident." He knew full well that General Chin could clear up all his questions. He nursed his drink carefully. "Why did the generalissimo offer his resignation last week but refuse to free Zhang even now?"

"Ah, the generalissimo wants to be a good host! It is important to be a good host! Enjoy, enjoy!" General Chin swept his hand over the table full of delicacies.

"Dragon-*ko*, you're a poor host!" Bright Crystal cried. "Why don't you help Mr. Strong and Mr. Dunning to some marinated beef?"

"Oh yes, of course, my apologies." Glorious Dragon focused his attention on Dunning. "This is a Shanghai favorite — impeccable texture and taste."

"Beef interlaced with, what, some flavorful fat? And what is the interesting taste?" Dunning was already distracted.

"The beef shank has been braised for hours in this special five-spice sauce until the meat has thoroughly absorbed the taste and aroma. The ligament and tendon also become so tender that they taste like fatty jelly."

While he talked, Glorious Dragon sensed an undercurrent of political intrigue. General Chin had dodged the American reporter's questions, and diverted him from the subject of Nanking, where the aftermath of the Xian incident was unfolding. The general had brought Strong here to distract him and prevent further prying into the internal maneuverings at the capital. The dinner was meant to facilitate General Chin's goal. Dragon understood the dynamics around the table. The life experiences of the different nationalities were fascinating. The Englishmen were interested only in trade. The flour tycoon, the Eurasians of the Power and Light, and the men from the Silk Council were all pillars of Shanghai industry, loyal to the National government. Eugene Ma was a very successful dealer of armaments. Using his German education and connections, he was able to sell German and Italian munitions to the Nationalists. The White Russian obviously hated the Communists. General Chin, as a member of the inner circle of Chiang Kai-shek, was also an ardent anti-Communist. Everyone around the table was pro-Nationalist except for Strong, an impartial reporter.

"Will the generalissimo honor his agreement?" Strong persisted. "The Japanese ambassador Kawagoe was in Nanking pressing for 'cooperation'!"

"There would be no Communists in China if the West had provided support." The White Russian slammed down his winecup. "After the Chinese Republic was established in 1911, the so-called democratic countries wanted only trade. Soviet Russia alone provided help. It is no wonder so many Chinese turned to communism!"

"The Germans helped the Chinese wipe out communism!" The wine stirred Eugene Ma. He was reminded of his fun-filled drinking days as a student in Germany. "General Alexander von Falekenhausen advised Chiang. He's a great leader for our democratic future!"

Glorious Dragon wanted to clarify that Eugene Ma's sense of democracy was based upon what Hitler said: "This is all for the PEOPLE." He tapped his lips and decided not to open his mouth.

"A Nazi general?" Wilson whispered, incredulous.

"A fervent anti-Communist!" General Chin reassured everyone.

"The generalissimo went to Xian on December 7 to meet Zhang. He thought Zhang would help him wipe out the Communists!" The flour tycoon picked up a jumbo shrimp. "Treachery! Sheer treachery!" He chewed up the shrimp.

"Perfidy!" the Eurasian from Shanghai Power and Light shouted.

"Treason!" Eugene Ma nodded.

"Why did Madam Chiang and her brother T.V. Soong go to Xian?" Dunning asked.

"Zhang and Mr. T.V. Soong have been friends from way back — since their student days, I think." General Chin turned his cup to Glorious Dragon, nodding and smiling — a signal to drink more. "It is in the national interest that they join the negotiation."

Glorious Dragon raised his cup, but Wilson frowned. He knew that instead of fighting the Japanese, Chiang Kai-shek had used American aid to wage war against the Communists. "Did Chiang Kai-shek agree to form a united front with the Communists on Christmas Day, just to buy his freedom?" Wilson asked.

"I'm ignorant like a foreigner," Strong joined in quickly. "If Marshal Zhang achieved his objective of uniting the Chinese, why did he accompany Chiang back to Nanking?"

"We're all upset by Chiang's kidnapping." Glorious Dragon took a sip. "Let's not worry about things we can't understand." In his mind, he wondered: *If Chiang honored his agreement to unite with the Communists, what would happen to foreign trade in Shanghai?*

Dunning was thinking along the same lines. "Chiang and the Soong family have been most accommodating to Western trade. How will the Communists proceed?"

"The Communists will not favor trade with the West," said the White Russian. "Chiang did a good job driving them into the barren Shensi Province."

Everyone knew that since 1930, the generalissimo had launched five campaigns to eradicate the Communists.

"I agree," added Eugene Ma. "The Communists were almost decimated during their Long March to Shensi." He smacked his lips. "The generalissimo must not let them recover."

"So you think the generalissimo will renege on the promises he made at Xian?" Strong looked to General Chin for an answer.

General Chin raised his winecup, waving it in front of the guests. "We're making far too much of this incident." He assumed the cheerful mask of the diplomat.

Glorious Dragon made a mental note. The generalissimo was trained in the Chinese classics — bound by the traditional ethics of a scholar. Should he honor his promise, and should the coalition become a reality, Japan surely would not accept a united China. If open warfare erupted between China and Japan, the foreign concessions would become sanctuaries of peace; real estate prices would skyrocket. A look into further investments in the area would not be amiss.

The Englishmen also found the discussion intriguing, but the Kaoliang was warm and the chicken in garlic sauce was superb. That dapper Dragon chap would surely clarify everything for them in the morning. So ignoring Strong, they readily agreed to learn the finger-guessing game Glorious Dragon suggested.

"You see, the game is quite simple," Glorious Dragon explained in a cheerful voice, his face flushed from the Kaoliang. "Both of us must shout out a number together from one to five. The rhythm picks up as you become familiar with the game, but for now, let's use this simple rhythm: one, two, three, shout . . . one, two, three, shout . . ." He smiled, waved his arms, and conducted the chorus of robust voices shouting numbers from one through five. "Now, as you shout, you throw out a fist for a zero, or a one, two, three, four or all five fingers." He gesticulated with his right hand, throwing out a fist, then one finger or more to demonstrate. "If the added number of fingers on the two competing hands equals the number that one of us shouted, you win. The loser drinks the wine."

"Oh-ho." Dunning laughed. "That's insane! Why should anyone play to lose?"

"It's only a game. Let's try." Glorious Dragon smiled. "Three," he shouted, throwing out two fingers while Dunning shouted "two" at the same time and threw out one finger. Glorious Dragon won and Dunning had to drink. A serving girl stood behind each guest and replenished the cup after each drink. Bright Crystal urged food on the guests.

It soon became apparent that Wilson often shouted the same number of fingers as he threw out. He formed the numbers with his lips even before he shouted, so he was losing and drinking heavily. Bright Crystal quietly maneuvered herself next to Wilson. Twice, she squeezed his arm and soothed him with her soft eyes; flashing her sweet dimples, she purred, "I'll drink for you." She motioned her serving girl to pour, and while the guests cheered and hooted, she downed her drink in one toss. "*Kang-pai*," she hummed. She drained her cup and held it in an upside-down position. The men cheered wildly; it was intoxicating to see a refined lady drink with such liberal gusto. Following her example, shouting "*Kang-pai, kang-pai*," they drained their cups. The guests were soon rendered rosy-faced and hazy-minded. Even Strong joined in the merriment. "This is very similar to a finger game I played as a child in the U.S. I can't remember what it's called now," he said.

The Xian incident was completely forgotten.

No one at the table, not even General Chin, was aware that although Bright Crystal and Glorious Dragon's first few cups contained liquor, they had drunk nothing but colored tea the rest of the evening. Their serving girls had been instructed to pour only for them, and in the excitement of jovial carousing, no one noticed. The Westerners couldn't tell one serving girl from another. They complimented Bright Crystal's generous capacity for wine.

The following morning, Messrs. Wilson and Dunning, thoroughly dazzled by the hospitality, acceded to all terms of the contract drawn up by Glorious Dragon.

Chapter 8

ARCHIE STRONG ENJOYED his evening on Avenue Joffre. Nevertheless, during the following week, he contacted all the party guests to discuss their understanding of the Xian Incident. When he called on Glorious Dragon, he was surprised to be invited by the young man to visit his sister and brother-in-law in Hangzhou. The beauties of the idyllic West Lake in Hangzhou had been renowned since the time of Marco Polo, so he accepted.

The diligence of the American reporter impressed Glorious Dragon. He understood the foreigner's confusion. He mulled over Strong's questions at the dinner table but could not respond without giving him a lecture on Confucian culture and ethical behavior. Although this was already 1937, the Chinese people understood that the emperor ruled with a mandate from Heaven based upon his exemplary life. Zhang would go down in history as the quintessential hero who had kidnapped the present emperor, Generalissimo Chiang Kai-shek, and forced him on a course of virtue — unification with the communists to fight Japan. Zhang would accept whatever punishment, including death, if required. For centuries, storytellers, singers and actors had celebrated such courageous men, in households, theaters, operas, tea-houses, wine shops and restaurants with slight variations on the theme. How could Strong even begin to understand the emotions simmering in the Chinese soul? Glorious Dragon would not know how to tell him. Should he take Strong to a

Chinese opera based on the same heroic theme? The falsetto voices of the singers on a bare stage would be trilling in half tones and would drive Strong away from his seat within minutes. No, he could not lecture Strong on Chinese thought and maintain a cordial relationship.

More to the point, Glorious Dragon wanted to know what Mr. Strong had already discovered about the recent events in Nanking. Would the generalissimo continue to keep Marshal Zhang under house arrest? Would he integrate the Communists into his army, and thus pose a serious threat to the Japanese occupation?

In a flash of inspiration, he decided that the American should meet his sister Purple Jade, who had so patiently taught him his classics. His brother-in-law, Righteous Virtue, had deplored Western powers' competing for Chinese territory and trade. He had rejected communism, Nazism and materialism, but he was familiar with Western manners. He lived the life of an exemplary Confucian scholar: conservative, with a learned contentment and pacifism. Glorious Dragon was confident Strong would benefit from a meeting with his sister and brother-in-law — two living embodiments of the finest in Chinese culture.

When Archie Strong entered the Huang family's first court, he took a quick breath, arrested by the sight of a dwarf cedar leaning toward a structure of porous Taihu rocks. The beautiful formation towered over a small pool where silver, gold and red carps swam. A covered walkway surrounded the courtyard on three sides, away from the front gate and spirit screen wall. Under an overhang of terra-cotta roof tiles at the entrance to the first hall, Righteous Virtue stood waiting for his guests. He was wearing an ankle-length brown silk gown with cream silk cuffs and trousers.

Strong was surprised that the mandarin spoke English. They took tea in the first hall and exchanged social pleasantries. Righteous Virtue suggested they visit the larger garden the Huangs shared with the Chous, his wife's maiden family.

"A walk in the garden is perfect after our train ride," Strong agreed. Righteous Virtue instructed the servants to relay the following message to Purple Jade: they would dine in the moon pavilion.

Leading the way, Glorious Dragon passed through a moon-gate faced with red-lacquered wood. The round frame offered a long vista across a lotus pond. A pavilion with latticed windows loomed in the right corner, towering over a blanket of budding azalea bushes.

"I often come here to view the lotus when they're in bloom," Righteous Virtue explained as they strolled along the covered walkway surrounding the lotus pond. "Their beauty reminds me of the spirit of our nation."

"How's that?" Strong raked his fingers through his brown hair.

"The lotus grows from mud, but the flowers remain pristine. That is how I hope our country will emerge from its present troubles."

Strong nodded. They had arrived at another moon-gate, made of terra-cotta tiles. He had an open view of a large glistening pond. Marble walks and bridges led to rock arrangements and open pavilions — studios for painting and reading and terraces of bamboo groves, budding fruit trees, and swaying willows. Strong was guided slowly through the walled-in garden, viewing it from different terraced heights and angles. Throughout the tour, Righteous Virtue pointed out the compositions of light and shadows, the balance of yin and yan. Water, stone, trees and flowers had all been carefully coordinated.

"I must thank you for allowing me to see this exquisite garden!" Strong exclaimed. Glorious Dragon smiled. Chinese etiquette would have called for a disclaimer, but he knew Strong was new in China; he accepted the compliment.

When they arrived at the moon pavilion, the table was set, and Purple Jade was waiting. She wore a silk burgundy jacket with subtle shades of violet woven in a small floral pattern. Purple satin piped the borders of the thigh-length robe, flowing loosely over a floor-length skirt of the same color. The skirt obscured her feet.

When the American guest was introduced, she got up, held both hands to one side at her waist, lowered one knee to the floor, and curtsied. She rose gracefully, then reclined. Archie Strong thought she looked like a princess from a storybook.

Purple Jade knew most Chinese immigrants to America came from Canton and Fukien Provinces, so Americans were familiar with Cantonese food. She had ordered the kitchen to provide a light supper of dim sum, but she included a specialty of the region, the crab meat shao lun bao (Small dragon dumplings).

Strong recognized the shrimp dumplings wrapped in thin rice dough right away. "These are my favorite when I go to New York's Chinatown for Sunday brunch!"

"Now try these shao lun bao." Glorious Dragon said. He carefully picked up a dumpling and placed it on a spoon. He added a few drops of Zhenjiang black vinegar, and some julienned young ginger and passed the spoon to Strong. "Try to eat it in one bite and savor the burst of juice mixed with the crab and meat filling."

"Ah, this is heavenly," Strong sighed. "How did they hold the juice inside such a thin piece of skin?"

"That's the cook's secret." Righteous Virtue smiled. "These dumplings have been made here for centuries."

Purple Jade sipped tea; the men drank beer and translated the conversation for her. As they ate, they discussed Chinese regional cuisine, garden design and architecture. They noted that while food differed from one region to the next, China had a common goal: to lead a quiet life in harmony with nature.

The conversation soon drifted toward the Confucian ideal of a simple, reclusive life away from the crass concerns of the material world. Strong heartily approved. He laughed and allowed that he too would love to be a recluse in such a home as this.

"But if I may ask my question," he began, his eyes flashing. "Do you feel strange that the Xian incident involved so much contorted maneuvering by your leaders? Why did Marshal Zhang return to Nanking with Chiang Kai-shek?"

"Ah, Zhang must return to give Chiang face," Righteous Virtue answered.

Strong had heard of the importance of face. "What can face do for Generalissimo Chiang, or for China?"

"Now that he was given face, Chiang must act like the paragon of Confucian virtue. We expect our leaders to act with honor. In other words, Chiang must fulfill his agreement and ally with the Communists to defend our homeland against foreign aggression!"

Strong wanted to know if the people wanted unity and democracy, but he remembered how America had long ignored Chinese interests and benefited from the British colonial trade in opium. He decided to concentrate on the Xian Incident. "So why did the generalissimo offer to resign? He knows the West supports him and he controls the best army."

"He must resign to regain face," Righteous Virtue said again.

"Doesn't his strength give him face? I've learned that the generalissimo is neutralizing Marshal Zhang's power by transferring his northeastern forces. These are now being absorbed into the Nationalist army in Hunan and Anhui."

"He must regain face by acting virtuous. Most Chinese detest the Japanese occupation," Righteous Virtue said. "All the armies must come under central government control. I understand even the Communist Red Army will become the Nationalist Eighth Route Army. I believe Chiang Kai-shek's son, Chiang Ching-kuo, will soon return from the Soviet Union to help integrate the Communists into our Nationalist government."

"Imagine, Chiang Kai-shek sent his son to the Soviet Union to study while he was being advised by the Nazis! I can't believe the Chinese will ever unite." Strong shook his head. He handled his chopsticks like an expert. He knew he was a quick study and thought he understood the contentious Chinese.

There were days when Purple Jade felt the suffocating worries of the Japanese threat and her divided country could wither the blossoms in her garden, but Strong gave her a chance to speak of her hopes. "Tell him our folk tale of the three defective sons-in-law." Purple Jade nudged her brother. She had often taught her brother through parables.

"My sister wishes me to tell you this story." He nodded to his sister and then to Strong. He took a sip of beer to clear his throat.

"Once upon a time, there was a man with three married daughters. One son-in-law suffered from an itchy scalp and had the bad habit of scratching his head in front of company.

The second son-in-law suffered from an itchy back and could not resist twisting to reach and scratch his back even on the most formal occasions. The third son-in-law suffered from a runny nose, and had to blow, despite the solemnity of any event."

Strong relaxed into his chair with his arms crossed before him.

"It so happened that the father-in-law had reached his sixtieth birthday and planned a sumptuous feast to celebrate. The noted gentry of the town had been invited. It seemed the sons-in-law were doomed to commit the gravest faux pas in front of the whole town. Not only would their improprieties bring disgrace to their families, but the father-in-law would lose face on his birthday. The daughters fretted and wrung their hands in dread of the feast, and their husbands promised to control themselves as best they could.

"The day of the party came, and all three daughters and their husbands went in all their finery. At the banquet, they sat together to give each other courage. The sons-in-law behaved admirably until the sixth course when they could no longer endure their itches and runny nose. They looked to each other and carried out their plan. The first son-in-law raised his voice to praise his father-in-law's virtues, then he volunteered to entertain the guests by relating an unusual adventure.

"'Last week, I went to gather wood in the mountains,' he said. 'Suddenly I saw a ferocious tiger on a ledge in front of me. I was so scared, I dropped all my wood, scratched my head, and wondered what to do.' He shook his hands toward the ground and dumped the load of imaginary wood. He scratched his head to demonstrate his story and satisfied his itch.

"The second son-in-law quickly took up the story: 'Ah, you shouldn't have wasted time to think! You should have run inside a narrow cave to hide!' He backed into a wall, rubbed his back against it, then squatted under the table and twisted into his seat, giving his back a vigorous scratching in the process.

"The third son-in-law could hardly breathe by this time, but he shouted, 'You two are not brave! Huh . . .' He took a breath and blew his nose in one big heave. 'I'll take my bow and arrow and shoot the tiger!' His arm swept up as he spoke. In one swift motion of drawing his imaginary arrow from his back and pulling the arrow from the phantom bowstring, he wiped his nose on his sleeve, demonstrating his skill. The guests enjoyed the pantomime and congratulated the old man on his witty sons-in-law."

Strong enjoyed the story but failed to see the point.

"You see — " Righteous Virtue took a deep breath, reluctant to have to explain again. " — all the Chinese political factions are like the sons-in-law. With all their imperfections, they cooperated to save the family face."

"Yeah, but they still suffer from the itches and the runny nose!" Strong retorted.

Purple Jade winced at the forthright American talk. She whispered to her husband, "It would be at least five years before the old man would celebrate another important birthday." Righteous Virtue translated for Purple Jade. "The 'face' gave the sons-in-law time to correct their faults."

"That's positive thinking, I suppose," Strong conceded. He looked at this self-contained fairy princess in her orderly garden and was more moved by the lady's gentle, obliging manner than by her logic.

"Of course, the situation does not allow for outside intervention," Glorious Dragon said with some vehemence. "If one guest encouraged the first son-in-law to sell the third one's arrows to cure his itchy scalp, and another guest encouraged the second one to grab them for the benefit of his back, then all that 'face' would turn to squabbles in no time."

Glorious Dragon's face was flushed with emotion; both Purple Jade and Righteous Virtue remained unnaturally still.

Strong knew that Western philosophies like democracy, communism, nazism all brought competition, war and suffering to China. By contrast, the old Confucian teachings of hard work, education, and respect for authority had given China centuries of peace and prosperity. This family, like most Chinese, valued the traditional way to solve problems within the family and nation.

The vehemence in Glorious Dragon's voice made Archie Strong uneasy. He thought he had taken a proper measure of Glorious Dragon. He saw him as a shrewd and opportunistic businessman. Suddenly he felt the man's intense antagonism toward foreign meddling in Chinese affairs. He held his tongue, because he had studied Chinese history in preparation for his trip. Although America did not own a concession on Chinese soil like the Europeans, none of the Western powers had been blameless. All had played a role in causing havoc within the Chinese body politic.

"Look, the moon is out," whispered Purple Jade in Chinese. She pointed to the brilliant full moon in the clear dark sky, hoping to defuse the tension. Strong looked at the broken, wrinkled moon in the pond before them and thought: *People at home will see only this reflection of a broken disk from my reports. They will never see that clear moon in a cloudless sky.*

Chapter 9

A SHAFT OF MOONBEAM stole into the room where Purple Jade sat rubbing her temples. Her feet were soaking in a basin of hot water. Outside her window, the silvery West Lake shimmered. Tender spring greens of bamboo framed her view, obscuring the shadows of distant mountains. The drumbeats of war seemed to echo in the darkness. An ominous thud in her head filled her with foreboding. Her heart raced, but she directed her thoughts to the light and her good fortune: She never had to move into her husband's home and live under the tyranny of a mother-in-law. She truly appreciated her husband's unconventional courage. Yes, she must ignore all thoughts of chaos. She would maintain the normalcy of her household.

Purple Jade sighed. Things changed so fast! No one suspected her involvement in the Prosperous Dream fire. The opium den was being rebuilt, as the drug dealers were unstoppable. The only good thing that had come out of that incident was her rescue of Little Six, who was thriving under the cook's supervision. The visit of the American reporter had been stimulating, but she was exhausted. With his big blue eyes, he seemed as guileless as an inquisitive child. He might have understood the Chinese's strong desire for freedom and independence as a nation, and perhaps even understood the individual family's ideal of reclusive living in a crowded country, but did he understand the drama and nobility displayed by Marshal Zhang and the generalissimo? She was not sure if a foreigner could ever savor the heart-swelling glory of "giving face," and subjecting oneself to the rule of "virtue." She remembered her husband telling her that Miss Tyler had studied Confucian teaching thoroughly. She had been in the country a long time. Both Mr. Strong and Miss Tyler would be invited to the birthday party, she decided. Perhaps the foreign lady could help Mr. Strong understand.

Her mind drifted to an unpleasant task that morning. The family of the drowned girl had claimed the body. Her name was Chen Snow Song. Apparently, it was a suicide, yet no one knew the cause of the tragedy. The girl lived in town with her widowed mother, and her family owned a small stationery store. She had been a scholarship student at the missionary school. As the mistress of a leading family in this region, Purple Jade would be obliged to receive the mother in her home in a few days. Her heart quailed at the unpleasant task. What words of comfort could she offer to a bereaved mother who was a widow? Why would a young girl want to kill herself? How could she be so unfilial as to leave her mother to grieve? How did a Chinese girl become so radical that she placed her personal emotions above her family's welfare? Her headache intensified. A persistent fear needled her. She assumed that Snow Song's Western education had played havoc with her values, just as it had with her daughter Golden Bell.

"Evening peace, *M-ma*." Golden Bell came in carrying an American magazine. She saw Orchid massaging her mother's back. "*M-ma*, I'm sorry I was rude earlier."

Her eyes fell on her mother's small, arched feet; they looked pale gray and puffy in the water. She winced.

Purple Jade misunderstood Golden Bell's emotion. She thought she saw shame. "Come sit by me, my hot-headed heart-and-liver."

"I brought you a Western magazine to look at." Golden Bell edged close to her mother and opened the magazine, shielding her eyes from the sight of the grotesque feet.

Purple Jade did not look at the magazine. Instead, she warmed to her daughter's closeness. "You're young and restless. If the weather is nice this weekend, would you like to go boating with us on West Lake? I intend to invite your Miss Spicy-Too-Hot."

"Great! It'll be interesting for you to get to know her."

"Yes, you're right," Purple Jade replied with a tinge of regret. She did not want to mingle with the foreign lady who had chosen to enter strangers' homes to educate strangers' children. However, years of self-restraint had forbidden her to show disdain. "Yes, it is time to meet her. We won't stay out long, because young ladies can turn into brown prunes in the sun."

"*M-ma.*" Golden Bell smiled at her mother's analogy. "If I work very hard and write a very good poem in Chinese for Father, may I have my hair bobbed?"

"You have such thick glossy hair; it is positively enchanting when you let it fall loose around you." She looked at her daughter hungrily, not wanting to spoil the harmony of the moment.

"Then you won't allow me to cut my hair?" Golden Bell recoiled from her mother.

Purple Jade shuddered at this sudden display of hostility. She groped for some understanding. "Fashions are always changing. Hair will grow back after it is cut, so I guess it is all right. Just make sure you tell the barber to save your long hair for me."

"Oh, thank you, *M-ma*, thank you. I thought you might reject all my wishes just because they seem Western." Golden Bell moved close to her mother again.

"My dear heart-and-liver, as you grow older, you will learn that the best weapons for a woman are tears and gentle persuasion." She held her daughter's hand, pleased that they were reconciled. "How you ask for something is as important as what you ask."

When Golden Bell stood up to leave, her mother reminded her: "You may take back your magazine. I've seen them before. The foreigners all look alike."

"But *M-ma*, Western women do not have bound feet!"

"Yes." Purple Jade took several deep breaths. She straightened in her seat. "Western women can go everywhere with their big feet, but they become too brazen from having so much freedom!"

"No *M-ma*, they're strong. They would never have allowed anyone to bind their feet!"

As Purple Jade looked at her crippled feet, her ideal of a virtuous, compliant lady seemed hopelessly inadequate. Except for the rescue of Little Six, her one incursion into the proactive ways of the modern world had ended in a fire that failed to save the town from the scourge of opium. "Your father is right. You are the future hope and strength of China," she said. "Unfortunately, you are a daughter and will marry into another household. Traditions do not change. A son must hold a man's head when he is placed into the coffin." The thought sent chills down her spine; she wrung her hands in agitation. "No man would perform this task without being named an heir!" She took out her handkerchief and clutched it tightly to calm herself. "Sons-in-law bearing a different family name cannot inherit. We're still without an heir."

"Things will change, *M-ma*. You'll see!" Golden Bell could not argue the obvious. She bade her mother evening peace and left.

As Purple Jade returned to Orchid's quiet attention, Silver Bell ran in.

"*M-ma.*" She forgot to bow and pay her respects first. "Peony told me Golden Bell will have her hair bobbed. May I have some money and have my hair cut in town?"

"Silver Bell, you know it is unbecoming to come without a greeting." Purple Jade frowned, still agitated by her first daughter.

"Evening peace, *M-ma.*" Silver Bell quickly bowed. "May I go into town?"

"Child, you mustn't allow your maid to tell you what to do. Peony, come in!" Purple Jade raised her voice. She knew the maid would be hiding outside the door. "What is the meaning of this?"

"Here I am, *Tai-tai.*" Peony stared at the ground. "I didn't tell the young mistress to ask for money. I only told her what Iris told me."

"Silver Bell, your sister has her fate in life and you have yours. There is no need to compete and compare what doesn't add or subtract from your virtue."

"But, *M-ma*!"

"Peony, do you admire the new hairdo?"

"Well, *Tai-tai*, I . . . I don't know." Peony twisted the corner of her tunic.

"*Tai-tai,*" Orchid spoke from behind her mistress. "I heard the new hairdo also involves electrocuting the hair, so it all stands out in curls."

Peony and Silver Bell looked at each other and became quiet. Orchid was not often wrong.

"My little heart-and-liver." Purple Jade drew Silver Bell near her. "What Orchid said must be true. The new fashions are very strange, especially on a Chinese girl." She smoothed down the stray hairs on Silver Bell's pigtails. "Peony, don't you dare stir up trouble, and make your young mistress drink vinegar. I'll see to it that you get a whipping."

"Oh *Tai-tai*, please spare me. I only thought to keep the young mistress amused!" Peony worried the corner of her tunic some more.

"*M-ma*, spare Peony or I'll behave just like Golden Bell. She thinks she's so smart now, learning English and science; she never wants to play with me anymore."

"Hush, hush, Silver Bell. Don't be brazen like your sister. I'll find you a good husband who will take our name, and you will be my comfort in my old age."

"*M-ma*, tell me again how you met my father!"

"Not now, dear heart, my footbath is getting cold, and we must all prepare for bed. After you've memorized your assignment from the Three Character Book, I'll tell you."

"Come, young mistress," Peony called to her charge happily, all thoughts of punishment vanished.

Chapter 10

A FEW DAYS LATER, the women of the Huang family gathered on the river dock to wait for Miss Tyler to join them for a boating party. It had rained during the night, but the sun burned away the morning fog. A gentle breeze scattered crystal sparkles all over the grass. Golden Bell's spirit soared in anticipation.

As the car approached, Orchid stole into the boat to avoid the chauffeur. Taking up the rudder under the canopy, she turned toward the center of the river and waited.

Ah Lee had second thoughts about his attempted seduction of Orchid. In truth, his methods seldom met with defeat. Orchid's diffidence and inexperience excited him beyond endurance. He tried in vain to catch sight of her again, to make amends; her inaccessibility had become another enticement. Finally he decided to approach Orchid openly. After all, he was from Shanghai; he would show her the alluring foreign ways. He had seen foreigners go courting with flowers and candies. He had brought along a bouquet and a box of cookies.

When Miss Tyler noticed the gifts in the car, Ah Lee explained that he brought the cookies and flowers for Orchid to enjoy during the boating party. The chauffeur's speech, with a few carefully inserted English words, impressed Miss Tyler, and his tactful romantic gesture touched her. After greeting everyone, she thought she would give the soft-spoken, mild-mannered chauffeur some assistance with the stuffy Huangs.

"Where's Orchid?" she asked Purple Jade in her accented Chinese. "I believe this young man has something for her!"

Orchid sat with her back turned, surprised to hear the foreign lady asking for her on Ah Lee's behalf. Burning with confusion and embarrassment, she crouched lower into the boat.

Ah Lee stepped forward. Bowing to Purple Jade, he let his eyes survey the crowd. "*Tai-tai*, I would like to row the boat for you. I've brought some cookies and flowers for Orchid to share with you on our boating trip." He looked around from face to face. "Where is she?" He thought Orchid might have been left behind for some reason. He wanted to rush back and take advantage of her lonely state. In another quick bow, he clutched the gifts closer to his chest, mumbling, "I wanted to give her these as a token of my affection." He smiled his debonair best and noticed the foreign teacher glowing with pleasure.

Purple Jade was aghast at this impudent, forward servant. No decent man with any sense of propriety would have been so bold, so crass. Imagine inviting himself to the boating party with all the women! And Miss Tyler had encouraged him! Speechless with anger, Purple Jade turned red and her hands trembled. Iris quickly reached over to support her.

"Ah Lee wants Orchid for a concubine!" Peony giggled and Silver Bell tittered.

"You are already married?" Miss Tyler asked in consternation. She could never tell the age of the Chinese. She had thought the chauffeur was a teenager.

"Oh, I have no woman in Hangzhou!" Ah Lee replied nonchalantly. "I've no more affection for my wife in Shanghai. Perhaps I should follow your custom and divorce her."

Miss Tyler turned pale. She couldn't tell whether Ah Lee was being shrewd or naive. She knew she had blundered disgracefully. The Chinese might consider the loss of face unforgivable, especially in a teacher. The mission badly needed the support of influential families, such as the Huangs. She would have to make amends and try to think like a Chinese — exercise her "breath of a guest." For now, she must remain quiet. When they would reach the teahouse on the island, she would apologize and buy tea. She would express thoughtfulness.

Iris herded everyone on board the boat and signaled Orchid to push off, leaving Ah Lee gawking on the dock. He finally saw Orchid, but he had offended the mistress of the house and Orchid would be inaccessible to him.

"Snobbish bitches!" Ah Lee murmured to himself. "I'll buy three slave girls to serve me here in Hangzhou! See if I don't!" He sped away in the car, leaving a trail of smoke and dust.

Orchid felt lighthearted and reassured by the turn of events. Now her mistress would protect her from the crude and presumptuous Ah Lee. She picked up the oars. With help from Iris and Peony, she rowed vigorously toward the pavilion where they usually took their tea and watched the songbirds.

Everyone sat stiffly, watching circles form around the oars at every dip. Iris pointed to the water lilies and tried to inspire some positive comments on the peeping spring buds. No one responded. Even Silver Bell and Peony were silenced by the palpable tension between the teacher and Purple Jade.

Golden Bell fidgeted in her seat, painfully aware that her teacher had been dishonored. Perhaps her studies with the American lady would now be in jeopardy. As the boat slid by a lotus patch, she tore off a leaf, shredded it into bits and threw them into the water. She held back tears of frustration.

Purple Jade sat watching the roaming water birds and wondered about Miss Tyler's motivation. The woman had come halfway around the world to teach strangers and meddle in other people's lives. Righteous Virtue once told her that the Westerners had even probed the universe and spent hours arguing about the number of angels that could fit on the head of a pin.

The Confucian tenet of Jen (benevolence) was more practical, thought Purple Jade. Subjects must honor their emperor, the sons their fathers, and servants their masters. Their manner might be formal, but their civility was based on solicitude, its enforcement grounded in moral suasion. In a crowded country, harmony prevailed when everyone was given face. She wondered how the chauffeur could slight his Chinese heritage and ignore the proper conventions.

Her thoughts wandered to that unfortunate girl in the river. The girl must have chosen suicide to escape some intolerable fate. Did the missionary school teach her obligations to her family? Of course not! Instead, it must have taught her that she had individual rights and privileges. These Western ideas led to egotism and fear of the unknown. Yes, she was right to keep her children away from the missionary school.

"Miss Tyler, why did you come to China?" Silver Bell asked, when she could no longer stand the frosty silence.

Golden Bell gave her sister a look of dismay. She wanted to shout "Shut up" but realized it would be another offense to her mother. She brought her hand to her half-open mouth, and tapped it to stifle her shout.

"I don't know, really," stammered Miss Tyler after some thought. "I came from generations of pioneers. I suppose I was infected, so to speak."

"What's a pioneer?"

"Well, a pioneer . . ." Miss Tyler thought this ingenuous child was fascinating. She saw her chance for redemption. "A pioneer carries new ideas, develops new land. I wished to be one of the first to learn from China."

Purple Jade gazed at the distant morning fog, which floated like tufts of silk wool near the mountaintops. She noted Miss Tyler's careful Chinese and appreciated her efforts to make amends.

"Did you know Chen Snow Song?" Silver Bell asked.

Golden Bell glared at her sister and plucked another lotus leaf from the lake.

Miss Tyler paled. "Yes. I really don't understand. We must have failed her somehow."

"Silver Bell, stop your impudent questioning!" Purple Jade interrupted. The barbarian lady was a teacher after all. She must not suffer further indignities before her students. "Chen Snow Song was a victim of fate. No one can control that!"

Miss Tyler held her peace. She knew this was not the time to object to such stoicism. Instead, she accepted the charity and whispered her thanks to her hostess, "Shai shai."

Everyone fell silent. Golden Bell looked with grateful surprise on her mother. She dropped her leaf and smiled at her teacher.

Orchid's cares evaporated with every movement of the oars. For days, her role in the opium den's fire and her entanglement with Ah Lee had left her feeling guilty at the deception. When they reached the island, she was ready to run and shout. "Oh *Tai-tai*, there are some fruit peddlers on the other side of the dock. May I go and buy you some lichee nuts?"

"Yes, go, Orchid." Purple Jade gave her a handful of coins. "Iris will help me to the tea pavilion." Purple Jade sensed her maid's relief and was pleased by her suggestion.

As they ordered tea, they could hear Orchid's clever bargaining floating through the air. "Oh, you old turtle, nobody wants to buy your rotten fruit. If my kind mistress weren't so softhearted, I might spit on your fruit. A hundred coppers, indeed!"

Silver Bell and Peony ran off to explore the famous Nine Rivulets and Eighteen Gullies, glad to get away from the adults.

"Forgive me, Mrs. Huang," Miss Tyler began. "I didn't know Ah Lee was already married. I thought it was romantic to see a young man go courting on a spring morning."

"Miss Tai-lar, you cannot be expected to know the private lives of servants, so please don't let that concern you."

Miss Tyler understood the Chinese translation of her name to mean "Spicy-Too-Hot." She assumed Purple Jade had difficulty pronouncing English names; she ignored the implication. She acknowledged humbly: "I shouldn't have assumed his intentions in so private a matter. I suppose I was swayed by his English and his Western manners."

"We don't consider a man's affection for a woman to be a spectator's sport," answered Purple Jade. "If he had asked for Orchid through a proper marriage broker, I might have considered."

"Yes?" Miss Tyler equivocated. Purple Jade's response was a total surprise to her. She had completely misread this woman. "You would give your maid to Ah Lee even if he already has a wife?"

"Orchid is like a daughter to me." Purple Jade flashed an elegant smile. "I would never give her to anyone so coarse and ignorant of proper decorum."

"You were offended because of Ah Lee's impropriety?"

"If a man cannot control his outward behavior, how can he be faithful to his inner truth? Hai . . . " Purple Jade sighed. "It is unfortunate. Ah Lee has been corrupted by city life, but he is an indispensable servant. It would bring the household great peace if he took a concubine from among the household maids and settled down."

Miss Tyler could not comprehend this strange logic. "I know the Chinese believe in arranged marriages, but I thought consideration is also given to personal choices."

Golden Bell, who had been listening intently, could not resist giving her opinion. "Westerners think it is immoral for a man to take a concubine."

"You talk like a barbarian, saying the first thing on your mind," her mother said, frowning. "What's wrong with having a concubine? My late mother, your grandmother, was a concubine. If a person is properly educated, personal choices should coincide with the welfare and prestige of the whole family!"

"Eighty coppers? I may still spit on your fruit!" Orchid's voice intruded on the conversation.

"Why, that's . . . that's cruel, and an insult to womanhood," Golden Bell stammered.

"Iris, tell your young mistress whether you think it is cruel to be a concubine."

Iris blushed. "I'm only a servant." She wrung her hands and looked down. "Concubines are not different from maids. If the master is kind, it is an honor to be chosen."

"Why Iris." Golden Bell stared at Iris open-mouthed. She looked to her teacher for help. "Miss Tyler?"

"Seventy coppers! Aiya, you think I'm your Buddha?" Orchid's exclamation flew against the peddler's entreaties.

"Westerners believe all men are created equal. Here maids can be married off to any poor farmer or laborer. A concubine has more protection," Iris said.

"There is a different system here." Miss Tyler nodded soberly. "We believe democracy and independence can uphold individual dignity. Perhaps it may not be possible here because people are born into classes and have a different understanding of freedom and equality."

Purple Jade thought this strange modern talk of freedom had only encouraged selfishness, ruthless competition and breakdowns like Chin Snow Song's. But it was time for her to be gracious, and not to point out the troublesome ideas the teacher was bringing to China.

"How could a lady manage without her maid?" Purple Jade asked. "It would be a great loss of face for a mistress of the house to bargain, as Orchid is doing for me now."

"Miss Tyler, you often complained that you have to pay double for everything," Iris added, eager to make peace.

Miss Tyler adjusted herself in her seat, uncomfortable with the drift of the conversation. She knew her students' confusion and conflicts of loyalty. She also understood the mother's concerns. However, she must not teach and lecture in front of the mother. She merely nodded to Iris in response.

Purple Jade wanted to ask how Westerners could think everyone was created equal. Surely men and women could not do the same things, and master and servants were born with different gifts! How did they arrange marriages and manage their households? She had heard of divorces and wondered who took care of the divorced women and children. She speculated on Western households, where women functioned without the solidarity of other women. Her heart ached for Miss Tyler in her single, lonely state. She decided not to ask any more questions. She accepted Miss Tyler's "different" system for civility's sake. She was satisfied that the teacher showed restraint, was not contentious, and had enough grace to acknowledge her desire to learn from another culture. Golden Bell was impetuous because of her youth. Her teacher was not to blame.

"All right, all right, fifty coppers for all these lichee nuts and three extra bunches of dragon-eyes too." Orchid's voice rang triumphantly over the pavilion. "You're fortunate today, old turtle!"

When Orchid came with the fruits, Purple Jade took Miss Tyler with her to feed the songbirds. Miss Tyler remembered the camera she had brought and took pictures of Purple Jade feeding the birds. Together they discussed the birds' plumage and habits. They agreed that while the birds were of different colors, and sang different songs, it was obvious that they enjoyed each other's company.

Purple Jade steered the conversation to Miss Tyler's work. They spoke of a foreign woman's difficulties adjusting to life in Hangzhou: starting a school and dealing with Chinese men who held the purse strings. Purple Jade took note of all Miss Tyler's needs and promised to speak to her husband about them. Finally, she asked, "You work so far away from home. Did your family object to your choice of profession?"

"No, it is a Christian tradition for women to do God's work inside and outside the home. People respect women who serve their communities at home or in the world, especially in nursing and teaching."

"Nurturing the young and dependent is also central to the teachings of Confucius, but you have an admirable tradition — allowing women into the community!" Purple Jade thought this might be their meaning of equality for women. The Chinese would not encourage a woman to be inquisitive, but she must be gracious. "I wish we could learn more of that from you," she said in earnest. Both women smiled, surprised to discover how much they liked each other.

Chapter 11

THE MORNING SUN shone on the terra-cotta roof tiles, and the flowering apricot tree formed lacy patterns outside the schoolroom. Golden Bell and Iris huddled around Miss Tyler. They stood behind a tripod, taking turns to peer into a viewfinder.

"The subject must face the light, and the camera must remain very still," Miss Tyler said. "Iris, go and stand by the apricot tree. Now, Golden Bell, come and take a look."

Golden Bell had to stand on tiptoes to look into the camera. She was almost half a head shorter than Miss Tyler.

"My! Iris looks as if she's been caught in a pink net!"

"That's the reflected light from the blossoms." Miss Tyler waved her arm. "Iris, move in front of the tree." After many adjustments, she motioned Golden Bell to come and look again. "We mustn't get branch shadows on her face. There!" She clicked the shutter.

"Oh, Miss Tyler, if the picture doesn't show your red hair and blue eyes, do you think you'll look more Chinese?" Golden Bell asked.

"Maybe not. My big nose will give me away." Miss Tyler twitched her nose, sending the girls into peals of laughter. "Now, Golden Bell, you go stand in Iris's place, and I'll take your picture."

"How do I look?" Golden Bell's long eyes sparkled. She straightened her blue brocade jacket and dark silk trousers.

Iris swung her pigtails behind her. "I've never seen myself in a photo before!" She giggled. "I can't wait for the picture to develop and show it to Peony."

Loud banging sounds came from Golden Bell's room. Roof tiles and walls shook and rattled. Teacher and students looked at each other and ran to inspect.

They found the scrawny, pigtailed Little Six waving her hammer and smiling. "I found this faucet. Now the young mistress will have water in her own room!" She beamed, showing her crooked teeth. She had already nailed the faucet to the wall behind Golden Bell's dressing table and placed a washbasin under the faucet.

Golden Bell and Miss Tyler looked confused, but Iris burst out laughing so hard she had to lean against a wall to steady herself. "Oh, ho, ho, Little Six, such a country bumpkin! What a dumb egg! Oh ho, ho, she thinks she can bring on the self-coming-water."

"I didn't ask permission first?" Little Six lowered her head. Immediately, she brightened and tried to turn on her faucet, "I wanted to surprise the elder-young-mistress." She twisted the faucet this way and that, almost wrenching it loose from the wall. No water came, and she scratched her head.

Giggling, Golden Bell explained: "Little Six is the new scullery maid. Mother found her begging on the street. I gave her some of my old play clothes. She meant to repay the kindness!"

"How old are you?" Miss Tyler asked.

"No one told me. Maybe twelve?" Little Six wrinkled her nose.

"More like ten, I'd say." Iris took the hammer from her.

"Come, come, Little Six." Miss Tyler gently pried the child's hands from the faucet. "You've done a gracious thing." She led her into the schoolroom where she tried to wash both their hands together. Little Six felt the running water and ran back to her faucet in the bedroom. She turned it and muttered, "Strange, magic. Water there, but no water here!"

Golden Bell and Iris laughed and giggled some more, but Miss Tyler said, "There are no pipes inside this wall. The water is carried by pipes, which probably start from a stream up in the mountain."

"No pipes? What pipes?" Little Six whined. "Pipes come into this wall? How did the mountain pipes come in here?"

"Perhaps we can all go out and trace the pipe route. You can help us carry my photography equipment, and we'll take some pictures."

"What is the foreign devil talking about?" Little Six shouted to Iris. "What pictures?"

"You know, a likeness of yourself on a shiny piece of paper."

"Oh no, no, people say your spirit is taken away with your likeness!" Little Six shrieked, shielding her face behind her palms. "My uncle went into the city — came back so sick, he almost died. Someone took his picture, and he only recovered after my mother burned his likeness!"

Miss Tyler did not know how to answer, but Iris shook her head in exasperation. She shouted: "That has nothing to do with it. Nothing to do with it at all! You dumb egg! Country bumpkin!"

"Well, we won't take your picture, Little Six." Miss Tyler herded the girls into the courtyard. "Look, here is the pipe from the schoolroom. Look how cunningly it is blended with the eaves of the roof tiles."

Miss Tyler carried her own camera. Little Six tried to pick up the tripod, but Iris grabbed it away from her. "You'll only drop it. What a dumb egg!"

The pipe led them to the kitchen then out into the large garden. "Oh I must go back. I must go in," Little Six cried when they were only a few steps out of the kitchen courtyard. "Cook will be so mad at me for being away so long. *Tai-tai* asked him to teach me ten characters a day. Sorry, young mistress." She curtsied to Golden Bell, wringing her hands. Golden Bell turned away, speechless with embarrassment.

"Sorry." Little Six looked at Miss Tyler, not knowing how to address her. Miss Tyler was just going to reply when Little Sixth tugged on Iris's sleeve. "Sorry, Iris-jei." She ran.

Iris grimaced, grumbling, "A dumb egg, what a dumb egg!"

Miss Tyler and Golden Bell walked into the walled-in garden with Iris trailing behind. They passed a moon-gate framed by a circle of rosewood. The view of the glistening lake welcomed them.

"Isn't this beautiful?" The teacher pointed out the calculated compositions of color and design. "You have a beautiful home."

Little Six's histrionics still bothered Golden Bell. She asked, "Miss Tyler, you told my mother that you came here to learn from China." She took a deep breath. "There are so many stupid people like Little Six. What can you learn in China?"

"Little Six is ignorant, not stupid." Miss Tyler smiled. "The whole world is full of people like Little Six. It is only when we are allowed to make mistakes and given time to correct them that we can learn how things work." She put down her camera and stood under a willow tree, waiting for Iris to come with the tripod.

"But China is so . . . so . . ." Golden Bell meant to say "backward," but she could not utter the word. She had always heard her parents prate about China being the most civilized nation, and that all foreigners ever wanted was to steal from her riches. "Cruel," she whispered instead. "Look what happened to Snow Song. I heard she didn't want to marry the man her mother picked for her."

Miss Tyler remained quiet for a long time. She finally said, "It pains me to think of Snow Song. I wonder why she did it." She cleared her throat. "Such desperation, throwing herself into the river."

"Suicide seems to be the only way out for a Chinese girl!" Golden Bell stamped her foot and spat out her outrage. "Mother never wants to learn anything from the outside world. The Chinese always want to do things the Chinese way." She swallowed but could not control her anger. "They want to make the women weak — they used to bind our feet. Now they bind our spirit — they won't educate us or make us equal heirs!"

"I wish the missionary school had given Snow Song more strength and the means to be independent." Miss Tyler sat down on a rock. "Changes always bring turmoil. I wonder if Snow Song's schooling confused her instead."

"Did you know her?"

"I knew her as a scholarship student." She frowned. "But I cannot possibly know the personal life of every student in our school. I wish I had known her better."

Golden Bell saw Iris put down the tripod and stop to catch her breath. "The Chinese do not allow servants and especially girls to learn the free thinking in your world!" Golden Bell groaned, shaking her upturned hands in frustration.

"That is more or less the same in the West," Miss Tyler said. "The servants never have time to study, and the women are supposed to be wives, mothers, and objects of pleasure or service. Men are encouraged toward personal accomplishments — to become thinkers, dreamers, doctors, lawyers, engineers, or soldiers." She enumerated them on her fingers. She sounded almost angry. "They do things, but a woman is suspect when she makes her work her life."

"But you went to a university, Miss Tyler!"

"Yes, things may change. Some years ago, American women marched and even went to prison to demand an equal vote. My university is one of the very first to have coeducation."

"Oh, I wish someday I'll go there also! Someday I hope to bring equality to women in this country!"

"Perhaps you will. I'll certainly recommend it."

"Oh, I wish my parents will let me go. I can't understand my parents, especially Mother! She suffered under the old system. She has bound feet. I can't understand why she still follows those old traditions!"

"Yes, I have noticed how the Chinese gentry are extremely proud of their cultural heritage. Your mother may feel they are betraying their ancestors and selling out their cultural identity when they accept Western values."

Golden Bell knew that values like democracy and women's equality arrived in China along with colonialism, so they had become identified with competition and aggression. Since the turn of the century, the Chinese had been humiliated and traumatized by Western invasions. Her own father had protested against the division of important port cities into foreign concessions.

"I suppose there is progress. Nowadays young girls do not have bound feet," Golden Bell mumbled.

"Oh, yes, I'm sure things are changing. However, democratic ideas are very new and unproved theories here. I'm surprised that your parents did not object when I started teaching Iris."

"Yes, I was surprised too."

"Educating the servants is obviously important to your mother. Did you notice how all the women in your household are friendly and can read a little?"

"Oh yes, I never thought of it. Mother sets an example. She has taught Orchid how to read and write."

"America is a land of immigrants. We are naturally more open to influences from other cultures. I imagine the Chinese, steeped in Confucianism like your parents, are resisting the chaos that may come with new ideas."

"Oh." Golden Bell hesitated. She wasn't sure she understood her teacher, but she knew her parents' cultural pride was not something she could change, no matter how hard she tried.

"And you?" Golden Bell was dying to ask whether Miss Tyler's parents considered her an heir, wanted her to marry, or objected to her choice of work. Her Chinese training prevented her from prying. Her mother would admonish her for the impropriety. Quickly, she changed her focus. "What do the women do after university? Are there many great women artists and scholars in America?"

"Most women marry and become enlightened mothers. But there are still very few women artists, novelists, or professionals working outside the home." Miss Tyler sighed. "Social values change very slowly."

"That's just what my parents always say." Golden Bell brightened. "Did your parents approve of your work?" She just had to ask.

"Missionary work is supposed to be a calling from God," Miss Tyler answered matter-of-factly. "I've always wanted to travel, take pictures and have the adventure of teaching young women. Missionary work spared me the fight against people who might object to my life choices."

"What people?"

"Well, people in power — those who influence popular opinion, and who can tell you what to do and what not to do."

"Like parents?"

"Sometimes."

Iris arrived with the tripod, and Miss Tyler hastened to place her camera onto it.

"Did you hear a calling from God?"

"No, I did not. Look at that moon pavilion reflected in the mirror lake!" Miss Tyler pointed. She moved her tripod to an appropriate vantage point. "It is scenes like these that called me. Of course, working with young women and getting to know your culture have been a constant challenge and delight." She peered into the viewfinder and clicked the shutter.

"Perfect!" She grinned.

Chapter 12

THE NEXT AFTERNOON Purple Jade sat with Orchid in the front courtyard, embroidering under the cypress tree by the small pond. She ruminated on Miss Tyler's gentle, confident ways and began to appreciate Golden Bell's fascination with the self-reliant woman. She knew Silver Bell also wanted to follow this path of freedom and independence, which only deepened her concern for her family's need of an heir.

Purple Jade wondered how Righteous Virtue truly felt about concubines and other Chinese traditions. Clearly, he had never shared Golden Bell's contempt of her bound feet. His attention to her every comfort was complete. She was his precious Jade who needed shelter and protection, not only from the coarse realities of daily life, but also from the "brutal repression of the old system," as he had said with fire in his voice. In spite of his immersion in the Chinese classics, his total identification with his cultural heritage and his respect for tradition, he not only understood the horror of foot binding, but also wanted to educate his daughters like boys.

Their most cherished moments were their chess games together. Whenever they played, he was a relentless attacker, but she was a worthy adversary. She had been a careful student of Sun Tzu and his treatise on the art of warfare. Under a luminous circle of gaslight, she followed his movements from intersection to intersection, throwing up tiny interferences until Righteous Virtue became confused, distracted and soon fell into entrapment. He acted surprised each time he lost, blaming his lack of concentration and impatience, but she knew he marveled at his quiet, outwardly subservient wife.

In the delirium of their first days together, she could feel him challenged and fascinated by her talent for writing poetry and her thorough immersion in the classics. When finally they made love, he was tender but clumsy, full of fear and guilt at having hurt her. She accepted everything graciously, as a maiden of good breeding should.

With a wicked wink, her mother had given her a pillow book illustrated with many unusual positions of lovemaking. She had intimated that it would be delightful for any man to go through the book with his uninitiated wife. But Righteous Virtue had not found the book amusing. He flipped through its pages and turned crimson. "Such pornography is unworthy of your fine character!" he fumed. He threw the book into the charcoal brazier, scowling. But then, sensing her distress, he said, "You are an ideal wife for my family. My coarser passions have been spent on the turmoil in this country. I have no mind for women."

Purple Jade wept. She apologized in confusion and fear. She had been taught that all men were sensualists. They loved good food, fine wines, and the gentle ministrations of women. For centuries, it was a challenge for a wife to keep her husband from dallying with the flowers in the willow world. Yet her husband never strayed. When he made love, he did it in haste as if from necessity.

While Purple Jade enjoyed their shared activities of the mind, her panic over their physical challenges drove her to confide in her mother.

"Be patient, my child," her mother counseled. "He has only just returned from his modern education in Shanghai. I hear that in the West, their gods can only be conceived in virginity, so he must think the noblest of human acts unclean. He thinks of you as a goddess still."

Purple Jade had been pacified then. Often, the sight of her husband sent her insides melting. At other times, she could not understand her feeling of emptiness. Her breeding, those long years devoted to learning propriety and the refinement of manners, made her diffident in this matter. She often wondered if her husband's Western education and its curious pronouncements on the sins of physical love had deprived her of a male progeny — a crucial Chinese blessing. Now the time for an heir was overdue.

Yes, a concubine for the family. She would ask her husband to take a concubine. Why haven't I thought of this before? The Huangs must have an heir to preserve the dignity of the clan. The endless wars to establish the Republic had consumed his energies. And now a simple young woman could distract him from his troubles and let him enjoy the rights of his manhood again. With an heir, Righteous Virtue would be made whole. Just as Chiang Kai-shek and the Communists had solved the national problems by following ancient shadows, she too must solve her family needs in the traditional way. The virtuous wife must provide her family with an heir. Still, the need to share her husband made her heart ache as if stabbed by a thousand needles, but she focused on the pains in her feet instead. She had resolved to do what was necessary.

After all, she herself had been the child of a concubine. Her mother was the daughter of a minor silk tradesman, and she was fortunate to have been chosen as a concubine for her father, a prosperous merchant and industrialist. When her father's favorite concubine, Fragrant Wind, died giving birth to Glorious Dragon, her mother had helped the barren first wife select another concubine for their husband. They had been wise to curb their husband's roving eyes and keep his interest within the family. Now it was her turn to do the right thing for her family.

She remembered another Tu fu quatrain that seemed to suit her mood:

I do not pity the flowers that are about to expire.
I only fear age hurrying me on when blossoms die.
Lush, blooming branches easily pass their prime.
I say to the young buds: let your petals open one at a time.

Silver Bell burst in on her mother's thoughts. Peony followed.

"Afternoon peace, *M-ma.*" Silver Bell bowed hastily. "*M-ma*, let me recite to you!" Words tumbled out of her mouth all in a rush:

"Origin of man,
Is always kind.
Nature brings close,
Habit channels away.
Dogs don't bark,
Nature will change."

Everyone laughed. No one could resist the pun. "Gou boo chou" (Dogs don't bark) sounded so close to "Cur boo chou" (If not taught).

"Silver Bell, recite the last couplet to me again."

Silver Bell laughed with the others, but she obliged.

"That's better."

"*M-ma*, I've memorized your assignment. Now tell me how you first met Father."

"Ah, it was more than eighteen years ago!" She always began the same way. "It seems like a story I once read. But I did experience it. My dear little heart-and-liver, one day you will be betrothed and wonder how your husband looks too. It's the moment all maidens live for."

"*M-ma*, you said no one is to see the betrothed until the wedding night!"

"Yes, Silver Bell, but my family is famous in the silk trade, and my father was very modern in his way."

"So Father is just like Grandpa Chou."

"No, no, Silver Bell, Grandpa Chou was a merchant. Your father comes from generations of scholars. It is a much more noble family. That is why I, your poor mother, cannot understand his modern ideas."

Silver Bell was about to argue when Orchid whispered, "*Tai-tai*, tell us again how you first saw the master."

"Oh, yes," Purple Jade began as she lay down her embroidery. "After I was betrothed, I heard how daring your father had been. He was a member of T'ung Meng Hui and helped Dr. Sun Yat-sen establish the first republican government in 1911. He was beaten and kicked unconscious when he demonstrated against foreign aggression during the May 4th movement in 1919. I wept whenever I thought I was betrothed to a ruffian."

"What's the May 4th movement?"

"Oh, let me tell you again! Both Japan and China helped the Allies during the First World War. After the war, the Allies gave the German concessions in our Shantung Province to Japan. That's how Japan came to occupy our land in the north east and called it Manchuria."

"Oh . . ."

"Yes, our last emperor was a Manchu. So your father was considered an outlaw against the emperor in the old days."

"Oh . . ." Silver Bell might have continued her query but Orchid whispered, "*Tai-tai*, tell us why your family pledged you to our lord anyway."

"We knew, of course, that he was the sole heir to the Huang family's many bamboo mountains and fine acreage around West Lake. My parents assured me that he was a scholar. Still, I would not be pacified until I had seen him."

"How exciting!" Silver Bell clapped.

"Yes, that was very daring at the time. My father arranged to reserve the whole second floor of the Louwailou Restaurant, and invited your father to tea. My mother, my personal maid and I went upstairs and peeked through the windows while my father met my master downstairs and toasted to the union of the two families."

"Did you see him?" Silver Bell asked.

"Oh yes. He came to the restaurant riding on a white horse. He had already cut off his pigtail that marked him as a revolutionary because all Chinese men had to wear a pigtail under the Manchu rule. I found his Western haircut strangely attractive. He had prominent bright eyes. His back was so straight and his chin so square, I knew right away he was a scholar. Of course, I knew my parents wouldn't betroth me to a ruffian, but after I saw him, I became a willing bride."

"Father is now in the legislative council!"

"Yes, after the Nationalist government was formed." Purple Jade smiled in contentment.

"I'll never marry anyone I don't like, *M-ma*."

"Well, marriage brokers and spies can help us find out all about each other's family background and smooth over the adjustments to each other's habits."

"Will Golden Bell choose her own husband in Shanghai?"

Purple Jade groaned, clutching her embroidery to still her agitation.

"Don't worry your mother with things that may never happen," Orchid warned. "Our master will see to it that she makes a proper match." Over the years, Orchid had acquired a measure of authority that added a certain grace to her natural candor. "Look, here comes our master now!"

Everyone noticed Righteous Virtue's rapid strut into the courtyard. He carried a wooden box in his right hand, while his left hand hoisted up the front panel of his blue silk gown. That freed him for his long strides.

"Come everyone, come to the schoolroom." He barely acknowledged the greetings from the women, marched straight past the courtyard and entered the schoolroom complex. Silver Bell and Peony followed. Orchid folded up the embroidery and helped Purple Jade to her feet. She offered her shoulder to support her mistress, as they toddled yards behind.

When Purple Jade and Orchid finally reached the schoolroom, Golden Bell and Iris had already joined the crowd around the wooden box. Righteous Virtue had strung some wires around a metal pipe in the corner and attached another to the electric light. He turned the two black knobs on the wooden box. Crackling sounds came, and then a sweet soprano voice sang:

> *"I love to whistle,*
> *Cause it makes me merry,*
> *Makes me feel so very.*
> *Wheo . . .eo . . .eo . . .eo . . .eo. . ."*

"Father, Father, let me see, let me see the little lady inside!" Silver Bell tried to pull the wooden box closer to her. She peered into the top section, which had small Gothic-style windows covered by a canvas.

"You silly girl." Golden Bell sneered. "No one so small can fit into this box and still sing in English."

"Can't they make people grow small the way they bound Mother's feet?"

"No!" Golden Bell almost shouted. "Foreigners don't do such cruel things."

"Peace, children." Righteous Virtue waved his hand. "This is a short-wave radio. We're tuning in to a station in Shanghai. Soon there will be a broadcast about the war."

"Hai . . . my lord, you've bought more magic from the foreign barbarians!"

"*M-ma*, not all foreigners are barbarians," Golden Bell said. "I can read in English now and I like their literature — especially Shakespeare."

"Be quiet," her mother retorted. "Have you swallowed the foreign magic whole and forgotten who you are? I'm speaking to your father. You'll answer when you're spoken to."

Sulking, Golden Bell turned away. Silver Bell smiled and turned up the volume on the radio. The voice sang the refrain again.

Righteous Virtue reached over to turn the volume very low. "I alone will handle this radio." He glowered. "Golden Bell, you must realize the foreigners have been cruel in their own way. They forced us to import opium and plundered our country. They imposed huge indemnities because the ignorant Tui Zi empress ordered the slaughter of missionaries."

"Missionaries help us." Golden Bell almost shouted.

"Maybe," her father said with a nod. "People like Miss Tyler are friends, but foreigners still collect our import and export taxes from the concessions they control. In effect, we've all been working for the foreign treasuries. Of course, we admire their firepower and their science, but we must not forget the bitterness we suffered. So, while I buy their new inventions, I dress and live like a Chinese."

"Wheo . . . Wheo . . . eo . . .eo" Silver Bell puckered her lips and whistled.

"Oh, my lord, look what your foreign magic has done. What will people say when they see Silver Bell make these noises?"

Righteous Virtue laughed. "Silver Bell, that is very good! Western children whistle when they're happy." He smiled. "Jade-*mei*, Silver Bell is very quick. You must allow her to go to the schoolroom to prepare for the Shanghai schools."

"Oh, my lord." Purple Jade reached for her silk handkerchief. Dabbing on her dry eyes, she prepared herself for the all-persuasive tears that would prevent Silver Bell from leaving her tutelage. "You're asking too much of me. Golden Bell is only fifteen, but already she talks like a stranger to me. Now you want to turn Silver Bell into a boy also."

"Hai, these times are too trying for your gentle soul." Righteous Virtue looked at his wife tenderly, but then quickly averted his eyes. It was crass to show his affection in public. "There is a war raging in the northeast."

"We've known war," said Purple Jade. "Fortunately, the land around here is fruitful. When one warlord or another was given face and was paid off, there was still enough for all. I've long decided to ignore what I cannot control. I do my best to maintain the dignity of our family."

"Yes, yes." Righteous Virtue turned up the volume again. "The news broadcast is on. Iris and Peony, take your young mistresses away. They won't understand the chaos."

Chapter 13

THE NEWS REPORT was in Chinese. However, listening to a disembodied voice was such a novel experience that Purple Jade could not understand what was being said. There was talk of Manchuria, the derision of the Japanese as the brown dwarfs of East Ocean, and something about death and rape. She covered her ears.

"Oh my lord, people always exaggerate to stir up passions. Japan still hasn't declared war. Why must we listen to such a devil's voice?" Purple Jade pleaded.

Righteous Virtue turned off the radio. The news was unbearable. "Ah, my poor country. The Japanese are ready to take over. What bitterness we've yet to endure."

"The wise sage said: 'Let there be peace first in the household, then the nation will be at peace.'" Purple Jade watched her husband's face closely, not wishing to sound flippant.

"But our household is in peace, Jade-*mei*," said Righteous Virtue. "Thanks to you. You always manage to smooth out the difficulties."

"You're too kind, my lord." With Orchid by her side, she felt competent. She decided to broach the problem that was uppermost in her mind. "Still, we have no son. Have you forgotten the ancient saying? 'Of the unfilial acts, there are three: The first is having no son!'" She slapped her handkerchief down on her lap, rallying her courage. "You will have to take a concubine!" she blurted out in one breath, surprised by her own candor.

Righteous Virtue stared at his wife.

"Jade-*mei*," he said finally, "you know the peace in this house will be shattered if I brought in a concubine. You are too gentle a soul. I have no heart for women when the country is in chaos."

Purple Jade knew her husband was right. A strange woman in the house — a mother to the heir of the Huang household — she could barely bring herself to imagine it. If the woman was brazen, she would have bitterness to swallow for the rest of her life. She blotted her forehead with her handkerchief. "My lord, I've been most unworthy. I have not given you a son. It is my filial duty to arrange an heir for this household."

"Jade-*mei*, I have told you often, it is not your fault we have no sons. Modern science offers no clear answers. At any rate, Golden Bell does very well in her studies, and you know how bright Silver Bell is."

"My girls are a joy to me also. But, my lord, once the girls are married into other households, who will perform the rites to honor our ancestors?"

"Jade-*mei* , times have changed. You know the saying:

> Good man is not trained to be a soldier,
> Good iron is not shaped into nails!

Today our country suffers for lack of good soldiers!" He stood up, held his hand behind his back, and paced.

"But, my lord, are we to behave like barbarians? Our sons have learned to wield the brush instead of the sword; we are a nation of beautiful calligraphers! Is a life of the sword worth living?" Purple Jade straightened her shoulders. She knew they stood on common ground whenever she deferred to their ancient culture. "Do you choose to ignore what is written in the Tao Te Ching? 'To think weapons lovely means to delight in them, and to delight in them means to delight in the slaughter of men. And he who delights in the slaughter of men will never obtain what he looks for from those that dwell under heaven."

"Hai, the Tao is certainly correct."

"You can pretend to educate the girls like your sons, but will a noble young man want to marry a Westernized girl and take on our name?"

"So you will not permit Silver Bell to go to the schoolroom, ever?"

"Never, I cannot. It is my duty to provide an heir for this family." Purple Jade clasped her hands tightly to still her hectoring heart.

"Jade-*mei*, you're binding her soul as surely as the elders have bound your feet."

The mention of her bound feet brought her anguish. Was it possible that she had crippled her daughter? These were strange times. If Silver Bell became Westernized, and no one suitable would take the family name, there remained only one alternative: "To get a son — you must take a concubine!" Purple Jade repeated.

Both of them paused to take a deep breath. Righteous Virtue's body sagged. For sometime now he knew that he enjoyed a marriage of compatible minds. He and his wife had successfully built a poetic, almost lyrical rapport, eschewing physical pleasure. For too long, his passions had been caught up in his concerns for his country. He had worried about the coming war and plotted with Glorious Dragon to safeguard the family fortune. He had ignored the problems of the Huang family inheritance.

"All right, all right!" Righteous Virtue turned to walk away. "Find me a gentle woman! I will not have cackling women quarrel in my house!" He pounded one fist into his hand.

"Thank you, my lord, thank you . . . she will be your coming birthday gift!" Purple Jade gave no outward sign of her conflicting emotions. She excused herself, and Orchid helped her mistress back to their quarters.

Orchid had heard the whole exchange in stunned silence. She marveled at her mistress's valiant restraint.

Golden Bell and Iris had been squatting under the schoolroom window. When Purple Jade emerged, they dodged. As soon as her mother was out of sight, Golden Bell burst into the schoolroom. "Father, how could you give in to Mother! This is barbaric! I can't believe it!"

Righteous Virtue had turned on the radio. He tuned the volume down. "Calm yourself, Golden Bell. So you've been eavesdropping?"

"I crouched under the window because I wanted to hear some news."

"You might have asked to stay. Such clandestine activity is unbecoming in a young mistress of this house."

"So I'm sorry!" Tears of frustration flooded Golden Bell's eyes. "But taking a concubine," she shouted. "How can you do such a thing?"

"Be quiet!" Her father raised his clenched fist, slamming the air in front of his chest. "How dare you raise your voice to me! You are too forward and brazen in a matter that is none of your concern. Kneel!"

Golden Bell fell on her knees, crying copiously. "Forgive me, Father. I . . . I thought you . . . you're modern and enlightened. You're not like . . . other men."

"Modern, enlightened," Righteous Virtue glanced ruefully at his daughter. "When I returned from Shanghai and learned I was to marry your mother, I felt offended because I was modern — enlightened." He paced the room in fitful turns and stops, pouring out his turmoil. "Don't you know the shame and degradation the foreigners foisted upon us? They forced us to sign treaties that divided our major cities into concessions. Haven't you heard that the park in Shanghai had a sign at the gate: 'NO DOGS OR CHINESE ALLOWED!'"

"But Father," Golden Bell cried, "I thought you admired Western science and literature."

"Hai, the Western colonists are not men of science and literature. They are mercenaries. They gave us opium, guns and cannons to beguile our youths. In exchange they took our finest silks, pottery, art and along with them — our self-respect." Overcome with weariness, he paused. "Though I think Westernization is inevitable, I have no intention of becoming a foreign slave." He wiped the sweat from his brow and continued pacing.

"I don't understand."

"Look at your mother. Our old culture taught her grace and refinement in everything she does. Whether organizing a kite-flying party or sipping tea while watching the snow fall, she has cultivated it into an art."

He raised his daughter from the floor and motioned her to sit as he paced, distracted. "Whatever the circumstances, your mother has never failed to be civil, considerate, and courteous. Her kindness is not demonstrative, like those of the foreign missionaries, but inborn and cultivated over thousands of years!"

"But the old culture also bound Mother's feet!"

He raised his voice. "We're not perfect!" He clutched the back of an ebony chair, and his knuckles turned white as he tried to control his anger.

"But what does all this have to do with your taking a concubine?"

"Traditions change very slowly. We have no heir."

"I don't understand how Mother . . . being a woman, you'd think . . . she would be soaked in vinegar."

"My parents chose a good wife for me. Your mother is virtuous beyond bounds; she subjugates her emotions to safeguard this family." Righteous Virtue stabbed a hand in front of his daughter; his voice rose to a shout: "How can this family remain an upstanding member of this community without an heir? In this your mother and I have always agreed: the family is the foundation of our society!"

"You've told me often that I am the future hope and pride of China. How will a son make a difference?"

"One day I hope it won't make any difference. Marriage does not guarantee you happiness. When I die, I will be comforted to know that you and Silver Bell have a strong family to stand behind you."

Sensing the charged atmosphere, Iris hesitated by the door. She took one step into the room and announced: "Mrs. Chen, the mother of the drowned girl, has arrived. *Tai-tai* has arranged to receive her in the third hall, owing to the delicacy of the matter."

Golden Bell rose and went to her father. He stood in front of the window, clasping his hands rigidly behind his back. She knelt beside him. She touched his hands and cried, "Forgive me, Father. I was rash, but I still don't understand."

Righteous Virtue, his eyes rimmed red, pulled his daughter to her feet. "Go, prepare for Mrs. Chen. Once I was impetuous and said similar things to my parents."

Chapter 14

MRS. CHEN WAS stout, her features swollen from excessive weeping. Clad in white sackcloth, the mourning garb, she knelt before the lord and *tai-tai*. She kowtowed and thanked them repeatedly for retrieving her daughter's body from the river and providing the generous sum for her burial.

Purple Jade received the mother with a quiet solicitude that always endeared her to her dependents. She called Mrs. Chen "*Mei-mei*" and asked after her welfare. She offered aid.

When the visitor was finally persuaded to sit, Silver Bell edged close to her mother, whispering, "*M-ma*, ask her what went wrong!"

Purple Jade held her daughter's hand but ignored her request. Instead, she again asked about her visitor's wellbeing.

"Everyone has been so very kind." Mrs. Chen began her narration amid quiet wheezes and sobs. "How could Snow Song choose death? It must have been the bitter fate I was born with."

Righteous Virtue, Purple Jade, the children, and the maids listened without comment, each with his or her own thoughts.

"My Snow Song was a delicate child, so happy in the missionary school. The foreigners gave her a scholarship." She stopped to wipe her eyes. "But she was also born with a cursed fate. Her father died three years ago and left us indebted to the kindness of our neighbors. The butcher is a widower and a kind man. Although he is twice her age, he makes a good living and adored the ground she walked on. She could have asked for the moon and he would have bought it for her. I pledged Snow Song to him. I thought she would want for nothing more in life."

Why, oh why can't she see that was what killed her daughter? Orchid asked herself. *Though I'm only a servant in this book-fragrant house, I know I would wish to die if I were not pledged to someone familiar with book-fragrant ways but to some old butcher!*

Waves of motherly empathy and fear swept through Purple Jade. She coughed to compose herself and sipped her tea to clear her throat. She offered her condolences but felt sure the girl's values had been distorted by her education. Such a girl would rebel against being forced to marry a butcher, even though her family owed him favors and valued him as a benefactor. The girl had been taught to place her own inclinations ahead of her family's welfare. She had been encouraged to gratify her selfish dreams and emotions.

"They were to be married this coming eighth moon, when the proper three years of mourning had been observed," Mrs. Chen continued. "But she was contemptuous of the butcher's earthy, country ways. Oh, such a twisted fate!"

Righteous Virtue groaned privately at the poor mother's ignorance. Her thoughts had been so distorted by grief that she had accepted ill fate as a decree of heaven. Somehow, he knew that Westerners would rail against tragedy, but his countrymen accepted fate as a predetermined script. He shuddered to think that the meekness he so cherished had also victimized his people.

"Oh, bitter fate! My Snow Song had learned so well in school. The foreign lady said she could even use forks and knives without any mistake. Such kindness!"

Mechanically offering tea and words of comfort, Purple Jade distanced herself from the woman's gratitude for useless customs.

"What are forks and knives?" Silver Bell whispered to her mother.

Purple Jade ignored her. "The gods are jealous of the good," she said in a flat tone. She urged more tea on Mrs. Chen.

"Ah, she was good, she was, my Snow Song." Mrs. Chen cried anew. "It must be the jealous gods. Otherwise, how could so much kindness bring such tragedy?"

"Was your daughter a good student?" Golden Bell asked. After all, the missionary school must teach more important things than table manners.

"Oh yes, so many things I could not understand. My poor Snow Song, if only she could have talked to someone, someone modern like you. We did not understand her fancy learning in English."

Golden Bell nodded, but she lacked the words to comfort the woman. If she had known Snow Song, what could she have done to prevent this?

Righteous Virtue discussed Mrs. Chen's future welfare with controlled precision. Purple Jade continued to offer her condolences while her eyes focused on their forlorn visitor. When it was time for the woman to leave, Purple Jade pressed a freshwater pearl into her hand. "Since she died in the river, she must be buried with its treasure."

"Oh-me-to-fo, the Buddhas bless your kindness. You have saved her from the fate of a wandering ghost, and now you have ensured the comforts of her afterlife." The old woman began to kneel again, but Orchid and Iris came to hold her up and lead her out to the frontcourt. There she was offered more tea, until a palanquin was hired to take her home.

After Mrs. Chen left, silence filled the room like the rushing springs that filled West Lake. Righteous Virtue coughed to relieve the tension. "Jade-*mei*, you have given honor to our household. Ask Orchid to send tea to my study." He left.

"I still don't know why she killed herself!" Silver Bell muttered in frustration.

"The glove must fit the hand," answered her mother. She patted her daughter's hand and looked archly at Golden Bell. "Western manners and learning do not fit with life in this country."

"She could have gone to Shanghai." Golden Bell faced her mother, still defiant. "She could have found work there if her English had been good enough."

"Shanghai is a big city," replied her mother. "Without proper contacts, she would have had to take a job entertaining foreign sailors."

"So she died to save her honor?" Silver Bell asked.

"Perhaps she thought so, my heart-and-liver. Perhaps she thought so."

"I can see why she didn't want to marry a butcher twice her age!" Golden Bell argued. "I bet that Mrs. Chen could get pretty forceful, planning to eat meat everyday."

"Hush, Golden Bell. The poor woman has suffered too much already. At any rate, have you not learned the sage's teaching that children are reared to take care of their parents in their old age? Her mother did what was necessary for their survival."

"All that will change," Golden Bell retorted. When her mother did not answer, she shifted wearily in the stillness and then excused herself. Silver Bell followed.

Purple Jade wobbled unaided into the courtyard. She needed fresh air. There, the outline of an opaque moon was etched against the bright blue evening sky. The colorless moon reminded her of her untenable position with Golden Bell. Her daughter would always admire the freedom of Western women but would not appreciate notions of family solidarity and personal sacrifices. For once, her usual fog of war worries dissipated. Instead, she felt a new throat-clutching anxiety about her family. The dull pain in her feet intensified her dejection, and she hobbled to a bench. Snow Song had killed herself because she did not want to marry an old man. Her husband was also getting old, but he needed a woman young enough to give them sons. Who might take on this role in the house? How could she accept a strange young woman with, perhaps, unsavory inclinations? Her husband had agreed to a concubine. Instead of finding peace, she felt the tumult in her heart reach a feverish pitch. She moaned and rubbed her feet.

Orchid returned with tea. Together, they watched the setting sun color the moon to a pink globe. In the darkening light, Purple Jade watched, entranced. Her dejection vanished as the moon shone brightly in the dusky sky. An all-important decision had been made — the time of floundering was over. They would have an heir!

Chapter 15

BACK IN HER room, Golden Bell wanted to kick and scream at the strange turn of events. The enigma in the river was simply another case of the old oppressing the young. She would have killed herself too if she had been forced to marry someone so repulsive. Now her father, who was a paragon of rectitude, had consented to taking a concubine!

When Iris came in with tea, Golden Bell pushed it aside. "We're all doomed. The old people will never change!"

"Lower your voice, young mistress. Both of us will be in trouble if your parents hear you ranting." Iris wiped away the spilled tea.

"Why is everyone here so resigned to calamity? Mother convinced Father to take a concubine, and she had only kind words for that old hag who probably drove her daughter to her death!"

"No one knows why Snow Song killed herself," Iris replied. "She might have a delicate disposition, as her mother said. After all, she did have obligations toward her mother."

"I don't understand you, Iris! You've studied with Miss Tyler all these years, but you're always taking Mother's side!"

"I'm grateful to your family for treating me like a daughter." Iris stood in front of her mistress like a sentry guarding the younger girl slumped in her chair. "You're dear to me like a younger sister, but I can see the burden and responsibilities of a family such as yours. So many lives are dependent upon your parents' wise decisions." She tapped her mistress softly on the shoulder. "Young mistress, your mother will choose the concubine. She is getting a helpmate. Your parents are right."

Their long years of companionship had bred a tacit intimacy. Golden Bell's heart understood, but her wounded pride would not yield. She began to cry. "Iris, do you mean our studies with Miss Tyler are for naught? Mother thinks our education is useless in this country! What are you going to do if mother wants you to marry a butcher or a farmer who can't even read?"

"Your parents will not marry me to a dumb egg." Iris handed her young mistress a towel to refresh herself. "I had been an orphan for three years before my uncle brought me into this house to serve you. I'm used to hardships." She watched her mistress closely. "If you can keep a secret, I'll tell you my plans."

Golden Bell brightened. "What are your plans? Tell me, tell me!"

"Nothing is definite, but the chauffeur said the foreigners in Shanghai want servants who understand English. They pay well, and I shall buy my freedom!"

"Oh, how wonderful! Of course, you must run away, because Mother will never let you go. Oh Iris, when I come to Shanghai I'll visit you, and maybe you will find me a job too."

Iris smiled at her childish mistress. She took back the towel. "Now, you must not breathe a word of this to anyone. At any rate, nothing has been decided. After dinner, you must go to your mother; bid her evening peace and apologize." She offered tea to her mistress again. "Your mother did a very noble thing. It couldn't have been easy."

"Father said the same thing. I know you are both right," she wailed. "But why should women be treated like chattel?"

"I don't know." Iris wrinkled her brow. "I don't think the Westerners have a solution either. Miss Tyler is single and that is not natural."

"Do you think Miss Tyler came to China because she is single?"

"I don't know. But she would receive more help if she belonged to a family."

"Perhaps Mother really had no other choice." A glimmer of empathy pierced the shell of her resistance. "Then she must have suffered terribly!"

Mistress and maid looked at each other and fell silent.

Everyone was very quiet at dinner that evening. Purple Jade retired to her room early. Orchid left to fetch the foot water.

Golden Bell, puffy-eyed from weeping, came to bid her mother evening peace. She saw her mother by the window in a pensive mood. She knelt. "I'm sorry to have been presumptuous."

Purple Jade raised her daughter. "Did you try to talk your father out of our decision?"

"Yes, *M-ma*. We argued. I didn't understand."

"Hai, it is a pity you are not a boy. I like your spirit." She hugged her daughter close. "But my heart-and-liver, life is not ideal. War or natural disaster can come unbidden. We can only try to do what is best for our family."

"Miss Tyler said America is strong because it adopts the best from many cultures. The women in America marched and received the vote. Now they are equal to men and can choose what they want to do with their lives!"

"Miss Tyler is wrong to teach you to think only of yourself! Your father is the head of the household, and I manage affairs inside these walls. No one is free to choose self-gratification. The family's welfare is the responsibility of both the man and the woman!"

"I don't think Miss Tyler wants to teach me to be selfish, but she is open to new ideas and would not stand for the oppression of women!"

"I cannot understand all this talk of equality. If people do not obey their leaders, and children their parents, how do we maintain order? Our country is struggling to survive, so we must first protect our own family. I admire Miss Tyler's devotion to her work. I'm sure she understands why we need an heir!"

Golden Bell leaned on her mother. "I misjudged your purpose. You're so brave."

"Fate has been kind to me." She nodded. "You and Silver Bell are my gems, and your father is a true Chinese patriot — just as the marriage brokers told us more than eighteen years ago." She rubbed her daughter's back to soothe her. "He cultivates inner peace through his studies and now he will regenerate his household. Surely, the country will be at peace soon." Gently nudging her daughter away, she stirred herself with effort. "How could anyone conquer a people with such moral strength?"

"*M-ma*, do you think the East Ocean devils will conquer us?"

"Never! We're a vast country. Our culture has endured many foreign dynasties." She sat down stiffly and took up her embroidery. "Like the silkworm, we twist and turn to form beautiful cocoons. Many of us will be sacrificed to weave the most supple silk."

"*M-ma!*" Golden Bell looked at her mother with new eyes. "I thought you were weak and fearful!"

"The future is in the hands of fate." Her mother shifted in her chair. "But for now, where are we to look for a suitable concubine?"

Deep in thought, Purple Jade worked on her embroidery. Orchid returned with the foot water and began to unwind the bindings on her mistress's feet.

"Orchid, who do you think might be a suitable maiden for our lord?"

"*Tai-tai*, the matter is too grave for your maid to consider." Orchid was used to being consulted in private but was shy about giving counsel before Golden Bell.

Sitting next to her mother, Golden Bell found herself drawn into the deliberation. "A maiden from a book-fragrant family will not come in as a concubine," she said. "It has to be a cultured maiden from one of the trade families or a virtuous maid who could help you manage the household."

"Yes, there's Lao Wang's daughter, Pearl. She attends the missionary school in town, so she is not totally uncultured. Lao Wang will be pleased, but Pearl may be too modern."

"Pearl won't do. She's too much like a sister to me. The same goes for Iris."

"*Tai-tai*, the water is not warm enough. I'll return with a pitcher of hot water right away." As Orchid turned, she brushed a stray hair away from her big round eyes which sparkled like balls of onyx. All at once, Purple Jade knew. She waited until Orchid left.

"Yes, of course, I have her at my feet every day!" Purple Jade exclaimed. "Orchid would make the perfect concubine. She has served me faithfully almost all her life. Although she's almost twenty-three, she is still young enough to bear many sons."

"The household will be in great peace," Golden Bell concurred. "You were only too close to see the obvious."

"Orchid will always be by my side. Yes, how could I have been so blind?"

Orchid returned with the hot water and soaked her mistress's feet.

Golden Bell looked at her mother's maid with new eyes and realized for the first time that her face had a pleasant round shape. "Orchid, in all these years, I've never noticed your round face. It is the traditional indication for happiness and prosperity."

"Elder young mistress, it's getting late. Please don't make fun of my looks."

"What remarkable eyes!" Purple Jade remarked. "Orchid, where did you inherit such big round eyes?"

Orchid looked at her mistress uncomprehending. "*Tai-tai*, this is the only family I can remember."

"The ancient Chinese beauties may have long slanting eyes, but the modern movie stars all have big round eyes. So that should be all right," Golden Bell said.

Burning with unfamiliar emotions, Purple Jade clutched her daughter's hand. Perhaps her husband might find the strange features pleasing also.

"Look at me, Orchid."

Orchid looked up, her round eyes flashing.

"My child, you have been like a daughter to me. I'd like you to remain in this house. Would you like to be our master's concubine?"

Orchid stared at her mistress in consternation. That was a stunning offer! To become a legitimate member of this family? And if she produced a son, she would become *the* mistress in this family. She burst out crying, "Oh my kind mistress, you do me too much honor. I'll do whatever pleases you."

"Rise, my child. Tomorrow Lao Wang will find another personal maid for me in the country. You will train her," Purple Jade said. Planning for the household always calmed her. "I shall present you to my lord on his fiftieth birthday. You will be my birthday gift to him." Purple Jade winked at her daughter. "Let's keep my choice a secret. We'll need so much help for the birthday celebration, no one will notice my new maid."

Golden Bell tightened her grip on her mother's hand. In spite of her playful tone, her mother seemed desperate. Looking at Purple Jade's deformed feet, Golden Bell stilled the reproach in her heart. Her mother had secured not only new arms and legs and now a new womb. Tears welled in Golden Bell's eyes. She controlled herself with an effort. Her own life would never mirror her mother's. She would fly with her big feet. She congratulated her mother, bade her evening peace and left the room.

"Thank you, *Tai-tai*, thank you." Grateful tears streamed down Orchid's cheeks as she fumbled for a handkerchief. *The lord is a book-fragrant gentleman, not a licentious lout*, she told herself. He had always been kind. She knew he would be gentle. He was much older, but Ah Lee's urgency was frightening. Chen Snow Song drowned herself because she would not marry a man twice her age. Her master was more than twice her age, but he was not a butcher; he was a fine, handsome man. Yes, the master would be patient. He would teach her the same way her kind mistress had taught her. Now her children would be heirs in this family. She would never have to move into some crude farmhouse. Orchid wept with elation. She could think of nothing that would threaten her new position in the Huang household.

"Here, take this." Purple Jade handed her a silk handkerchief. At the sight of Orchid's dewy, firm complexion, she moaned within: *Oh youth, oh my lost years*! Her eyes moistened. She pronounced very loudly to strengthen her voice: "Tomorrow Lao Wang must begin to prepare your new quarters. We'll clear out and decorate the storage rooms next to the lord's library. I'll summon Dragon to bring me the finest silk. We will begin your trousseau."

"*Tai-tai*." Orchid massaged her mistress's feet in the hot water. "You've been more than a mother to me. You've given me a permanent home and a place in this book-fragrant household. Should I bear a son, I shall still remember my origin and your kindness."

"Dry my feet, my child. It won't be long before another maid will do this for me. I know your heart and I'm pleased that you see the honor." Purple Jade had resumed her mask of dignity. "Set up the chess board and invite my lord here for a game of chess tonight."

Without another word, Orchid finished her tasks and left. Her heart was bursting with joy. Now this was truly her home. What an honor she had been given!

"Oh-me-to-fo," Orchid silently prayed to the Buddha that night. "Bless my kind mistress, and bless me with many sons to repay the kindness of this house!"

Throughout the chess game, Righteous Virtue and Purple Jade felt distracted. Neither husband nor wife had mentioned the topic of a concubine again, but Righteous Virtue was uncharacteristically tame in his moves on the board. What a woman! he marveled. *How she is going to reward me for my fifty years' honest endeavor!*

Try as she might, Purple Jade found it hard to weave the webs of entrapment that had been the strength of her game. *Everything I love and value will be lost if we do not have an heir*, she reminded herself. *Orchid, the perfect gift, will meet the needs of the family. I must avoid facing Orchid alone in the days to come — the thought of her bright wide eyes, sprightly step and firm young features already set my stomach churning. Purple Jade, keep yourself busy! Please, please, concentrate on your game!*

Chapter 16

IN 1937, THE YEAR of the Ox, the Chinese Communist and Nationalist parties began negotiations for a united front against Japan. On the twentieth day, the fourth moon of the lunar calendar, Righteous Virtue celebrated his fiftieth birthday, buoyed by the hopeful mood of unity that pervaded his household and nation.

Banners and red lanterns inscribed with the symbols "FU" and "SHOU" ("good luck" and "long life") festooned every hall. Potted miniature willows and flowering cherry trees (ping jing in Chinese. bonsai in Japanese) filled the house with warm hues. Sparkling silver vases, jade carvings and precious porcelains proclaimed this an auspicious day. Miss Tyler set up four tripods in four locations. She slipped from one position to another, recording the whole affair on camera from different angles.

Relatives and guests had been arriving all morning long. Those who came in motorcars and rickshaws had to dismount on the street, as they could not drive past the low stone sill under the front gate. Palanquins carried visitors through the gate. Winding past the spirit-screen wall facing the street, they alighted in the front courtyard. Waiting palanquins, rickshaws and motorcars lined the outside walls of their house and garden.

Righteous Virtue greeted the male guests in the front hall. In the library, gifts were presented to Lao Wang, the accountant, who duly recorded each one. The more intimate friends and relatives, accompanied by Righteous Virtue, paid their respects by bowing before the ancestor tablets.

Female guests were taken to either the second or the third court depending on their relationship to the family. Purple Jade received her intimates in the third court.

In the afternoon, two large ebony chairs draped with bright red brocade were centered on a platform in the first hall. Red silk cushions with glossy embroidery padded the seats. Paintings of Huang ancestors on two large scrolls hung behind the chairs. A houseboy lit a string of firecrackers on a bamboo pole two stories high, commencing the ceremonies.

"Oh, it's time to start. It's time to start!" Silver Bell shouted over the crackling explosions as she covered her ears.

"Oh, I just love rousing heat!" Peony replied, already flushed with excitement.

"Where's *jei-jei*?" asked Silver Bell. "Mother said we have to be seated together, over there." She pointed to the two smaller ebony chairs flanking the large ones.

Silver Bell wore a skirt of rose-colored silk, and a brocade jacket of the same color, with tiny plum blossoms embroidered in silver. Her braids had been wound with silver and rose ribbons. Not a single stray hair marred her peachy face and flashing eyes.

The guests began to assemble in the frontcourt. Glorious Dragon had invited Archie Strong. Strong was wide-eyed with curiosity and delight. He thanked his host for including him in this unusual splendor.

The rustling of lustrous silks and richly embroidered brocades filled the bustling courtyard. Strings of pearls, jade earrings, emerald rings, hairpins of jade dragonflies, coral butterflies, gold and silver combs, precious stones shaped cunningly into flowers of glistening hues, bracelets of gold, jade and carved ivory — all vied for attention.

Ladies milled about, dispersing their fragrance with a gentle flutter of their fans. The older women seemed to prefer fans made of ribs of carved ivory. Some men brandished black-lacquered fans, inlaid with tortoise shells; younger ladies giggled and flirted behind fans made of lacy sandalwood. Purple Jade carried a transparent silk fan of embroidered butterflies. The stitches were so fine that whenever she waved it, the butterflies seemed to glide through translucent air. The sweet scents of jasmine, rosewater, night orchid, lotus and lilac wafted through the air.

The garden pavilions were equipped with mahjong tables, games of chance and chess. Musicians strolled along the many courts playing Chinese mandolins — the pi-pa, the two-string violin — erhu, and the bamboo flute. Jugglers and magicians performed amid circles of guests who laughed and clapped.

All at once timbrels rang out and flutes soared in a vigorous tune as the drums of the hired band banged to demand attention.

The bandleader chanted: "The Master and *Tai-tai*, please be seated." Righteous Virtue, who was resplendent in a navy blue gown of gleaming silk, led Purple Jade to the throne-like chairs. Purple Jade looked stunning in a lavender skirt and a light jacket of soft mauve. An embroidered golden phoenix dominated the jacket.

Next, Righteous Virtue's stepmother and half sisters were announced, followed by the Huang family cousins. They bowed before their hosts in turn, and stood behind the chairs.

"Where's *jei- jei?* Go look for Golden Bell." Silver Bell nudged Peony.

As she spoke, Golden Bell appeared besides her, wearing a lime green silk skirt and mint green jacket with a row of jade buttons clasped by golden frogging.

"It's about time you appeared. Where were you?" Silver Bell hissed, poking her sister.

"I was helping to prepare the bride," whispered Golden Bell.

"Who is she . . . who is she?"

"Mother strictly forbade anyone to breathe a word about it; there are too many people in the house wasting mouth water and spreading what is not true."

"Oh good *Jei-jei*, please tell me, tell me!"

"Well, all right, everyone will see now in a minute anyway." She adjusted the jade pin on her newly bobbed hair.

As soon as she whispered the secret into her sister's ear, Silver Bell hopped on one foot, then the next, clapping and laughing.

Golden Bell covered her sister's mouth. "Don't spoil it for everyone else!"

The Chou family's relatives were announced. Glorious Dragon and other cousins similarly joined the relatives after paying their obeisance.

Then the younger generation was called forth: "The young mistresses of the house, please be seated." Golden Bell and Silver Bell stood before their parents; they knelt and kowtowed. They were seated on the ebony chairs flanking their parents.

The music cascaded in trills, then swelled to a spirited crescendo while relatives and friends paid their respects formally to their hosts. After the youngest cousin had performed his rite, the music reverberated a full ten minutes more. The bandleader cleared his throat and announced in a booming voice: "Let the concubine be presented."

A door opened, and a hush descended upon the guests. Orchid emerged, dressed in a rose red gown, the color more pink than the true red that was draped on the chairs. It was the appropriate color for a concubine's wedding.

Orchid wore pearl and ruby star bursts in her chignon. No veil covered her face, as was the custom for the usual bride. Thanking Buddha under her breath, Orchid blushed as she prayed repeatedly to be blessed with a son. Her heart warmed remembering the chests upon chests of silk gowns, jewelry, quilts and embroidered silk comforters Purple Jade had prepared for her dowry. She knew that few young women in this region would be more richly endowed.

As Righteous Virtue watched Orchid approaching with her great sparkling eyes, he devoured her firm young features with a hunger he had not known before. Waves of both panic and exuberance swept away his initial shyness. He had a numbing thirst. He had not known such passion since the days he had marched in the streets of Shanghai, and shouted slogans against the foreigners.

"Is this foolishness or biology?" he asked himself. Then he remembered his own clumsiness. He had been Purple Jade's champion and protector. His love for his wife had crystallized into a friendship so consuming that he felt innocent of sex. Perhaps he had known all along that his wife would choose Orchid — her sweet, discreet servant and companion. Yes, he had also been fond of Orchid. Now she would do well to bring harmony within the household.

Purple Jade noticed her husband's excitement. Her heart was sore with jealousy. *Oh, let that red-eyed monster pass from my consciousness*, she prayed. She had learned from experience that by simply accepting the validity of her feelings, she would be calmed. *Yes, it is natural to drink vinegar and feel uneasy, but we will have an heir*, she reminded herself. She tilted her head toward her husband and whispered, "I have given her a pillow book."

Righteous Virtue nodded and touched her hand in gratitude. Purple Jade felt the electricity in the touch, but knew that although she might seem naive to a sophisticate, she had forever bound to her the love and respect of her husband. The red-eyed monster reared its head for another brief moment at the sight of her beautiful gift. Indeed, she could hardly recognize the radiant Orchid. The monster would always be there, she knew, but she had already mastered her inner turmoil. She never would allow it to disturb the peace and harmony of her house. She straightened in her seat and sat poised for her role in this dramatic moment.

Orchid came before them; she touched her head to the floor and remained prostrate. Righteous Virtue's heart skipped a beat. He had been reluctant to accept a concubine from his wife. Now, the wisdom of Purple Jade's choice struck him with full force.

Murmured waves of approval came from the guests. Some clapped and shouted, "Good. . . good."

Purple Jade descended the chair platform. She touched Orchid on the head and asked her to rise. Taking Orchid by the hand, but avoiding her eyes, Purple Jade led her to her husband. "My master," she said with a clear ringing voice, "may this, my present to you on your fiftieth birthday, bring many felicitous blessings to this house."

Righteous Virtue rose. Giving his wife a secret smile, he bowed and led her, followed by the concubine and his daughters, to the ancestral shrine. There they kowtowed in deep obeisance. The wedding ceremony and the birthday reception ended.

The guests assembled in the large garden, where dining tables were set up in the rambling pavilions and terraces. Before the meal, a golden tray with a flask of wine and two golden cups was brought to the head table. A servant girl held the tray, and Orchid stood with her head bowed as she filled the cups with wine and presented the wine to her patrons in turn — Righteous Virtue first, then Purple Jade — as a sign of gratitude and respect. The quiet ceremony over, the feasting began. The male guests threw their fists in finger-guessing games. A poetry slam broke out around another table. Hangzhou was renowned for its gourmands and poets. The ladies ate daintily, anticipating the usual dozen courses of finest delicacies. The succulent Dongpo pork was named after Su Dongpo, the famous local poet. Live jumping shrimp immersed in Shaoxing wine was the specialty of the region. For months, the servants had saved the shrimp in a special basket suspended in the river. Long noodles, which symbolized long life, were served instead of rice. Dessert featured the traditional long-life peaches, which were peach-shaped steamed buns filled with bean paste. The green leaves and red blush of the peach were painted with vegetable dyes.

A stage occupied one end of the large open pond. Against a backdrop of a plain white canvas, a troop of Shanghai opera singers presented "Havoc in Heaven, the Adventure of the Monkey King." Ladies swayed to the music while they ate; the men reeled with the wine they had imbibed.

Mr. Strong joined Miss Tyler, who was sitting with Golden Bell and Silver Bell. Mr. Strong couldn't stop eating morsel after morsel of various dishes, exclaiming all the while how these were not the Chinese dishes he had known. When the beggar's chicken arrived, Strong thought a ball of clay had been placed in front of them. The server cracked open the clay with a little hammer and lifted a tightly wound bundle of lotus leaves onto a blue and white plate. He broke the seal on the leaves, and a whole chicken emerged with a heavenly aroma of herbs and mysterious seasonings. The chicken had been doused with Shaoxing wine, and stuffed with mushrooms, rehydrated dried scallops, onions, garlic, lotus seeds, and sweet rice. Everyone plucked off the tender chicken meat and took spoonfuls of the stuffing. Strong was so busy eating and exclaiming his excitement that Miss Tyler had to touch his arm and tell him that the girls would like to explain the opera to him.

Although Miss Tyler spoke Chinese, Chinese opera — sung on a bare stage in high falsetto voices — was alien to her. She found the music dynamic and the acrobatic skills of the dance pantomime intriguing.

"The men wave blue banners to portray sea waves," Golden Bell explained. "That man standing with the oar is on a boat."

"The Monkey King wears red on his face because red represents courage and honor," added Silver Bell.

"Do the costumes also represent different things?" asked Miss Tyler.

"Oh yes," replied Silver Bell. "Perhaps I can come to the schoolroom next week and tell you all about it."

"That is very kind of you." Miss Tyler winked at Golden Bell. "But tell me, Silver Bell, how do you feel about having a concubine in the house?"

Golden Bell turned crimson with embarrassment. Her sister answered, "It is wonderful because we'll have an heir!"

"I do have a great deal to learn from you." Miss Tyler sensed Golden Bell's dismay. "Western culture is so different from your fine traditions that I must be a careful teacher of my own and a good learner of yours."

Miss Tyler turned to translate her Chinese conversation with Silver Bell to Mr. Strong.

"Righteous Virtue speaks excellent English," Strong whispered. "How did he get his wife to give him a concubine?"

"Mr. Huang is a founder and trustee of our missionary school," Miss Tyler answered. "I've been tutoring in this house for more than five years. I understand this was Mrs. Huang's idea."

"What?!" Mr. Strong looked into Miss Tyler's eyes to make certain she wasn't joking.

"My student told me that she had insisted upon it. Mr. Huang gave in only because it is the proper thing to do here to ensure an heir!"

"I'll be darned!" Mr. Strong slapped his lap. "His wife looks like a fairy princess. Is she crazy? No one would believe that, even in my Sodom and Gomorrah — New York City!"

"They'll understand even less in Syracuse, New York." Miss Tyler blushed and lowered her head to speak into her napkin. "Purple Jade is a great lady. She has ensured the harmony and perpetuation of this family."

"I'll be returning to the States next month. When are you due for leave?"

"This will be my twelfth year in China. The longer I stay, the less I want to leave." Softness graced her hazel eyes. She had come to love these gentle, hospitable people, and she had accepted their stoic ways. She had arrived here to teach, record her experiences in pictures and perhaps convert them to Christianity. Instead, they had changed her.

Strong took note of Miss Tyler's radiant face as she looked at her students and wondered at the devotion of this missionary woman. He judged her to be about forty-five. What was she doing here? He still could not fully understand the Xian incident. Now, the Huang family's solution to getting an heir sounded insane! Aloud, he said, "Here's my card. Please call me sometime when you're on leave. I'd like to interview you and perhaps you can explain the propriety and logic of concubines in New York. My God, what am I saying?" He ran one hand over his hair and wiped his forehead with his handkerchief. "My wife will flip if she hears this. I mean, you will present the Chinese point of view, of course."

"Yes, of course!" Miss Tyler pocketed his card and turned to face the reporter. "I hope you'll allow me to speak of Chinese culture in broader terms. To have a concubine is an honest, open expression in this male- dominated society. In the West, we're subtler. The French have their mistresses and we have our prostitutes and other outlets for men. I'm afraid it will be a long time before we Westerners will accept the reality of how the so-called fairer sex has learned to cope."

Strong smiled and shook her hand. "It has been a pleasure meeting you. Perhaps someday we'll talk again when you're back in the States."

Righteous Virtue, Purple Jade, and Orchid came to the table to toast their guests. Miss Tyler and Mr. Strong thanked their hosts and wished the family peace and prosperity.

Miss Tyler remembered the presents the girls had prepared. She nudged Golden Bell to remind her. Silver Bell produced her flute and played a fetching tune with a lively rhythm, while Golden Bell recited to the accompaniment:

"The flower is a maid of comely beauty;
Drifting down the brook of life, she does her duty,
The flower of virtue is a comely beauty!

Anchoring roots to a tree that is already flowering,
Joy and felicity precariously towering;
May love and happiness find safe harboring!

The flower is a maid of comely beauty;
Floating down the brook of life, she does her duty,
This flower of virtue is a comely beauty!

Man of upright virtue does his filial duty;
In Hangzhou, our fabled city,
That peace and purpose be restored with surety!

The flower is a maid of comely beauty;
Sailing down the brook of life, she does her duty,
This flower of virtue is a comely beauty!"

Everyone clapped and cheered, urging the sisters to repeat their performance. Purple Jade smiled, brimming with pride. She had orchestrated all the elements to a perfect pitch. All the activities flowed with integrity and grace; the months of planning and hard work had come to fruition.

Righteous Virtue announced: "I am honored by your presence and your many gifts. Let it be known that from now on, Orchid shall be named Huang Comely Brook."

Never uttering a single sound, Orchid, with her head lowered and blushing throughout the evening, bowed deeply in thanks. She was led away to her bridal suite.

The night sky lit up. The fireworks had begun. There were peonies, chrysanthemum, lilies and other varieties in successive flowery display. Purple Jade rested her hands on Silver Bell's shoulders, flushed with satisfaction.

"The time of flowering is here!" she said.

BOOK TWO

The Dragon Uncle

Chapter 1

BRIGHT CRYSTAL APPLIED make-up in her bedroom. Glorious Dragon, sprawled on her Western-style four-poster bed, read out loud the headline: "Three Divisions of Japanese Army Opened Fire on Beijing." He sat up straight. "July 7, 1937 is a black day indeed."

"I hope the fighting won't spread." Bright Crystal carefully penciled in her eyebrows.

The mirror reflected a hand-painted scene of egrets among marshy reeds and twisted pines. A shade of bamboo slats deflected the noonday sun. A fan droned softly overhead. The beige and green decor tempered the searing Shanghai heat.

"You know, there is no formal declaration of war." Glorious Dragon put down the paper.

"General Chin went to Lushan a week ago," Bright Crystal said. She tilted her head this way and that to make sure her brows had the desired curve.

"Chiang Kai-shek's summer capital? What's he doing there?"

"He's with Chiang, and they're meeting with Mao Tse-tung and Chou En-lai."

"So the Xian Incident brought the Communists and the Nationalists together. No wonder Japan attacked; they don't want to see China united." Glorious Dragon's eyes followed Bright Crystal's every move.

Bright Crystal lined her lips lightly with a burnt carmine pencil. "General Chin thought Marshal Zhang had forced a shotgun marriage. It won't last." She filled in her lips with a rose sheen. "My humble opinion is that the Chinese people now demand their survival as a nation. No party with a thought to future leadership would dare collaborate with the Japanese. What do you think?"

She turned to look at her lover, pursing her lips like a coquette. For one brief moment, Glorious Dragon was uncertain whether she sought his opinion on her lipstick or on her reasoning. All his discussions with Bright Crystal had involved her brilliant deductions. Yet no one felt threatened by her intelligence. Glorious Dragon liked to compare her artfulness with his sister's erudition.

Purple Jade's mind was clothed in a mantle of dignity; more often than not, she deferred to the opinions of the men around her. In spite of her learning, she appeared naive, innocent and humble. Bright Crystal, on the other hand, seemed vain, superficial and fickle, yet her perceptions were incisive and full of pragmatic wisdom. He would have gladly taken directions from her without her feminine guile. They were birds of the same feather. Life was an elaborate intrigue and conversation a challenging game to both of them.

In a rush of emotion, he kneeled behind his Crystal and embraced her slender waist. Snuggling his nose against her fragrant neck, he teased, "So how shall we prepare for the coming storm?"

Giggling, twisting her arm around to tickle Glorious Dragon, she forced him to release her. "Why are you wasting time here in broad daylight?" Still laughing, she picked up the silver-handled brush, and stroked it vigorously across her hair, so Glorious Dragon could not resume his nuzzling without being hit. "Everyone will want to rent in the foreign concessions as war approaches. Buy up as much real estate in this neighborhood as you can, and put the rest of our money in foreign banks!"

"Yes, young mistress." Glorious Dragon stood erect, brought his hands together and bowed deeply as if paying obeisance to an ancestor. "Shall I evict everyone on Avenue Joffre and buy up the whole French concession in your name?"

Laughing giddily, Bright Crystal poked Glorious Dragon with her brush, and spelled out her instructions as if carrying on a frivolous banter. "Just remember the important part: Everything in the foreign bank accounts must be in your name and mine. Real estate ownership is kept on public record, so it should be in the names of reliable relatives. My father must hold some apartments. The rent will take care of him in his old age. When the fighting begins, your relatives, too, will be safer here."

"I've been scouting the neighborhood for weeks now." Glorious Dragon looked for his shoes. "No one wants to sell, and what's available is impossibly overpriced. No one would consider renting you an apartment without several gold bars for key money."

"So you've looked already, eh? When the fighting gets near, foreigners will want to go home. Buy then!" Bright Crystal's voice became somber. "But have you diverted funds to the foreign banks?"

"No." Glorious Dragon found his shoes and sat down near the door. "I'll attend to that tomorrow. I should advise my sister, brother-in-law, and all the Chou cousins in Hangzhou to do the same. Plus, my sister's family has a very friendly American tutor. My brother-in-law will make sure to deposit our funds into small regional banks in America that can avoid our government's sanctions. We may have to make some donations to the missionaries, though."

"Good planning! You are so good to your sister and her family."

"Aside from you, she is the only family I have."

Their conversation was interrupted by a knock on the door. The servant girl announced that a Mr. Eugene Ma had arrived.

"I didn't invite him," Crystal whispered.

"But you flirted with him." Dragon scowled.

"Yes, in front of General Chin and all of you."

Dragon understood their necessary roles. He bit his lip and motioned to Crystal that he was slipping out the backdoor.

Within half an hour, he was ringing the front doorbell and asking to see Crystal.

"Oh, Dragon-*ko*, great to see you." Crystal laughed and shook his hand. "Eugene is here to reassure me that we need not worry about the Japanese invasion."

Dragon shook Eugene's hand. "Fancy meeting you here, Eugene. I came to glean some information from Crystal—just in case General Chin had provided deeper understanding."

"General Chin thought Zhang had forced a shotgun marriage. It won't last." Crystal parted with the information as if she were telling Dragon for the very first time. Both Crystal and Dragon were used to brandishing Chin's name in front of other men enamored by Crystal. This was their best protection.

"I agree," Eugene said. "I was just telling Crystal that the political council in the Hopei-Chahar region has just apologized to Japan. They want to help the Nationalists fight the Communists!"

"Thanks to your Italian planes, the Nationalists will put up a good fight." Crystal smiled sweetly, glossing over all the political complications.

"Is your information correct?" Dragon asked.

"Of course. I also told Crystal that my German contacts introduced me to the Italians, and I gave them a large order to buy their planes." Eugene snapped his fingers as if to boast how easy it was to clinch the deal.

"Congratulations! The air force will really help our National cause. Your German education probably helped." Dragon knew very well that Eugene spoke German, but he asked, "Do you speak German?" He was playing the humble card — giving Eugene another chance to brag.

"Of course I do." Eugene sipped his tea, but if Crystal were his mistress, he would have asked for beer.

"Imagine having such an excellent education." Dragon nodded.

Crystal beamed her admiring smile and said, "Oh Eugene, you must call me and tell me whenever you get more information. General Chin never tells me enough. I hope he'll come here soon." This was a hint for them to leave.

After some pleasantries, Eugene kissed Crystal's hand and bade her goodbye. "Guten Tag," he said. He clicked his heels together and bowed.

"I'm coming with you, Eugene." Dragon also kissed Crystal's hand and gave her a secret wink.

As the two walked away arm in arm, Dragon said, "Congratulations Eugene! Let's go for a drink. That sale was a masterful score!"

"Yes, yes." Eugene smiled. "I'll treat." He was more than pleased with himself.

Dragon could not help imagining how Mr. Strong would have enjoyed the political confidences they had just shared.

Dragon returned to Crystal's house for lunch. As they ate, Dragon continued their morning discussion. He asked, "So

Eugene maybe correct and Japan may soon withdraw. What do you think?"

"No, I think Nanking will repudiate the apology by the political council in the Hopei-Chahar region this time."

"Why?"

"I think the Chinese people do not want a Japanese overlord. After the drama of the Xian incident, every Chinese knows about Chiang's bargain with the Communists. As I said this morning, I think the Chinese people all want their survival as a nation. No party with a thought to future leadership would dare collaborate with the Japanese."

Dragon nodded in agreement. He knew his sister would have come to the same conclusion because she was trained in the classics, just like Chiang Kai-shek. He hurriedly took a few bites and left the table.

"Where are you going?"

"I have a secret mission."

"What mission? Are you going to check out the properties owned by foreigners?"

"There is really no time to lose." He winked and bade his lover good afternoon.

Glorious Dragon's father began life working for a silk trader. He traveled up and down the Yangtze Valley to buy the best cocoons. Soon he won enough respect and good will to start his own business — all the while amassing a fortune. Later he established factories in Shanghai, and expanded into the export market. He was already an old man when Glorious Dragon was born.

Fragrant Wind, his favorite concubine, died giving birth to Glorious Dragon. The old man was furious at his loss. He took to smoking opium and refused to even look at his only son.

As a young boy, Glorious Dragon seldom saw his busy father. Successive numbers of teachers had been hired to prepare the only son in the classics. But Dragon always managed to make his teachers resign. One left because the boy had dissolved a handful of salt into his tea. Another left because he choked on the pepper Dragon left in his lunch. The last one literally ran out the door because the mischievous child set off a string of firecrackers right under his seat. Dragon was the target of his father's constant rage and disappointment. But no one disciplined him because he was the heir, and his father resorted to his pipe after his fiery rage tired him.

Purple Jade, the child of another concubine, was always there for him. She was thirteen years older and taught Glorious Dragon everything as one child taught another — all in the spirit of play.

"But I'm not as smart as you are, Jade-*jei*!" Glorious Dragon said.

"Oh no, you're naughty, but you're smarter!"

"Surely you're more fond of learning. Father often bellowed that he wished you were his son!"

"That's because I never felt the kind of pressure that a son gets. Whenever I made a mistake, I would giggle and the teacher would smile. As you know, girls are not expected to study. But once I read the Tang poets, nothing could stop me. The teacher thought I was strange! But Father was delighted. He encouraged me. He had suffered so much himself — he was almost illiterate. You mustn't blame him for his harsh ways."

Purple Jade was like that — self-deprecating and unwilling to find fault with anyone. If she could not explain the source of her suffering, she would blame fate.

Glorious Dragon, by contrast, looked back at his father's abusive outbursts and the cruel practice of binding his sister's feet and blamed the old ways. He hated the classics, which required memorization without comprehension. He loved his sister and admired his brother-in-law, but could not understand why they stuck with the old stifling ways, where traditions dominated.

Yet, much as he strained against the old culture, he was shackled emotionally to his family. The thought of Purple Jade's noble presence in the family compound filled his heart with tenderness and peace.

He remembered the scene at his father's deathbed. In his delirium, the old man called out his favorite concubine's name: "Fragrant Wind, Fragrant Wind . . . Old Chou is coming."

In a moment of lucidity, he held on to his son's hand. "Glorious Dragon, my son, my son, how I neglected you!" His face grew red, and his breathing tentative. Purple Jade moved closer to calm him.

"No, let me!" He motioned her away, clutching desperately at his son. "She was like me, my Fragrant Wind, your mother. Her father gave her to me because . . . because his fields had been flooded." He smiled with obvious pleasure. "I didn't have to, but I accepted her. Saved him an extra mouth to feed. Accepted her as my concubine. She was smart, grateful. She went with me to select the finest cocoons. I . . . I shouldn't have blamed . . . blamed you. Oh, how I miss her. If she had lived, perhaps . . . I could have stayed away from the pipe . . . but now you must take care of our family."

His father died a few days later, but the old man's words left an indelible mark on Glorious Dragon. He could no longer be indifferent when war or opium threatened his family's honor or safety. In spite of his disregard for tradition, he managed his family business with intense commitment.

He shared all his family concerns with Bright Crystal. She had also grown up without a mother. Her father would have taught her to cook, but he had followed his heart instead and allowed his only child to choose her own path. She was fortunate not to have been highborn and thus bound by old restrictions. She chose to pursue her own interests wherever her inclinations took her. Glorious Dragon admired her honesty and courage, but he never told her of his new insatiable urge to wreak havoc in General Chin's opium dens. He knew that her ignorance was her protection.

Chapter 2

WHAT DISGUISE SHOULD I use for the opium den this time? Glorious Dragon stomped around Bright Crystal's parlor, wondering.

The idea of planning to disrupt another opium den and hurt General Chin's pocketbook always kept his heart thumping. Twice before, he had caused substantial damage in two locations. He bought drinks for foreign soldiers, and when they became intoxicated, he provoked them to raid the dens. Cursing, they charged into the smoke-filled rooms, brandishing their half-empty bottles and breaking them on the proprietors' and smokers' heads. In the ensuing melee, he had no trouble sneaking away.

When he first arrived in Shanghai, he had sampled several dens just out of curiosity. However after smoking a pipe or two, he realized he did not enjoy the languorous state that followed. What fascinated him were the nubile young women in slinky *cheongsam* who served the patrons. Glorious Dragon stopped going after seeing the seedier parlors, which employed young boys and prepubescent girls. Now, every time he thought of Little Six and General Chin's involvement, he wanted to smash more opium dens.

"You look like a fettered hound. What's eating you?" Crystal had entered the room.

"Nothing."

"How's the contract with Babson and Westcott coming?"

"I'm not sure."

"Do you want me to ask General Chin to help?" As soon as the words were out of her mouth, she knew that it was insensitive of her to mention Chin.

"No! Never accept a favor from him!" Glorious Dragon ran to the piano and pounded on the keys with his fist.

"Please stop." Bright Crystal covered her ears. "I can't stand it! I'll buy you a gong to drive away the devil in you!"

Glorious Dragon continued pounding. He could think of no other way to relieve his frustration and anxiety.

Bright Crystal snuffed out her cigarette. "I'll go get some iced tea." She walked out, touching Glorious Dragon's back as she passed.

General Chin had a wife and two concubines in Nanking. Although he had many other mistresses in other cities, Bright Crystal was his prized possession. Her natural charm and modern social skills were invaluable to Chin's numerous business transactions. He thought of himself as a liberal, generous man. He subscribed to the popular understanding that women were toys — though surprisingly clever at times. He permitted the young men in town to hover around Crystal, allowing an occasional indiscretion.

Bright Crystal could not question General Chin's values or his control over her life. She did what she could to safeguard her livelihood. She enjoyed whatever limited independence she had, although her relationship with Glorious Dragon had grown beyond the bonds of a casual affair. Their affection for each other defied prudence; their casual game of love had developed into a dangerous entanglement.

"General Chin is not a person to be dismissed easily, even though I no longer need his financial patronage," Bright Crystal often told Glorious Dragon. "I loathe serving him. The situation is intolerable!"

"He has such a stranglehold on our happiness!" Glorious Dragon turned to hug her. "What can we do?"

"Let's run away!"

"Let's go abroad. We have contacts in America and Europe and can seek refuge there!"

"Oh, that would be wonderful!"

"But how can we apply for passports without Chin's knowledge?"

"If his secret police got wind of our plans, he could easily kill us."

"Where can we go?" Together they collapsed into the bed, each restless with mounting apprehension, tinged with passion. "Even if we went overseas, we could not escape his long arm."

"We might still meet his assassins in a strange land." Dragon snuggled close and began licking her ear and taking off her dress.

"The general is an old hand at political intrigue."

Still, with the threat of war hanging over China, they knew they needed General Chin's connections and information to counter whatever fate had in store for them.

"The new maid in the house . . . " Glorious Dragon took off his shirt. "Is she reliable?"

"Yes, Little Lotus is completely trustworthy." Crystal helped him out of his pants. "My father made sure of that."

"Oh Crystal, Crystal." He kissed her breasts while she freed herself of her underwear.

In the midst of lovemaking, Dragon cursed General Chin and the other fatuous young men captivated by Bright Crystal's charm.

"No one touches me the way you do," Crystal murmured. "I need the other men around so General Chin still thinks that you're just one of them."

"No doubt all the others are afraid of Chin." He pushed her hair away from her face and slowly kissed her every feature. "We belong together."

"Yes, my father and you are my family." She returned his kisses. Her hands traced his spine and played with his hair.

Soon they were calmer, but the drizzle of dread returned. Crystal asked: "Speaking of family, did you ask your sister's family to move here?"

Dragon got up to put his clothes on. "My brother-in-law agrees that we are safer in the foreign concessions because everyone will be considered non-belligerent. But he would never agree to move here without work waiting for him."

Having lived with the dread of an imminent government collapse and the uncertainty of war, Crystal swallowed hard to drown out her anguish. She rallied her wits. "I heard the army needs uniforms," she whispered calmly. She could not tell him that her source of information was General Chin.

"Oh Crystal," Glorious Dragon kissed his lover and started to peel off his clothes again. "You take such good care of me!"

Glorious Dragon allowed several weeks to slip by without implementing his new plan to cause havoc in an opium den. He did not feel safe repeating his old methods. Twice, he had brought a group of drunken foreign soldiers to disrupt a den. Someone might have suspected that the only Chinese man in the party was the instigator. This time, he must put on a disguise and cause the destruction all by himself.

Persistent gunfire alerted everyone that the Japanese now sat in the harbor. The streets of the International Settlement began to fill with refugees. They lay next to their meager belongings on the sidewalks, sat on the steps of the big banks and insurance companies, and crowded on to the wharves. On August 13, 1937, the Chinese air defense came out in force, strafing the enemy warships. People clogging the congested streets craned their necks to catch sight of the planes. Everyone expected to be safe in the foreign territories. They thought the Japanese would not dare to bomb the Western powers.

The oppressive summer heat, the crowds on the street, and his unpleasant destination drove Glorious Dragon to the limits of his genial nature. The mere thought of visiting an opium den made him ill. However, he also saw the confusion on the streets as an excellent opportunity to carry through his plan.

Dressed like a coolie, and buffeted by all the pushing and shoving on the streets, Glorious Dragon almost lost track of where he was. But he found the tenement owned by General Chin, known for its second-floor opium parlor. He ran up the rickety stairs in a fury.

When he entered the lobby, his eyes adjusted to the perpetual dusk. The proprietor was resting by the front desk, vicariously enjoying the drug by inhaling the sticky sweet smoke. Cursing, Glorious Dragon shoved the debilitated man and hollered, "I must look for my father!"

In the cavernous room, heavily painted young women hovered over reclining bodies. When they spotted him, they recoiled from him and tried to soothe the smokers. On the opium beds, sweaty, naked torsos gleamed in the heat. Glorious Dragon kicked off the hurricane lamps, flipped over the furniture and stormed through the room while several men appeared from nowhere ready to restrain him.

He broke lose from them and dove into a private alcove. There, an old man with glazed eyes, clad only in loose dark trousers, lolled over his pipe.

"You, degenerate turtle!" Glorious Dragon bellowed, knocking the pipe away from this total stranger. Foaming at the mouth, the man sat up. His scrawny hands came up automatically to shield his gaunt face. His unfocused eyes peered from dark sockets. With a terrified whimper, he collapsed back into the bed, averting his face from Dragon's rage. For a moment, the security men stopped, thinking that the outraged son had found his father — an important patron.

"Get up!" Glorious Dragon commanded.

The body did not move, and Glorious Dragon could not lift the slippery torso.

"You're a curse to your ancestors! Your mother's milk rots in your mouth!"

Suddenly, a thunderous boom rocked the whole building. Windows exploded; sunlight burst into the room; falling plaster, tumbling bricks, billowing smoke and dust filled the atmosphere; flames sprang up everywhere. People screamed and scrambled out from their beds in a rush for the door. Glorious Dragon felt the floor give way beneath him. The body of the old man hurtled toward him.

When he woke, he was in a hospital bed. Bright Crystal was beside him, sponging his arms and legs. When she saw him open his eyes, she gave a soft shriek of joy.

"Are you all right? Oh my Dragon, I thought you were dead! There were so many casualties in the streets!"

Dragon nodded and smiled.

"Are you in pain?"

"No." He shook his head.

"Those imbeciles! The Chinese air force dropped two bombs on the International Settlement area by mistake! One was in front of the Cathay Hotel, and the other actually went through the Palace Hotel. They say two defective planes caused the mistake. I say their commanders are defective. They're either stupid or corrupt!" She continued ranting while bathing Dragon.

"A bomb? The den did not catch fire?" Dragon moaned. For a moment, he had thought his rampage had started the fire.

"A bomb! Dropped by the Chinese air force by mistake! What were you doing in the opium den?"

Glorious Dragon turned his face toward the wall.

Amid her sobs and gentle dabs, Crystal informed her lover that most occupants of the opium parlor had survived. Many had suffered shock and smoke inhalation, but had only minor scratches.

"Fortunately, the tenement building was stronger than it looked," Crystal said. "You have several broken ribs. Someone said you were looking for your father." She looked puzzled. 'But your father died a long time ago!"

"I was confused. It was so hot." Glorious Dragon looked on her effervescence with a wan smile. He was ashamed to lie to his Crystal. He turned his eyes away from her dewy face. "You look lovely when you're all wound up."

Suddenly he realized what she might have done to save him. "Did you get General Chin's help to find me?"

Bright Crystal dropped the sponge in the basin, stunned by the tone of reproach in his voice. She threw herself, crying, onto his chest.

Glorious Dragon held her. He stroked her hair, murmuring to her, and controlling the despair in his own heart so that his Crystal could be soothed by his even, steady breathing. "Hush, hush," he said finally. "We're together. That's what matters."

He lifted her chin and rubbed her wet cheeks with his fingers. "Now, you'll smile for me." He gave her a naughty wink. 'Have you thought of this as a God-sent opportunity? Many foreigners will want to leave. Now we can buy all the real estate we want."

Bright Crystal smiled. No, she hadn't thought of it.

Chapter 3

IN HANGZHOU, LIFE had resumed its usual rhythm after the birthday festivities. One morning in August, Purple Jade sat by the small pond in her courtyard embroidering under the cypress tree.

"Uncle Dragon is coming, Uncle Dragon is coming!" Silver Bell skipped in trilling.

"Yes, my heart-and-liver." Purple Jade looked up, "Your Dragon uncle is coming from Shanghai to have dinner with us."

"M-ma, may I please go with Father to meet Uncle Dragon at the station?"

"Of course, Silver Bell," her mother said with a smile. "Maybe Golden Bell would like to go with you."

"Oh goody! I'm going to tell *jei-jei*." Silver Bell skipped away clapping.

She almost bumped into Comely Brook entering the courtyard.

Orchid, renamed Comely Brook at the wedding, became pregnant shortly after her marriage. Her body took on a rounded womanly aspect.

"Look at our second *tai-tai*, Winter Plum," Purple Jade said to her new personal maid. Her own eyes avoided Comely Brook, who was a picture of blossoming health. "She has sprouted good fortune. She's lovely to behold." Purple Jade never allowed a negative note to slip into her speech. Whenever the sight of Comely Brook made her feel old, she would reproach the red-eyed demon. She would only speak of blessings coming to the family.

"Yes, *Tai-tai* has been blessed," replied the maid. "Second *tai-tai* has sprouted double good fortune."

"With so much harmony in this house, I'm sure we'll have a son this time."

"Morning peace, *Tai-tai*." Comely Brook curtsied. "I just came from a walk in the back garden. The mulberry tree is filled with leaves now. We forgot to take the silkworm eggs from the cold house after the birthday celebration."

"Brook-*mei*, how often must I remind you not to call me *tai-tai* as before. When the young master arrives, he will be embarrassed his mothers do not address each other properly."

"*Tai*, I mean *Jei*. . . Oh, that's not important." Comely Brook blushed. Her heart quivered whenever she thought of the kindness of her former mistress. Yes, Purple Jade had been her mother, sister, teacher, friend and mentor. But she would always address her as Mistress. "I'm not used to such honor." She lowered her head. "The young master must know you are his true mother."

Oh-me-to-fo, let it be a son! Comely Brook prayed silently several times a day. To bear an heir for the family would be a kindness repaid. A son would elevate her present status. Indeed, a son would mean power and honor! But what if . . . no, she wouldn't think of it. Another daughter would mean ingratitude, disloyalty. Oh, best not think about it.

"Yes." Purple Jade savored her eminence and was glad that her moment of sore-hearted envy had passed without a hint of betrayal. "We shall have a son. Did you say the mulberry tree in the back garden is already full of leaves?"

"Yes, *Tai-tai*. We're at least four months late. The weather is so warm now, the eggs should hatch in a few days."

"Winter Plum, go and help second *tai-tai* take down the eggs from the cold house. She shouldn't strain herself in her condition."

"*Tai-tai*, we saved an extra sheet of eggs last year. Should we prepare three baskets?" Comely Brook was happy to resume her role as assistant.

"Yes, I shall supervise the preparation myself," Purple Jade responded. "Ask my daughters and their maids to join us in the south workroom by the back garden."

Later, the baskets were lined with soft rice paper; twigs were attached to the baskets to make three treelike tents. The eggs looked like tiny sesame seeds, thickly speckled on strips of paper. Purple Jade placed them in the baskets.

"Silver Bell and Peony will come for the first watch in the morning; Golden Bell and Iris should come around noon; second *tai-tai* and I will do our embroidery here in the afternoon. Since it is already August, there is no need to cover them at night with silk blankets. Let's hope there won't be any violent summer storms to upset the baskets." Purple Jade gave the orders, which were essentially the same from year to year.

Several days later, tiny black, antlike worms emerged. Soft goose-down feathers were used to brush them off the egg paper. Feathers and paper flowers, the silkworms' traditional ornaments, were then inserted all around the basket.

The women went into the back garden to harvest mulberry leaves. Silver Bell and Peony giggled and laughed as they climbed the mulberry tree. They picked the tenderest young leaves, and rushed them into the south room to shred them for the baby worms.

"M-ma," Silver Bell called from the mulberry tree, "is Uncle Dragon coming this evening?"

"I think so, my heart-and-liver," her mother replied. The watery morning sun bathed the garden in a soft flossy hue. A few bees buzzed amid the flowering honeysuckle. A cloyingly sweet fragrance filled the air. Purple Jade stretched and walked among the younger women. By now, she was used to the looser binding on her feet, and walked with deliberate hammering motions.

The birthday-cum-wedding propelled her adjustment. During the hectic months of preparation and celebration, adrenaline had helped her play the role of wife, hostess, and mother of the bride. And now, without Orchid to lean on, she had grown used to walking on her own. She enjoyed the freedom of movement, and the sense of total mastery in her household. Her newfound power and independence felt almost supernatural.

As far as she knew, no daughter-in-law in any traditional home had the privilege of having a separate home built to her specifications. But Righteous Virtue had insisted upon this Western practice. He suggested the simpler architectural lines of the early Ming period. Their house was designed with a traditional north and south orientation. Wing-like, earthen-tiles topped the angular lines of posts and beams separated by plain white walls. Rosewood antique pieces added warmth to their living quarters. Ancient scrolls of calligraphy and watercolors, done by generations of Huang ancestors, adorned the walls. Classic blue and white porcelain urns holding miniature trees and flowering bushes were displayed throughout the house. The gardener periodically changed the exhibit when plants reached their full glory. In this back garden, Purple Jade was delighted to feel her growing feet stomping past the budding potted hibiscus, ready for show.

"I want Uncle Dragon to see our new worms." Silver Bell resumed her patter, recalling her mother from her labyrinthine thoughts. "Do you think he'll pay more for our colored cocoons this year?"

"I don't think the colors make much difference to the weavers," Purple Jade answered. "The factory is very clever with dyes, but I'm sure you could charm your uncle into paying more for anything."

"Oh M-ma, I can't wait to see the cocoons. Last year I saved one pink, two light green, and several yellow ones. The moths from those cocoons produced our eggs. This year, I hope all will be rainbow-colored!"

"That's not likely. The colored cocoons are rare mutations. Of course, if we do get colored cocoons, that'll be very lovely indeed. Perhaps your uncle Dragon will order the silk untouched, and we could weave a scarf for you."

"Oh that would be so beautiful—"

Golden Bell ran into the garden with a letter in her hand. "M-ma, M-ma, Iris ran away!"

"What?" Purple Jade gasped. She shook her head as her hand swept the air in front of her. "No! We never mistreat anyone in this house. She must have gone into town without telling you."

"No, M-ma." Golden Bell handed her a letter. "I didn't see Iris all morning, so I went to look for her in her room. This is the letter she left me."

"*Pss*, the brazen vixen. The letter is written in English!" Purple Jade thrust the letter back to her daughter.

"Well, Iris studied with me every day since Miss Tyler came." Golden Bell smiled. "She's probably better educated than all — I mean Silver Bell."

Everyone knew she meant to say "all of you," since no one else could read the letter.

"Give me the letter." Purple Jade stood erect, straightening her shoulders. "Your father will read it tonight and decide what to do." She would not give her daughter the opportunity to flaunt her audacious foreign learning.

"Iris has gone to Shanghai," Golden Bell almost shouted. She handed her mother the letter with a flourish. "She says she's grateful and will write again when she finds work. She took my pearl earrings that I promised her long ago."

"Ungrateful minx! She stole your earrings too? What will people think when they hear of such treachery in this house?" Purple Jade fidgeted with a plum branch. "Why didn't she ask for her freedom? People will say we've been mean masters." She would have stamped her feet for effect, but a wave of pain in her legs forced her to sit.

"*Tai-tai*, perhaps Iris was drinking vinegar. She might have hoped to become the concubine," Comely Brook said, giving her mistress a sidelong glance.

"Iris is already eighteen." Golden Bell pouted. "The way you fought Father about keeping me home must have made her feel like an imprisoned bird."

"That is your interpretation." Purple Jade glared at her daughter. "It is bad form to make a fuss about Iris. We have lost enough face as it is. The servants will snicker behind our backs."

"I'll go to Shanghai and find her. I'll talk to her."

"You will do no such thing! It is your father's fault that the maids have become so uppity. We can't call attention to this disgrace, but we must do something to show the servants this will never happen again!"

"*Tai-tai* is absolutely correct." Comely Brook came forth with her usual support. "You see the two young mulberry trees there? We've forgotten the gardener is Iris's uncle. He has cultivated these trees for three years, though we have more than enough leaves from this one tree for our small crop of silkworms. Perhaps some apricot trees might be prettier and more useful in this back garden."

Purple Jade understood at once. "Winter Plum, go get the gardener!"

When the gardener came, he knelt before his mistress and touched his head to the ground. "*Tai-tai*, forgive my unworthy niece. After two generations of service in this household, my family and I had no idea that Iris had become so brazen. It must have been that new chauffeur. He puts disloyal ideas into her head!"

"One serving maid in this house is a small matter!" Purple Jade replied in a stern voice. "Golden Bell gave Iris her freedom. You're certainly not to be held responsible for your niece."

"Thank you, *Tai-tai*." The gardener kowtowed again.

"But gardener, why do we have three mulberry trees in this garden? Are you cultivating them to sell the leaves? Tell all the servants that such skimming is not to be tolerated! Chop down the two small mulberries there and replace them with two apricot trees!"

"Yes, yes. *Tai-tai* is most wise. The apricots will be prettier." He touched his head to the ground once more. "Somehow, the mulberries had taken root. I've let them grow without thinking."

"Then see to it right away."

"Thank you, *Tai-tai*, for your kindness. All the servants will see the fallen trees and I shall inform the master if we hear anything about Iris."

When Righteous Virtue came home, the women immediately surrounded him. Golden Bell, Silver Bell and Purple Jade spoke all at once.

"Father, Iris ran away!"

"Father, the silkworms hatched today."

"My lord, I ordered the two extra mulberry trees cut, and two apricot trees planted."

"Wait, wait, one at a time. It's good news the silkworms have hatched, but what's this about Iris running away, and why do you want to chop down the mulberry trees?"

Purple Jade produced Iris's letter. "Iris left this note to Golden Bell. We think she has run away to Shanghai. We also found Iris's uncle cultivating two extra mulberry trees in the back garden as a cash crop for himself." Purple Jade opened her silk painted fan and gave it a perfunctory flutter. She seldom needed to give an accounting of her housekeeping practices, and certainly never before her daughters. She needed air and looked to Comely Brook for support. Comely Brook came forward quickly to stand beside her former mistress, and fanned both of them with her big paper fan.

Purple Jade continued: "I normally permit a certain amount of private enterprise among the servants, if it doesn't interfere with the proper maintenance of our household."

Righteous Virtue accepted his wife's explanation without comment. He read the letter and laughed. "Ha, Iris writes beautiful English! I wish Silver Bell had taken advantage of Miss Tyler's tutoring."

"This is no laughing matter, my lord," Purple Jade protested in an injured voice. "All this foreign learning brings nothing but trouble into this house."

"Times have changed, Jade-*mei*," her husband answered. "You did right to discipline the gardener. All the servants will understand this as kindly punishment; you've saved our face." He beamed proudly on his clever wife, but Purple Jade averted her eyes. She brought her fan to cover her mouth, giving Comely Brook an imperceptible smile of gratitude.

"However"— Righteous Virtue began to pace —"Iris is obviously a bright girl. It is important to have grateful allies rather than spiteful renegades in these uncertain times. I'll ask the chauffeur what he knows about this affair, and we'll get in touch with her. Dragon might use her in his silk factory in Shanghai."

"Please, Father, ask Mother to send me to school in Shanghai." Golden Bell tugged on her father's sleeve. "Uncle Dragon and Iris both will look after me."

"Those two will be the worst influence on a young maiden!" Purple Jade slapped her fan shut.

"Hush, Golden Bell." Righteous Virtue touched his daughter's hand, but looked steadily into Purple Jade's eyes. "The East Ocean Devils are already attacking Shanghai; they'll overrun Hangzhou in no time if Shanghai falls. We may all have to hide out in the foreign concessions for safety."

"So we'll all have to go to Shanghai!" Comely Brook cried with a start, surprising herself. Her voice echoed the same thought in every one's mind. No one noticed that it was Comely Brook's first comment on any family deliberations.

"Oh, goodie!" Golden Bell and Silver Bell exclaimed almost in unison.

"Oh, my lord! This, this is impossible!" Purple Jade stuttered. The serenity of her house made the fighting in Shanghai seem very far away. Even when the warlords were feuding, she hadn't left home except for a few trips to the monastery that provided safety while strong, armed men and servants guarded her house. Back then, safety had been much easier to attain than most people imagined. The contending parties had created a system whereby a little manipulation, an offer of food or money, would allow them to strut their might, while avoiding the loss of blood in real battle. Those who suffered were too proud to give face or too stubborn to share their wealth.

Directing her fan toward Comely Brook, Purple Jade muttered: "To leave this home . . . in Brook-*mei's* condition . . ." Her eyes filled with tears.

"Now, now, nothing is decided. I must pick up Dragon from the station at five." Righteous Virtue was not eager to discuss such weighty problems then. "Why don't we all go for a ride in the car on this lovely summer day."

"Oh, Uncle Dragon is coming! Uncle Dragon is coming!" Silver Bell chimed.

"Yes, Dragon will know more of what's going on. He hasn't been home for a long time. I wonder what's kept him away?" Purple Jade paused. The long months of preparing for and enjoying the festivities had been blissfully free of anxiety. The pestilence of war had seemed miles and miles away. "I don't feel like a ride now."

"I'd better stay with *Tai-tai*," Comely Brook said. "You'll need space in the car for luggage." It was like her to be thoughtful and practical. She also wanted to avoid Ah Lee.

"All right. Let's go, girls!"

The train had just arrived when the Huangs reached the station. Chou Glorious Dragon was one of the first to emerge. Amid a sea of passengers clad in dark cotton tunics and baggy trousers, Glorious Dragon stood out in his three-piece suit of textured raw silk. His boater hat rose almost a head above all the other passengers. He swung his walking stick, and the golden chain of his watch sparkled between his vest pockets.

"Uncle Dragon, Uncle." The girls waved from the car as the chauffeur went to pick up his luggage and Righteous Virtue greeted him.

"Welcome home, Dragon-*dee*." Righteous Virtue smiled affably. "You show no sign of your recent brush with the immortals."

"You didn't tell my sister my accident in the opium den, did you?" A shadow crossed his sunny face.

"No, but what were you doing there?"

"Oh, I was in the wrong place at the wrong time." Glorious Dragon turned away to look at his luggage. "I happened to be passing the building when it collapsed. My sister does not need to worry about my bad luck."

"No, of course not."

"Thanks." Dragon shook his brother-in-law's hand. Though his half-sister was almost like a mother to him, he shared the traditional masculine desire to protect her. He would not know how to explain to her his continued raids on General Chin's opium dens and his traumatic experiences in the city.

Glorious Dragon tossed the chauffeur several coins. "Find yourself a rickshaw to go home. I'll drive the car." He looked at the girls and smiled. "Ah, Golden Bell and Silver Bell, my Shanghai mistress will turn into a vinegar bottle if she hears that I've been riding with such beautiful young ladies."

"Oh, they're no better than other young women." Righteous Virtue dismissed the compliment with a swish of his hand and beamed broadly. Tradition required a disclaimer on any compliment, though he agreed with his brother-in-law. His daughters were exceptional beauties. He could not see any man resisting their charm.

"Virtue, pardon my criticism, but such old-fashioned modesty is unbecoming to a modern man like you. Your girls are gorgeous!"

"Ah, young girls are a true worry today. Let's hurry; your sister has prepared a feast." He hoisted the front panel of his Chinese robe and climbed into the back seat. The chauffeur adjusted Glorious Dragon's suitcase and left.

"Who wants to sit up front with me?" asked Glorious Dragon, and held open the passenger side door with a bow.

"I will! I will!" both girls chimed.

"All right, Golden Bell, you sit in the passenger seat and Silver Bell, you sit on my lap on the driver's seat."

"Oh my, Uncle Dragon, you'll teach me how to drive?"

"Is it safe to have Silver Bell driving, Dragon? She is only nine." Her father frowned.

"Open your heart, Virtue. I guarantee! This town is not Shanghai. Everyone will just gawk or run away when they see a car coming." He lifted Silver Bell on to his lap, and placed her hands on the steering wheel. "Here, Silver Bell, you take charge of the steering like this; squeeze the rubber horn like this when you see anyone in the way."

"I'll help you pilot; do the shifting, and step on the pedal." Her uncle pried her hand away from the horn that she was busy honking.

While Silver Bell steered, Golden Bell giggled and chirped about Iris and the mulberry trees. Righteous Virtue looked on nervously from the back seat. He had not burdened his wife with the coming demands of "*Tao Wren*" (running from chaos.) He was pleased his brother-in-law had lightened the atmosphere and did not alarm the girls.

Passersby smiled, pointed to the merry car, and ran out of the way. Glorious Dragon felt he had made the right entrance for his coming mission.

Chapter 4

"OH DRAGON-*DEE*, YOU'VE finally come." Purple Jade greeted her brother with genuine pleasure. "You look so trim in your new foreign suit!"

"Don't I look as if I've just stepped out of *Vanity Fair*?" Glorious Dragon turned around for everyone to admire him. He had lost weight during his hospital stay, but his carefree manner belied his ordeal.

"Dragon-*dee*, you have no shame! I don't know another Chinese like you. *Vanity Fair* indeed! They all look like the devils!" Purple Jade scolded, but her eyes were glowing.

"Jade-*jei*, our ancestors still control you and Virtue-*ko*." He laughed, twirled his walking stick, and sauntered before them with open arms. "There are opportunities all around us. I'm having the time of my life!"

"So I see." Purple Jade swished her fan. "You always seem to bring rousing heat wherever you go."

"And why not?" Glorious Dragon ripped open a package. "Look what I brought you — champagne from France via Shanghai. They call it the bubbly. It'll make the most solemn man giggle!" He flourished the bottle and held it aloft for everyone to see.

"Oh Uncle Dragon, may I try some?"

"No, Silver Bell," her mother answered. "You're giggly enough as it is! Winter Plum, go get the set of jade wine bowls. We have to celebrate."

"Ah, I forgot to bring you the champagne glasses." Glorious Dragon did not seem disturbed by the omission.

He carefully lined up the precious wine bowls when they arrived. The thin green stone looked translucent and fragile. "What craftsmanship!" he exclaimed, standing back a moment to admire the bowls.

The girls screeched and giggled as the bottle was popped open and foam came spurting out.

"See, your mother is right! You're giggling already, and you haven't even tasted the bubbly." Their uncle teased them with darting glances while he poured the wine.

Hiding their mouths behind their handkerchiefs out of propriety, the girls giggled some more.

"Drinking champagne in these fine jade bowls reminds me of Iris." Glorious Dragon toasted everyone. "Did Golden Bell tell me in the car that she ran away to Shanghai and left a note in English? Fancy that!"

"M-Ma wouldn't allow me into the schoolrooms, but Iris was with Golden Bell all these years."

"Hush, Silver Bell. Dragon, can you use her in your factory?" Righteous Virtue asked. "It's not proper that anyone from our house should turn into a bar girl."

"Can I use her? A modern young woman who knows English? She'll be invaluable in my dealings with foreigners and the export bureaucrats."

Golden Bell shot her mother a triumphant look. She was ready to shout: "See, I told you so," when Comely Brook rested a firm hand on her shoulder. Golden Bell turned to look at her. Comely Brook formed a silent "no" with her lips and shook her head ever so slightly with a gentle sway of her rounded body. As the elder young mistress of the house, Golden Bell could remonstrate with the concubine. But following Comely Brook's steady gaze, she saw her mother's uncertain, forlorn eyes and kept still.

"She has to be taught to use forks and knives and learn proper Western manners, of course. All the businessmen will be so impressed!" Glorious Dragon slapped his lap with enthusiasm. "I think I'd better adopt her as a niece, before someone else hires her."

Righteous Virtue nodded. "Winter Plum, send for the chauffeur. He should be home by now."

"Dragon, I suppose you know what you're doing." Fanning herself vigorously, Purple Jade frowned. "In truth, Iris has been much like a sister to Golden Bell, and this would give us lots of face."

She passed a bowl of wine to Comely Brook and motioned her to sit and drink with them. Orchid was not in the habit of sitting down with the family, but she was Comely Brook now, and Purple Jade always made a point of being solicitous. Comely Brook nodded her thanks and sat demurely beside Golden Bell. Purple Jade sipped her wine, happy that her resourceful brother would take care of this "disgrace" in her household.

After the chauffeur bowed to everyone, Righteous Virtue addressed him: "Ah Lee, we know you have many friends and relations in Shanghai. We believe Iris has gone there." He spoke with just enough gruffness to give weight to his mild words but avoid all recriminations. "We've always treated her like a child of the house. Now Mr. Chou has agreed to adopt her as a niece. Please help us get in touch with her."

"You're most generous!" The chauffeur bowed again. "The Buddha will bring blessings on this house, master." He smiled, relieved that his complicity in the matter had been overlooked.

"Well then, please use your influence and see that the message is delivered."

"Yes, master. I'll do all I can." He left.

"Now you must all come to Shanghai and attend the adoption ceremony." Glorious Dragon swept his arms across the room.

"Why can't we bring Iris home and have the celebration here?" Purple Jade slapped her fan shut.

Glorious Dragon took a deep breath. He wanted to swing his arms and bellow out his determination to risk everything to bring all the Huangs to safety. Instead, he spoke softly. "The chief purpose of my visit today is to bring our families to a foreign concession in Shanghai." He had seized on the adoption celebration as a means to lure his sister out of her home, but he could no longer maintain the illusion. "The news from the war front is very bad indeed. The enemy seems to be gaining ground." He sounded sober and very grave.

"Dragon- *dee*." Purple Jade opened her fan again to hide her agitation. She paused to compose herself. "Our country is so vast, and we've often known war. Nothing has changed the stability of this household."

"The East Ocean devils are brutes. They rape and kill indiscriminately."

"Surely no one will touch an old woman like me or a pregnant lady like Brook-*mei*!" Purple Jade clutched her fist to her pounding heart, grappling with the contrast between the ordinary and her knowledge of war's carnage.

"I do not wish to frighten the young ladies, but the truth must be told. The situation is urgent." Her brother wiped his mouth and continued, "Lao Ting, our uniform shipper, has personally seen beastly acts performed against not only young women, but children, animals, and even old women in their sixties!"

"*Hai*, what war can do to people," Righteous Virtue said in his gentle voice. "My classmate Liu went to school in Japan. He said the Japanese are the cleanest and most orderly people he has ever known." He stood up to pace, lowered his head and avoided eye contact with anyone.

"There is no use lamenting. We must act quickly. The enemy is already at the mouth of Shanghai Harbor. They can march in any day. If I were you, I'd go to the French concession tonight!" A rush of blood added color to Glorious Dragon's champagne-reddened face. The urgency in his voice electrified the room.

Purple Jade turned pale. Spasms of heat and chill ran through her body. "Dragon-*dee*, surely the wine has gone to your head!" She bit her lip. She did not want to panic in front of her children. "How can a household leave immediately? Where shall we live? What are we to live on?"

"Dragon and I have been planning for this for some time," answered her husband. "I never told you because we hoped this move would never become necessary. But Dragon is correct. We have no time to lose. Golden Bell and Silver Bell should go with Dragon tomorrow. I'll tell the chauffeur to have Iris meet them in Shanghai. The rest of us will arrange the transfer of our furniture and valuables, and we'll go when we can."

"You can always return when the fighting is over." Dragon added to soften the blow.

"Oh Uncle Dragon, have you arranged a school for me in Shanghai?" Golden Bell asked, her eyes flashing with excitement.

"Can I bring my silkworms to Shanghai?" chimed in Silver Bell. "I saved the colored cocoons last year. This year, all my cocoons might weave a rainbow on the basket tent!"

"Hush girls." Purple Jade gave them an acid glance. She held her breath and kept quiet for a long time. The prospects of rape and pillage had pervaded the air for a long time. Yes, she must be prudent and prepare for temporary adversity. Yes, she would return once the fighting was over.

"Do we have a place to move to?" she finally asked the men.

"Yes," answered her husband. "Dragon says he has bought a small foreign house for us on Petain Road in the French concession."

"What? What kind of house, where?"

"A two-story foreign house on Petain Road. It is named after a famous French general."

"Bei-tan, Precious Pawnshop Road? I don't believe a general could have a name like that. It must be an inappropriate street to live on!" She sounded flippant, but it was the only objection she could think of. Purple Jade tapped her fist on the table. She looked to Comely Brook for agreement.

Comely Brook looked confused, but she nodded.

"Jade-*jei*, you must know by now the translation of sounds can have very strange meanings." Her brother moved to sit beside her. "You could say that Bei-tan also means 'Precious, Should Be,' a more fitting meaning for our present purpose. However, I know you will be pleased to know our cousin Der Wei's family and cousin Chou Ling both live in our Chou family-owned houses in the same French section, on Gavaine Road."

"Gau-en Road? High Grace Road is a good name. When is cousin Ling moving?"

"Next week, perhaps sooner. You'll be only a few streets away, with plenty of time to visit."

"Dragon-*dee*, you can always make the best of everything. No wonder my lord wants you here to convince me of this temporary move." Purple Jade smiled uncertainly. "In order not to disrupt the household here, let's just say we're visiting our city home to celebrate Iris's adoption. Golden Bell and Silver Bell, get ready to pack. Tomorrow, you may leave with your uncle Dragon."

"Oh M-ma, you must have more *cheongsam* made for us. Everyone in Shanghai wears those modern sheaths. We'll look so old-fashioned in our jackets and skirts!" Golden Bell pleaded.

"Yes, of course," Purple Jade replied without thinking. The modern Hangzhou ladies also were wearing the sheaths. She turned to give Comely Brook a slight nod. Her sister-wife would remember to take care of another detail necessary for their life in the city.

"Hooray, we're going to Shanghai! We're going to Shanghai." Silver Bell skipped out of the room and pulled along her smiling sister. "Uncle Dragon is taking us."

Purple Jade gave specific directions to Comely Brook and to Winter Plum and other maids to start packing for their sojourn in Shanghai.

Chapter 5

WHILE THE FAMILY ate, the men tried their best to maintain a normal demeanor. They knew instinctively they must defuse the tension caused by their radical decision. The girls chatted about what they thought they would need in Shanghai. Purple Jade answered perfunctorily and made charts in her head about what to bring. Somehow, the customary dread lifted from her shoulders. The needed action released her pent-up weariness.

"How can we afford to buy a house in Shanghai with our farm income?" Purple Jade asked her husband when dinner was over and the girls were sent to their rooms to pack.

"To begin with, I cleared three mountains of our bamboo crop last year," her husband replied. "Dragon helped me sell it for the war effort."

"For the war effort?"

"Yes, you know all construction uses bamboo scaffolding, and porters use bamboo poles to carry food and ammunition. We have a precious commodity. We invested the profits in his uniform factory."

"Thank you, Dragon-*dee*. You are resourceful!" Purple Jade smiled. "But what's this uniform factory? I thought we are in the silk business."

After Comely Brook poured tea for everyone, Purple Jade beckoned her to sit beside her.

"Oh yes, I helped to develop silk parachutes. But our national air force is so limited, we can never prosper with just that." Glorious Dragon reached for a cup of green tea to settle his stomach after the sumptuous dinner. "My mistress, Bright Crystal, told me our National army needed uniforms, so I started a factory."

"Useful information, even if it came from a mistress," Purple Jade mused.

"How did your mistress acquire such information?" Righteous Virtue raised his teacup. He looked intently at his brother-in-law over the curling steam. He slurped the tongue-searing tea . His lips never touched the cup. The ancient custom of drinking hot tea in summer brought him instant relief. The tea refreshed his breath and soothed his digestion. It brought him a full head of cooling sweat and dispelled his post-prandial lethargy.

"She is also the mistress of General Chin Bar-tau." Glorious Dragon relaxed into his chair and folded his arms over his nervous stomach. He must sound casual and not betray any hint of the disdain he felt for Chin.

"Oh Dragon-*dee*, sharing a mistress! You are swatting a fly on the tiger's head!"

"I heard Chin is Generalissimo Chiang's bodyguard and head of his secret police. He's extremely powerful." Righteous Virtue wiped his brow. Anxiety now annihilated the tea's cooling relief.

"I . . . I thought he also had a hand in the drug traffic." Purple Jade's voice shook as she remembered the fire they had caused in the Prosperous Dream. She grabbed Comely Brook's hand.

Dragon took up his teacup again and blew on the hot steam. "Wonderful tea." He winked at his sister. He knew exactly what would cross her mind. "I hope someday you'll meet Bright Crystal. She entertains well-connected people — acquires all the useful information."

"My lord" — Purple Jade turned to her husband— "did you know Dragon was so tangled in politics?"

"Dragon, your sister has good judgment. Never mix politics with business!" "Oh I can follow the politics all right." Glorious Dragon took another sip, looking well composed. "You own the business!"

"I do?"

"Oh yes." Glorious Dragon nodded. "You see, when I heard the uniform contract was out for bids, I told them my brother-in-law owned a uniform-manufacturing facility."

"But I do not own nor understand the workings of any factory!"

"We're all befuddled by your wheeling and dealing, Dragon-*dee*. I hope you're not involved in anything illegal." Purple Jade felt her heart pounding. She looked to Comely Brook for support.

"Master Dragon and General Chin must be friends," Comely Brook whispered in her mistress's ear. "No one knows we went near the Prosperous Dream."

"Oh, everything is on the up and up," her brother replied. "I rented a 'go down' on the Bund and lent you all my workers from our silk factory for one day. I had some difficulty renting sewing machines, but I managed to get enough." He laughed. Yes, he would use any information from Chin to benefit his family and hurt the general.

"We were lucky," he continued. "The contracting official was very impressed when we toured your plant. He happens to be a graduate of St. John's University and knows your name. I told him that since you work for the local legislative council here, I manage the East Asian Uniform Company for you."

"That is partly true." Righteous Virtue looked puzzled. His wife had turned crimson from worry, but he did not want to appear ungrateful. "After all, you do manage our share of the money in East Asian Uniform, which has been profitable."

"So you had the contract before the uniform company existed!" Purple Jade could not quite understand the scheme.

"What better investment can you get?" Glorious Dragon gesticulated with both hands. "I have a contract in hand." He formed his right hand into a fist. "Then Virtue gave me his money." He formed his left hand into another fist. "I went to the bank for the rest." He clapped his hands and proudly pronounced: "We now own the most modern uniform factory in China."

"All this is far too puzzling for me." Purple Jade rose to bid them good evening. She would leave the moral quandary to her husband for the moment. She grimaced as her mind raced ahead in anticipation of their temporary flight. "Continue talking. I must pack for the girls. Brook-*mei*, come help me." The women bowed to bid good evening. They left with their heads huddled together, consulting each other on what to pack.

Purple Jade, Comely Brook and Winter Plum stayed up all night, sewing gold coins and small jewelry pieces into the girls' clothing. Bedding and other lesser items were packed hastily into large trunks, marked for the luggage compartment of the train.

Glorious Dragon and Righteous Virtue discussed finances far into the night. Glorious Dragon advised the Huangs to sell as many land holdings as possible. Righteous Virtue resisted, arguing that this would be a violation of ancestral trust.

"Remember the American missionaries' offer to buy the hill near West Lake?"

"Yes, to build a church, but I refused. It is too close to our ancestral burial ground."

"Since you will move your family into the French concession, you must protect your ancestral grounds by placing them under American protection. Get an agreement from the church that they will respect your burial rights, then sell them the land. Ask them to deposit the funds in an account for you in America."

"There is something to what you say about placing the graves under American protection, but my family and I shall never leave our homeland. Why should I place our money in a foreign country?"

"The way I see it, our country is headed for a great upheaval. We've just changed a dynasty, and the East Ocean Devils are gobbling up our land. The countries in the West are also on the verge of war, but America seems to stand by itself. They're a vast country like ours," he added, opening his arms wide. "After all, they did not acquire land concessions from us. Remember I had asked you to introduce Miss Tyler to me. I have already moved most of my funds there. They are held in trust for your daughters."

"Thank you, Dragon-*dee*, for thinking of my daughters. Truly I feel like a useless fool these days. I'm doing everything to protect my family, but all my actions go against the principles I so cherished." Heedless of his show of emotion, Righteous Virtue stood up to pace, fuming: "When I was in Shanghai, I was a leader of the student protest movement. You were still very young in 1919. You may not remember. In the spring of that year, the Western powers met in Paris and totally discounted the Chinese 'Bitter Labor' contribution to the Allied forces during World War I. They awarded the German concessions in our Shantung Province to Japan."

"So, that's how they came to occupy the land and named it Manchuria!" Dragon exclaimed.

"Yes." Virtue stopped to wipe his sweaty face with his handkerchief. "I marched with the other students and agitated for a complete boycott of Japanese goods. This May fourth movement turned me against all foreign intervention in Chinese affairs."

"That must have been really exciting!"

"Exciting? Well, fury can be exciting. I was young and patriotic." Virtue started to pump his fist into the air while he shouted. "*No more extraterritorial rights! No more foreign concession*!" When he lowered his fist, his eyes were blank and he stared at the ground. "Now, I'm going to place my family under the shelter of these same concessions." Tears flowed down his cheeks. "Dragon-*dee*, I've always enjoyed your company — admired your pluck. But I'm uncomfortable with your business methods. I know my family owes you our lives, and your sister will rightly admonish me for my ingratitude. Never have I felt such helplessness, such anguish in my heart."

Glorious Dragon considered the gravity of the moment. He had become westernized in Shanghai; he felt uneasy when he saw a grown man in tears. He reminded himself that it was a time-honored Chinese tradition to use tears to express patriotism and loyalty. He let the thought rest. Playfully, he asked: "Virtue-*ko*, have you ever seen a marionette show?"

Righteous Virtue wiped his face again. The question puzzled him. "Yes, in Shanghai. It was frivolous."

"Well, you and my sister are marionettes that have been manipulated by old Chinese traditions. To me, you represent all that is good and innocent in our ancient culture. But you'll be crushed in these times of chaos. I'm a free man who loves your marionette show. I'm not without the basic virtues of Chinese charity and humanism. I practice 'jen' in my pragmatic way."

"Your honesty and courage only accentuate my timidity. I look to the East and West, and vacillate." Righteous Virtue stood rigid and stared at the ground. "I hold myself in contempt — envious of what I despoil. *Hai*, what is this world coming to."

"Virtue-*ko*, the hour is late. We must prepare for the big move soon. It is best to humor my sister and agree that this is only a temporary visit. We can buy the necessary furniture in Shanghai. You and I both know it may be a long time before we'll return here again — if at all." He paused.

When he was sure his brother-in-law had regained his composure, he instructed: "Arrange for this emergency. After all, the survival of your family is the first duty you owe to your ancestors."

Righteous Virtue looked about the spacious hall filled with ancient scrolls of calligraphy, watercolors, gleaming rosewood furniture and ancient porcelain vases. He pounded his fist against his open hand. "My grandfather, my father and I have all grown up in Hangzhou. These halls are the first fruits of my independence." His voice rang with angry despair. "I know your judgment to be shrewd and correct. I must sell as much property as possible and turn it into liquid assets, but who am I" — he paused to wipe his eyes — "without my roots?"

"If America seems too far, convert as much money as possible into English pounds. Ask your old classmate Chang Tar Guo of Chekiang Bank to manage it for you in their Hong Kong branch."

Righteous Virtue nodded in bitter silence. Glorious Dragon sighed. He hoped his brother-in-law had acceded to practical reality.

As the two men bade each other good night, Righteous Virtue bowed deeply to his younger brother-in-law.

"Dragon-*dee*, you're wise beyond your years. My emotions have blinded my common sense. I shall do what I can to follow your advice."

Glorious Dragon quickly returned the bow. "My honored Virtue-*ko*, I cannot shoulder such esteem. As you know too well, it is difficult to ride with the dragon!"

Chapter 6

THE NEXT DAY, Purple Jade ordered palanquins to take the Huang women to the station. Palanquins were seldom seen in Shanghai. Residents of the bustling city vilified their ancient languid grace. Purple Jade thought it appropriate that her girls should have another leisurely ride to enjoy the local scenery, temper their excitement, and cultivate the necessary patience and reserve.

The train station was a hive of swirling people and a jumble of luggage. News of war had set people in motion. When the palanquins arrived, Ah Lee was unloading their luggage from the car. Purple Jade lingered to pay the porters while Silver Bell hopped off the palanquin, skipped over the crossbar where the porters shouldered their load, and dashed toward the luggage.

"You pissing bitchy slave girl!" the porter cursed, spitting after Silver Bell.

"What?" Purple Jade gasped, glaring at the porter.

"That pissing bitch passed her female ass over my shoulder bar!" He spat with disgust. "May she suffer the same evil fortune she brought me!"

The porter alternately spat and cursed, disregarding the distressed mother in front of him. Purple Jade wrung her hands and fidgeted in silence. Comely Brook heard the commotion and entered the arena. Assuming her servant's voice, she shouted: "Shut up, you old turtle! Don't you know you've just carried the great ladies of the Huang household?"

The porter ignored Comely Brook and continued his mutterings. He held out his hand to Purple Jade for compensation: a female had stepped over his crossbar, and in so doing, had blemished its honor.

With a groan, Purple Jade handed over the extra coins and fled. She ran toward the men checking in the luggage and stumbled. The sting of reality hit her: Outside the protective walls of her house, she was but another female, a chattel to even the lowliest porter. Reluctant to upset her husband and the girls, however, she held her peace. Her tears would not come even when the girls boarded the train. She stood transfixed for a long time, weak with fear and pale as the white silk kerchief she held.

Unaware of the indignity she had suffered, Righteous Virtue assumed that her stillness was due to her unaccustomed separation from her daughters. "You'll be united with the girls very soon, Jade-*mei*."

Comely Brook clung solicitously to Purple Jade, not knowing how to assuage her mistress's sorrow. She prayed more fervently now for a son. Yes, she would preserve her noble husband's family line to avenge her mistress's humiliation. All would be made right upon the birth of her son — no, "their" son.

Several days later, Purple Jade, Comely Brook and Winter Plum left for Shanghai. Their house in the French concession was technically on foreign land and would remain safe from Japanese depredation. Purple Jade brought only what was essential to her personal needs, refusing to move antiques and family treasures, "since," as she insisted, "the visit will be temporary."

Righteous Virtue remained behind to sell property and settle accounts. He shipped more heirlooms to Shanghai every day and told his wife that there might be looting during the war. Proper furnishings were necessary to maintain "face" in their Shanghai house during their short sojourn in the city.

When Shanghai Harbor had been under siege for one month, Righteous Virtue gave detailed directions to the servants to manage the house. He departed, his car stuffed with family valuables. At the last moment, he included one small basket of silkworms, now already fat and snowy white. The gardener supplied a box of mulberry leaves wrapped in a cool wet cloth.

The car crawled through village streets, hugging the ancient north-south canal that had carried silk to Beijing for centuries. The chauffeur finally reached the highway between Nanking and Shanghai. As they approached the city, they heard muffled gunshots. The Chinese were piteously deficient in firepower, and the Japanese navy lobbed bombs into the Chinese sections.

"The East Ocean Devils do not dare bomb the foreign concessions," snorted Ah Lee. Righteous Virtue did not reply. He was used to the chauffeur's jaunty ways. In his youth, the novelties of the city had always drawn him into a whirlwind of activities — intoxicating but also exhausting. Now tension strained his taut muscles. He closed his eyes and inhaled deeply. Better to let the chauffeur think him asleep, he thought, than see his anxiety.

Shops and windows were all shuttered in preparation for the violence to come. Sandbags fortified stately buildings. Few people were about.

Suddenly an ocher flash lit the eastern sky. Their nostrils filled with smoke. Righteous Virtue opened his eyes. The gray concrete buildings were silhouetted against a dusty pink sky. He listened for the bomb, but could not distinguish the rumble from the pounding of his heart. There was a gnawing flutter in his stomach; he lit a cigarette with shaking hands.

"That's a big one!" Ah Lee exclaimed. "But I've seen bigger!" He had made several trips to the city within the last weeks.

Righteous Virtue did not know how to respond to such bravado, but he was thankful for the confidence with which the chauffeur threaded the car through the streets leading to the French concession.

The streets came alive as they neared the foreign territory. There had been a migration of people and beggars toward the safety zone. Defeated, shuffling figures filled the streets among temporary lean-tos. The odor of human sweat, cooking grease, and street dust penetrated the car.

Ah Lee blasted his horn and slowed the vehicle to accommodate the dense crowds. Importuning hands quickly surrounded the car. To give alms now would be to incite a riot.

Soldiers came, brandishing their rifles. The crowd thinned, but some hardy bodies clung to the car. A soldier yanked at the collar of a frayed cotton jacket, and a whole strip of cloth came off like peeling paint on a dilapidated wall. The man fled, hugging what remained of his clothes to his chest. Several men began laughing. The tension broke; the ragged men dropped off the car.

Righteous Virtue gave the soldiers a guilty, furtive glance as he passed out two packs of cigarettes. The soldiers quickly cleared the way for them.

The chauffeur stretched himself with impatient languor, his bravado restored. "They're lucky the soldiers let them stay. They'd be sitting ducks if they were forced to return to the Chinese section."

Righteous Virtue averted his eyes from the dispossessed masses. He hid behind clouds of cigarette smoke, and cursed the education that had left his emotions vulnerable to the plight of these benighted human beings. The chauffeur, with his callused sensibility, was better equipped for survival.

As Virtue stared ahead through a haze of smoke, he saw a woman picking lice off her daughter's hair. They sat at the mouth of their lean-to, basking in the sun and watching the bombs hit the Chinese sections. There was such lyric tenderness on the woman's face that Righteous Virtue started with sharp recognition. This could have been Purple Jade doing Silver Bell's hair!

Chapter 7

WHEN GLORIOUS DRAGON returned to Shanghai, he exaggerated his public attention toward Iris to divert suspicion. He would not visit Bright Crystal without Iris. Bright Crystal understood his prudence, and Iris was briefed on how to play her role. She began her induction into high society.

These new precautions were necessary, because when Crystal was feeding Glorious Dragon his supper in the hospital one evening, a stranger opened the door, stared at the loving scene and said, "Sorry, wrong room!"

Several unexpected incursions followed, and Dragon became aware of strange men hovering near him when he exercised outside his room. He realized with a shudder that Bright Crystal's passionate care had been a serious blunder. General Chin must know by now that he was her lover and not a "*tang* cousin." He and Crystal were brazen to act like hosts in the house the general had provided! With Shanghai under fire, it would be easy for General Chin to kill them both. But why didn't he? Perhaps the general still required Crystal's services. She could turn the foreign business contacts against him. Perhaps the general was just biding his time, letting them live in fear and humiliation.

Glorious Dragon had left Shanghai to urge his sister to leave Hangzhou as soon as he was discharged from the hospital. Iris's presence was a fortuitous gift.

One day, Glorious Dragon received an urgent call from Bright Crystal. She was weeping hysterically. Her personal serving girl, Little Lotus, had been raped behind their house by two ruffians. They also sent a message to her mistress: "Never see your lover again, or suffer the same fate!"

The young lovers met immediately. They were paralyzed with fear and indecision. "You mustn't come here any more," Bright Crystal cried, tears streaming down her face.

"The Japanese may take Shanghai very soon," Glorious Dragon whispered. "They will neutralize General Chin's power."

"It won't be easy living under the Japanese! General Chin still has underworld connections." Bright Crystal wiped her face, smearing her make-up. "Shouldn't we both run away now?"

"Where should we go?" Glorious Dragon began to pace. "I can't join the Communists in the northwest, so the most logical place is overseas!"

"Who will take care of my father if I leave?"

"And who will manage the Chou family businesses?"

"General Chin often brags about his long arm of influence." Bright Crystal sobbed. "He can always have us assassinated overseas. I know he believes in revenge." She trembled uncontrollably.

They stared at each other, mute with anxiety. All their defiant frivolity evaporated.

Glorious Dragon folded his Crystal into his arms. Finally in a tight, angry voice he said: "We'll stay and wait, but we must not meet again." The stakes were too high for everything he held dear.

Bright Crystal nodded in silence and packed a bag for her Dragon. Weeping and shivering, she intuitively understood his anger — the helplessness of a fearless Dragon.

Glorious Dragon avoided Avenue Joffre from that day on, posting bodyguards around himself wherever he went.

When Righteous Virtue finally arrived at the house on Petain Road, the insular peace and warm greetings cheered him.

"My lord, you've finally come. Purple Jade and Comely Brook bowed their welcome in tandem. Purple Jade and the girls looked fresh and taller in their modern sheaths. Comely Brook, however, had reverted to wearing her pajama-style work clothes. With her expanding girth, she was happy to forgo her fancy sheaths in favor of the simple cotton outfits she made herself. Righteous Virtue smiled broadly, muttering his praise: "You all look wonderful, wonderful."

"Father, look at the piano uncle Dragon bought us!" said Golden Bell.

"Oh Father, you brought my pets! Look, they didn't grow much during the last months! Peony must have neglected them!" Silver Bell rushed the silkworm basket to the library and cleared out the rice paper littered with the worms' droppings. She lined the basket with fresh paper and replaced the worms. She then picked up a few and held them against the window light. The worms were now snowy white, but not translucent and pink, which meant they were not ready to make cocoons.

"I don't think Peony fed them regularly. Look how they weave their heads back and forth looking for leaves!" Silver Bell quickly spread out the fresh supply her father brought. A soft crunching sound sifted through the human voices.

"My lord, what was the state of our home when you left?" Purple Jade asked. In the cramped disorder of her quarters, she yearned for the serenity of her Hangzhou home.

"Everything is under lock and seal at home, but already we hear the distant rumble of guns," answered Righteous

Virtue. "There is sad news from the Northern Village. Hoping for leniency, the villagers formed a welcoming party for the East Ocean Devils. They waved the Japanese white flag and treated the soldiers to wine and meat. But the soldiers demanded women, and the people didn't have enough time to hide." He looked at his family, uncertain if he should continue.

"Tell us all," his wife said. "It is worse to leave things to the imagination. We hear the guns and wait in apprehension."

"You can hardly imagine such horror — rape and rampage all over. Our national army lacks the firepower to protect us, but the peasants are resisting valiantly. *Hai*, there is such suffering and loss." He sighed, looking at the worried faces of the women dear to him. "We're safe in the French concession. Technically, this is French territory, so the East Ocean Devils would not dare to commit atrocities here. We did right in coming here."

"Our home is in the hands of fate now," Comely Brook said as she served tea. "I've moved all your personal belongings to your room upstairs, my lord." Household chores occupied her mind.

"I've learned to handle the stairs slowly, with no unnecessary trips," said Purple Jade. "Brook-*mei* and I share a room now and the girls and Iris share the third bedroom."

Purple Jade dutifully gave a positive picture of their lives in this small house. As the virtuous wife, she would neither burden her husband with her feeling of stifling confinement, nor whine about the thin walls and her negligent daughters who sometimes talked too loudly in their room. Many days and nights she had sat up longing for the scent of bamboo, cherry blossoms and cedar. On moonlit nights, she remembered the hourly change of shadows playing outside her windows. She yearned for an accounting. Did they buy the spring wheat to brew the special liquor? Did the cook smoke the hams? Did they catch enough fish to salt?

With an impatient flourish of her hand, she smoothed the side of her hair. "As you must have heard, Iris is working as a receptionist in our factory, and the girls are doing well in the Chinese-Western school."

"The McTyeire School is very hard, so I've been tutoring Silver Bell in English," Golden Bell added.

"Is she a good student?" her father asked.

"Oh Father, I can sing all the songs from the movies!" Silver Bell ran to the piano. "Uncle Dragon is so much fun! I can't read the music he bought me, but I can always pick out the tune. I've been practicing every day! Let me sing for you:

'*Come, come, I love you only, my heart is true . . .*'"

Her father laughed. "Golden Bell, does she know what she's singing?"

"I'm not sure," answered Golden Bell mystified. "She is always more interested in the music."

"Hush, Silver Bell, your father needs to rest. What are you singing anyway?" asked Purple Jade.

"Oh, it's about a calm, calm peaceful evening." Golden Bell improvised, giving her father a conspiratorial look.

"My lord, the girls have gone to so many movies! I think it is shameless and *sour meat* to watch the foreign devils hug each other and dance with hardly any clothes on. But Dragon loves to indulge the girls, and there is so little for them to do in this small house."

"It is amazing how Silver Bell can pick out the melody with her right hand and improvise with the left. Has she had lessons?"

"No," answered his wife. "Should I inquire about getting a teacher for her?"

"No, it doesn't seem necessary. Jade, you've managed well. The girls are thriving here, in spite of the chaos outside." Righteous Virtue smiled and sipped his tea. He was feeling at home already.

His wife nodded. "I do hope the silkworms will remind them of home and who we are."

"Oh thank you, Father, for bringing the worms. I do miss climbing the mulberry tree. But Father, I simply adore Jeannette McDonald and Nelson Eddy!" gushed Silver Bell.

"My favorite is Loretta Young!" Golden Bell said. She brought her father a scrapbook of movie-star photos and playbills.

"*Lo-eh-lee-tai-Yah!*" Purple Jade said, trying to pronounce Loretta Young's name.

Righteous Virtue smiled and the girls laughed.

Golden Bell called out: "That is 'Sixth Moon's Sun'! Mother, your Chinese translation from English sound is so funny!"

"Really, I don't see what's the use of bothering. They all look the same: such big eyes, noses, and mouths. It is most uncouth to have so many pictures taken showing all those teeth!" Purple Jade grinned in mock horror.

Everyone broke up laughing again. "Oh Mother, you'll have to go to the movies more often!"

"Now that you're here, my lord, we should hire a cook. So far Winter Plum has been a 'one foot kick': cooking, cleaning, and washing. Perhaps we should bring Peony here to help. It is safer for her here as well. Brook-*mei* is working too hard — "

A loud banging at the door interrupted her. Glorious Dragon rushed in with a large package under his arm.

"I'm in danger!" He huffed. "Girls, go into the library. Sing as loudly as you can and lock the door. Jade, Virtue, don't let anyone get in there! I have no time to explain." He ran past them into the servants' quarters.

Winter Plum ran in shouting: "There are soldiers in the front and back streets everywhere. Some are at the front door now!"

"Oh my lord, the East Ocean Devils have come! Girls, go! Do as your uncle said." Purple Jade herded her daughters into the library. The girls locked the door. Silver Bell banged on the piano and sang as loudly as she could:

"*Come, come, I love you only . . .*"

Righteous Virtue went to the window to look. He mumbled: "No, they can't be the East Ocean soldiers. They're wearing the uniforms from our warehouse." He opened the door.

"I am Huang Righteous Virtue of the Hangzhou legislative council. Why are you here?"

"We have General Chin's warrant to arrest Chou Glorious Dragon. He has committed acts of high treason! We've seen him enter the house!"

Righteous Virtue could not utter one word of protest as the soldiers brushed past him and strutted into the house. Purple Jade and Comely Brook stood guard in front of the library door, stretching out their arms to block the soldiers. Inside, Silver Bell finished one song: "*Oh come, he— ro mine.*" Then she proceeded to a new tune: "*Give me some men, who are stout-hearted men . . .*"

The soldiers faced the two women immediately. "Open the door; we have orders to search the house!"

"Oh spare them, they're my only daughters!" Purple Jade began to wail. "Take me, take me, I am an old woman."

"Take me!" Comely Brook threw herself at the captain. "I'm a pregnant woman. Your ancestors will curse you, you beasts!"

Taken aback by the hysterical women, the soldiers turned to Righteous Virtue. "Please calm the women! We're not the East Ocean Devils. We won't harm your daughters."

The women cried and wailed, releasing weeks of tension and fear. Righteous Virtue attempted to calm them. When they were finally led away, the soldiers found the library door locked from the inside. The girls continued to sing. They ignored the knocking and commands to open the door.

The soldiers bunched together and rushed the door with their shoulders. Purple Jade and Comely Brook screamed as the frightened girls banged the piano in a frenzy, though no more sounds came from their mouths.

The door caved in with a loud crash as the soldiers fell into the library. They found the two trembling girls huddled by the piano, a basket of silkworms on the table, books and movie star pictures by the chairs, and no place anyone could hide.

"Where is Chou Glorious Dragon?" the captain demanded.

Everyone looked on with terror-filled eyes, but no one answered. The captain spat in disgust and ran out of the room. A quick search was made of the rest of the house. In the end, the captain said: "The spy was mistaken. We must have entered the wrong house. Our deepest apology." The soldiers bowed as they left the house.

While the house was in turmoil, a soldier had slipped out the back door. He had helped the guards on the back street disperse the curious throng that had gathered. When Glorious Dragon reached the end of the street, he melted into the crowd, hailed a pedicab, and took off his uniform. Soon, he arrived at the river and disappeared.

Chapter 8

"IT SEEMS I'VE arrived just in time. I'll have to manage the factory somehow without Dragon," Righteous Virtue said, wiping his damp brow. "It must be General Chin's order to arrest him."

The women were shamefaced at the spectacle they had caused. Still shaken by the ordeal, Purple Jade mumbled: "These stories of rape and disaster must have unnerved me. I didn't even notice that the soldiers spoke Mandarin with a southern accent."

"My poor country." Righteous Virtue avoided looking at the embarrassed women. "The East Ocean Devils are devastating our land, while our best soldiers are settling quarrels between jealous lovers!"

"Does anyone know where Uncle Dragon is?" Golden Bell asked.

"It is best not to know," her father answered. "In fact, I'd better put up a reward by the East Asian Uniform for any information leading to our manager's arrest!"

"Dragon is so clever." Purple Jade grimaced. "He told us to do just the right thing."

"I think the bundle under his arm must have been a uniform from our factory," Comely Brook added.

"That is such a clever way to escape." Golden Bell giggled.

"I wonder where he is?" Purple Jade looked from face to face, sharing the bewilderment.

While the Japanese laid siege to the harbor, refugees from surrounding towns and villages poured into Shanghai, clogging the streets of the foreign concessions. As bombs and guns exploded, a parade of men, women and children plodded the tree-lined streets, their possessions strapped to their backs. Men were haltered to wooden carts, their veins bulging from their necks. They strained under their burdens of tables and chairs and looked for a safe location to set up camp. Other family members pushed from behind, repelling the grasping hands of the desperate.

People with untreated wounds and lurid deformities lay everywhere — under trees, against buildings. Some sat in a stupor, catatonic from shock, trodden by crowds, harassed by flies. The blind stared into passing faces, holding out broken bowls, moaning for alms. Men with missing limbs told tales of horror: the bombs that fell from the sky maimed and mutilated with a swiftness they could not comprehend. The elusive enemy stayed miles away, killing with impunity, sitting in the gun turrets of battleships or airplanes. The stench of unwashed bodies, excrement, oozing wounds, blood and saliva permeated sidewalks. The more robust homeless swarmed like buzzards, harassing those who looked more prosperous. Hungry children snatched whatever edibles they could pry loose from clutching hands. Many uprooted plants and others gnawed on tree bark.

Aggressive hustlers set upon those in motorcars. They threw themselves into the car's way, spitting and lunging at the vehicles. Ah Lee carried a short whip to deter the troublemakers. His invectives and the lashings of his whip chilled Purple Jade. The dispossessed mobs filled her with both pity and repugnance. Totally unprepared for the scenes of desperation she saw around her, she felt the anger and frustration of helplessness. Bereft of her old home, she shared in the pathos of this wartime calamity. Yet she was thankful for the chauffeur's callousness: Righteous Virtue must leave for work every day; food must be purchased for the family.

The English officers sat in their armored cars to keep order. Sikh noncommissioned officers brandished rifles. The wretched Chinese vagabonds gawked at the maroon-colored turbans and shrank away. The French flourished their tricolor all over their concession, informing one and all that this was French territory. The muscle men of the Chinese underworld repelled the mobs. Thereafter, Purple Jade forbade any unnecessary trips by any member of the family. They became virtual prisoners in their own home.

While her daughters attended the McTyeire School, Purple Jade spent many hours teaching Comely Brook the Tang Poems. In spite of herself, Purple Jade became aware that she was often annoyed when Comely Brook did not know her lesson perfectly. One day, the lesson seemed to be more tortuous than usual.

"Dumb egg! Go fetch me some tea!" She slammed down her book, her voice shrill and sharp. Comely Brook ran out sniffling, her head lowered and her back hunched. Purple Jade had never called anyone a dumb egg to her face, and she had never used that tone of voice on Orchid before. For a long while, Purple Jade sat fidgeting and fuming, unable to understand her loss of temper and Comely Brook's difficulties. She could not bring herself to prepare an apology.

After what seemed like an hour, she wrestled with a restless, bitter stomach, and barged into the kitchen, where she had never ventured. The kitchen was empty, and the warm, damp air felt greasy. She stumbled into Winter Plum's narrow bedroom abutting the kitchen and found Comely

Brook and Winter Plum sorting the laundry and whispering together.

"Oh *Tai-tai*!" Winter Plum gasped. "What brought you down here!"

"Orchid." Purple Jade reverted to her old way of addressing her former maid. "Where is my tea? We haven't finished our lesson." She noticed her slip of tongue, but enunciated her words clearly and precisely, maintaining her customary reserve and dignity.

"Oh *Tai-tai*." Comely Brook looked up, her round eyes moistening. "I thought our lesson was over!" Her eyes conveyed regret, but not surprise. She hurried into the kitchen to prepare tea. "*Tai-tai*, go rest yourself. I'll be up in a minute."

Although Purple Jade now addressed Orchid as "Brook *mei-mei*," Orchid had never ceased to address her mistress as "*Tai-tai*." Orchid lived upstairs now, but she remained Purple Jade's personal maid and helped Winter Plum with the housework. In this small foreign house, the "upstairs" world of dressing up, being alert, and learning to read the classics gave her a constant nervous tremor. Unconsciously, she sought the company of Winter Plum and the solace of the familiar work area. Despite the privileges of her elevated status, she preferred her old routines.

Purple Jade glanced at the laundry in Winter Plum's small room and felt absurd. She had nothing to say to the working-women before her. She hobbled upstairs murmuring, "We'll finish our lesson another time."

Her slow climb up the still unaccustomed stairs made her wish she could scream or rant instead of presenting a facade of respectability. She realized, at last, that she was the useless, helpless woman she had always feared she might become. Living in a small, strange house in a nasty city, and so very close to the activities of the maids, especially Orchid, made her realize the illusion of her status: It was artificial and did not really matter. The sight of Orchid's burgeoning stomach was also a constant reminder of her pointless dignity. With the sounds of war ringing in her ears, the necessity for an heir seemed trivial, and the responsibility for another human life became a menacing shadow in her mind.

Unable to articulate her deepest wound, she realized that although Comely Brook served her as before, the change in their relationship was permanent. Without a separate suite of rooms for herself and sharing a room with Orchid, Purple Jade could not help but be aware of the nights when Comely Brook left to service her husband. She imagined the activities going on down the hall, and wept silent tears of rage, training herself to pretend not to hear the muffled conversations and noises coming from beyond the walls. She tossed and turned all night in her solitude, unable to quell her remorse, her self-reproach. All her anguish had erupted in her uncharacteristic outburst at Comely Brook. She recognized the corrosive effects of jealousy and how it was devouring her inner peace. She tried to accept her feelings. She resolved to take responsibility for the harmony in her home and to maintain the dignity of "their" coming son. Still, she always had time on her hands — idle time that did not encourage serene contemplation.

"I must go home. I must get out of here somehow!" she said aloud.

Weeks later, her persistent longing for the river, the bamboo, and the graceful lull of her old home finally broke Purple Jade's stoic reserve. The Japanese blockade of Shanghai Harbor had continued into its third month. The everyday chores and the numbing anxiety over impending disaster made the stalemate of war appear less threatening. One evening, the girls read and Comely Brook sewed. Purple Jade set up a game of chess with Righteous Virtue.

An hour into the game, Righteous Virtue moved his cannon sideways four steps and removed his wife's soldier. He thought he held her general in check.

Purple Jade moved her horse diagonally to block his cannon. Her husband charged his chariot across the board taking her chariot. "Jade-*mei*, your concentration is slipping."

"I know, my lord." She sighed. "It would have been so different playing in our courtyard under a moonlit night. This house is stifling." She moved her other chariot in front of his cannon to safeguard her general.

Moving his chariot sideways, Righteous Virtue took her premier. Purple Jade moved her soldier one step near the boundary. "Now that you're here, perhaps I could go back home and check on things. I'd like to bring Peony here to help Brook-*mei*. I'm uneasy about leaving her at home. This blockade could last a long time."

"I'd rather have the whole family stay together. We must hide out during this time of confusion." Moving his chariot five steps, he removed her horse.

Purple Jade's cannon jumped over her soldier and took his cannon. "I could go by sampan from the English section and be back within a week. I cannot sleep nights, dreaming of the cypress in our court." She was sweating uncharacteristically. The volcanic unrest in her soul threatened the unity of her family. She must go home to heal.

Righteous Virtue saw his general under the gun and moved his official to protect his game. "You've had this all planned, haven't you?" He scratched his head marveling. "This is a winning stroke."

Purple Jade moved her horse diagonally into the corner intersection of his inner wall. "Yes, I had it all planned. Everything will be in order after my return home." She spoke with a quiet assertion, but her hands trembled, and she clasped them tightly in her lap under the table.

"Yes, you've won again." Righteous Virtue sat back sighing, while his eyes surveyed the board. Purple Jade's horse now threatened his general at an angle. If he moved an official to block the way, her cannon could jump over it and take his general. "Yes, Jade-*mei*, you knew what you were doing."

"Thank you, my lord. I know the Hangzhou bamboo shoots and other produce have often plied the waterways to Shanghai. Iris knows a fisherman familiar with the route. She will accompany me tomorrow. Brook-*mei* will serve you while I'm away."

Early the next morning, Purple Jade packed a small suitcase and with a light heart, and set out for the river. The Hwangpo's stench made her retch, but darkness concealed the details of deadly flotsam crowding Shanghai Harbors. Iris was not keen on the trip, because she was fast becoming an independent woman in this city. But she acquiesced out of loyalty to and sympathy for the woman who had been more nurturing than her mother.

As the boat drew near the dock of her house, Purple Jade grew lightheaded from the fresh air, glimmering water, and layers of interconnected rooflines drawing ever closer like the flight of winged birds in formation. The gently rising courts of her house melded harmoniously with their surroundings: the walls, gardens, and roofs seemed to have grown like essential appendages in a landscape of towering bamboo groves, beetling rock boulders, hovering willows, and the flowing river. Yes, she was coming home. She banished all thoughts of the impending war and her promised return to Shanghai within the same week.

Chapter 9

IN THE WEEK that followed, Japanese infantry columns in Hangchow Bay broke through stands of stubborn Chinese fighters. Chinese forces pulled back, allowing the Japanese to push inland, threatening Nanking, the nation's capital. Using Shanghai's excellent harbor facilities, the Japanese navy began landing war equipment and supplies. Stories circulated around town: Chinese civilians would be conscripted as slaves and used as coolies to push and pull the formidable Japanese arsenal — miles and miles of artillery pieces, tanks, carts, and cases of grenades, and firearms.

On Petain Road in the French concession, the Huangs had grown accustomed to hearing the guns of invasion like so many firecrackers popping. Fighting for control around Shanghai intensified. Rivers and roads were no longer safe for passage.

The Japanese captured Nanking on December 13, 1935. News of the holocaust reached Shanghai. People could hardly believe the savagery. It was rumored that the large Chinese infantry was promised leniency, but once they surrendered and were disarmed, the massacre began. Wave upon wave of men were pushed off cliffs, beheaded, gunned down, and buried alive. Thousands of old men, women and children shared their fate. Other young women and boys were rounded up to service the Japanese soldiers. They were tortured, humiliated, disfigured and slaughtered. The massacre lasted for six weeks.

When Hangzhou learned of the approaching enemy, Miss Tyler opened her mission to all the women who sought sanctuary. Iris urged her mistress to go.

"You go, Iris," Purple Jade commanded instead. "Miss Tyler will have her hands full. You can help. Ask the gardener to empty our grain storage and bring the mule cart with you. They'll need the food supply."

"Oh kind mistress, I can't leave you," Iris stammered with tears in her eyes. "The soldiers are brutes!"

"There's a secret compartment behind my chest of drawers. If the soldiers come, I'll hide in there. I must stay and guard the house," Purple Jade answered with quiet determination. She had thought of just this possibility when she decided to stay. Her father used to have regular contact with the Japanese in his silk trade. She was told that they were a most refined and cultured people. Purple Jade thought the stories of atrocities must be grossly exaggerated.

Purple Jade directed all her furniture to be covered and supervised the loading of mule carts with grains, hams, and salt. She sent Iris and the gardener away. She felt no fear, only tiresome irritation. Peony remained to take care of her mistress. In an emergency, she would hide in the rafters of the cold house. Little Six refused to leave "her grandpa" — the cook, who remained to guard the house with the rest of the male servants.

On December 24, Japanese soldiers captured Hangzhou.

A sturdy log, nearly a foot thick, barred the front door. As the rumble of soldiers drew near, Purple Jade sent Peony away to hide after she slipped behind her chest of drawers backed against the hollow in the wall. A thick grove of bamboo outside concealed the bulge from the exterior. Small vents facing the bamboo grove aired the narrow space, which had stored the family diamonds, lapis lazuli, jade and topaz.

All evening she hid in the stifling silence and watched the evening star twinkle between the bamboo canes. Suddenly, a nightingale shrieked in nervous flight, and Purple Jade knew danger was at hand.

In one deafening blast, the front door crashed down. A score of soldiers dashed into the house. In their hands were torches. Smoke and fire colored the night sky.

Loud screams, angry shouts, and piteous wails filled the air. Tramping throngs milled outside.

"Help, help!"

"Little Six, Little Six, where are you?" the cook called.

"Water, someone, please, the front hall is on fire!"

"Water . . . water . . ."

Another blast rattled the wall of her hiding place. Purple Jade hugged herself to still her trembling. From her sanctuary, she heard the screaming of the tortured men: "They all went to the mission house . . . They all went to the mission house . . ."

Peeping out of her vents, she saw soot-smeared soldiers casting ominous shadows across the wall. A soldier chased down Ah Joy, the newborn puppy, and pierced it with a bayonet. He swung it over his shoulder. Blood dripped down his back as he rushed across the hall.

"*Oh-me-to-fo*," Purple Jade wailed softly, beseeching her Buddha. Her decision to linger had been worse than foolish. She heard the soldiers enter her room, searching for women, valuables, food, and wine. Finding none, they vented their rage in other ways. They threw the porcelain bowl on her night table across the room and shattered it. Trunks and cupboards were ransacked, their contents scattered over the floor. A rifle flashed, discharging a round into the firm dark wood of her Ming desk. A stray bullet flew through her narrow closet. No one heard its hollow passage. Purple Jade cowered in the corner, rigid with fear.

"Eee-yah . . . kind Buddha, let me die! Eee-yah . . . save me!" It was Peony, screaming for help. Stamping feet and grunting noises all rushed toward the cold house.

"Swallow that!" It almost sounded like Chinese.

"Kill me! Kill me . . ." It was Peony, choking and screaming.

Purple Jade fidgeted, sobbing with pity, while distant groans, wild laughter, and swearing guttural snarls tormented her. The bamboo soughing outside was like an echo of her despair. She had been responsible for Peony's plight.

Crammed in her closet, she watched the night walk across the bamboo grove. When all was still, a bright star appeared among the bamboo leaves. It was the morning star. Quietly she stole from her hiding place. The fire had damaged the entire house. Only her sooty compound was untouched by the flame. In the smoldering rubble, she found the two servants who had come to put out the fire: the porter, disemboweled; the doorman, beheaded. Flies swarmed around their blackened bodies. Purple Jade wobbled away, her icy fear numbing her senses.

Near the kitchen and the cold house, half a dozen drunken soldiers lay snoring. Little Six lay twisted and torn, dark red oozing blood smeared all over her torso. Purple Jade would not have known the macabre bundle as the child she once rescued had she not recognized the suit of clothes given her when she first came into the house. The cook lay dead beside Little Six, his right arm stretched out toward the child.

Purple Jade edged to the kitchen door. Peony, bent over with pain, was reaching for rat poison. Purple Jade dashed forward and stayed her trembling hand.

"You're young and I'll help you heal. Our country needs you."

With fiery eyes, Peony spat out her revenge. "The poison is for the wine. They can't live without it!"

Without a word, her mistress obeyed. Purple Jade carefully broke the seal on their jugs of finest wine and stirred in the poison. With an expertise she did not know she possessed, she sealed the jugs again. A strange calm descended upon Purple Jade. She half-carried and half-dragged Peony out the back door. They trudged the mile toward the dock.

A small throng of townsfolk was already there. A local fisherman recognized the lady from the Huang household and helped them into the boat. Purple Jade pressed an antique jade pendent into the hands of the fisherwoman. The oars splashed; the shore sprang back.

Over the water, smoke continued to build. Furious black clouds billowed upward from the town, settling over the causeway. Waves of humid, soot-laden air enveloped the Huang and Chou family compounds in acrid gray.

Standing riveted on deck, Purple Jade could not recognize her home. The bamboo grove by her house across the water still looked green and glistened in the charcoal haze. To her right, she saw claws of fire brooding over the eastern end of town. Remembering the images of the blackened dead, she retched.

In an instant, the burning air inside the bamboo erupted. Pieces of flying cane burst into small tongues of fire, trailing dense sooty smoke. Popping explosions mocked the celebration of fireworks, which had so often heralded the festive events of her life. The lyricism of home and hearth turned to ashes right before her eyes. Purple Jade turned from the heinous sight and asked, with lead in her heart, to be taken to Shanghai.

"Huang tai-tai, You must change into a fisherman's suit if you wish to pass into Shanghai Harbor." The fisherman's wife handed over her best suit.

Without protest, Purple Jade exchanged her brocade robe for the rough cloth suit of a fisherwoman. Charcoal soot was smeared over her face to hide her smooth pampered skin. When the Japanese patrol boats came by, the fisherman placed her in the lee of the boat, cleaning fish. With her small feet tucked underneath her and her delicate hands covered by the blood and entrails of fish, she became just another fisherwoman. Peony slept with the fishermen's children. Her pale, sick face drove away all who came to inspect.

When the boat arrived at the English section of Shanghai, Purple Jade sent a message to Petain Road. The East Asian Uniform Company hired a small sampan and transferred the lady and her maid to the factory. There, they changed into ordinary street clothes and hired a pedicab to take them to the safety of the French section. Purple Jade noticed that the Japanese had cleared away the refugees.

Day and night, Purple Jade devoted herself to nursing Peony. She studied her collection of Chinese medical books, consulted Chinese doctors, and sent the chauffeur to all corners of Shanghai to purchase the necessary ingredients. These included loquat syrup, ginko nuts, ginseng, lotus root mixed with milk and steamed, jujube and goji berries, apricot seed, oxlip and raspberries fried in wine, scallions, Menthol, dried buds of the white lotus, dog rose, knot grass steamed and sun dried, peach pits and honey. Purple Jade brewed the medicine herself and fed it to Peony, while the rest of the family tiptoed around them in hushed concern. Comely Brook noticed Purple Jade's lapse into moments of unnatural stillness. She offered tea, brought her embroidery, or asked for instructions on household matters. She watched her mistress closely, but did not mention anything to alarm the others.

In her quiet moments, Purple Jade recited her Tu Fu poems to seek serenity:

Ten thousand petals swirl to diminish the spring.
Adrift in the wind, they sadden me.
I watch the last flowers about to fall before my eyes.
The hurtful wine passes my lips but does not ease my pain.
Two kingfisher birds nest happily in a ruined pavilion,
Pair of stone unicorns guards the tombs of high ministers.
It is a law of nature to pursue pleasure.
Why have I let old goals entangle my body?

When Peony recovered, she became restless. She had neither the heart nor the concentration to do the reading and writing assignments Purple Jade gave her. During her occasional trips to the factory, Peony learned of the peasant resistance movements in northern interior China. She made it known that she wished to join them. Purple Jade objected. In the end, Purple Jade and Comely Brook prepared a jacket for Peony, with gold coins and jade pieces sewn inside.

As the household stirred to life one morning, they found Peony was gone. She had left without a word, so their ignorance could shield them from blame. Suddenly, Purple Jade felt overwhelmed by the strain of her traumatic experience. While Peony was there, she had resumed her old role as the family doctor. She had a purpose and an important task. She was able to maintain her composure. Now inconsolable, she took to her bed.

Purple Jade slipped into delirium, reliving the horrors of her time in Hangzhou. In her deranged shouts and mumblings the family came to experience vividly the atrocities at home. The girls tiptoed around the house. They whispered to each other and tried to understand what they could not. Their father commanded them to study hard, and they buried their anxiety in schoolwork. Righteous Virtue sought help from the doctors. The American doctor prescribed sedatives, which enveloped Purple Jade in a drowsy stupor. The Chinese Dr. Tsui approved the same medicines that Peony had taken. Comely Brook resumed all personal care of her former mistress. She concentrated on preparing the choicest herbs — those she knew Purple Jade would use. In time, the violent outbursts subsided. It was a full month before the household returned to normal.

When Righteous Virtue realized his wife's depression had been tempered by caring for Peony, he wisely persuaded Dr. Tsui to accept Purple Jade as an intern in his practice of Chinese medicine and acupuncture.

For centuries, the practice of healing in China had been passed along family lines, its secrets guarded like family fortunes. It was unheard of that a woman should be admitted into this elite society. But Dr. Tsui had recently lost his wife and a young son during the Japanese bombing. He had been impressed with Purple Jade's thorough self-instruction in herbal medicine. In his bereavement and confusion, he consented.

Every morning Purple Jade left by rickshaw for his clinic, where the doctor soon found her in full command of his Chinese pharmaceuticals. The many drawers and bamboo cylinders of powdered oyster shell, cuttlefish-bone, ginseng, shark fins, turmeric, orange peel, camphor, cicadas, dried sea horses, magnolia flowers, licorice roots, deer antlers, ashes, sulfur, saltpeter, and varieties of ferns and mushrooms were all thoroughly catalogued, numbered, and arranged in impeccable order. Purple Jade worked quietly, observing with infinitesimal care the taking of pulse, the measurement and positioning of the acupuncture points for various ailments. No longer useless, and grateful to be admitted into such sacrosanct knowledge, her mind became focused and disciplined.

Iris returned one day under full Japanese escort. It appeared she had done a commendable job helping Miss Tyler run the mission. She had helped nurse the wounded and treat the enemy soldiers who had been poisoned. The Japanese were grateful, but Purple Jade eyed her presence with unease. Still, Iris's work at the uniform factory ensured safety for them all.

Righteous Virtue did not wish to call attention to himself. He sold his car and rode a bicycle to work. He came home exhausted every evening.

Two East Ocean soldiers stood guard at the bridge where Righteous Virtue had to cross each day to reach his factory. Every Chinese was required to bow to the soldiers as he passed their posts. The humiliation was intolerable.

Righteous Virtue secretly placed part of the factory in full production to make uniforms for the Nationalists and shipped them down to Hong Kong. Whenever possible, he included guns and ammunition for transport to Chungking. New to the ways of the town, the Japanese still found waterfront activities confusing. Righteous Virtue's subterfuge brought back the excitement of his youth. At times, he felt both strangely animated and depleted by his actions.

Chapter 10

AFTER THREE MONTHS of intense fighting, the Japanese had taken full control of Shanghai by early December. General Chin departed. Bright Crystal languished in uncertain malaise. The Chinese underworld still held power in all corners of the city, and Bright Crystal knew General Chin had close connections to these gangs. She had heard nothing from Glorious Dragon, nor did she know how to reach him.

Several times she picked up the telephone to call Purple Jade, but every time she disconnected before speaking. She was certain Purple Jade would overlook her errant reputation. She knew instinctively that they shared their love for "her Dragon." She yearned for a mother's shoulder to cry on, but Iris had told her Purple Jade's horrendous experience in Hangzhou. How could she alleviate such a loss? It would be unthinkable to burden her further with concerns for Glorious Dragon. She paced her rooms with restless hunger. Yet, when she sat down to eat, she had no appetite. Listless and vapid, she shunned the mirror, became careless of her daily toilette. Alarmed at her appearance, her father created masterpieces in his kitchen to restore her spirits.

One summer day in 1938, a dust-covered vagabond knocked on the back door of Bright Crystal's house. The stranger had long hair and a ragged black beard that gave him a ghoulish appearance. His flea-ridden rags hung in shreds around him; he stank of sweat, dirt, and rancid food.

When Little Lotus, the serving girl, opened the back door, she slammed it shut and shrieked in alarm. The vagrant shrugged and squatted beside the door to wait.

By mid-morning, Bright Crystal's father opened the back door to set on his day's marketing. The beggar stood, towering over the rotund chef. Falling to his knees, the beggar called, "Ba-ba!" — the name Bright Crystal had always called her father.

With a loud gasp, the father recognized Glorious Dragon. Without another word, he pushed him into the kitchen. Once inside, he berated the serving girls and shouted for hot water, food, and scissors.

Informed of her Dragon's return, Bright Crystal screamed with relief and delight. She wept and laughed, babbling with questions and exclamations about his condition as she held him close. She felt his protruding ribs; she kissed his cheekbones and hollowed eyes. His condition sent her trembling — their precarious existence made real to her. Glorious Dragon clasped her to him, murmuring, "There, there, I'm home."

Bright Crystal clung to him and would not let go.

Finally calmed, she took over his "restoration." She scrubbed and trimmed him in a hot tub. Between sips of soybean milk, Glorious Dragon allowed himself to be lathered, shaved, and fondled as Bright Crystal began to massage him gently with her fingers. Smelling of soap and disinfectant, he soaked in the bath, drinking wine. Bright Crystal offered him a bowl of plain, soupy, soft rice.

"First, you must have something easy to digest," she said, wiping his mouth as she fed him. "Look at you," she teased. "Your shoulder blades look like a coat hanger!"

"You can't imagine what I've been eating!" Glorious Dragon obligingly opened his mouth and swallowed everything. "A meal of grubs and grass was a treat!"

"Oh my poor Dragon." Bright Crystal put down the bowl to wipe her tears. Glorious Dragon pulled her into the water. Splashing and squealing with urgency, he helped her remove her clothes.

As they toweled each other dry, slowly examining each other's bodies, they tumbled to the floor. Sitting back on his heels, Glorious Dragon held her at arm's length. "Oh my Crystal, I can't believe how beautiful you are!" Her soft, creamy body was all he could see. He lifted her thigh, and kissed her. Reaching the clouds and rain, her heart raced and she wanted to shout.

"You have penetrated my whole being," Bright Crystal whispered. "Don't ever leave me again!"

They spent long hours talking of their experiences during the past frightful months. Bright Crystal wept to hear the suffering Glorious Dragon shared with the dispossessed. They could not blame Japan alone for all China's problems. The warring factions within China encouraged foreign depredation. Japan happened to be the closest and hungriest predator. Corruption was rampant within the Chinese government. Its scorched-earth response to the Japanese advance also caused widespread suffering.

"The Chinese government opened the Yellow River dikes, causing the flood," Glorious Dragon said with disgust. "Then they blamed the act on the Japanese."

"Of course it's the Chinese government," Bright Crystal responded with an emphatic jab of her nail file. "The Japanese were already marching into the interior. Why would they send their advancing army into disarray?" She worked on her long-neglected nails. "Where were you during the flood, my Dragon?"

Glorious Dragon ate from a breakfast tray in Bright Crystal's bed. He wolfed down a pork bun, and proceeded to slurp loudly on soft bean-curd soup, seasoned with chopped, spicy mustard roots, ground dried shrimps and seaweed.

"I went to Hangzhou after I left Shanghai. Knowing General Chin's long arm of influence, I did not stay long. Lao Wang still had a close grip on our household affairs. He supplied me with money for my escape."

Crystal perfumed herself and applied make-up.

"When the dikes broke and the flood came, I had already moved on toward my mother's village, hoping to find something about her origin. Oh my Crystal." He stopped eating. "You can't imagine the misery! Thousands died. Many more thousands were reduced to gnawing on tree bark. Dysentery and cholera set in . . . oh, Crystal, you've never seen such hollow-eyed children, skeletal, emaciated men and women. The bastards who committed such deeds are the true traitors, whatever they call themselves!"

"So, you gave away your money and became one of them?"

"There was no food to buy! Within a week, I exchanged everything I owned. When I learned that the Japanese had occupied Shanghai, I walked all the way back." He saw Crystal's tear-stained eyes and beckoned her to join him. Reclining in shimmering silk sheets, they leisurely traced their fingertips over each other's arms, legs, lips and nipples.

Bright Crystal whispered into Glorious Dragon's ear: "I think Iris has a Japanese boyfriend. They met in Hangzhou, when Iris helped to nurse the wounded in Miss Tyler's mission. There were so many poisoning cases among the soldiers that the *Kempetai*, the Japanese secret police, came. Iris's boyfriend is a lieutenant, but strangely, he was born in the United States. He sounds terribly interesting. We must invite them here, and place ourselves under *Kempetai* protection, so we'll never need to fear General Chin's underworld connections."

The mischievous glint returned to Glorious Dragon's eyes. "Yes, yes, now you'll be freely, openly mine!"

After several weeks, Iris brought Lieutenant Akiro Kamasaki to Avenue Joffre. Lieutenant Kamasaki, born in California, was most taken with the English-speaking Iris. To him, she was a radiant angel of mercy, nursing wounded Japanese soldiers as well as the Chinese.

Both Glorious Dragon and Bright Crystal had preconceived notions of what a Japanese looked like. They had expected a short, bow-legged man, with sly slits of eyes and an irascible temper that expressed itself in guttural grunts. It was therefore a pleasant surprise to meet Lt. Kamasaki, dressed in a gray three-piece suit. He was even taller than Glorious Dragon. His large, somewhat bulging eyes lent him the expression of a curious imp; his slightly protruding mouth was overshadowed by a handlebar mustache. When he changed into tennis shorts, he was noticeably more hairy than most Chinese. He was an excellent tennis player. Glorious Dragon noticed his forceful serves.

The game over, they lounged on the rattan couches in the sunroom and enjoyed a drink.

"You're tall like an American," Glorious Dragon said.

"My parents like to attribute my height and weight to the American milk and meat I was raised on. I think it is simply a case of the recessive gene, plus my muscle-building exercises," Lt. Kamasaki replied.

"Perhaps your parents were correct. You said you stopped growing after you returned to Japan," added Iris. Her thin cherry lips quivered as she glanced toward her lover.

"Oh yes, but by then I was already eighteen-years-old." Kamasaki smiled. "I had stopped growing at sixteen." He admired Iris's quiet reserve and quick intelligence. He was also touched by the open gratitude she felt for her former masters.

"So, if you were born in America," Glorious Dragon mused, "how did you get into the Japanese military?"

"It was not easy being Oriental in the United States. The Americans can't tell one Asian from another." He looked fondly into Iris's glowing face. How calm and liquid were her eyes. "I was often called a 'Chink.'" He continued, "a 'yellow bastard,' a 'sly-eyed scum'! We could live with the name-calling, but our neighbors did not want us around. Japanese immigrants were not allowed to own land, but since I was born in America, my family bought some land in my name. We worked hard and our farm prospered. Our neighbors did not do as well. First, our dog was poisoned; then our barn caught fire. One night, a tractor mysteriously crushed some of our crops. So it went, one disaster after another. We reported these incidents to the police, but they took no action. They said they could find no evidence of mischief. My parents began to fear for our lives. We sold the farm for a song and returned to Japan ten years ago." The lieutenant shrugged.

"We in China thought the Americans were helping Japan." Glorious Dragon wrinkled his brow. "They sell you all the scrap metal and gasoline you need."

"It is our money they respect!"

"Trade benefits both parties," Crystal said.

"Yes, the Westerners want to trade." Lt. Kamasaki gave a bitter short laugh. "I still have some very good American friends on a personal level, but Europe and America are not ready for racial equality."

Kamasaki stood and started to pace. "Do you know that during the Paris Peace Conference in 1918, Japan asked for 'acceptance of the principle of the equality of nations and the just treatment of their nationals?'" His voice rose in anger. "This basic doctrine of human decency was rejected by our idealistic President Wilson — out of consideration for the feelings of our southern senators." He looked on the puzzled faces of his Chinese friends and corrected himself. "Excuse me, I should say 'their President, and their southern senators.' We're conversing so fluently in English, I thought I was back with my American-Chinese friends."

"So you're not totally used to being a Japanese," Glorious Dragon spoke gruffly to conceal his pity for the young man's confused identity. Kamasaki looked no older than twenty-six.

"I guess not." Lt. Kamasaki sighed. "None of my compatriots know this, of course. My mind and heart are in America, which has rejected me. Japan is supposed to be a Confucian state, like China, but they have renounced the rule of 'virtue' and become seduced by the might of the sword."

As they looked at him with undisguised sympathy, he stopped abruptly and shouted: "I said 'they' didn't I? Well, I've been drafted into the army and I'm now a part of it all."

"No Akiro," Iris spoke in a hushed voice, "you've helped so many Chinese. You said you had grown up with many Chinese-Americans!"

"Yes, I have." He had witnessed the destruction his army brought. It pained him to consider the victims — his racial brothers.

Bright Crystal kept still throughout the conversation, taking measure of this young man who had struggled so hard with his conscience while he participated in the crime against her country. "When a society discriminates against a person for his color or her sex, humanity is blighted!" She spoke with such force, everyone turned to look at her.

There was no need to elaborate. She had spoken for them all.

Chapter 11

SEVERAL WEEKS LATER, the villa on Avenue Joffre was again aglitter with lights. This time the finest Japanese sake was heated and served to accompany the twelve-course Chinese dinner. Iris came with Lieutenant Akiro Kamasaki and some of his colleagues.

Kamasaki had prepared his Chinese friends for a meeting with Lieutenant General Goto. Goto had come from peasant stock and had spent forty of his fifty-five years in the military. Hard work and clever war strategies brought him high rank and honor, but he never acquired cosmopolitan charm. He looked like the stereotypical dwarf bandit that most Chinese envisioned— short and bowlegged. He spoke very little English, so Kamasaki translated for his superior. Captain Fujii and two of his assistants spoke perfect Mandarin with a Manchurian accent. They had been stationed in Manchukuo for years and had acquired a taste for Chinese living. They much preferred the many complicated spices of Chinese food. Following Japanese custom, they removed their shoes at the front door. They admired Bright Crystal's Western-style parlor — the piano and the comfortable sofas. The spacious Chinese dining room, the elegant, sturdy, but intricately carved rosewood tables and chairs all impressed them.

The Japanese had the same finger-guessing game for drinking wine, and the Chinese hosts soon learned to say: "*Ichi, ni, san, shi, go*" (Japanese for "one, two, three, four, five").

"We have so much in common." Glorious Dragon raised his cup for a toast: "In Chinese, we say *'yee, erh, san, sze, woo.'* Otherwise, the throwing of fingers and fist is the same! Amazing!"

There followed an amiable enumeration of common elements in both cultures. Japan had adopted Confucian philosophy and literature during the third century. So the concepts of filial piety and loyalty to the emperor were shared experiences. In daily life, both countries used chopsticks and soy sauce, and everyone enjoyed the Chinese banquet. Whenever General Goto was fuzzy on the meaning of some phrase or sentence, they resorted to writing Chinese. The Japanese "Kanji" script had been adopted almost unaltered from Chinese ideograms, making the understanding between the Chinese and Japanese around the table complete.

"With so much in common, I wonder why the Chinese would not accept our doctrine of '*Wang Tao*'?" General Goto smiled and asked Glorious Dragon.

"*Wang Tao*" literally translates to "Kings' Way." It is the ancient Chinese teaching of obedience and filial service to the king. In the Japanese interpretation, it was their design to restore China under the rule of the sometime Manchu child emperor P'u Yi, whom they had installed in the puppet state of Manchukuo. The Chinese outcry against this titular head was universal. General Goto had brought up the subject to gauge the political inclination of the Chinese at the table.

Glorious Dragon did not take the bait. He would not be drawn into an unpleasant discussion. Instead, he smiled and said: "Let's not go into politics. Tonight, we'll drink to our new friendship!" He proceeded to play the finger-throwing game with an aide.

General Goto soon joined in the raucous drinking. But his jovial spirits were soon disturbed by a call. The telephone was brought to him. He listened. Answering with grunts, and an occasional "*hai*," he slammed down the phone with disgust. "They're sending me some arrest warrants to sign." The general drained his cup as he spoke. "Some Chinese are getting very bold. They're shipping war materials to Hong Kong for transshipment to the Nationalists. Send the papers in to me when the messenger comes."

Lt. Kamasaki translated for General Goto as Bright Crystal left the dining room to instruct the doorman. Iris excused herself and followed.

"Crystal." Iris drew Bright Crystal aside in the hallway. "Mr. Chou's brother-in-law, my employer, has been manufacturing and shipping uniforms and whatever war materials he could lay his hands on down to Hong Kong. I'm sure General Goto means to sign his arrest warrant!"

"Oh no," Bright Crystal answered in hushed anxiety. "What are we to do?"

"We can't call the Huangs," Iris said urgently. "Such things are not to be trusted to the telephones. The Japanese have ways of listening in."

"My Dragon will want to go and help Righteous Virtue escape." Bright Crystal paced the hall like a cat. "Would Lt. Kamasaki be offended if we got all the Japanese drunk? We cannot afford to have your lieutenant upset."

"It will be hard to get Akiro drunk, but I'll find a way to tell him to pretend. He often complains that his colleagues get drunk and do irresponsible things. I'm sure he will be willing to help the Huangs, for my sake."

"Go back to the banquet before they become suspicious. Leave everything to me." Bright Crystal disappeared into the kitchen.

When the Japanese messenger arrived on his motorcycle, the doorman directed him to park it outside the front gate.

"The general was not pleased with the disturbance," he was told. He was then led to a back parlor where a feast of food and sake waited for him on a small table. The soldier was sorely tempted, but following protocol, he asked to speak first to General Goto. He was told to wait.

The soldier had come from sentry duty, and the ride on the motorcycle had further chilled him. The scent of warm sake wafted up from the little table. He edged closer. Suddenly, he heard footsteps. He drew away and straightened himself in preparation for a salute.

The footsteps stopped near the door and a female voice trilled, "No, no, General Goto, you really must not." A lady giggled. There was the hard breathy sound of an urgent male, entreating in unintelligible Japanese. The soldier smiled knowingly, while the doorman entered with his head lowered in mock embarrassment.

"The general wishes you to rest a while and wait."

The soldier relaxed and dug into his feast. A serving girl arrived repeatedly to refill his wine.

When the Japanese had become woozy from their drinks and were settled into their limousine ride home, Glorious Dragon headed for his sister's house. Since his return to Shanghai, he had concentrated upon recuperating. His appearance late at night was a great surprise to the Huangs. He had a new chauffeur and a new car. His shoes shone under clean white spats; he looked smart in his wool suit. He asked that they should not wake the children.

"Oh Dragon-*dee*, you're looking so well!" Purple Jade exclaimed. She wiped her tears of relief. "Where have you been? We've been so worried about you!"

"In these times, homeless people wander around the whole country. It is easy to melt into the crowd," answered her brother. He had decided he must be brief with tales of his traumatic journey. He must curb all emotions. He must attend to the urgent task before him. "I've been back to Hangzhou. The news is not good."

"I do wish we could go back." Purple Jade shook her head to blur the images of destruction heaving through her head. "Dragon, is it possible to rebuild?"

"No, you cannot go back," said Glorious Dragon with a sigh. "Jade-*jei*, Virtue-*ko* is a famous patriot; it won't be safe for him to go back. They're executing resistance leaders every day."

He turned to Righteous Virtue and said casually, "I hear you've been doing some very daring things!"

"Have you, now?" Righteous Virtue responded, feeling proud. Few people could appreciate his courage as much as his daredevil brother-in-law. "I've continued to produce Nationalist uniforms and ship them to Chungking via Hong Kong."

"Yes, so I've heard." Glorious Dragon took another sip of tea. "You're working double shifts — slipping them right under the Japanese's noses."

"Did Iris tell you this?"

"No, I wish she had. She's not used to questioning your decisions. The Japanese have already issued warrants for your arrest! With hundreds of workers in your plant, didn't it occur to you that someone might be tempted by the enemy's reward money and report you as a patriot?"

"Oh my lord, you never told me about these activities. You're in grave danger!" Purple Jade exclaimed.

"I know there are risks, but I thought I had picked only the most trustworthy workers. How can I sit here prospering while the country suffers? Is your information reliable?"

"After the East Ocean Devils entered Shanghai, I returned to Bright Crystal. She's as lovely as ever and entertains dignitaries with such flair." Glorious Dragon smiled. "She's some lady!"

"Some lady, sure! She's a traitor!" Righteous Virtue struck the table with his fist, and stood fuming.

"Hold your temper, Virtue-*ko*." Glorious Dragon's voice belied his own anger. "We owe all our family fortunes to this brave lady and now you owe her your life!"

"What?"

"She has delayed your arrest, but they know of your activities and they will come for you very soon."

"My lord, you must flee with your next shipment." Purple Jade was dry-eyed but her voice trembled.

"No, you must flee tonight! Everyone here can plead ignorance to what you were doing," said Glorious Dragon.

Righteous Virtue began to pace. "The family must all go with me. I can't bear the thought of endangering you. You come too, Dragon. We'll start a new factory in Hong Kong."

"Hong Kong is English," Purple Jade reminded him.

"The people are Chinese!"

"But my lord, they are Cantonese. They speak like foreigners!"

"Learning a new Chinese dialect is a small price to pay for freedom."

"You're my lord," came her whispered reply. "I shall go anywhere you wish. With my bound feet, I have never enjoyed freedom. Now Brook-*mei* is big with child. We will endanger our son . . ." She could not continue.

"Virtue, I cannot leave Bright Crystal," said Glorious Dragon. "Also I have obligations toward the Chou family silk factory. You must leave immediately, and the family will slow you down. I'll take care of my sister and your family."

Righteous Virtue continued pacing, unable to accept the coming separation. After a long pause, he faced his brother-in-law: "Thank you, Dragon. We owe you debts we can never repay." He beat his right fist into his left hand in frustration. "How are you to take care of two families when the uniform factory is closed?"

"I was going to spare you the news, but the silk factory is prospering because the Japanese air force is in great need of parachutes. It won't be difficult for me to secure a contract to manufacture uniforms for them."

Righteous Virtue banged both fists on the wall crying: "Dragon, you have driven me too far! You're forcing my family to depend on traitors!"

Purple Jade paled.

Going to the window, Glorious Dragon stood for a long while, staring into the dark skywell. He answered in a steady voice: "Virtue, I have told you when we were in Hangzhou: it is not easy to ride with the dragon. When I see an opportunity, I shall send you parachutes, along with whatever useful information I hear. You know General Chin is still powerful with the Nationalists. In their eyes, I am already a traitor."

Righteous Virtue's tears came freely now, amid apologies, words of farewell and endearments. He saw Purple Jade crawl upstairs on her hands and knees. He ran to the stairs.

"I'm sorry," she sobbed, "but it is the fastest way I can climb the stairs."

"No, no, no," her husband replied. "I shouldn't have . . ." He kneeled and lowered his head into her lap. "Forgive me. I couldn't stand by . . ."

"Yes, you are the true Righteous Virtue of our nation!" Purple Jade rose and walked upstairs. She clenched her fist and put on her old mask of dignity.

When Purple Jade and Orchid came down with his small suitcases, Righteous Virtue had already composed himself. Avoiding eye contact, and with a few words of farewell to his two wives, he accepted his bags. "Tell the girls that I stole away so they can truly claim ignorance of my activities. I'll write to them." He left with Glorious Dragon.

When Silver Bell came down to the library the following day, she saw a snowy mountain of cocoons glistening in the morning sun. The worms had climbed the branches weeks before and done their work. With the house in upheaval, no one had thought of them. When the children were told of their father's absence, they were stunned into silence, but tears flowed down their cheeks. Silver Bell ordered hot water and soaked every cocoon in it. It would not be right to save some for eggs now that they must buy mulberry leaves. She was determined to reel each cocoon herself. She would weave a silk scarf for her father even if it took her the rest of her life. She had just turned ten and, like the cocoons, no one seemed to have noticed.

BOOK THREE

Distant Love

Chapter 1

THE HUANG FAMILY read and reread Righteous Virtue's letters after he reached Hong Kong. Purple Jade wrote to her husband twice a week, repeating all the important information, and hoped that he would receive at least one letter per month. The mail was not reliable during wartime.

When the Chinese New Year came, the house on Petain Road remained quiet because Purple Jade thought it wise not to receive guests outside of the immediate family. She and the girls went to cousin Chou Ling's home on New Year's Eve, where a ten-course feast was prepared for all the Chous. Cousin Der Wei had become more addicted to opium than ever. He required his pipe after dinner. The Huangs went home at ten. Purple Jade promised her daughters firecrackers as soon as their uncle Dragon would arrive the next morning.

Comely Brook prepared "goodie" boxes for the girls to be placed beside their pillows. They now shared a bedroom. The first thing they did on New Year's morning was to eat sweets that would bring good fortune in the New Year. They compared their contents.

"See what I have here — dried lichee nuts, dragon eyes, candied lotus seeds, green olives, apples, kumquats, and tangerines. These are the same as those we used to have in Hangzhou," Silver Bell said to her sister. "Look, here is a package of golden candy coins!"

"Open one. The chocolate inside is delicious," Golden Bell said. "I think these come from America."

"Yes, yummy! I wonder why we never had them in Hangzhou." Silver Bell licked her lips. She unwrapped another gold coin. "Still, I miss the drums, the music, the dragon dances, the fireworks, and all the noisy fun at home every New Year. Do you remember the time the sparklers burned a hole in my New Year's jacket? No one could scold me because no angry words are allowed on New Year's Day." She chuckled. "Peony and I had such a laugh watching the fussy second *koo-ma*'s face when she had to compliment me on my twirling sparklers and ignore the hole in my new brocade jacket!"

"Oh, life was so stifling in Hangzhou! I wonder if Hong Kong is just like America. Isn't it a British colony just as America used to be? I wonder if everyone speaks English there."

"I don't know," replied Silver Bell. "Write to Father and ask him. Tell him Brook *Ma-ma* is wonderful. She is helping me with my silk-weaving project."

"I'm not going to help." Golden Bell pouted. "No one understands me here except Iris. It is not only that no one understands English, but they can't understand me even when I try explaining things to them in the most proper Chinese!" She jumped out of bed. "Come, look out for me. I'm going to use the bathroom."

"Wait, Mother bought chamber pots for every room and ordered everyone to use them!"

"We used the bathrooms when Father was here!"

"Don't get us into trouble! Mother said we must use the pots to help old Chen fertilize our garden!"

"All these old-country ways drive me crazy!" Golden Bell stamped her foot.

"You're the only defiant one!"

"I'm going to write and tell Father about all this nonsense!"

"Do you think Father will agree with you?"

"Of course he will. He is a modern man. I'll also ask him to buy us an automobile."

"You're right." Silver Bell nodded. "I heard Uncle Dragon tell Mother the uniform factory is prospering."

"It is really infuriating that Mother should buy a rickshaw and hire old Chen to pull it." Golden Bell shook her upturned hands in exasperation. "Old Chen must have been a farmer near Hangzhou. Look at our front and back skywell. He has turned the few square yards of dirt into vegetable patches. He insists it is a waste to flush urine down our modern toilets." Golden Bell ran out of the room.

When she returned, she said, "Old Chen is not going to get my contribution when he knocks on the back door every morning and evening asking for fertilizer!"

"Ugh! The smell is terrible!"

"Old Chen is not even a good rickshaw puller." Golden Bell started dressing. "He is so feeble and pulls so very slowly. When I'm in a hurry to go some place, he tells me Mother has errands for him on the way."

"I think Mother is being kind. She doesn't want him to pull for long stretches without a rest, so she lets him pause to buy her needle or thread or something."

"But Old Chen puts on such airs. He takes an eternity to get us anywhere!"

"I know!" Silver Bell exclaimed. "In school, Mrs. Curtis told us rickshaw pulling is an insult to human dignity. It is work for a beast of burden!" She smiled at her sister. "Help me write an English letter to Father. If we both write, perhaps he will ask Mother to buy us an automobile. Then we won't feel ashamed to invite our friends home, and they won't think we are such country bumpkins. After all, this is a very fashionable section of town!"

"Hmm, a good idea! I'll help you write in English. Father will be impressed." Golden Bell spent more time with her sister now that Iris lived in Bright Crystal's house. "Let's tell him that Liang Red Phoenix has been elected president of our student body. Her father has a very successful business somewhere. She goes around town in the most smashing Packard automobile. The license plate says number eight, so we all call her Packard eight. Even the American teachers sometimes call her by that nickname because it is easier for them to say things in English than to say Liang Houng Foung" (Red Phoenix).

"We must remind Father to give us English names."

"I've told the school that Father is a graduate of St. John's University, and that he will give us appropriate English names. We don't have to depend on the teachers to name us." Golden Bell tilted her chin up and looked down on the room as if speaking to her classmates.

In Purple Jade's room, Comely Brook was making their beds. Purple Jade said, "I hope Dragon will bring Bright Crystal when he comes. I'm certain we owe her our livelihood."

"Bright Crystal is afraid to taint the Huang family name with her reputation." Comely Brook plumped up a pillow.

"What a noble soul! It is no wonder Dragon adores her."

"It does make you wonder, doesn't it?" Comely Brook was now in her eighth month of pregnancy. Still doing all the housework, she paused frequently to rest. "The respectable ladies around cousin Chou Ling's mahjong table do nothing but gossip all day, and they are received by the highest in society. They sneer and snicker about ladies like Bright

Crystal, who is a true heroine." She winced and stretched, then twisted to rub her back.

Purple Jade noticed her discomfort. "Let me give you a back massage."

"Oh, no, *Tai-tai*," Comely Brook waved her mistress away. "I'm fine. You're already working too hard."

"I'm not going to Dr. Tsui's clinic today. I need to practice." Purple Jade smiled. "I will not try my acupuncture on you. I'll only follow the control points on the meridians of your back. My feet may be crippled, but I am developing strong hands."

Purple Jade placed several quilts on her desk and instructed Comely Brook to take off her clothes. For one brief moment, Purple Jade was transfixed as Comely Brook stood holding her protruding stomach with both hands, totally unselfconscious. Her flesh shone creamy and smooth in the daylight. Her full breasts and rounded belly seemed oiled by the life within her.

So this is my magnificent gift to my husband, Purple Jade thought. In her youth, her sense of propriety had forbidden her to examine her own body. The pain of her bound feet was also a constant distraction. Yes, she had been denied sensual joys all her life.

She helped Comely Brook to lie comfortably on her side.

As Purple Jade proceeded with her massage, she recounted her new experiences to Comely Brook in the same way she used to talk about her painful feet with the now renamed Orchid. "Dr. Tsui is a very progressive man. He insists that all acupuncture needles be boiled for fifteen minutes after each use. He has acquired many charts from the Westerners to help me study anatomy."

The gentle but firm movements of Purple Jade's hands elicited soft groans of pleasure from Comely Brook.

"There is also a priceless collection of ancient anatomical models and diagrams in his clinic. These wooden and ivory figurines show the meridians of one's body, and how chi travels through them. I practice inserting the acupuncture needles in the wax figures made of bronze on the inside, with holes for the proper acupuncture points. Now show me your middle finger."

Comely Brook extended her middle finger as directed.

"No two persons are of the same size or shape, so we estimate the location of the proper points by a flexible *tsun*, measuring the length of the middle bone on your middle finger." Purple Jade measured Comely Brook's middle bone against her own finger. "Now, here is the point for the relief of your neck." She pressed on it for a few minutes. "Brook-*mei*, I've become so accurate in my work, Dr. Tsui has allowed me to treat real patients!"

"Thank you, thank you, *Tai-tai*. You've found the right point!" Comely Brook sat up and swiveled her neck.

"I'm still deficient in the arts of pulse reading and tongue examination."

"I definitely feel more relaxed."

"Most patients don't trust a woman to diagnose their illness. I also lack confidence in stating my opinion." She massaged Comely Brook's shoulders. "In acupuncture, Dr. Tsui is usually there to confirm my location. Somehow, the patients do seem to appreciate a gentle feminine hand." Purple Jade motioned Comely Brook to lie down again.

"No, no, *Tai-tai*. This is enough. I'm fine. I feel wonderful." Comely Brook still found it hard to think that a few short months ago their roles were reversed.

Purple Jade had similar thoughts. "All your life you've massaged my feet, while I led such a sheltered life. Now I'm exposed to human suffering daily. Yet truly, I feel my days are stimulating and challenging." She lowered her head.

Comely Brook was overcome by emotion. She fell to her knees and grabbed Purple Jade's hands. She wept and kissed them. "*Oh-me-to-fo*, may the Buddha bless them." She held them to her cheeks.

Purple Jade assisted Comely Brook to her feet. "Hush, Brook-*mei*, get dressed." She was beginning to feel uncomfortable with the strange pleasure she felt at the sight and touch of Orchid's body.

Comely Brook became aware of her unseemly outburst in the face of her mistress's serenity. Her mistress was adept in directing her toward manners of probity. She started to dress.

"Virtue-*ko* has instructed me to send you to a Western physician," Purple Jade said in a steady voice. She had long ago resolved to be a pillar of strength in this household of women. "We know he is a learned man, who has great faith in the Western sciences. Brook, do you think the Western Ocean Devils know anything about the feminine art of giving birth?"

"No, I don't think so."

"Cousin Chou Ling took a tour of the hospital when it was opened to the public. She saw hearts, brains and even a fetus pickled in jars!"

"The West Ocean Devils may be used to cutting up people because they are too familiar with knives. They use them every day during their meals."

"Mrs. Lee told me that sometimes Western hospitals cut open the women and remove the babies," Purple Jade continued. "Mrs. Chang said that sometimes the children are gouged out of their mothers by tongs. The tongs are shiny and short, but almost exactly like the kind we use to grasp and handle charcoal. Do you think it wise to have our heir born in a place like that?"

"No, please don't cut me open!" Comely Brook cried.

"I would never let anything like that happen to you."

The steel in her mistress's voice reassured Comely Brook. She finished dressing, and took on the same placid tone as her mistress. "It is better to stick to the methods of old. I would feel more comfortable at home."

"Yes, I shall write to our husband and tell him I'll send for old Tsai *Ma-ma* from Hangzhou. She delivered both Golden and Silver Bell. She is old but experienced, and now, I also can help."

Both women beamed.

"Uncle Dragon is not coming until noon," Golden Bell informed her sister. "Let's write to Father now."

Silver Bell took out her pen and paper. "I'll write what I can in English, and write the rest in Chinese. You can help me change it to all English when you're done with your letter.

"Write 'Dear Dad.' American children call their fathers 'dad,' so that is what we shall call him from now on."

"Isn't it hard to learn English?" Silver Bell asked. "I get so confused. For instance, why do they pronounce know' and 'no' the same way but spell them differently?"

"It's strange, isn't it?" Golden Bell proceeded with her own writing. "I'm telling Father about Old Chen, but I'll also tell him that sometimes Mother still stares into space and has moments of deafening silence." She read from her letter. "'She goes to Dr. Tsui's clinic every day, and studies her herbal medicine every night. She looks tired even though she says she likes her work. Without a household of servants to manage, minus the social obligations of Hangzhou, she is a different woman. I'm sure it's her love of learning that's sustaining her spirit. Perhaps it also provides the balance and sanity of her mind. I hope time and an open mind will heal her sorrow.' What do you think? Do I sound like an adult?" Golden Bell asked her sister. "Father must know I appreciate Mother's problems, but he must also see how exciting it is for us now that we are in Shanghai." She leaned over and corrected her sister's sentences.

"That sounds fine. I'll tell Father that Mrs. Williams gives me piano lessons in school," Silver Bell said. "Do you think Father knows why I must practice so many scales? Everyone prefers the songs I play. But Mrs. Williams says that if I do not practice my scales, I'll never be a good pianist. Mother thinks the teachers are gods, but have you ever heard of a great pianist who plays scales?"

"No. Tell him we both want to be Christians." Golden Bell pointed to the place where her sister was supposed to write.

"OK." Silver Bell was delighted that her sister was giving her so much attention. "Golden Bell, should I tell Father — I mean Dad — that I had to ask Mother's permission for our baptism, because you have already made Mother angry, refusing to go in the chamber pot? No, maybe I should leave that for later." She erased it. "I'll tell him I sing in church, and we both agree it is only right that we should be members. I love to sing "Amazing Grace" and "Onward, Christian Soldiers." Do you think Father knows these songs?"

"The first one is pretty — so sweet. It makes me want to cry." Golden Bell smiled. "The second one is a marching song. Father might even have sung it while riding his white horse during the revolution. I think you've learned more English from the songs than from the books in school." Golden Bell shook her head. "I wouldn't tell him about that, though."

"I'll tell him I'm reeling our cocoons to make a silk scarf for him. Mother said we'll need to buy more cocoons from Hangzhou soon," Silver Bell said. "Well, I'd better tell him it is Brook *Ma-ma* who is really doing most of the work. She is so wonderful. She often asks me to teach her songs and allows me to feel her stomach. Once, I felt the baby kick! Oh, Golden Bell, I can't wait to see the baby! Do you think Father would mind if I give the baby half of his scarf? I'll definitely teach him how to play the piano!"

"I'm not afraid to tell Father that I refuse to help weave his scarf." Golden Bell sneered. "I'm saving some of my allowance from Uncle Dragon to buy him a set of fountain pens, so that every time he writes, he'll be reminded that I am the future and promise of China, just as he said I should be."

"Should I tell him we hate the foul-smelling herbal drinks Mother brews for us every week? No, I'll say we both hate the drinks, but we gulp them down to please her."

"Oh I don't think you need to bother Father about what Mother thinks is nutritious."

"I know you are secretly proud of her, because you tell everyone in school our mother is a doctor."

"Never mind." Golden Bell waved the thought away. "How are we going to tell Father about Iris?"

"What about Iris?"

The doorbell rang, and Golden Bell went to answer it. "It must be Uncle Dragon. He'll advise me. Bring down the firecrackers. We're starting our New Year!"

Chapter 2

GOLDEN BELL MET Glorious Dragon at the door. "Uncle Dragon, Uncle Dragon, Iris wants to marry Lieutenant Kamasaki! What are we to tell Mother and Father?"

"Tell your father the truth." Glorious Dragon drew his niece away from the front door. "He is a liberal man of learning. He will not hold nationality against any man."

Silver Bell came out with a string of firecrackers.

"Tell your father that Iris met a Japanese lieutenant when she was helping Miss Tyler in the Hangzhou mission. He holds some type of administrative position, so he was never involved in any atrocities." He strode toward a rake and tied the firecrackers to its handle.

Silver Bell gawked. "Iris met a Japanese!"

"I've met Lieutenant Kamasaki," Golden Bell informed her sister. "I was impressed. He was born in America — still carries his Western ways, but he and his family have gone back to their Japanese roots."

"A Japanese! Imagine that!"

"We speak in English. I honestly can't understand why we call the Japanese 'brown dwarfs of the East Ocean.'" She rolled her eyes. "Lieutenant Kamasaki looks just like a tall Chinese scholar — fairer than our peasants who work in the sun all day. Oh *Mei-mei*, it is so very romantic! He knows Iris was my personal maid. He is fascinated by our family."

Silver Bell nodded. "But what will Mother say?"

Glorious Dragon drew the girls away and lit the firecrackers. He huddled close to shield them from the fiery sparks. "Tell your mother Lieutenant Kamasaki is Mr. Kam, that he was born in Fukien and educated overseas, so he does not speak our dialect. Tell her they met through Iris's work in the factory." He looked up and saw that the firecrackers had brought his sister to the upstairs window. "Silver Bell, remind me to tell you another episode of the Monkey King making havoc in heaven when we get inside." He took out two red envelopes from his coat pocket and gave one to each girl.

Purple Jade noted that her daughters had neglected to kowtow in thanks for the New Year's lucky money in the red envelopes. When she came down to greet her brother, he was already deep into his story. "The Monkey King was floating down from the airplane on a parachute designed by our factory."

"Happy New Year, Dragon-*dee*, said Purple Jade. "I see you are improving on the classics!"

"Oh, *M-ma*, we prefer his story," Silver Bell cried.

"Happy New Year, Jade-*jei*." Glorious Dragon stood up to bow. "You'll like the ending of my modern version also. Well, the Monkey King flew to the East Ocean and bombed out their Sun God! Everything blew to high heavens just like the fireworks at your father's birthday party."

"Oh, wasn't that the best party we've ever had?" Silver Bell clapped.

"That would put a glorious end to this war, wouldn't it?" Purple Jade laughed.

Comely Brook served tea and the traditional sweets for the New Year. Glorious Dragon said: "The girls miss festive celebrations. I want to take them to a movie, or better still, take all of you to the Park Hotel to watch people dance."

"Oh goody!" The girls ran upstairs to change.

"You are really overindulgent, Dragon-*dee*. When you're not here, it is only Silver Bell's music that enlivens our house." Purple Jade smiled.

"Today is special. I've booked a table in a European restaurant for our New Year's Day dinner. But before dinner, we'll go to the tea dance. You and Brook *mei-mei* must both get changed!"

There were public executions of thieves and Chinese patriots on the streets of Shanghai every day. The Japanese left the headless bodies to rot in the open, so that passersby would learn to fear their conquerors. Glorious Dragon instructed his chauffeur to take a circuitous route to avoid the gruesome sight.

At the hotel, everyone enjoyed watching the dancers. The girls tapped their feet, swayed with the music and gazed longingly at the action on the dance floor. Purple Jade allowed Glorious Dragon to teach her daughters a few steps. Exhilarated by their brief dancing lesson, the girls were reluctant to leave.

On the way to dinner, they were still giddy from the excitement, and so were surprised when their car became mired in an impossible tangle of pedicab, rickshaw, and bicycle traffic. Suddenly, people tumbled all over each other, clearing the way for a Japanese military convoy. A dozen soldiers on motorcycles led the way. An open van followed. A huge white flag, emblazoned with the red sun of the East Ocean, fluttered over the cab. More than a dozen men were in the van, with their hands tied behind their backs. White banners flew from the sides of the van stating the crimes of the prisoners: Traitors," "Thieves," "Enemies of the co-prosperity sphere." Some of the men hung their heads low; others wept. A few others looked like educated gentlemen. One young man had chalky pale skin, glowering eyes, and a scowl of defiance on his face. He looked like a student. Another man wore a Western suit. His dark eyes burned with rage. Purple Jade turned pale. She thought that either one of them might have been her husband, thrown in with common criminals, to be executed like one of them.

The man in the Western suit began to shout: "*Chun Hwa Ming Kwo Wan Sway! Chun Hwa Ming Kwo Wan Sway!*" (Long live the Republic of China!) People on the street took up the chant, raising their fists. The women were moved to tears.

"The Japanese wish to instill fear in our hearts," Golden Bell said in a steely voice, "but instead we are roused to even greater heroism."

Purple Jade turned to her brother to thank him for her husband's freedom. But he averted his eyes, and began singing an English song with Silver Bell. Purple Jade remained quiet. She realized that this was his way of soothing his conscience — trying to keep his head above this flood of national shame.

When they entered the European restaurant, Silver Bell exclaimed: "The tables are set with so many shiny weapons!"

Glorious Dragon explained that one knife was for spreading butter, another for fish, and the one with a sharp scalloped edge was for cutting meat. One fork was for uncooked raw vegetables, one for fish, and another for the meat. One spoon was for the soup, another for coffee or tea afterward.

"We won't have tea with our meal?" Comely Brook asked.

"You'll have it when the last sweet course comes."

Everyone nodded, but they were confused. Glorious Dragon held up each piece of silverware before he used it, so they could follow and use it the same way.

"The weapons are heavy!" Silver Bell whispered.

The salad of raw vegetables was too strange for the women. They pushed their lettuce around their plates and watched Glorious Dragon.

Purple Jade turned to discuss financial matters. "Dragon-*dee*, since Virtue is no longer working in the uniform factory, you are solely responsible for its enormous profits. We really should not take half of it."

"Since these are war profits, I know Virtue will not approve." Glorious Dragon crunched his raw carrots. "However, none of us wish to see the profits fall into enemy hands. Let me set up accounts for the girls in America."

Purple Jade nodded. To argue would be a reproach to her brother. This plan would be a face-saving option for all concerned. "For myself, I will take the necessary yens for our household expenses and no more."

When the soup came, Comely Brook exclaimed, "They do everything backward — not saving the soup for the last course!"

Everyone enjoyed it nevertheless. The crusty bread, spread with butter, was a favorite.

"*M-ma.*" Silver Bell slurped her soup. "Golden Bell and I want to be baptized!"

Glorious Dragon motioned her not to slurp.

"Your teachers have been most kind to you. I don't wish to seem ungrateful," her mother replied. She took a breath and was just going to speak again when Silver Bell chimed in: "Oh goody! I'll have to wear a white dress at the baptism. Brook *ma-ma*, will you make me a dress like the one on the American doll Father gave me?" She found it hard to drink soup without making a sound. "Do you think they will ask me to sing during my baptism? I do wish Father could be here to see me."

"Wait." Her mother put down her spoon. "It is cold outside. I'm afraid pouring water over your heads will give you a chill. Your teachers will probably think I am an uneducated, ignorant woman, but I never liked Western ways."

"Oh, *M-ma*!" Golden Bell rolled her eyes.

Everyone waited while the servers cleared their soup dishes.

"Your mother is right. Christianity is very strange." Glorious Dragon held up the fish fork and knife when the fish was served. "We believe children are born kind and can be educated to remain good, but they talk of children being born in sin. I cannot find one streak of meanness in either of you."

"The Christians looked to a simple carpenter to bring them peace." Purple Jade was pleased to have her brother's support. "Perhaps they should go wash the heads of the East Ocean Devils to bring peace to this tormented country."

Silver Bell brought her knife to her mouth. Glorious Dragon stopped her. "You must either switch the fork to your right hand or eat with the fork stabbing the food with the left hand."

Golden Bell also struggled with her utensils. "This is a ridiculous way to eat!" She laughed.

They found themselves full before the main course arrived.

A waiter wearing a tall puffy hat wheeled in an enormous piece of meat. He waved a huge knife, and rubbed it against a round steel sword. Silver Bell expected him to do a sword dance; she found the sound of grinding steel frightening. The waiter put down the sword and took out a long fork. With a flourish of his shiny knife, he carved out slabs of meat that appeared quite raw.

"It must have come from some freshly killed animal. Look, the blood is still flowing," Comely Brook whispered in awe.

The waiter scooped up the blood, and poured some over the meat before serving them. As if in one voice, the women claimed to be full — unable to eat another bite. Golden Bell ate a tiny portion just to keep her Uncle Dragon company. Purple Jade and Comely Brook escaped to the restroom.

In the restroom, Comely Brook promptly disgorged her entire dinner. "The sight of all that blood unnerved me," she panted. "Ugh . . . imagine eating red flowing blood!"

"My stomach is upset too," Purple Jade answered. She brought water to help Comely Brook rinse her mouth and massaged her back.

When they had regained their composure, Purple Jade sighed in resignation. "The girls are exposed to so many new things in Shanghai. I'm grateful Lao Wang sent us Old Chen to pull our rickshaw. At least I know every place he has taken the girls to. It is also convenient to have a man around to take care of the essential errands."

Chapter 3

Dear Jade-mei:

Your letter brought me great peace. I'm happy to learn that you are all well in Shanghai, and busy with your many pursuits. Your study of herbal medicine is most impressive, and I believe the herbs can be a superior preventative for illness. Your compassionate care of Comely Brook also moves me. Your personal attention will nurture her in a way no medicine can. You have maintained our family integrity in these confusing times. If our nation had more men and women of your moral caliber, we would have nothing to fear.

Your arrangements with Dragon are wise, and perhaps the best under present circumstances. I've written to him and expressed my gratitude for his care of my family. Since he is providing for the children's financial future, I've made large contributions to our national struggle in his name. He is in fact a true patriot. He is prudent and most sensible not to bring Bright Crystal into our house. Our daughters are at an impressionable age. They may want to emulate Bright Crystal's glamour. I'm writing another letter to the girls so they may understand my thoughts on their welfare.

My only request to you is to send Comely Brook to a Western physician for an examination. I understand your concerns. As you know, most women at cousin Ling's mahjong table are not educated, and do not understand the wonders of modern medicine. When Golden and Silver Bell were born in Hangzhou (Jade-mei, I can't believe they're already sixteen and ten!), there were no Western doctors there. Now you are in Shanghai. You must take advantage of the finest the world has to offer. Trust me, I only seek the best for my family. I've written to Dragon, and asked him to find a woman doctor for Comely Brook.

The Chinese doctors only feel your pulse, examine your tongue, and look into your eyes. The Western doctors examine all the woman's private parts, so you must reassure Comely Brook that it is all very proper, and that I approve. I think a woman doctor will help to ease her mind. There aren't many women doctors in the world. However, I've heard that there are a few in Shanghai. I would advise you, Golden and Silver Bell, all to have a check-up with the woman doctor as well. Jade-mei, as you are now practicing Chinese medicine, it would be of added intellectual interest for you to experience the Western methods. You must have noticed how strong and vigorous the Western people are. Our nation has been trampled upon long enough. I'm sure your experiences will confirm my belief that we must not encourage our daughters to be weak and helpless.

Your studies in acupuncture are truly impressive. Our ancient art has been most successful in pain alleviation. By comparison, Western medicine is far behind in this regard. Perhaps your work in acupuncture will some day enlighten the world regarding the benefits of this ancient science. I am speechless with awe whenever I think of you as a working "doctor." Indeed, you exemplify the perfect woman in our culture: nurturing, gracious, considerate and self-effacing. Good luck in your studies. My heart bursts with pride for you.

Jade-mei, we all wish for a son. But moral principles do not govern procreation. Now that our country has no laws to protect us, the question of inheritance is moot. I shall be just as pleased to have another daughter. Deep down, I feel the soul of our nation is feminine. We are a gentle, artistic people devoted to the enjoyment of life. We conserve, suffer, endure, and we survive to procreate. Another daughter will bring me great joy because she will reaffirm the life principle that is the foundation of our culture. If the child is male, he will be called Brilliant Way; if female, she will be called Jade Bell. She should be named after you because she is truly a gift from you, and I hope she will learn from your strength as well as your decency and thoughtfulness.

Consistent with my belief in bringing good health to my family, I urge you to practice modern hygiene at home. Since ancient times, the Chinese have had a high infant mortality rate, and I believe proper hygiene will correct that. From now on, all toilet activities must be confined to the bathrooms. After the baby is born, all the utensils must be boiled in hot water as you do for your needles in the clinic. No one is to feed the baby by passing food from one mouth to another. If the baby cannot chew the food, it is not needed. In this, I am thankful that Comely Brook is not one of those vain modern women who need to hire a wet nurse for her baby. A young mother's milk is nature's best food, and a lucky baby is one who has a healthy mother. I read that modern science recommends cod liver oil for everyone. Check with the doctor if you need a prescription. Comely Brook, Golden, and Silver Bell should all take it. Jade-mei, you should take some too. It will please me greatly to learn that my family is in good health. As a point of intellectual curiosity, are there any Chinese pharmaceuticals that correspond to cod liver oil?

I am also happy to hear that Iris has a suitor. She has reached marriageable age, and we shall have properly discharged our responsibility toward her. Should she decide to marry, we must be generous with her dowry. She is now an adopted niece, and an indispensable hand in the administration of the factory. Since the factory does business with the enemy, some of them may attend the wedding. I do not wish the family to attend the public wedding. Dragon will represent the family. Instead, the family should have another celebration in a Chinese restaurant with all of Iris's relatives from Hangzhou. I know the girls will be disappointed, but this is my command: that they will attend only the family celebration.

In view of the coming social activities, perhaps you might ask old Chen to cultivate some flowers in our front and back skywell. He sounds like a noble old soul. I commend you, Jade-mei, for hiring him and providing for his welfare.

I am deeply moved by Silver Bell's efforts to weave a scarf for me. A piece of homespun silk will be a true reminder of my Chinese soul. I shall wrap my favorite books and your poems in it, and if the cloth is long enough, you should keep half. But the weaving will take too long and it will bring lint into the house. So I suggest that you ask Dragon to have the factory finish the job. I know it will be made from your cocoons, and so much of your love, thoughts, and effort have already gone into it.

Now a few words about my life here in Hong Kong. I have decided that I am not an industrialist. So instead of starting a factory, I have found a position writing editorials for the New Island News. *I also help in various aspects of editorial work, so I commence work at five in the afternoon and return home around dawn. I am still staying at the East Asia Hotel. The schedule suits me fine. I am thrilled by the opportunity to read the many foreign publications available at the news agency. In many ways, I enjoy my work so much that I am ashamed to take a salary.*

In some ways, life here reminds me of the heady excitements of my student days. But I am no longer young, and my heart is with you in Shanghai. When Comely Brook has delivered, and the baby is old enough to travel, I will arrange with Dragon to bring you here.

Hong Kong is a British colony, but most faces here are Chinese. It is also a tropical island. I know it will mean another move and more adjustments for you. I am already considering housing for us. Since the island is so small, most families live in apartments. There are some lovely apartments on Robinson Road. (Purple Jade, try not to translate the name into Chinese and judge whether it would be an auspicious place to live. Western names translated into Chinese have strange comical meanings.) This is on the mid-level of a mountain called Victoria Peak. The peak area is often shrouded in mist and is very damp, but the mid-level has wonderful ocean views and catches the cooling breezes. However, for one who is used to a house with many courtyards, the apartment may feel confining. There will be no gardens. All the rooms will be on one floor, but the view can be breathtaking.

One other alternative is Happy Valley. There are many lovely houses on Blue Pool Road, much like the one you are living in now. They are larger, and I think we'll all be able to have separate rooms. They also have larger gardens, and one can cultivate tropical flowers. But being in a valley, it can get very hot in the summer. You will have to adjust to the heat. I am excited whenever I think of your arrival. There are so many things I want to show you.

With my warm regards to you and Comely Brook,

Respectfully,

Righteous Virtue
The 27th year of the Republic of China
The First Moon, 26th day.

Chapter 4

Feb. 25, 1938

Dear Golden Bell and Silver Bell:

Your English letters please me. I'm particularly happy to learn that Golden Bell is helping Silver Bell. The strength of our family depends upon the unity and mutual assistance of all members. The strength of a nation is based upon the strength of its families. In you I see the triumph of our cultural values, and know our national humiliation will be avenged some day.

I have asked your mother to follow Western standards of hygiene, because of a baby's low resistance to germs and infection. You both could help by cleaning up after yourselves, without waiting to be served. As you are both fond of Western manners, you must know that Westerners do not have personal maids, and everyone contributes to the necessary chores around the house. The essence of our culture is to learn grace and virtue, to nurture the young and the dependent, and to live exemplary lives. You two must set good examples of personal care and hygiene, which you are learning in school, so that the baby may grow up in a healthy environment.

In Hangzhou, using chamber pots in our home of many courts was never a discomfort. Now your mother is out of the house most of the day, and may not be fully aware of the inconvenience in our cramped city quarters. She is making a valiant effort to adjust to our drastically reduced circumstances, and is naturally inclined to preserve as much of her home atmosphere as possible. Both of you must learn forbearance and patience.

Golden Bell, I've asked your mother to have old Chen cultivate some flowers in the front and back skywells. Western ladies wear gloves when cultivating their own gardens. Perhaps you could consult your science teacher and decide upon the types of flowers suitable to the Shanghai climate. You could be old Chen's helper. Teach him some scientific methods, and learn something from the old peasant, who will feel honored that you should take an interest in his endeavors.

Rickshaw pulling is a life-saving profession for old Chen. Your mother has made sure that he is not strained, and a man is never a beast when he is given face and security. We all have our burdens in life. Some psychological burdens are far more intolerable than physical ones. Given a choice, I would gladly pull a rickshaw for gentle mistresses like you than be exiled here away from my family and my roots.

The Packard is a very beautiful car indeed. One day I should like to own one, when the country is at peace, and we are reunited. I'm learning how to drive now, and I shall love to drive you wherever you choose. In fact, Golden Bell will soon be old enough to learn to drive. I shall be glad to teach her. But the time is not now. It is in poor taste to parade one's good fortune in times of national shame and suffering. Remember our devastated home and separated family. Do we have so much to be cheerful about? It is rumored that in the northeastern provinces under enemy control, your "Packard Eight's" father is a prominent businessman. I don't know if he is involved with the opium trade, but these provinces are flooding our country with so much cheap opium that the poorest rickshaw puller can afford a smoke. (Again, your mother is wise in hiring old Chen. He doesn't smoke.) You only need to look at your mother's cousin Yu Wei to see the effect of this business. Yes, the enemy would love to see our nation reduced to a people of degenerate drug addicts. Think clearly children: is it such an honor to be named after the license plate of a car?

I do apologize for not providing you with English names earlier. Golden Bell, you will be called Victoria. Your undaunted spirit and insatiable desire for learning promise a bright future for our country. Tell your mother that this is the name of the last English queen. During her reign, the English Empire prospered. Your American teachers can call you Vicky for short.

Silver Bell, I have no understanding of music education. However, teaching is not an easy task. I'm sure your teacher will not teach you what is not necessary. Practice your scales, and perhaps someday you will tell me whether it has helped your piano playing. I'm naming you Sarah, because I like the sound of this old biblical name.

Regarding baptism, I can understand that both of you wish to be like your teachers. But the Chinese do not believe children are born in sin. We shall discuss this further when you come to Hong Kong. You will be older then, and if you still feel you need a religion to guide you, I shall not oppose. It is a pity that Christianity came in with the merchants of colonialism. I do believe our Chinese morals would be reinforced by their doctrine of charity. This is essentially the same as our concept of jen *— the foundation of a harmonious society — but it is difficult to practice* jen *in times of war and hardship. The Western idea is strengthened by the added incentive of a heavenly reward. Living in Hong Kong, I'm also enjoying Christian charity and the protection of colonialism, so I cannot find fault with Christianity. I would like to know that you want baptism not because it is fashionable but because you understand and truly want to practice the basic belief of charity. Though your mother is not a Christian, she practices* jen *in the Christian way — especially for old Chen. Golden Bell, you need to be more like your mother to become a true Chinese Christian!*

Golden Bell, it is best that your mother does not know Mr. Kamasaki is Japanese. You remember how ill she was after she returned from Hangzhou. The shock of learning Iris's association with a Japanese may cause her to relive the trauma of losing our home. I know there are many admirable individuals from every nation in the world. Still, Mr. Kamasaki is in our country because of the war. For that reason, none of you are to be seen with him in public. You will visit Iris in her home, but never when there are other Japanese friends around. This is my strict command, and you shall obey without exception. Iris has chosen her path in life. I wish her well. It is the arrogance of youth to think that they can defy conventions as well as centuries of war and enmity. They will have a difficult road before them. I should be surprised if Iris will find acceptance in the Kamasaki family, even in private. The Japanese have adopted much of our fine culture. In both of our cultures, marriage is a union of families. Unless they choose to live overseas forever, life will not be easy for them.

When the baby is born and can travel, I mean to bring you all here. If there are any Cantonese girls in your school, you should learn some Cantonese from them. Hong Kong is a British colony, and you'll find the schools here very different from the American missionary school you now attend. The many Western nations have cultures as diverse and distinctive as the Chinese culture is different from the Japanese, the Korean, or the Vietnamese. Many new adventures await you. It will please me greatly to know you're behaving like the brave new women of China: independent, strong, helpful, but gentle and kind. You're my hope and faith in the future of China.

Your loving father,

Righteous Virtue

Chapter 5

WITH THE GIRLS in school and Purple Jade working in Dr. Tsui's clinic, life in Shanghai was highlighted by many interesting events.

One Sunday, Purple Jade received Old Tang, a distant Chou relative who now managed cousin Yu Wei's household. It was Old Tang's habit to flourish his handkerchief, dab his forehead and twitch his nose when he wanted to make a point. With one hand resting on a stack of boxes beside him, he waved his white handkerchief and gave a perfunctory pat to his face. He said: "Huang *tai-tai*. I've brought you some valuable jewels and furs."

Purple Jade felt like laughing at the man's assumption that she would be interested in these ostentatious items. "You are too kind. I hardly have need of such fine things nowadays."

"Your adopted niece, Iris, will be marrying an important man." Old Tang wiped his wiggling nose. "Let me show you what I have."

He opened the first box. Purple Jade gasped. It was a pair of ancient jade blades, worn during court ceremonies by the chief counselor to the Manchu emperor—the centerpiece of a group of court jewelry collections in her cousin Chou Yu Wei's house. The blades were more than a foot long and eight inches wide, tapering to a three-inch oval near the top. The emerald green was hand-polished to a translucent sheen of only an eighth-of-an inch thick.

With dramatic flicks of his white kerchief, Old Ting told of cousin Yu Wei's increasing opium addiction and how cousin Chou Ling also resorted to pawning the family heirlooms and furs for her expenditures at the gaming table. Purple Jade quickly agreed to buy the important pieces, all the while calculating how she would justify such purchases to her husband. In the end, she added a leopard coat that was cousin Chou Ling's pride and joy. It would be a great loss of face for all the Chous if someone outside the family should be seen wearing it. To avoid recrimination and safeguard the family treasures, Purple Jade would use the fur to line her winter silk robes, so no one need ever know. Of course, she would never display the jewelry.

Golden Bell thought her father's suggestion for planting flowers in the skywells was a wonderful idea.

"What do people plant in their gardens in Hong Kong, Mrs. Curtis?" Golden Bell asked her biology teacher.

"I'm not sure. Something tropical, I suppose."

Confused about the British colonial culture and the American colonial past, Golden Bell thought people in Great Britain and America might share the same habits and enjoy the same gardening patterns. She asked again: "How about America? Do they plant tropical flowers too?"

"I suppose they do in the south."

"What do you think the English and the Americans might grow here?"

"England is a very small country in the north." Mrs. Curtis took out a map. "Let's see if we can find a place in America that has Shanghai's climate."

Golden Bell huddled close. "See here." Mrs. Curtis pointed. "Shanghai is about the same latitude as Savanna, Georgia, in the United States." She rummaged through her bookcase. "Here is a book on Georgia. You may find something about its vegetation."

The school bell rang, and Mrs. Curtis had to leave for the next class. "Chinese gardens are famous for their elegant designs. The cherry blossoms, peonies, night-blooming cereus all originated in China. For best results, I would consult a local gardener for something indigenous."

Golden Bell's heart ached when she remembered their garden in Hangzhou. She had been so busy absorbing novel Western ideas that she had seldom given a thought to her home. Now the memory of her playful days among the lilies, roses, jasmine and azaleas filled her with longing.

She learned that the state flower of Georgia was the Cherokee rose, though the picture in the book did not look like a rose. Golden Bell asked Old Chen to plant roses, peonies and other flowering bushes in their front skywell. Golden Bell consulted with Old Chen about where and when such a flower should be planted. She was frequently seen in the garden showing Old Chen pictures. Old Chen now considered himself a gardener more than a rickshaw-puller. He ran faster whenever they approached home. Each morning he knocked on the door and presented the Huang women with a fresh bouquet for the house. He always had a special flower for Golden Bell, because he had been given so much face by her consultations. The girls wrote: "Father, you are right about how people can be beasts, but Old Chen is certainly not one of them."

Purple Jade was so proud of her daughter that she proclaimed to her husband: "Our Golden girl has matured!"

Purple Jade thought Mr. Kam a very fine young man. But he had many traits that she could not understand. She asked her brother: "I noticed that when he bows, he does not hold his hands together the way we do, but lets them fall on his knees like the East Ocean Devils."

"Mr. Kam must have had to work with the enemy so much that he has taken to their ways."

As Mr. Kam did not have a family in Shanghai to arrange for the bride's gifts, he paid the Huangs a handsome bride price. The sum was so generous, Purple Jade was reluctant to accept it. Glorious Dragon assured her that Mr. Kam was wealthy and most grateful that the Huangs had given Iris such a fine education. Purple Jade spent all the money on the wedding and Iris's trousseau.

In spite of tension about Mr. Kam's identity, the wedding was a success. The Huang women were particularly happy to see so many familiar faces from Hangzhou. Iris's uncle, the gardener, and his family stayed in Petain Road for a whole week.

Purple Jade was grateful that her husband had ordered the family away from the public wedding in the city registry. Iris wore a white gown, and Purple Jade could not help thinking how strange it was for her to be married in the mourning color. Comely Brook spent hours fixing the veil and the silk tulle around the skirt. The girls were disappointed that they could not attend the Western ceremony. They thought Iris's white silk gown was gorgeous. She looked like a movie star. At night, Iris was dressed properly in her red gown — all embroidered and beaded. Since she had been officially married that morning, she did not wear the red headdress, but wore red flowers in her hair instead. Everyone proclaimed Mr. Kam a lucky man.

"What a shame the war has prevented his family from attending!"

"His relatives should have seen this pretty bride!"

No one would have guessed that Iris had been a maid. Since the groom's friends had gone to the public wedding, only the Huang family relatives and friends attended the banquet that evening.

As Mr. Kam did not attempt to speak Shanghainese or the Hangzhou dialect, most guests shied away from him. His wealth and obvious lofty status overwhelmed Iris's relatives. They socialized among themselves. All appeared dignified, properly attired in the finest robes that Purple Jade had bought for them with Mr. Kam's money. Iris was happy that she was given so much face.

Purple Jade confided in Comely Brook, "Our ancient saying is absolutely true:

Buddha needs a coat of gold,
Man is dignified by the proper clothes."

Everyone was surprised to see Miss Tyler. She had suddenly grown old. Her hair had turned white, and Lao Wang told the Huangs how her vigilance and generosity had saved his daughter and countless other women from defilement. Iris had helped Miss Tyler organize the women into nursing squads to care for the wounded Japanese and Chinese alike when Hangzhou was raided. Now the people considered Miss Tyler their savior.

"When the East Ocean Devils came, I should have sent Peony and Little Six to her," Purple Jade whispered to Comely Brook. "Rich or poor, male or female, we are certainly born equal in our needs and suffering. If our husband does not object, I will approve Golden Bell and Silver Bell's conversion to Miss Tyler's religion!"

The girls were stricken to see how sad and worn their teacher looked.

"Have you been ill, Miss Tyler?" Golden Bell asked.

"No, I've been just fine. But the Methodists in New York want to transfer me to a seaport where I can be evacuated easily."

"Will you be coming to Shanghai?" Silver Bell's eyes lit up.

"Or Hong Kong?" Golden Bell added.

"Maybe, maybe." Miss Tyler smiled. "Say your prayers, and all will be well." Somehow, her colorless tone did not sound reassuring.

When the Hangzhou kinsfolk told of the fear and destruction caused by the enemy, Comely Brook told them about the Japanese family that had moved next door.

"The woman looks rather sickly and pale, but the little girl is very sweet and has come visiting several times, bringing gifts. Somehow she found out that Silver Bell understands English. They have managed to communicate in a common language!"

The country folks made tittering noises, predicting disaster if the girls became friends.

"We threw away the gifts of course, but Silver Bell tasted a piece of cake and said it was filled with bean paste, just like some of our sweets."

None of the Huangs had ever seen the father, but some nights they could hear him when he came home drunk and beat his wife. Old Chen wanted to go and help the woman, but since they were East Ocean people, Purple Jade thought it best not to interfere and not show too much neighborly concern.

"I went to visit with some flowers from our garden one day," Comely Brook said. "The man was gone, but the woman was dusting and polishing a beautiful Ming desk. It looked just like that Ming desk *Tai-tai* had in her Hangzhou room, with the curved sides and a wing-like top."

"They're all the same — robbers and killers!" someone responded.

"The poor woman almost cried when she thanked me for the flowers." Comely Brook nodded and looked embarrassed. "She pointed to her little girl and said in halting Chinese, 'only a female!' She was all bruised on the face." Comely Brook patted her face here and there. "But her house was full of Chinese antiques, and everything was immaculately clean."

"It is such a shame that the Japanese people have taken so indiscriminately from our culture." Purple Jade sighed. "Our ancient arts would surely add grace to their lives. Unfortunately, they also added brute force to our traditional scorn for the feminine Sex. Brook-*mei*, we must feel sorry for that woman. We can call that man a brute, a thief, and an enemy, but she has to care for his loot and honor him as a husband!"

Lt. Kamasaki did not understand the Chinese spoken all around him. He thanked Ms. Tyler for her care of the Japanese soldiers, but he insisted that Japan's principal aim was to drive out the white men and form a united Eastern culture with the Chinese.

Golden Bell grew impatient with Miss Tyler's polite silence. She rolled her eyes and said in English, "We prefer Christianity from the white man rather than your brute force."

Lt. Kamasaki immediately apologized for the crimes of his country. "The irony is, my army thought that the terror would create a subjugated people, but instead they have united your country, given you a true sense of nationhood."

Suddenly there was a great commotion at the front of the restaurant. Somehow Lao Wang, the accountant, found out Iris was marrying a Japanese. "Why should a Chinese flower get stuck to a pile of East Ocean dung?" he shouted again and again.

Glorious Dragon quickly had him restrained. Two men dragged him off to his bed in the hotel. Glorious Dragon returned to apologize. "Lao Wang is drunk. He's reliving the horrors of the Japanese invasion!"

Purple Jade did not understand the meaning of Lao Wang's howling insults. She also apologized. "Our country folks have suffered too long. Everyone, please forgive the rowdiness."

Both girls felt sorry for Iris now. Since Lao Wang knew Mr. Kam was Japanese, everyone in Hangzhou would know eventually, and Iris would never be able to visit her old hometown again. The girls still considered Lt. Kamasaki wonderful — a different sort of Japanese, but they thought it would be difficult even for Iris to socialize with people who had behaved like beasts.

The next day, Purple Jade examined the accounting books Lao Wang brought for her inspection. She questioned him on his uncharacteristic outburst during the wedding celebration.

"I'm red-faced from shame." Glorious Dragon had coached Lao Wang well, strictly forbidding him to breathe a word about Mr. Kam's true identity. "*Tai-tai*, please forgive my poor capacity for wine." He looked Purple Jade straight in the eye. "My stomach can no longer tolerate festive food. For months, we've all been living in semi-starvation."

"That's all right! I understand." Purple Jade trembled with embarrassment. "I should have known everyone is barely subsisting."

"Yes, I have stopped collecting rents from the tenant farmers because the East Ocean Devils are levying such heavy taxes, but what can anyone live on?" Lao Wang cried openly now.

"You've done the right thing." Purple Jade ordered some of her family heirlooms to be sold and gave clear instructions as to how the money should be distributed among her former retainers.

Chapter 6

PURPLE JADE TOOK Comely Brook to see the female obstetrician Glorious Dragon recommended. They were kept waiting a long time in Dr. Rankling's office. Comely Brook stretched and fidgeted.

"Look." Purple Jade pointed to the examination table. "This is the perfect height for a massage." She motioned Comely Brook to lie down. She rubbed and squeezed her back and shoulders.

Before Dr. Rankling walked in, she watched them quietly by the door. When they finally introduced themselves, Purple Jade was most pleased that the doctor spoke very good Shanghainese. The doctor was gracious, soft spoken and asked many questions about Chinese medicine. After giving Comely Brook a thorough pelvic examination and pronouncing her healthy, she led Purple Jade on a tour of her facility.

Purple Jade noted Dr. Rankling's gray hair and decided she might be in her fifties. She was impressed by the painstaking care Westerners took in disinfecting and cleaning all their instruments. When they met a male colleague in another office, Purple Jade was surprised to be introduced as "a Chinese doctor." She was also fascinated by how the male doctors treated Dr. Rankling as an equal. For the first time, she could see that Western ways would be liberating — that her daughters' modern education could lead them to accomplishments in important professions. Imagine, both Golden

Bell and Silver Bell might become doctors someday! It was intoxicating to think that such possibilities could be open to her girls.

Purple Jade invited Dr. Rankling to visit Dr. Tsui's clinic. When she arrived, Purple Jade thought Dr. Rankling looked pale and haggard.

"Are you feeling well?" she asked.

Dr. Rankling shook her head. "I'm used to my migraine headaches."

"Do you have a remedy for your pain?" Purple Jade thought the woman needed bed rest.

"No. Western medicine lacks a cure for my pain. I refuse to take an opiate."

"Have you tried Chinese medicine?" Purple Jade asked.

"No, but do you have a cure?"

"We think so. It works for most people," Purple Jade replied.

"Right now, I'm ready to try anything!" the doctor cried.

Purple Jade massaged the doctor's neck and head muscles, explaining the Chinese theory of *chi* and how it traveled through the meridians of the human body. Then she applied pressure on points near the top of the eyebrows, the center of the nose, on the temple, the jawbone and behind the ear on top of the neck. Dr. Rankling expressed much relief after the massage. She wanted to try acupuncture to alleviate her headache. Purple Jade sterilized the needles. Dr. Rankling noted that the process was the same in Western medicine.

Purple Jade twirled a needle in the *hegu* — the soft fleshy part between the thumb and the forefinger — known as the joining of the valleys. In a matter of minutes, Dr. Rankling drifted off to sleep. When she awoke, she touched her face and different parts of her body. "The pain is gone!"

Purple Jade smiled.

"I feel warm and relaxed all over. Amazing!"

Dr. Rankling invited Purple Jade to assist her in the delivery room. Purple Jade agreed. Many evenings, when Dr. Rankling was called to deliver a baby, she telephoned Purple Jade to assist and personally came by in her motorcar to take her to the hospital. She introduced her as "my super doctor," and never failed to mention that Purple Jade alone could take away her migraine. The nurses in the hospital called her "the small feet doctor." They became familiar with the sight of Dr. Rankling ambling into the hospital and Purple Jade trotting enthusiastically beside her.

Once in the delivery room, Purple Jade donned a surgical gown and alongside Dr. Rankling, underwent a thorough scrubbing. She helped massage the woman's stomach and maneuver the baby into proper position. This often led to natural deliveries, without having to resort to surgery. Also, Purple Jade came to realize that while the Western doctors used instruments to help in deliveries, they did not hurt the babies in any way. As a woman, she was used to handling blood, but she was impressed to see that the Westerners planned each surgical operation in meticulous order, and every move was carried out with precision and grace.

Purple Jade assisted at Jade Bell's birth, and Comely Brook was greatly comforted by her presence. The labor lasted ten hours, but the birth was completely natural; no instruments were used, and she was not given a sedative. Purple Jade gave her massages, and Dr. Rankling taught her deep breathing.

Purple Jade's heart fluttered wildly as the baby's head emerged. Tears coursed down her face, and she wanted to shout and sing at the miraculous sight. These days, her twittering restless feelings had been replaced by surges of sweet tenderness when she successfully assisted in deliveries.

The baby girl had Comely Brook's sparkling big eyes, but Purple Jade felt Jade Bell was her special child, because she had been responsible for her birth in so many ways. The baby was also a symbol of her rebirth — her new life in medicine and self-reliance. Everyone in the family called the baby Little Jade.

Comely Brook wept upon learning that she had given birth to a girl. "I've been ungrateful! I did not give you an heir!"

"This is mostly my fault." Purple Jade held her hand. "You expected a boy because I encouraged that thought."

Purple Jade was determined to celebrate the birth as though the baby were a boy. Comely Brook and Little Jade stayed in the hospital for seven days, so they did not have the third day ceremony at home. The family sent red eggs to all the relatives in Shanghai. Lao Wang in Hangzhou also was instructed to distribute red eggs to their friends, relatives, servants, and tenant farmers.

Everyone found the baby adorable. At one week, she could already lift her head and stare with her big cow eyes. Shortly after one month, she lifted herself up on her arms and turned herself over! Following Western fashion, she was not wrapped in swaddling cloths, and Purple Jade was amazed to see how strong and healthy she appeared.

After all the fuss about wanting a son, Purple Jade was surprised that she was happy with another daughter. Gender seemed insignificant after the loss of her home in Hangzhou. Now her passion was her work.

In her free time, she loved to watch Little Jade. She had never felt free to watch her own two daughters as infants because she had been so anxious and always bedridden with pain. Now she was relaxed. Comely Brook was young and rich in milk. It was a sensual and satisfying experience just to watch her nurse. At two weeks, the baby had a face like a round peach. Purple Jade noticed a dimple on her right cheek when she cried or smiled, and her eyes were as bright as the West Lake on a clear autumn day.

The baby cooed and gurgled when she heard singing. Silver Bell sang to her by the hour, and asked if the baby could sit outside to watch her when she played jump house. She thought Jade Bell was much more fun than any of the dolls she'd ever had!

Cousin Chou Ling called one day and insisted that Purple Jade bring Comely Brook and the baby to her house for a game of mahjong. All her women friends wanted to see Jade Bell. Purple Jade could not refuse. She did not want to appear superior, giving herself the air of a snobbish "doctor."

When she entered the main hall that evening, Mrs. Chang rushed forward to examine Jade Bell nestling in Comely Brook's arms. All through dinner, the ladies gave favorable comments:

"What a lovely doll!"

"How soft and milk-fragrant she is!"

"How alert she is when she is awake!"

"She seldom cries."

"She already knows her family."

"She smiles when anyone talks to her!"

Throughout the evening, Mrs. Chang tried to draw Purple Jade's attention to her own pallid, sickly four-year-old son, seated on the lap of his nursemaid in a corner near the window. The boy frequently hid himself behind the blue chintz curtains and seemed disinclined to play. When he spoke, he lisped. He refused to look anyone in the eye. When he whined for his mother, she hovered over him. He had a raspy cough and runny nose. Mrs. Chang lamented that no medicine seemed to help his chronic condition.

Purple Jade wondered why Mrs. Chang wanted to display the poor listless boy. The child would be always at a disadvantage in any society. Was Mrs. Chang perversely using this strategy to deny his infirmity? It embarrassed Purple Jade to receive compliments for Jade Bell in front of Mrs. Chang. Most guests avoided the boy. Various opinions were whispered concerning his behavior.

"This boy has tuberculosis."

"He is mentally deficient!"

"He may have been born with ill fate!"

"He may not live long!"

Once dinner was over, Comely Brook was sent home with her sleepy daughter. Mrs. Chang asked, "Jade, since Orchid's baby is female, will you pledge her to me as a future daughter-in-law?"

Purple Jade felt chilled by such a horrible prospect. She shrugged to disguise her panic. She was unable to respond. She assumed Mrs. Chang was acting out of kindness, since everyone knew that the Huangs had wanted a son. A family that already had two daughters would be eager and grateful to get rid of a concubine's daughter.

Mrs. Chang had also called Comely Brook, Orchid — a pointed reminder that the baby came from a worthless maid. She offered a modest bride price, though very generous, considering it was wartime.

Absorbed by her mahjong game, Mrs. Chang mistook Purple Jade's silence for consent. She said, "We shall have to choose an auspicious day to formalize the troth."

Purple Jade was cold with fury. She knew that Mrs. Chang was behaving properly according to the old traditions — ensuring for herself the services of a future daughter-in-law despite the poor chances of her son's survival. She mustered all her self-control to thank Mrs. Chang. "But my master is a liberal, modern man. He would not approve."

"Huh . . ." Mrs. Chang huffed. "Your husband likes to turn away good fortune. He left his factory to go to Hong Kong, didn't he? Well, what can you do?"

Purple Jade lowered her head and did not answer. The other women probably thought she was embarrassed, but to herself, she thought, *I've come to admire my husband's Western ideas. I have changed. I would feel totally heartless to take Little Jade away from Comely Brook and give her to a sick little boy. Should the boy become an invalid or die, the baby will be Mrs. Chang's slave for the rest of her life.* Purple Jade paled at the thought. *Yes, I would be proud if all MY three daughters became doctors like Dr. Rankling.*

Glorious Dragon took all the cocoons from the house to their factory. The factory sent back a beautiful piece of silvery gray silk. Held in the sun, the silk shone with light shades of the rainbow. Since the cloth was more than three yards long, they sent Righteous Virtue a very large square in which to wrap his poems. The rest was made into three scarves. Comely Brook embroidered a rose on the scarf for Golden Bell, and Purple Jade embroidered a peony on the scarf for Silver Bell. Later, she also embroidered an orchid on the scarf for Jade Bell.

Purple Jade was happy to see Golden Bell and Silver Bell spend more time together. The Japanese girl next door was obviously lonely, but Purple Jade could not allow a friendship. With Little Jade in excellent health, Purple Jade felt it was time to leave Shanghai, and join her husband in Hong Kong. She knew she would miss her associations with Dr. Tsui and Dr. Rankling, but her place was by her husband. A family needed its master, and her husband had been pleading for a family reunion.

Iris agreed to live in their house while they were gone. Purple Jade told her husband that she favored the house on Blue Pool Road in Hong Kong because she was still uneasy in high buildings. Glorious Dragon had taken them to the Palace Hotel on the Bund. The tall building and the elevators made her stomach flutter. Though the view was outstanding, she felt she was perched on a cloud. Her small feet had grown larger, but the bones of her last two toes were permanently crushed, and she would always be unsteady on her feet.

The girls were increasingly in awe to see the change in their mother. She had always been poised and self-possessed, but now she was more confident — not so unnecessarily deferential. Her friendship with Dr. Rankling had altered her entire outlook on women's place in the world, and her daughters were impressed. Still, life was different without their father. When Uncle Dragon came, he took everyone to tea in the hotels and to watch people dance. Sometimes their mother and Comely Brook accompanied them to the movies, but Purple Jade refused to give parties on birthdays and other celebrations when the master was not present. She was careful not to broadcast themselves as a household of women. They all understood that their society was not ready to accept a woman as the head of a family. Everyone was ready to go to Hong Kong. They could hardly wait!

Chapter 7

IN EARLY JULY 1938, the Huang women and children, including Winter Plum, left Shanghai by steamship. Everyone was seasick, but the young ones soon adjusted to the lulling motions. For most of the journey, Purple Jade stayed in bed.

The ship sailed into Hong Kong Harbor before dawn. They were so excited, none of them could sleep. The girls came on deck and clutched the railings.

"Sarah, look!" Golden Bell cried. "There is Hong Kong Island." The girls had agreed to practice using their English names, even when they spoke in Chinese.

"Oh, Vicky." Silver Bell sucked in the bracing salt air. "Hong Kong looks like the Christmas tree in school!" She hugged herself. "This is a fairy land! Look at all those rows and clusters of lights going up to the top of the mountain!"

"It is the most beautiful sight I have ever seen! This must be a tropical paradise!" Golden Bell pulled her gray silk scarf over her head.

"Oh, I'm so excited, I can hardly stand it!" Silver Bell stood on one foot and then another, and did a little hop and dance. "I wonder if Father is waiting for us down there in the morning chill."

"He's probably just finishing work. Remember, he works for the newspapers."

"Look, the tug boats are coming to guide us to the dock."

When the ship finally docked, the passengers had finished their breakfast. Customs, immigration, and police officers trooped on board. The Caucasian officers in their crisp, neat uniforms impressed the girls. The immigration officials wore spotless white. The police wore khaki shorts and short-sleeved shirts. Each police officer carried a revolver, slung casually from his belt.

In the lounge, a long line of Chinese awaited an inspection of papers. The air turned hot and stifling under the mid-morning sun. "So hot and sticky!" Comely Brook said to Plum Blossom. They took turns fanning the baby and Purple Jade. Children whimpered and adults fidgeted, chatting in subdued irritation. Droning electric fans muffled their mounting noise. The khaki-clad policeman brandished his nightstick barking, "Please stay in your queue! Stay in your queue!"

A family of Europeans entered. They walked straight to the front of the line, where the white officers smiled and greeted them and processed their papers immediately.

"Why aren't they lining up like everyone else?" Silver Bell asked.

"They must be important people," replied Purple Jade.

"No." Silver Bell wiped her forehead. "I played with their little girl yesterday. She said her father is a clerk in the Jardines Company."

Still another European family was given preferential treatment.

"Whites are treated differently here." Golden Bell clenched her fist.

"Speak quietly, children." Her mother shaded her eyes against the intense tropical sunlight. "I've heard of the white man's arrogance. These people are not like Dr. Rankling and Miss Tyler. Hong Kong might be different because it is a British colony."

"Most people are Chinese, so what's the difference?" Silver Bell pouted.

"The difference is that Great Britain is not at war with the East Ocean Devils." She fought an impulse to close her eyes—not knowing whether it was the indignities or the glaring light that pained her. "Anyway, it is imprudent to display your emotions. If you want to see your father again, please keep quiet."

Both girls fell silent. Another European appeared. He directed a porter with two cartloads of boxes, stamped with bold letters: "FRAGILE!" "ANTIQUES!" "HANDLE WITH CARE!" He held out a stack of papers for the customs officials, who shunted aside a waiting Chinese family. It was obvious that the white man would not trust his precious cargo to the luggage handlers. He was going to take a long time to go through customs. The Chinese in the long line began to murmur and fidget. The officer held out his nightstick with both hands. Extending it in front of his chest, he continued to shout: "Stay in your queue, stay in your queue."

The Huang girls grew sullen and peevish. Their morning vision of living in a tropical paradise vanished, and the heat and humidity intensified their bitter realization that they were once again a subjugated people — second-class citizens in their own land.

"Number-one boy!" The haughty police inspector snapped his fingers at a middle-aged ship steward wearing a white Chinese jacket. "Bring lemonade for everyone. We'll have many more hours of processing here." He scowled at the line of Chinese.

Silver Bell asked, "Why does he call that man a 'boy'?"

"I don't know. Perhaps he made a mistake." Her sister edged toward a shady spot between the lounge windows. "I'd love some lemonade."

"Look at all the hair on that foreign devil's arms and legs!" Winter Plum whispered to Comely Brook.

"It is no wonder we call them barbarians," Comely Brook replied under her breath.

"Don't get near them. They smell to high heavens!" Winter Plum tried to sound superior to counteract the arrogance of the white men. She fanned herself.

"When people have active sweat glands, it is difficult for them to control their odor. That would apply to the Chinese as well." Purple Jade motioned toward everyone on line.

Comely Brook eyed the hairy inspector with disgust. "The barbarians smell particularly bad when they've had whiskey and raw meat!"

"The barbarians also take meticulous care to stay clean and neat. We Chinese have a great deal to learn from them." Purple Jade spoke somberly, remembering the antiseptic smell and sparkling orderliness of Dr. Rankling's hospital.

"Number-one boy, get more boys to help you serve!" The officer commanded as the steward came forward pushing a cart loaded with glasses and several pitchers of lemonade. The steward looked vacant. He did not move.

"Go!" the officer bellowed. His face deepened in color. "These Chinese have to be taught everything?"

His remark ruffled a man behind the Huang family. He asked in a clear voice: "How is it possible that these people came from around the world to buy our antiques, but think we need to be taught everything?"

When the steward left, a thin Chinese man in a Sun Yatsen suit spoke, "Brothers and sisters of our country, let's help ourselves. Since there aren't enough glasses, each family will share one or two."

People mumbled. The cart was pushed up and down the line as the Chinese helped themselves to the lemonade.

When the steward returned with several helpers, they were no longer needed. The officer pretended he hadn't noticed. The steward came forward, bowed, and asked with exaggerated courtesy, "Sir, is there anything else I may do for you?" To the Chinese he gave a sidelong glance of pleasure.

"Bring the officers some iced tea," the officer barked. He strode away.

A man behind them spoke to the Huangs. "The white officer acts like a petulant child." He tilted his goatee toward him. "His arrogance is irritating everyone. The British masters are foolish to alienate the natives at this time."

"He called the steward a 'number-one boy' as if he were a superior master." Golden Bell seethed.

"No, young lady," the man replied. "The superior master would call a servant 'old Chen' or 'old Wong,' because he knows that a servant given dignity will render good service. When a man is called a boy, he is robbed of his manhood, and someday he will behave like an irresponsible boy. The officer is sitting on a volcano here."

The man bowed to Purple Jade: "I'm Shih Tar Hai, from Jiang Su Province. My business is in Shanghai. I'm going to buy English wool in Hong Kong."

"Most happy to meet you, Mr. Shih." Purple Jade returned the bow. "My husband works for the *New Island Daily News* here. Thank you for enlightening our daughters."

"Did you say Hong Kong is a volcano?" Silver Bell asked, wide-eyed with alarm.

"Bow to Shih *ba-ba* first, Silver Bell," Purple Jade reminded her.

"Shih *Ba-ba.*" Silver Bell bowed. "Are we on a volcano?"

Golden Bell shook her upturned hands in exasperation. "Not your kind of volcano!"

Mr. Shih smiled. "Native discontent can create an explosive situation. The white man must have the cooperation of the Chinese if he wishes to remain here."

"I hope they get our cooperation," Purple Jade mumbled. "The British are so haughty. The Japanese promised us a 'co-prosperity sphere.' No wonder so many Chinese want to cooperate with them."

"Oh yes, that is just what Mr. Kam . . . said." Golden Bell checked herself just in time. She turned quickly to face the customs table. "Why, it is almost our turn."

She need not have worried that her mother would discover the identity of Mr. Kamasaki. Looking out the window, over the custom officers' heads, Purple Jade's heart swelled as she caught sight of her husband pacing on the far side of the dock. The straw-colored bowler hat was uncharacteristic, but the simple cream-colored Chinese robe was unmistakable. The way the hands were held — gently knotted in the back — the slow pacing with the abrupt turn were distinctive. Purple Jade's months of loneliness, the sense of her solitary burden, and the memory of the nauseating ocean passage evaporated. She stared for a whole minute as if her breath had failed her. Totally unselfconscious, she stretched both arms before her and let out a soft moan, her eyes welling with tears. The eyes of her family followed her yearning arms, and the girls began to shriek in recognition.

Golden Bell's excellent English sped up the immigration process. They were soon cleared for disembarkation.

As the family came on shore, Righteous Virtue rushed forward with outstretched arms.

The girls raced ahead to hug their father, who looked tanned and happy. Purple Jade tarried behind. Righteous Virtue strode smiling toward her. She bowed. He clasped her trembling hands. "Now that my family is back together, I'm a whole man again."

Purple Jade savored the protective grasp of her husband's hands. Her composure restored, she turned and took Little Jade from her mother's arms while Comely Brook and Winter Plum bowed. The heat and the wait had exhausted the baby. She was now sound asleep. Opening her eyes for a brief moment when she was transferred into Purple Jade's arms, she smiled.

"Look at our new daughter!" Purple Jade beamed. Her husband returned Comely Brook's bow and looked fully into the baby's sleepy pink face. "Ah, this is Little Jade. I'm thankful for this new life." He smiled and mumbled almost to himself. Indeed, the dewy face before him had awakened the wild vigor of his youth. He turned and placed his arms around his elder daughters.

He led the girls with their luggage to a waiting cab. Winter Plum supervised another. The baby and Comely Brook got into yet another cab with more luggage, as Righteous Virtue led the convoy with Purple Jade, driving his Buick with the remaining baggage.

Fatigue and the joy of reunion mingled with all the strange sensations of a new place. Purple Jade felt overwhelmed but noted that her household had been reduced from courts of flowering cherry, scented cedars and murmuring bamboo groves, to four dusty and rattling motor cars. A bittersweet smile graced her lips as she looked at her husband. She thanked her Buddha that her family, the vital force that sparked her fervor and maintained the sanity of her life, remained intact. Silently she prayed that she might again find another sympathetic soul like Dr. Rankling so that her involvement with medicine might continue. Yes, she implored her Buddha, let her new activities complement her family life, and she would be complete.

Chapter 8

ALL MEMBERS OF the Huang family began to learn the Cantonese dialect. Purple Jade studied it with special intensity. She knew her inability to communicate would doom her practice in medicine. Her association with Dr. Rankling had been the tonic of her cosseted life. She did not want to feel useless again. Although she had her own room now in their rented house on Blue Pool Road, Comely Brook was the housewife in this small home. She saw only one role for herself — "the small feet doctor."

Over the chessboard on a quiet evening, Purple Jade extolled Dr. Rankling's virtues to her husband. She expressed her sympathy, admiration and respect in oblique terms.

"Doctor Rankling's gray eyes were often hooded by her migraine headaches."

"I know. Her affliction led her to your acupuncture."

"She has wavy hair, cut short and blunt, just above her ears."

"Long flowing hair is usually more attractive in a woman." Her husband concentrated on the game board.

"But Dr. Rankling is imbued with the spirit of service. Her short hair is more convenient. It does not require the kind of fussing long hair demands."

"Perhaps that is why she's not married." Righteous Virtue laughed with a touch of sarcasm. "There are many young women working as secretaries in Shanghai and Hong

Kong. Most of them putter away in their jobs until they find a husband."

"They look very smart doing useful work."

"Some of them may look glamorous, but your intellectual depth and Comely Brook's simplicity far surpass the vagaries of modern fashion."

"I wonder what kind of upbringing encouraged people like Miss Tyler and Dr. Rankling to become so generous and unstinting in their service." Purple Jade rested her head on her palm, stopping the game. "By serving in China, their generosity is directed toward strangers, not their families!"

Righteous Virtue stared at his wife. Their common pride in their heritage had been so pervasive that neither of them considered the flip side of the coin: the tyranny of excessive family cohesion. Traditionally, all munificence outside the family was considered secondary.

"Of course, I could never turn away from the needs of my family." Purple Jade returned her attention to the chessboard. "But would I be neglecting my duties toward you, my lord, if we found another woman doctor, like Dr. Rankling, with whom I might continue my apprenticeship?"

"Of course not, Jade-*mei*! Brook-*mei* is an able manager at home. I'm proud of your services in medicine. I'll look into finding a woman doctor." He beamed at his wife, happy with his own liberal inclinations.

"I have begun my studies in English, but it might be years before I can speak to the foreigners."

"I can probably find you someone who speaks Cantonese." His eyes turned to the game board and found his general under siege. "Ah, Jade-*mei*," he exclaimed with a short laugh, "you're the mainstay here!"

A week later, Righteous Virtue learned of a Dr. Margaret Crozier, a pediatrician, who was conversant in Cantonese. Purple Jade telephoned for an appointment for Little Jade's physical.

Dr. Crozier, only thirty-two years old, was trained in midwifery at Charing Cross Hospital, London. She branched into pediatrics in the colony, where certification procedures were lax and Western doctors in great demand.

She had come to the colony five years ago with her husband, who was a senior cadet — or a "griffin", as the British called them — for the Taipans of the Swires House. The European community in Hong Kong enjoyed a life of elegance and luxury, made possible by an abundance of cheap servants and an unregulated economy. The popular gossip among the colonists was that the slant-eyed Chinese women possessed alluring wiles and a secret sexual prowess. Once established as wives or concubines, they wallowed in a life of material pleasures.

Dr. Crozier had learned sufficient Cantonese to deal with her serving staff and her patients, but she had neither the time nor the inclination to investigate the ways of this Oriental culture.

Purple Jade did not expect Dr. Crozier to be a victim of mysterious pains, like Dr. Rankling. However, she did assume that all Westerners who spoke Chinese, in their adopted land, would be sympathetic toward Chinese customs and curious about Chinese arts.

On the day of the appointment, Purple Jade dressed with special care. A light sprinkling of rose water scented her chignon. She wore no other jewelry or ornaments, except for a rare and luminous bracelet of purple jade. She chose a navy blue sheath of light Shantung silk, cut in the modern style of a *cheongsam*, the slits opening from the ankle to a modest height just below the knees. The supple silk was embossed with the ideograms *fu* and *kway*, the symbols of good luck and fortune. The *cheongsam* hung straight and loose on her slightly rounded frame, lending her an aura of subdued dignity. The only flaw in her appearance was her shuffling gait. She wore cloth shoes several sizes larger than her feet, with cotton stuffed in the empty front portions. She relied on a deliberate scuff of her heels to lift her feet when she walked.

Comely Brook wore a casual cotton print tunic and loose baggy pants to suit the October warmth of the tropics. She held Little Jade in a sling on her back like any *amah* who carried her charge. As soon as they entered the pediatrician's office, she untied the sling and put the baby in her arms.

Dr. Crozier's light brown hair was parted in the middle, and swept up into two pompadours raised high above her forehead. Her high-heeled shoes, erect posture, and lofty hairdo made her look like a tall statue floating above her cigarette smoke. When the Huangs entered, Dr. Crozier left her mahogany desk, snuffed out her cigarette, and offered her hand to Purple Jade.

The regal, pretty young woman enveloped in a cloud of smoke surprised Purple Jade. But she shook the young doctor's hand and bowed deeply. She thought the show of respect was necessary because this glamorous woman, like Dr. Rankling, might become her advocate and provide guidance.

Dr. Crozier did not return the bow as would befit a younger woman. Instead, she stepped briskly over to Comely Brook, and lifted Little Jade from her mother's arms onto the examination table. She addressed Purple Jade without turning to face her: "Ask the baby's *amah* to leave the room."

Comely Brook held on to Little Jade's hand as she stood beside the table. She smiled at the doctor, but remained murmuring to the baby, comforting her in these new surroundings.

"Comely Brook is the baby's mother."

"Oh, my apologies!" Dr. Crozier looked puzzled. "Proceed to undress the baby," she said to Comely Brook and then turned to Purple Jade. "And are you an aunt?"

Purple Jade was aware of the Western disdain for concubines, but she did not want to lie and mislead a future colleague. "No, I'm the senior sister-wife."

Dr. Crozier lifted her head in surprise. She focused her full attention upon them: an audacious female mandarin with an impassive face and a short, mousy woman who looked like a servant. Purple Jade paled under such direct scrutiny; she turned to look at the baby.

The doctor's eyes glowed with curiosity. "Your husband took this young woman for a concubine?"

Purple Jade went dumb with embarrassment.

Noting Purple Jade's imperfect Cantonese, Dr. Crozier repeated her question. "Your husband took this concubine? How barbaric!"

Purple Jade was not prepared for this conversation. She could see the doctor's blue eyes widen in surprise and her pink smooth face turn glossy. The cold fluorescent light caught a glimmer in those clear limpid eyes that carried no hint or shadow of pain.

"No, but, yes. He accepted Brook from me as a birthday present." She spoke to the ground.

"You what? That's impossible!" The wide round eyes fluttered in disbelief. "You did this out of your own free will?" The doctor forgot the half-undressed child and returned to her desk to light another cigarette.

"But that is not why I came.' Purple Jade wanted to change the subject. She gave up trying to keep her composure with this pretty statue in a cloud. With a deliberate effort, she softened the harsh Cantonese accents with her melodious

Hangzhou murmur. "I have studied Chinese medicine and learned the ancient methods of acupuncture and massage. I assisted Dr. Rankling." She stopped, shocked at herself. It was vulgar to prate, to dwell on one's accomplishments. Besides, Dr. Crozier was not listening. She did not seem to understand the mumbling in her Hangzhou accent. Tears of panic and shame welled into Purple Jade's eyes.

"Are you sure your husband did not have to force you?" the doctor asked. She drew deeply on her cigarette and enveloped herself in more smoke. "You can report him to the Social Services Bureau."

Comely Brook looked up with a start. Purple Jade's eyes grew large with alarm. She knew her soft murmur in defective Cantonese must have confused the doctor. She had heard that the English thought the Chinese were barbarous and practiced uncouth customs.

"Hong Kong is English. We believe in freedom of choice. You certainly should not have to tolerate this cruel condition." Dr. Crozier looked down from her lofty height and was surprised to find both women weeping and preparing to leave. "Oh Lord," she cried. "Please calm down! There is no reason to be upset. You've had the tradition for so long!" She snuffed out her cigarette and prepared to return to the baby.

Comely Brook snatched Little Jade away from the doctor's hands. The two women shuffled off, their faces contorted by fury and shame.

Chapter 9

ON THEIR WAY home, Purple Jade followed Comely Brook into the pedicab wondering, *Why did I behave in such an unseemly manner? It was against all propriety that I should brag about my limited experience in medicine, and so soon after meeting the pediatrician. My usual finesse seemed to have been swept away under the young doctor's forthright expressions. I should have swallowed my pride and invited her to tea, I should have allowed time to cultivate our relationship. But it is too late now. Why did I feel hurt when she pitied me? But I feel the hurt even now.*

What had the pretty doctor said? "We believe in freedom of choice." Yes, Dr. Crozier and Dr. Rankling were free to choose the medical profession. That choice was not open to me in my society. I can remember a time when I wept and even envied my brother who was able to study in Shanghai. What would it be like to be trained as a doctor? Surely my perceptions would be different. My choices for my family would not come back to vex me now. It seems ridiculous now that a year and half ago I undertook the distressing and delicate office of finding our family an heir.

Comely Brook sensed her mistress's unease. "The doctor is too young!"

"Yes, she is very young, very pretty, and perhaps also very clever."

"But she's rude to say those things."

"Westerners tend to speak straight from the shoulder. We're not used to their ways."

"She said we're barbaric!"

"We call foreigners barbarians, too. Perhaps she does not understand our emphasis on education, patience and social harmony."

Comely Brook understood. To maintain harmony and give comfort, a cultured woman like her mistress would have practiced detachment and taken the time to understand a new situation. "The doctor must not have come from a book-fragrant family!"

"What makes you say that?"

"Why, her clothes are all crispy new! The new rich are always wasteful! Remember how Ah Lee used to show off the fancy suits his foreign master gave him? The foreigners discarded them simply because they were tired of wearing them. Why, the suits were practically new!"

"Yes, Brook-*mei*, even in our noblest homes, fine clothing was passed down from generation to generation."

"Ah Lee also made a habit of giving away bits of fancy wrapping paper to the maids so they could fold them into birds, flowers and animals and decorate their rooms. Once, even Silver Bell accepted some because Ah Lee said his wife cleaned the Shanghai foreigners' house and took the paper, which the foreigners had thrown away. Imagine throwing precious paper away every time they opened a present!"

"Yes, Westerners are wasteful, but the Chinese misuse other human beings, and especially female resources."

"What do you mean?"

"We call servants *Yon jen*—people for use."

Comely Brook could not understand why her mistress defended the foreigners, but many ideas were beyond her comprehension.

"I'm not sure I understand. It is my fate to be part of the Huang family!" Comely Brook sat tall in the pedicab. "Surely there is no shame in loving service."

"Of course not." Purple Jade nodded. *Perhaps it was Comely Brook's fate to be a domestic vassal.* She did not know how to clarify her ideas.

The pedicab driver let out a soft moan. He groaned and hunched into his handle bar as he pedaled up a steady rise leading into the hills of Blue Pool Road. Purple Jade watched the sweat pour down his bare shoulders. His muscles strained and bulged as he propelled the tricycle under the tropical sun. Sitting in the shaded cab behind, Purple Jade thought: *How much more disgusted I should have felt seeing inhuman treatment. Our society bound my feet.* It all seemed so plain to her now. Except for the freedom to write poetry, her education had stifled her creativity, her need to explore and understand the world. *Oh, how I enjoyed my rare occasions of independence and active accomplishments! My ride to destroy the opium den and my work with Dr. Rankling were the only highlights of my confined life.* "I read that many Western women are now learning how to drive," she said aloud.

"Oh, I wish I could drive!" Comely Brook exclaimed. "The Dragon master can do so many things just because he can drive." She also seemed to remember their raid on Prosperous Dream.

Purple Jade sighed. *With my bound feet, the joy of mobility would always be limited for me. Why did I accept such limitations? Perhaps the fear of new influences blinded me. Instead of complaining and seeking vindication, I made my home a fortress for the teachings of our ancestors. All my sacrifices for the good of the family were my true conceit. The liberating Western values that came with war and Chinese humiliation became a personal tragedy. Didn't Miss Tyler mention that America grew strong by taking in new immigrants and the best of their cultures? But I refused to see the benefits of an open society where foreign ways were assimilated. The sage taught the golden rule of the mean, but I indulged in such cultural pride that I failed to see this same hubris causing war and destruction.*

The pedicab swerved and cruised down the center of the road to avoid potholes. A motorcar brushed past them, honking furiously. The Caucasian driver leaned out the window to gesticulate and curse. The pedicab driver swerved to the side. He cursed back, spitting at the car. Both Purple Jade and Comely Brook grabbed on to Little Jade and the cab ever more tightly as they rode over the bumps on the road.

"Some Westerners are so snobbish!" Comely Brook muttered a curse of her own. "Remember how the foreigners were allowed to cut in line on our ship when we first arrived in Hong Kong?"

"Yes. Still, we must embrace the Buddhist teaching of loving tolerance and dispersing good wishes upon every human and living creature, because we believe in the essential unity of life."

Comely Brook was calmed by her mistress's usual kindness. "Yes, I remember hearing the young mistresses sing Christmas carols, sending good wishes upon the whole earth. But some foreigners like Dr. Rankling and Miss Tyler must also have studied the Buddha's teaching."

"Yes, I suppose. I wish we could have spent more time exploring our common ground with the Christians."

"But the Westerners say people are born equal. If every rickshaw puller wanted to live like the nobles, what ruthless killings and debauchery would result!" Comely Brook was still trying to understand.

"Yes, anarchy would ensue if people had no idea what equality meant." Purple Jade answered, surprised that Comely Brook had thought of such matters. "Still, Westerners believe that everyone has a right to an education. If we can agree with their concept that each person is endowed with thoughts and feelings worthy of singular attention, more opportunities and development would surely follow."

In Hangzhou, secure in her rank and status, her conduct and snobbery had seemed like a moral perfection. She saw it all now with a clarity that had eluded her. *How presumptuous I was with Orchid! If Orchid had been accorded all the rights and dignity of a human being as the Westerners saw it, it would have been inconsiderate, indelicate and irrational of me to give her to an older married man! What madness and blindness led me to do such a thing! Yes, service to the needy must be my way to descend from my pedestal.*

"While you nurture the family in your way, I must devote my life to serving in a different way." She reached out to hold Orchid's hand.

"You mean working with pregnant women as you did in Shanghai?"

"Perhaps." Purple Jade sighed. "But Dr. Rankling is still in Shanghai."

Purple Jade could feel their frustration. Yes, Western ideas led to many new understandings. She could see it now: *Giving my husband a concubine was most propitious in Hangzhou, but under the new light of a strange culture, it is monstrous and barbarous. Dr. Crozier had called it cruel. If only I had not been so proud, justifying all my actions by cultural pride. Oh, I should have learned something from Miss Tyler's tutoring!*

I cannot allow the problems of dislocation to pass into my husband's hands alone. I practically forced Virtue to take a concubine! Comely Brook and the baby are not my flesh and blood, but I love them — like a mother? Not really, more like a father. I should have chosen my younger brother as a model to emulate. Glorious Dragon disregarded all old conventions, but followed the dictates of his mind and heart. In the end, aren't love and friendship the paramount virtues? Yes, I will make sure that Comely Brook and the baby receive the proper respect and care in my society. By the terms of our culture, I did not commit any hideous crime. But . . . She turned to release Little Jade's thumb from her mouth, and to reassure the young mother. "Yes, Brook-*mei*, the Western women work very hard to make sure our days of insignificance are over. We must not allow our anxieties to impede our progress."

Comely Brook was confused. She could not understand her mistress's words. How can anxieties get in the way of progress? Perhaps her mistress was being kind as usual. In intellectual matters, she was afraid to ask for specifics. Her mistress read books and carried on conversations that were incomprehensible to her. At last, she determined that what her mistress meant by progress might have come from her work with Dr. Rankling in Shanghai. Yes, she must somehow help her — allow her mistress to enjoy the same work she did in Shanghai. This visit with the pretty doctor had caused them anxieties. The doctor was too young. She had breached the necessary decorum that would have given them face. She was certain that the doctor's failure to suppress her surprise and her obvious insensitivity to the customs of the land had intimidated them. Hazily, she thought it had something to do with herself and Little Jade. Her mistress had elevated her to the status of a sister-wife. This was a more magnanimous gift than money. The old phantom of wishing for a son came back to rebuke her. To her, there was only one way to gain respect. She resolved to have another try for a son. She prayed again to be blessed with an heir. Perhaps then even foreigners would have to give them face.

When they returned home, Comely Brook helped Purple Jade out of her silk gown and into her comfortable cotton sheath. She knelt before her silent mistress and broke into sobs. "*Tai-tai*, I've caused you shame."

"No, please stand, Brook-*mei*," Purple Jade whispered. "Some foreigners are ignorant of our ways. We don't seem to understand each other, and we have not learned from each other."

On a rainy morning a week later, Comely Brook rushed into the room where Purple Jade sat reading. "*Tai-tai*, *Tai-tai*, there is a medical emergency. Come down and meet the elder Old Fan." She smiled broadly, in spite of the urgency. She looked so triumphant that Purple Jade did not protest, but allowed herself to be led toward the living room, where a man in a workman's short jacket and baggy trousers stood holding his straw rain cape and hat.

"Old Fan is a fisherman. His wife has gone into labor. They don't have enough money to consult a real doctor." Comely Brook babbled on as they descended the stairs. "Some days ago, I told the fish stall owner in the market what you did in Shanghai, and today, Old Fan came."

Old Fan did not lift his head when Purple Jade entered the room. He knelt and knocked his head on the floor. "Huang *tai-tai*, my wife is in great pain. The baby is not positioned right. The midwife doesn't know what to do."

"I'll come with you," Purple Jade responded at once.

Comely Brook quickly rounded up a raincoat and umbrella. "Old Fan has a rickshaw waiting." She handed her mistress the old medicine bag, which she had secretly prepared some days ago. "I have included acupuncture needles, sterilizing equipment, rubber gloves, and the various ointments for massage."

Purple Jade smiled. "Tell the lord where I am when he wakes. Brook-*mei*, you are a gem."

"I hope you do not mind tending to a fisherman's wife!"

"No Brook-*mei*, her needs are just as real as those of book-fragrant families. There were many indigent patients in Dr. Ranklin's hospital."

Old Fan rose and bowed his thanks repeatedly. He led Purple Jade to the rickshaw and ran beside the puller leading them to the harbor.

A waiting sampan ferried Old Fan and Purple Jade to the houseboat in Abedeen where Old Fan lived. The gentle rain-misted air obscured the vast sea. Purple Jade was reminded of her boat rides on West Lake, and the fisherman's family who had brought her to Shanghai after her home was destroyed. She looked at Old Fan, and realized that he was in fact a rather young man, deeply sunburnt. Seams lined his forehead, nearly burying his deep-set eyes. Buckteeth dominated his face, which had an expression of profound tenderness. As they drew near the houseboat, Old Fan's wrinkles sank deeper at the sound of his wife's screams.

Purple Jade held on tightly to Old Fan's hand as he helped her to the houseboat. She took no notice of the disorder in the small cabin. She knelt before the screaming woman.

"*Shh* . . . try not to thrash." Her soothing voice and strong firm hands calmed the woman. She ordered the midwife to boil her needles. She inserted two needles into each leg, one a little below the knee, and the other slightly above the inner aspect of the ankle. Soon the patient became peaceful. Then Purple Jade began to massage the woman. Rubbing Tiger Balm ointment on her hands, she instructed the laboring woman in deep breathing while she gently pushed and manipulated her pelvic area for what seemed like hours until the child's head descended the birth canal. She washed her hands and put on a new pair of sterile rubber gloves. She reached for the head and coached the mother to push and breathe.

Old Fan shook and wept, when his son was placed into his arms. Purple Jade was too elated to notice her sore arms and sweat-drenched body. The delivery had taken four hours. Her knees felt raw from rubbing the floor. Tired but ebullient, she quietly ordered the midwife to bathe the baby and tidy up the small chamber. She refused any payment and asked only to be taken home.

Once home, Comely Brook quickly prepared a hot steamy bath for her mistress. The girls tiptoed around their mother in awe, and Purple Jade knew she had found her calling. She had no words to describe her feeling of satisfaction and fulfillment — she had calmed the searing pain of the mother and brought a new life into the world.

Every morning from that day on, Old Fan left a choice fish with the fish stall owner in the market for Winter Plum or Comely Brook to come and take home to her mistress.

Chapter 10

IN SHANGHAI, GLORIUS Dragon resumed his life of glamour. He missed his sister and his nieces, but the Huang and Chou factories were now busy with orders from the Japanese. His many business enterprises and social commitments consumed all his energy. He abandoned his bachelor apartment and openly hosted dinner parties in Bright Crystal's villa on Avenue Joffre. Dragon and Bright Crystal talked frequently of marriage but procrastinated their union. So many of their friends had known them as *tang* cousins that they felt awkward acknowledging their long years of deception.

One evening, as Glorious Dragon returned home from work, he found two Japanese sentries stationed in front of Bright Crystal's house. A white flag with the red sun of Japan fluttered from the arch over the great steel door. The soldiers refused to admit him.

"General Goto's order!"

Glorious Dragon left, not daring to utter a word of protest. He went to his sister's house, where Iris now lived with Lt. Kamasaki.

No one knew that General Goto was enthralled by Bright Crystal's sophisticated taste and saucy elegance. Glorious Dragon realized that he and Bright Crystal needed Goto's political protection. After gaining so many contracts from the Japanese army, they were now in his debt.

Inside her villa, Bright Crystal ordered tea, shrimp dumplings, and other Chinese savories that General Goto favored. Following Japanese custom, General Goto removed his boots at the door. He apologized for his uninvited presence, stating with exaggerated graciousness that her household was the most comfortable he had ever known.

He sank his scrawny body into the deep sofa, but his short legs did not reach the floor. His calves stuck out over the edge, while his stockinged feet dangled in front. When he took out a cigarette, Bright Crystal leaned forward to light it, as she used to do for her important guests.

General Goto sucked on his cigarette, saliva foaming in one corner of his mouth. With one long breath, he exhaled to blow out the match and in the same instant caught hold of Bright Crystal's jeweled hand. He narrowed his beady eyes to look at her through the smoky veil but left the cigarette dangling from his lips. With his free hand, he drew her arm down with a vigorous tug. Crystal tumbled to the floor, tripped by his projecting legs. She had twisted out of the way just in time to avoid falling into his lap.

Bright Crystal was accustomed to dealing with the indiscretions of drunken men, but General Goto was obviously sober. Though filled with rage, she knew she must hold her tongue. She lowered her head briefly to hide her disgust. When she raised her head, her eyes glowed with annoyance, and she gave a sharp, exasperating cry:

"What a clumsy fool I am!" Her voice rose to a shrill shout. "Little Snow, bring a wet cloth. I just dropped a match on General Goto's uniform."

General Goto was startled by the loud cry, but before he could resume his pursuit, Little Snow had come in. He had to relinquish Crystal's arm and allow the serving girl to wipe away the small soot mark on his pants.

"Oh, General Goto, you must be annoyed by my stupid blunder." Bright Crystal regained her composure. She sat on a winged chair across from the general and lit a cigarette.

"Enough. That's all right." Goto brushed Little Snow away with a scowl, irritated that his act of seduction was interrupted.

"General Goto, you must stay for dinner and let me redeem myself." Bright Crystal knew very well that the enemy had no intention of leaving, so now she would play the gracious hostess. "Little Snow, tell the kitchen that General Goto and his guards will stay for dinner with Lieutenant and Mrs. Kamasaki, Mr. Chou and myself. Oh, of course, the guards are to be fed in the back parlor." She gave her orders with a swish of her hand and spat out puffs of smoke as if exasperated by such mundane details.

"I didn't know you were expecting guests. Lieutenant. Kamasaki did not mention anything."

"I arranged it this morning with Iris." She lied. "I have a new gown that I want to show her."

"I've been patient." Goto had decided to show his hand. Bright Crystal understood in a flash that the swaggering brute was about to proclaim his affection in broken Chinese. She must not allow him to continue.

"I've been patient too." She looked at General Goto sideways. "I hope you're not working Lieutenant Kamasaki too hard. They are supposed to be here by now." She walked toward the phone as she spoke and dialed Iris's number before the general could object.

"Hello, Iris? What has delayed you? General Goto is joining us for dinner!" she said as soon as the phone was answered.

"Uncle Dragon is here," Iris said. "The soldiers at your door would not let him in!"

"Glorious Dragon was held up in the office, and you are coming together?" Bright Crystal spoke very loudly. She did not pause to listen to the assurance that all three would come to her rescue.

General Goto, frustrated by Bright Crystal's teasing playfulness, was also aroused. He snuffed out his cigarette. His uniform's stiff collar chafed at his neck; he whipped open the first few buttons on his jacket. "Damn! I wish I had a soft kimono here." In one quick maneuver, he slipped his feet to the floor and proceeded toward Bright Crystal. Fondling her breast, he said, "Let's make it official. Tell Kamasaki that I'm taking General Chin's place." He laughed. He hadn't expected Bright Crystal to be so compliant. She was behaving in the most beguiling manner. Even as she talked on the telephone, she smiled at him, allowing her dimples to quiver.

"Oh General Goto, you mustn't now . . . What will the servants think." Bright Crystal cooed coyly, half to the general, half into the phone. "Well, Iris, I can't talk. Come as soon as you can." She hung up.

"From now on, Mr. Chou will not be allowed in this house!" General Goto growled urgently. He pulled Bright Crystal into his arms. He had received intelligence that Glorious Dragon was not actually a cousin but a lover. He had plans to take care of Dragon very soon.

"But I invited him long ago." Bright Crystal extricated herself firmly.

"That owner of the uniform company writes bad propaganda in Hong Kong. Mr. Chou cannot be a manager anymore. We will take over the factory!" General Goto did not mean to reveal his intention, but he felt the need to gloat.

"Oh!" Bright Crystal was too shocked to respond. Her heart was beating wildly, and her mind raced ahead. She knew she must buy more time. Fawning to placate the general, she whispered smiling, "We must not be hasty. You must be comfortable here. Give me a week. I'll have your kimono and a tatami room ready." She looked at him with a meaningful wink. "Only one week."

General Goto was more stirred than ever. He had waited a long time to make this move. But Lt. Kamasaki's uncle was a major general, and Goto did not wish to offend the lieutenant. He was uncertain how Bright Crystal and Glorious Dragon were related to Iris Kamasaki. It was not easy to collect information. Since the lieutenant was in the *Kempetai,* bypassing his authority on espionage was highly irregular. He'd had to select a special agent, and after eight months, he still lacked a clear understanding. The agent insisted that Mrs. Kamasaki was once a servant in a country manor. But that seemed preposterous! Who had ever heard of a maid speaking English and quoting Shakespeare? The agent must have listened to envious gossip. General Goto was impressed by Iris's social graces and secretly admired Lt. Kamasaki's unusual choice of a wife. He recently had learned that Bright Crystal, Glorious Dragon and Iris were not related, and that General Chin had been Bright Crystal's sponsor. Clearly, Lt. Kamasaki would have no right to interfere, now that General Goto had decided to take over the sponsorship.

He turned away from Bright Crystal with a smirk. "I'll wait one week and no more!" He paced the room in irritation. It would not do to have Kamasaki see him under the spell of a woman. "I'm coming back in one week, exactly! I expect my quarters to be ready for me." He turned abruptly, preparing to leave when Bright Crystal extended her hand for him to kiss.

"Do you have to leave?" Bright Crystal purred. "We are all going to be so disappointed!" She smiled and set her dimples into full view. "Please, General Goto, leave a few guards at the front gate to protect me!" She knew it would be better to have the guards openly stand watch, keeping away Chinese spies.

General Goto left feeling very pleased with himself. He speculated that perhaps Bright Crystal had been hoping for his protection all along. Mr. Chou might not be her lover after all. Dashing young men were seldom faithful or constant. But General Goto hoped she wasn't expecting to marry him, since he already had a wife in Japan. Ah, that Kamasaki's American education had spoiled the women, he thought. Bright Crystal must be fishing for a husband. Yes, it would be more comfortable to have a Japanese-style house to share with Bright Crystal. He would give her a week to get ready. Where could she go? He gave a casual order to the two guards at the front gate to note the identity of all visitors.

Bright Crystal, highly agitated when General Goto finally left her house, lit one cigarette after another. Feeling defiled and uneasy, she knew her coquettish behavior, which had so captivated the men around her, had now trapped a viper. Over the years, she had cultivated the movements of her mouth, her eyes, her dimples, and the gestures of her hands. She even learned to control the lifting and arching of her brows. Her charm had brought her financial security, social influence and even passionate love. But she now realized that she was playing with fire, and Glorious Dragon had been drawn into her destructive flame. When at last her friends arrived, she collapsed into Dragon's arms, babbling, apologizing and ranting her outrage.

The crisis brought Bright Crystal's father from the kitchen, who joined them in their deliberations. Everyone agreed that Glorious Dragon should go into hiding immediately. If a way could be found, they should both escape to

Hong Kong and then America, where they might begin life anew as a common working couple.

"No, I cannot go until I personally avenge my country in one battle," Glorious Dragon proclaimed after some thought. "I'm sorry, Akiro, if this will cause you trouble. Your military government and some of our corrupt generals have inflicted so much pain and destruction that I simply cannot run away without lifting a finger to help."

"We know you have already helped a great deal," Iris said. While others might speak of Glorious Dragon as a sycophant to the enemy, she knew he had given generously to the support of all the kinsfolk in Shanghai and Hangzhou.

Lt. Kamasaki shrugged and paced. He wanted to smuggle Glorious Dragon and Bright Crystal onto a ship for Hong Kong, but he could not help his friends fight his army.

"My Dragon is correct." Everyone was surprised to hear Bright Crystal's support. "We must redeem ourselves on the battlefield." She lowered her head. Her eyes were full. No one could doubt her resolve.

Her father moved close to her. He held her hand and nodded mechanically as if in a trance. "I understand. Old Yuan told me the German consulate has been looking for a cook. I will go and apply. You have done more for your old father than I could ever hope for."

"Oh *ba-ba*, you are a dear." Crystal wept in her father's arms.

"Akiro." Glorious Dragon stood up to face his friend. "You and Iris must leave now. What we need to do cannot involve you. We appreciate what you have already done for us."

Iris and Lt. Kamasaki looked on their friends with admiration, anxiety, and sympathy. "There is a cargo freight liner leaving for Hong Kong in a month's time. If you want to get on it, try to send this to Iris at the uniform factory." Lt. Kamasaki took off his American high school ring. "This will be your secret password. Then check into the International Hotel under the name of Mr. and Mrs. Kam. I'll get in touch with you then."

Bowing, the men shook hands while Glorious Dragon thanked his Japanese friend again for his help. Iris and Bright Crystal lingered in each other's arms.

In the evening, Bright Crystal called General Goto and requested that he send construction workers and painters to refurbish her house. The guest suite on the second floor must have new sliding screen doors and window shades; the finest tatami mats must be ordered for the floor; bathroom fixtures must be changed into the Japanese style, and the whole house given a fresh coat of paint.

Flattered by her elaborate plans and preparations, General Goto agreed not to visit. He would wait to be surprised at the end of the week. Glorious Dragon and Bright Crystal talked far into the night and planned their escape.

The next morning, Glorious Dragon left openly in his limousine, going straight to the banks to transfer most of his funds to America. At the last bank, he sauntered into the men's room and peeled off his Western wool suit, revealing a crumpled cotton tunic and trousers. He slipped out of the bank with the noonday crowd and disappeared. His chauffeur reported him missing after waiting for him the whole day in the bank's parking lot.

General Goto sent droves of workers and one spy. He was recognized at once because he was the only one who smoked and paced more than he worked. Whenever Little Snow or Little Lotus brought the workers food and drink, he took the first and largest helpings. Soon the serving girls brought the workers beer and wine.

Bright Crystal came out to inspect the workers the first afternoon. She held a perfumed handkerchief over her mouth as if the dust was overpowering. The small dash of pepper in her handkerchief made her sneeze, tear, and cough. She ran back to her room and called General Goto. Little Snow pinched her nose together and spoke for her mistress, complaining of the dust and the cold she was catching. She asked for more workers to speed up the work.

The next day, the whole house became more confused than ever with the added workers. Bright Crystal emerged from her room coughing and sneezing to inspect their progress. She could barely reach the staircase because of the severity of her sneezing attacks. That afternoon, she changed into a maid's cotton suit, and stole down to the kitchen to bid her father farewell. She walked out her front gate like a housemaid carrying a basket. The guards at the door took no notice; so many servants and workers had been passing all day.

The maids brought food and drink to the spy and flirted with him. They complained about the extra chore of nursing a sick woman.

While Bright Crystal was supposedly sick in bed with a cold, Little Snow continued to call General Goto everyday in her pinched voice and discoursed on her health, the house, and what she most wanted the general to buy for her.

"Oh, a Rolls Royce would be divine!"

The general huffed, puffed, and temporized. "I am not a rich man, but I will try."

Early in the morning on the fifth day, Little Lotus ran to the spy in alarm. Bright Crystal was missing from her room. The frightened guards had no idea how she could have eluded them. No one had entered or left the house last night. Both the front and back doors had been guarded, and the high walls surrounding the garden were covered with shards of broken glass on top.

Three nights earlier, a man in a worker's suit had met a maidservant by the dock of the Hwangpo River. They took a sampan and were carried to Hangzhou. There, they got help from Lao Wang and caught a train. By the fifth day, Glorious Dragon and Bright Crystal had reached Changsha, in Hunan Province.

Chapter 11

ON THE TRAIN Bright Crystal asked, "Why are we going to Changsha?"

"The rail line between Hankow to Canton is an essential supply route for the Chinese guerrilla forces in the region. Changsha is a key rail center," Glorious Dragon explained.

"How are we to fit into their war plans?" Bright Crystal snuggled close, resting her head on her Dragon's shoulder. It was hard to find comfort on the hard seat of a rattling train.

Glorious Dragon moved to one end of the seat. He spread out his jacket to cushion Crystal and drew her head down to rest on his lap. "One of my classmates from high school, Tall Man Wu, is an administrative assistant to General Hsueh of the Ninety-ninth Army. Changsha is under its protection."

"Have you been in touch with Tall Man Wu? Does the army want us?" Bright Crystal yawned.

"Yes." Glorious Dragon played with her hair. "I have been secretly buying and shipping arms and ammunition there. You sleep and rest."

When they finally arrived in Changsha, Tall Man Wu welcomed them warmly. As they drove in town, Crystal felt cheered by the sight of children running and laughing in the marketplace. People gossiped and joked on the streets, but a rancid smell of raw meat and vegetables filled her nostrils.

They were offered a suite of rooms in a mountain retreat away from the bustling town. Glorious Dragon protested. He had come to fight; he would not be treated like a guest benefactor. Bright Crystal concurred, and they were moved into a peasant's home closer to town.

The mud-floored hut featured a crude table, several stools, and one armchair. The door and windows were hewn from slabs of pine, and rice paper served as windowpanes. The buffeting cold winds of November whistled through the hut's many crevices. Bright Crystal hopped onto the *kan* as soon as she entered the house. The *kan*, a platform bed, was built with bricks and cement. Cotton quilts on the surface helped to soften it. Several times a day, a peasant came with charcoal or wood to feed the fire in its belly, so the *kan* was also where they warmed their tea. Though Bright Crystal missed her city comforts, she was determined to make herself at home in this rude cottage.

From their mud-walled hut, Tall Man Wu led them to the supply depot, which was clustered behind the frame and brick buildings near the town's south end. A high earthen wall surrounded the compound with trenches on all sides. They toured the trenches. Crystal learned the names of different firearms in the depot and Dragon peppered his friend with many questions on the details of the operations. Tunnels connected this part of the fortress to the administration building, where they took their meals in the officers' dining hall.

They were also initiated into the beaten paths of short cuts and safe passages that led into the sandbagged embankments and other fortifications around town. There were reports of skirmishes nearby. Everyone anticipated a major battle. They soon became accustomed to the sight of soldiers walking about with guns strapped to their backs.

Since neither Bright Crystal nor Glorious Dragon was familiar with firearms, Tall Man Wu taught them how to use the carbine, the submachine gun, and the grenades.

Everyday they practiced target shooting in the numbing cold. Soon, they no longer jumped, when they heard explosives.

The soldiers wore cotton-quilted winter uniforms. When the pair first changed into the bulky gray garb, they pointed to each other and laughed at their rounded shapes. "We're like two rolls of stuffed sausages!" Bright Crystal cried. Now they wore the practical uniform day and night to keep warm and be ready for action at any hour.

"I still don't think I can handle a gun, my Dragon," Bright Crystal whispered as she cuddled in her lover's arm on the *kan*. They gazed at the thatched roof, where a frame of parallel twigs supported a thick mat of hay. The clean smell of drying hay pervaded the room, and the novelty of simple, Spartan living seemed romantic.

"When the enemy comes, I want you to go to the mountain retreat. You're not combat-ready," Glorious Dragon answered. He was more cold and tired than he could ever remember, but he never felt more tender and grateful toward Crystal. He had not expected her company in this venture. They had never discussed patriotism, but they must have shared the same thoughts.

"No, I'll stay by you, my Dragon. You're no more combat-ready than I am." Dragon was about to protest when the siren sounded. They leapt from their nest and ran toward headquarters to obtain their instructions.

They rushed past soldiers shouting and scrambling into their positions in trenches and lookout points. When they reached the general's office, the tense and solemn faces of the officers sobered them. All eyes were riveted on the conference table. Instead of being covered with the usual array of ashtrays and teacups, it now had a large map with a jumble of telephone and electronic equipment pushed to one side. No one noticed Glorious Dragon and Bright Crystal when they slipped into the room.

"Our scouts have reported a Japanese forward platoon south of Yochow. Here." General Hsueh pointed with a marker. "We believe the platoon is backed by several armored divisions. So we can expect a Hitler-style blitzkrieg within twenty-four hours." He sank down into an armchair, exhausted by the hours of vigil-keeping and deliberation. He motioned Tall Man Wu to carry on the instructions.

"Our mission, as you all know, is to safeguard Changsha and keep the rail lines open all the way to Canton." Tall Man Wu, towering over everyone, traced the rail line on the map with his pointer. His imposing voice was firm but soft, belying his large muscular frame.

"Lieutenant Liu will go to Yochow with his brigade to set up communication links with headquarters. Lieutenant Chang, take two brigades to assist in the evacuation of Changsha. Other brigades have been dispatched to man the trenches and move ammunition."

Everyone seemed to have been prepared for this emergency. Tall Man Wu looked around the room and lifted his chin to dismiss the lieutenants. He raised his hand in a casual salute as everyone left to carry out their assignments.

Glorious Dragon realized that the command had not given him a combat role. He confronted Tall Man Wu and demanded action.

"I'm sorry, my friend. I know you want to see action, but we are already in your debt for the ammunition you sent. You and Bright Crystal must remain in the headquarters to coordinate the communications coming in."

Glorious Dragon understood the urgency of the situation. Since Bright Crystal had steadfastly refused to be separated from him, he must accept the relative security of the headquarters. His venturesome spirit felt thwarted, but there was his Crystal — a protective angel or a millstone around his neck. He accepted his orders with a sullen nod and trudged toward the communications room, pulling Bright Crystal along with him.

All afternoon, Lieutenant Liu reported on the advancing enemy's movements. Bright Crystal brewed tea and quietly served everyone. All at once, they heard droning planes overhead. Gunshots erupted like thousands of firecrackers. The ground shook. A sudden roar of fire engulfed the building in great tongues of orange and red.

"Run to the shelter! Run to the shelter!"

"What happened? What happened?"

"Were we hit?"

"Worse! Some bombs hit the ammunition pile near our entrance."

A bitter wind whipped the fire onto the bone-dry timber, and turned the thatched roof into a bonfire. The entire town was soon ablaze.

In the communications room, a wild scramble ensued. "Help me move the equipment into the tunnels," shouted the man next to Dragon.

Smoke choked the rooms, as beams and pillars split and collapsed all around them. Dragon scooped up his radio and groped his way toward the tunnel, calling Bright Crystal to follow him.

Gray forms screamed and pushed around him. Everyone and everything seemed to be moving, crashing, coughing and crying. Glorious Dragon followed the crowd, totally confused. He clutched the radio to his body and stumbled ahead. As soon as he reached the cool damp tunnel, the soldiers behind him closed the trap door to prevent the smoke from descending. Another soldier passed Glorious Dragon his canteen for a sip of water.

Dragon dropped his equipment in alarm. "Bright Crystal, where is she?" He scanned the murmuring dark forms and shouted, "Crystal, my Crystal, are you here?"

Most soldiers knew the visiting Shanghai couple who had come to help. An unnatural hush followed Glorious Dragon's anxious call. Glorious Dragon battled his way to the trap door. Restraining hands grabbed him.

"It's a furnace up there."

"You won't survive."

"You can't find her."

"You'll bring in the fire."

"You'll kill us all!"

Glorious Dragon yelled and pleaded to be let go. Kicking and scratching, he could barely be restrained. The soldier with the canteen tore off his shirt and wet it. He tied it loosely around Glorious Dragon's head and helped him to the trap door. He splashed the remaining water over Glorious Dragon and commanded: "Keep your face to the ground."

Once out of the trap door, Glorious Dragon broke into a crouched run and retraced his route of escape, which by now had become an inferno. Fiery splinters fell about him, singeing his wet clothes and scorching his bare hands. He coughed and bellowed for his Crystal.

A distinctly feminine moan rose behind him. He stumbled back and saw Bright Crystal on the floor. A fallen beam had pinned her legs. He kicked the beam. In one tug, he had pulled her free. He dragged her along, shielding her with his body. They finally reached the trap door. "Open the door! Open the door!" he screamed, stomping on it with all his might. He lost consciousness.

When he awoke, he was in an underground room. A nurse came to help him drink. Tall Man Wu hovered over him and smiled when he saw Glorious Dragon regaining consciousness.

"Where, where is my Crystal . . ."

Tall Man Wu grimaced, his face contorting. He tried to hold back his tears and choked. He turned away. Glorious Dragon sank back into his bed, with silent tears of despair. He understood.

"She died speaking of you. She even smiled, because she was so proud." Tall Man Wu's voice wobbled. "You must feel honored to have such love and respect."

Glorious Dragon did not respond. He turned his face to the wall. His whole body writhed. Tall Man Wu instructed the nurse to sedate his friend and left to direct the war.

Glorious Dragon felt a warm breeze on his face. The budding spring flowers and tender greens sprouted all over their garden in Hangzhou. He was playing shuttlecock with Bright Crystal, kicking it back and forth with the front and sides of their feet in expert rhythm. Purple Jade stood in the pavilion counting, clapping, and laughing like a teenage girl.

He twisted his torso and swung his right leg behind him in a nimble skip and hop to give the shuttlecock a vigorous back kick. The shuttlecock flew like a missile and hit Bright Crystal in the eye. Glorious Dragon awoke in a sweat.

There was a dull rumble, which grew louder. "Is this the sound of a motor? Where is it coming from?" Glorious Dragon asked the dimly lit room, unaware that the nurse was attending another soldier in the gloom.

"We have already repelled two waves of enemy attacks. I think a full armored division must be coming."

Reality dawned upon Glorious Dragon. He sat up with a sudden jerk. He had come here to fight. Now Bright Crystal was dead; why was he lying here in comfort? He did not ask for instructions. He got up from his bed and dragged himself out of the tunnel. He stumbled into the trenches. Passing through the supply depot, he stuffed his pockets and the inside of his belted jacket with hand grenades. The depot was deserted; all the able-bodied men had gone to meet the oncoming tanks.

When he emerged from cover, a wind cleared Glorious Dragon's head. As far as he could see, the town had been scorched to the ground. Swirling winds of dust and ash blurred the faces of the soldiers crouching along the trenches. He surveyed the crowd, but could not recognize anyone. Someone pointed in the direction the armored division would be coming from, and he saw the mound of half-torn brick wall where he could take cover and intercept the advance. He walked with calm deliberation toward the half wall and ignored the shouts of warning. He was leaving the farthest outpost of town where no one could cover him.

Glorious Dragon cowered near the wall and heard the rumble of oncoming tanks shaking the ground underneath. Rifle fire broke out somewhere. He felt bullets zinging over his head, zapping and pinging off the surrounding brick wall.

He groped for a hand grenade and felt for the pin. In the rush to get into position, Dragon did not notice how stiff and strangely uncooperative his hands had become. He felt no pain. The cold had frozen the burns, but he could barely feel where the pins were and he could not maneuver his fingers to pull them. He also knew he could not grasp the grenades and therefore would fail to throw far. In his panic and frustration, he yelled so loudly, his voice echoed through the valley. Suddenly, he remembered his dream and the idyllic garden of his childhood. He remembered how he once cried when he broke his rubber slingshot. Purple Jade comforted him as usual and taught him to swing his shots with a strip of silk ribbon. Desperately, he unwound some of his hand bandages and fashioned a cradle for swinging the grenades. A bitter smile graced his blackened lips.

The boom of big guns was now everywhere. The crashing sounds of tank treads and whirring engine warned him of the approaching tanks. In the short intervals between explosions, he peered out from his crouched position and watched the tanks approach in a rough V-formation. The lead tank advancing on his left would be about ten yards away and slightly to his back, he surmised. He would have just enough time to turn and lob another grenade on the second tank coming to his right. He rushed out, a grenade already in the cradle of his sling. Pulling the pin with his teeth, he swung the grenade expertly on target, hitting the lead tank. There was no time to savor his success. He sprang around, cradled another grenade in his sling, pulled another pin with his teeth, and swung the grenade at the second advancing tank. The grenade fell short of its mark as the tank growled past him. He took cover behind the brick wall and waited for the third tank to come from the left.

Meanwhile, the second tank turned. A cloud of dust and smoke from the battlefield shielded its action. The soldier in the turret trained his sights directly on the brick wall where the grenade swinger had been hiding. He fired. Incredibly, the grenade swinger emerged from the cloud of smoke like an apparition. He was whistling as he moved toward the tank.

"This one is for you, my Crystal!" Glorious Dragon shouted as he marched jauntily forward. He broke into the most popular patriotic tune of the time:

*"Arise, those who would not be slaves,**
Use our blood and flesh
To build a new great wall."

Perhaps the enemy soldier paused in his turret because he was surprised. When Glorious Dragon stood still to reload his slingshot, the blast from the big gun sent him rolling onto the ground, but again it had missed him. He was already too close to the tank. The man in the gun turret had lost sight of him. The soldier from the tank would have to emerge to shoot him. Glorious Dragon crawled painfully forward.

"Arise, arise," he sang as loudly as he could to obliterate his pain. "We are united . . . go forward, forward . . ."

Coming in close, he pulled the pins on two grenades with his teeth, and holding them against his chest, he rolled under the tank.

A deafening explosion filled the air.

In November 1938, the Huangs learned that the Imperial Army of Japan had confiscated their uniform factory. Instead of regret, both Righteous Virtue and Purple Jade felt only relief. The guilt of war profiteering had ended.

Iris wrote to say that Glorious Dragon and Bright Crystal had disappeared, leaving everyone to wonder where they were hiding. General Chin still held sway in Chungking, so the Huangs secretly hoped to see the lovers in Hong Kong.

In January 1939, Tall Man Wu sent Purple Jade a letter and a plaque from the Nationalist government, commemorating her brother's bravery and announcing his death. Not only had he donated large supplies of arms, he had destroyed two tanks all by himself. His feat of valor so stirred the soldiers on the battlefield that they rose from the security of their trenches, held their caps in their hands, and silently paid tribute.

Among the personal effects returned was an American high school ring, which Golden Bell remembered seeing on the small finger of Iris's husband.

The entire household grieved for Glorious Dragon. Comely Brook made a black armband for Righteous Virtue. The female members, including Little Jade, wore small, white, button-shaped yarn flowers in their hair to denote a family in mourning.

Purple Jade slipped into delirium. In her crazed howling, she told the winds that Glorious Dragon had been more than a younger half-brother. She had nurtured him like her first-born child, and her only son. She thanked his spirit and wailed that in recent years he had cared for her and her family, much as she would expect a son to do. "Yes, Glorious Dragon, my precious little brother, my baby" she cried, "you are more, far, far more than a filial son. Whenever you came, you brought laughter with your wit," she keened with torrents of tears. "Oh sunshine, sunshine, your generosity is the sunshine for our family!" No one could calm her. She stumbled around the room, thrashed and moaned. "Your warm affection intoxicated our hearts, and your playfulness was my youthful renewal! Oh, why, oh why are you taken away from me?" She shoved everyone away, and no one dared interrupt her ranting, even though she scared the children and they had to be kept out of her range. After almost a week of drinking the herbal brew Comely Brook prepared, Purple Jade lapsed into silent bouts of depression. She stared into the void and refused to be fed and bathed. In time, Purple Jade was able to weep together with Comely Brook, Golden Bell, Silver Bell and Righteous Virtue. They proclaimed Glorious Dragon a modern patriot. He was a quintessential Chinese in his resourceful struggle for survival. He had used native cunning to maintain his independence. With his dedication, he had more than fulfilled his filial duties toward his family. He chose death and honor rather than a life of servitude or cowardly escape. Why was fate so blind? Purple Jade's mind could not fathom a reason; nor would her heart yield its pain.

One day she announced that she was ready to return to her work. Comely Brook quickly notified the boat people. Soon, the demands of her work restored her equilibrium. She carried on, hiding her silent tears every night, not wishing to burden her family with her special loss. Once again, Tu Fu's poem gave voice to her grief.

Sounds of anguish— hush, hush.
You entangle the strands of my heart.
Is there regret or lament when a man of valor pledges his life to his country?
Deeds of renown are emblazoned in the unicorn pavilion,
Bones of soldiers decay into oblivion.

Chapter 12

NINE MONTHS PASSED as life settled into a steady rhythm for the Huang family in Hong Kong. Purple Jade regularly attended to the medical needs of the boat people in Aberdeen. The choicest seafood was her tangible reward.

Their house had been furnished with the practical simplicity of the tropics — tables and chairs of bamboo and rattan. The only touches of luxury were potted plants and embroidered silk cushions. The walls sweated in the damp, torpid air, forcing Purple Jade to remove the ancient calligraphy and paintings during the summer months. Nothing brightened the bare plastered walls of the living room then.

In early September 1939, the girls began another school year in the Catholic convent school, where the nuns wore hats with flaps that flared out like butterfly wings. They spoke French in the convent, and English in the convent school.

At first, the new Catholic environment confused the girls. Silver Bell often had questions for her mother. "Sister Felicie said there is only one God, and the Catholic Church is the only true church." She fidgeted in her rattan chair, which squeaked and rustled as she moved.

"The Jade Emperor in heaven has many courtiers. Naturally, the followers of each courtier will want to claim they are the true, loyal ones," Purple Jade explained as best she could. "The Catholics and the Protestants must be behaving like rival factions in the heavenly court." She sat very still. The noise of Silver Bell's flimsy chair annoyed her. The ever-oppressive humidity threatened to ignite all her nameless anger. She forced herself to be calm, refusing to criticize her children's teachers. Teachers were spiritual parents. She had witnessed the destruction of her home and hearth, but she would not demolish her remaining values — however lifeless they might have become in this strange land. She had tried valiantly to make this her home. She lifted her palm-leafed fan and heaved a heavy sigh.

"But Sister Felicie said that the Jade Emperor is an idol. The Catholic God is the only true one," exclaimed Silver Bell. "What I can't understand is why Sister Felicie's Catholic God is the same Christian one as Mrs. Curtis's Protestant God in Shanghai, but somehow the Catholic Church can claim to be the true one." She continued to twist and turn in her chair and began picking at a loose cane.

"Don't pick at the chair, Silver Bell," her mother chided. "The sage said: we must be generous and benign of heart." She fanned herself. "By cultivating oneself, we can regulate the family; by regulating the family, we can govern the state; by governing the state, we can bring peace on earth. When order and kindness direct the world, heaven will be pleased. All the intrigue in the Jade Emperor's court is really none of our concern."

"Oh, *M-ma*." Golden Bell rolled her eyes. "You're still quoting from the old books!"

Purple Jade nodded. Indeed, her answer would have sufficed in Hangzhou, but her home had become an ancient stage set that tumbled. She must tell her daughter something that made sense in these changing times. "I remember Miss Tyler telling you about their freedom of religion. Like us, the

Americans want to take the best from all religions and look for harmony."

"But *M-ma*." Golden Bell shook her head. "You two are talking about two different things. Confucian scholars are concerned only with proper behavior on earth, but the Christians want to go to heaven."

"*M-ma*, Golden Bell is right." Silver Bell pulled a splinter from the chair, making it creak even more. "Sister Felicie said life on earth is not important. We must become like the Chinese bamboo, so that God may use us to build houses, furniture, carry loads, and be messengers of Christ, like . . . like . . . water pipes."

"I have read that bamboo is a symbol of the Chinese." Purple Jade sighed, remembering the cool breezes, the fresh scent, and the rustling melody of her bamboo groves by the river. Then the sight of black, sooty lengths of popping bamboo entered her mind. She closed her eyes firmly as she drew herself upright in her chair with a deep breath. She fanned herself in agitation. "I think it is a poetic symbol. Like the bamboo, we are a people who will bend but will not break. We are resilient. We have a natural thirst for life and family; that is what brings us peace."

"I shall remember your comparison, *M-ma*." Over the years, Golden Bell had learned to appreciate her mother's patient, steadfast virtues. She also grew to understand her mother's suffering, her strength, and her service to the boat people. Instinctively, she knew her mother's classical learning was the steel in her gentle soul, and somehow the family would prevail under her guidance. She gave her sister a reproachful look with a motion of her hand and changed the subject.

"Look *M-ma*, I'm doing some sketches of the many types of plants in our garden. I still don't know their names. The books in school are useless." Golden Bell took out her sketchbook to show her mother.

"Why can't your biology teacher help you?" asked her mother.

"Our school books all come from England, so they describe the plants of the temperate zone. Hong Kong is tropical. Father will have to take me to the Chinese Correspondents' Club library. I will compare my drawings to the pictures in the books and find out their names." Golden Bell held up a watercolor sketch of a Royal Poinciana tree that shaded most of their front garden. "Isn't this the most exquisite tree you've ever seen? The blanket of red blossoms on top is like a huge umbrella. It is so dramatic!"

"What a lovely sketch!" Her mother was delighted with the diversion. "If I didn't know better, I'd say you had practiced calligraphy and Chinese painting all your life. We'll frame this after you've found out the name of the tree."

"*M-ma*, you're so appreciative. Somehow my teachers always find faults."

"Are you having trouble in school? Didn't we give you a good foundation in English?"

"Well, my writing is all right, but my pronunciation of English is 'so American' as my teacher, Miss McCarthy, says." Golden Bell lifted her chin, imitating Miss McCarthy's haughty pose.

"American missionaries run the McTyeire School. Perhaps you also have seen too many American movies." Her mother shook her head. "Is there really such a big difference in pronunciation? You'll be graduating next summer. Will this affect your grades?"

"I hope Miss McCarthy doesn't hold it against me, but she does make a fuss about it. Yesterday, we had to dramatize a poem by Longfellow." Golden Bell stood up. She stretched out one arm and held an imaginary bow in the other. She drew on the invisible bow and arrow. "This is how Miss McCarthy sounds:

I shought an arrow into the ai--are,
It fell to earth I knew not wher-ah."

Silver Bell rolled her eyeballs skyward. She giggled and clasped her hands to her chest, and collapsed onto the rattan sofa, as if stricken by the arrow. Little Jade toddled over. Imitating her half-sister, she rolled her large dark eyes and tumbled to the ground, giggling and squealing with joy. Everyone laughed, and Comely Brook clapped.

"Perhaps you should give up some American movies!" Purple Jade said. "If you want to graduate with honors."

"I may not have to." Golden Bell sighed. "The English cannot continue their snobbish ways once they are at war in Europe. England has . . ." The news from school was that England had declared war on Germany. She did not want to be the bearer of bad news. Her father would know best how to tell her fragile mother. She quickly continued, "England may declare war on Germany. There is talk in school that many English families are preparing to evacuate."

Purple Jade felt a chill at the news of coming war. A sudden fog swirled in her head, but with the children around she was able to maintain her equilibrium. "Your father and I have talked about sending you to America." She took a deep breath. "We have written to Miss Tyler and she has suggested Syracuse, New York, where she came from."

"I don't want to leave you!" Golden Bell answered, blinking back tears. She turned away to pick up Little Jade and tickle her belly. She smiled and cooed at the baby as she tried to regain control.

"Golden Bell still has another year before she matriculates!" Silver Bell chimed in.

"I'll cut down on the movies, *M-ma*." Golden Bell smiled for her mother. "The theaters here have to play 'God Save the King' before each film. All this colonial stuff kills half the fun of seeing Loretta Young anyway." She shrugged and gave a nervous laugh.

"What is the name of that actor, the one who played the lover of that Camellia Flower Girl?" Comely Brook was ready to be distracted.

"Oh, that's Robert Taylor." Silver Bell rattled up from her sofa.

"*Lo-bar-tai-la!*" Purple Jade translated. "Oh, this one is Turnip Too Hot!"

The girls began laughing uproariously. "Oh, *M-ma*, if only Miss McCarthy could hear you!"

"Come to think of it, do you think our own Miss Spicy Too Hot might be related to this Turnip Too Hot?"

"*M-ma*." Golden Bell laughed so hard she could barely answer. "Miss Tyler and Mr. Taylor are as different as our Miss Chen and Mr. Chang!"

"Well, well, the foreign devils have their confusion too." Purple Jade smiled. She knew she could always create a jovial mood whenever she gave a ridiculous translation of an English name. "Girls, go finish your homework. Tonight is your father's night off. He wants to take us out for a ride and let Golden Bell practice her driving."

Purple Jade felt better when the children's concerns occupied her mind. It was important that she always appear strong. Also, her strenuous work among the boat people often obliterated all her thoughts of "that other life" in Hangzhou. But in the bosom of her family, she sometimes thought the incredible pain of losing Glorious Dragon and her home would overwhelm her. The shadows of war and separation hung around her. She gasped for breath and steadied her voice: "It's been stifling all day; we'll enjoy the evening cool. Later, we'll stop by the Chinese Correspondents' Club. Golden Bell will work in the library while we take tea."

Chapter 13

IN THE AFTERNOON, peals of laughter and song awoke Righteous Virtue. He looked out the window and saw Silver Bell, followed by Little Jade, each hefting a small tree branch over her right shoulder. Their right palms cradled the branches like a rifle butt. Their left arms swung smartly by their sides while they marched around and around under the Royal Poinciana tree, singing at the top of their lungs:

"Some talk of Alexander,
and some of Hercules.
With a tra-la-la-la-la,
To the British grenadiers!"

Little Jade strutted resolutely behind Silver Bell on her short legs. Her hair was bunched together in the center of her crown like a small sprouting fountain over her white flower barrette. Her splayed walk made the fountain sway and bounce to loud squeals of "tra-la-la, tra-la-la."

Righteous Virtue could not help chuckling. He went downstairs and called to the girls. When they came running, he squatted down and scooped up Little Jade.

"Oh Father, Father, *M-ma* said you're taking us for a ride tonight!" Silver Bell skipped beside her father as they walked toward the house.

"Yes, I am. Do you know what you are singing, Silver Bell?"

"Tra-la-la, tra-la-la," said Little Jade, licking her fingers.

"Oh Father, it's such a rousing song. I learned it in school. Don't you think Little Jade and I march ever so smartly?"

"Yes, but isn't it strange that Chinese girls should imitate British soldiers?"

"Evening peace, my lord." Purple Jade bowed. "What are you talking about — British soldiers?"

"Silver Bell sang a song of the British grenadiers. I thought it might not be appropriate."

"Perhaps it is now." Purple Jade handed her husband a hot towel. "After all, the British Empire protects us."

"Ah, yes, if only I could have more faith in their might." He let Little Jade squirm out of his arms. Seated on a cane chair, he wiped his face. "The English are only interested in their homeland. They won't send more troops, and they're counting on that obsolete fleet in the harbor to deter the Japanese." He returned the towel to his wife and banged one fist into an open hand. "They think only the white man can fight. Why, the Hong Kong Defense Force has hardly any Chinese in it! They think it is a waste of time to give arms to the Chinese and train them!"

"The Chinese are too smart. We'll leave the fighting to those with the firepower."

"You may be right about that." Her husband accepted tea from Comely Brook, who was pregnant again. "Brook-*mei*, please take the children away, and go rest a while. I have important news to discuss with Jade-*mei*." He stared at his tea and averted his eyes from both wives.

Comely Brook paused. Purple Jade usually included her in their family deliberations, even though she was mostly a listener. Though a concubine, and therefore one of the mistresses of the house, she still served Purple Jade and attended to all her needs as if she were her personal maid. Still, she was now the principal manager of the house while Purple

Jade worked with the boat people. She never discussed her household concerns with her husband, but ministered to his needs when he returned from work in the morning. She never questioned his commands. Without a word, she ushered the children outside.

"Mind, Jade-*mei*, this is not to my liking. Today, England declared war on Germany. We received the news early this morning. All English dependents in Hong Kong have been ordered to evacuate."

Purple Jade shuddered. She had hoped that Golden Bell's news from school was mere childish speculation! She sat down slowly and fanned herself. Her complexion turned red, then pale, then red again in waves of anxiety and panic. She had long anticipated what her husband was now saying. "Jade, you have more relatives in Shanghai, and we own our house there. You have to start preparing the family's return." He broke off, knowing the devastating effect of his words.

Righteous Virtue had stumbled into bed in the morning and had not announced the news to his sleeping family. For more than a year, he had struggled with his ambivalence. He had hoped and prayed that England and America might join in the war against Germany. As Japan and Germany were now allies, the Nationalist Chinese could then count on Western help. Many days and nights he sat dreaming of a fantastic invasion of occupied China by the combined forces of the American, British and Chinese armies. The absurdity of his dreams mingled with his guilt over the hardships his family would suffer under this path to liberation. His national pride struggled with his wish for peace and safety. He often discussed with his wife the possibility of English involvement in the European war. Now that England declared war, Hong Kong — a British Crown colony — was vulnerable to Japanese invasion. Righteous Virtue was reluctant to bring news of possible war and separation to the family. Yet he felt strangely exhilarated by the anticipation that some decisive action might be near, now that Japan had blundered into such powerful Western enemies.

"I understand." Purple Jade's voice rang out, strangely resonant in the rented house of evening shadows. "Golden and Silver Bell must eventually leave and go to study in America. Your editorials are rife with anti-Japanese sentiments, so we cannot remain here. You must flee to Chungking. The babies cannot tolerate the rigors of war in interior China."

Inwardly, she was deeply shaken. Without her husband and her flesh and blood around her, would she be able to maintain her equilibrium? Once her daughters left for higher learning, as they must, she could become a true helpmate to her husband in the interior. Oh, to share in his active struggle against the East Ocean Devils! She dared not dwell on such heady possibilities.

Righteous Virtue was thinking along the same vein. "I could start a small newspaper in the interior to rally for our national cause, and you could start a clinic."

They smiled wistfully at each other. Her mind quickly steered away from temptation. She had urged a concubine on her husband; she could not blame him. With her bound feet, her furtive reach for freedom would never have been possible without Comely Brook's near-silent support. Yes, she was committed to Comely Brook in a way that transcended class, tradition, and power. They were fellow victim-slaves who had stumbled upon a central nerve in human relations — there is joy in kindly service, and peace in loving acceptance.

Her voice took on urgency. "Brook-*mei* is only a concubine. The child in her and Little Jade will have no status in Shanghai. I must return with them and protect them. I'm as much responsible for their lives as you are." The shimmer in her eyes betrayed her brave words. "The silk factory in Shanghai is floundering under Japanese control, but they are still buying raw silk from Hangzhou. The Chou family will need my help."

She saw herself and Comely Brook as the two white gulls in Tu Fu's poem:

A hawk hovers in empty air.
White gulls drift along the river in a pair.
The hawk swoops in the wind with ease,
The two gliding with the currents still in peace.

Morning dew warms the grass.
Revealing a spider web of brass.
Nature mirrors the affairs of man,
From which ten thousand sorrows span.

Righteous Virtue realized in a flash that his wife, at forty-one, was a true beauty. Her charm was imbued with integrity and courage, but it was shielded, as if under glass, by her formidable reserve. Her hair was graying, her skin still supple and smooth, her eyes liquid but so still. In any crowded room, her imperturbable civility, her patience, and her sweet insistence on pleasing was an island of tranquility and grace.

He looked again, astounded. She sat calmly with her hands clasped in her lap. The setting sun lit up sparkles on the silver in her hair, but her eyes were luminous as slow-welling tears caught the light. Righteous Virtue etched her image into his mind.

He was weary, and longed to rush forward to hold her, but he restrained himself with an effort. Her dignity and formality were the foundations of her strength. He must respect and protect them. He gave his wife a desolate, longing glance. "Jade-*mei*, we'll stay together as long as we can.

Let's hope the Japanese will not expel the English from Hong Kong. I'm loath to desert my family again, but I do not have the cunning or the necessary guile to deal with the enemy." He turned to face the evening gloom.

"My master, you must not shoulder the blame of war, the force of fate." Her placid voice smothered the feverish tumult within her. "You have no alternative, when it is a choice between your integrity and collaboration with violence and murder." Her anemic tone masked the darkness in her heart. Silently she recited a Tu Fu poem to herself:

Darkness shadows the mountain road.
I gaze from my study above the water gate,
Streams of cloud rest upon the cliff,
And a lonely moon tumbles among the waves.
A line of cranes winds overhead in silent flight,
A pack of wolves fights over food below.
I have not slept, grieving the war.
Who is strong enough to right heaven and earth?

"I've written so many editorials urging the British to rouse the natives here." Righteous Virtue's knuckles on his clenched fists turned white. "Oh no, they can't spare more troops, but why won't they arm the Chinese? They refuse to listen to our intelligence from the mainland! *Hai*, the British don't trust the Chinese to do anything!"

"Do you think the East Ocean Devils will dare to defy the British fleet here?"

"I won't be surprised if they do. The fleet consists of nothing but rusty buckets." Righteous Virtue sipped his tea. "I place my confidence in the American fleet out in Hawaii. They will not stand for an attack on the crown colony of their traditional ally. While they are guarding the Pacific, I hope Hong Kong will be spared."

He balanced the teacup on the cane tabletop and looked morosely at his wife. "Sometimes I'm at a loss trying to understand the Western democracies. I'm told that the German and Japanese warships are still refueling from American lighters in the Shanghai harbors. The Americans prosper by selling scrap metal, gasoline and other war materials to Japan. They think they can feed a mad dog and not be bitten!" He gave a short bitter laugh. "It is no wonder so many Chinese fall for the Japanese line of 'Asia for Asians.' It makes sense." He looked guilty. "In . . . in a global war, the United States is still the safest place. Perhaps we should send Golden Bell to America this year instead of the next."

"Yes." Purple Jade's voice trembled. She tried to ignore the pain in her chest. "We should begin our inquiries, and the paperwork." She turned away, unable to contemplate her daughter's departure. There had been, and would be, many more sleepless nights of tearful examination. She had turned the matter over in her mind so often that she was now firm in her belief that this was the only safe option. Golden Bell still had another year of high school. Should she leave right now? Should they send Silver Bell as well? She remembered Peony and did not dare let her emotions dictate her daughters' fate. Trembling with uncertainty, she lifted one hand to touch her brow.

Yes, I must visit the Ling Ying Temple on Lan Tao Island. Perhaps the Buddha will help with a propitious decision, oh-me-to-fo. It would be a blessing if Golden Bell could finish high school and stay home another year. She fanned herself slowly and gasped for breath. In a timid voice she asked her husband, "Do you have news from the mainland?"

"Yes, the Nationalists are settling in for a long struggle. The Japanese are keeping up the massive air strikes on the civilian population around Chungking." He sighed. "I try to send in supplies, but it is getting more and more difficult." He wiped his sweaty brow and his voice lightened. "Last March we completely routed the enemy at Tai'erzhuang. We repelled them at Changsha, and though the Japanese control all the big cities along our eastern coast, they don't have the use of our railroads." He smiled. "Our guerrilla action is most successful. We harass the enemy with small firearms, then melt into the countryside."

"In a large country like ours, that is the only way to wear down the enemy." Purple Jade swept her arm in a wide arch in front of her. "We attack when they least expect us and withdraw when they're prepared."

"You've been reading Sun Tzu's *The Art of War* by Sun Tzu." Righteous Virtue nodded. He wanted to savor the triumph of their old methods. "In the white man's eye, this is a war of interminable attrition. They think we are cowards because we won't fight openly. But they are wrong! We shall prevail. I just hope we don't have to devastate our country in doing so."

Purple Jade lowered her head; the image of her charred home and courts in Hangzhou hovered before her. The thought of never seeing her brother's bright face again gnawed at her heart. A vacant glaze blanked her eyes. Her husband whispered to help restore her composure.

"Jade-*mei*, I've promised to take the family out for a ride after dinner. Let's get ready."

Chapter 14

PURPLE JADE RECEIVED the news of Comely Brook's second pregnancy with a sense of nameless malaise. With their home in ashes and their land under Japanese control, the family's need for an heir was over. She had come to accept the randomness of gender after assisting in so many births. Some families were never blessed with a son, no matter how hard they prayed, while other families could never beget a daughter.

Comely Brook's obvious elation at her second pregnancy baffled Purple Jade. But when Comely Brook confided that she prayed for a son, Purple Jade recognized her desperate effort to become "valuable." Her simplicity and overwhelming devotion moved Purple Jade. She decided to conceal her growing doubts and resolved to bolster that glimmer of possibility that a son might still make a difference. "A son surely will add more yan elements to this household so dominated by the yin," she said.

Somehow, a deeper part of her refused to hope. She turned her back on domestic management and left Comely Brook in full command. In her days of deformity, Comely Brook had brought dignity to her life. Now she would make certain Comely Brook received her due in full measure.

Was Comely Brook ever like a daughter to her? No, she was always fond of her, but she had also taken her for granted. Yes, she had used Comely Brook; not cruelly, but she had used her — just as she now used her own arms and legs. Thinking of her frequently sore arms, Purple Jade wondered why Comely Brook never complained. Like an old married couple, she and her maid had become one person. Right or wrong, they had adapted to the old conventions and acquiesced to life. War brought them some measure of freedom, but annihilated all refinements. Fate had set their lives on a congruent course. She must not permit the mere hint of jealousy to slip onto her countenance or into her words. Their activities must grow from need to necessity to essential harmony because Comely Brook was also her new womb. Indeed, their partnership was the very center of her being.

As for her two daughters, she loved them with an intensity that frightened her. Golden Bell seemed to have been wise from birth. She learned the Chinese classics at Purple Jade's knees with such voracity that Purple Jade was elated, astounded, and later, deeply wounded when her Golden glory preferred Western learning. Golden Bell's quick adjustment to Miss Tyler and her keen perception of Western values had annoyed her. She had tried desperately to protect her daughter from a culture that she herself did not understand. Now she knew Golden Bell was astute. She must send her to America where her daughter might flourish in safety. Since the family's move from Hangzhou, their mutual respect had grown — their time together crowded with consultations, intoxicating challenges, and the tenderness of confidences.

And oh, how her spirits had soared and fallen on Silver Bell's songs. The gift of music to the house of Huang was most gratuitously endowed. Purple Jade could not fathom the sources of this talent. She herself could not carry a tune; nor had she ever known her husband to hum or play an instrument. The cadence of their poetry was the music Silver Bell never shared, yet her little girl had trilled her way into her soul. Purple Jade's responses to her "little heart-and-liver" were inexplicably physical and unrestrained. Her deepest recesses ached and she became aware of a maudlin depression when she noticed Silver Bell sprouting tiny breasts. The flowering of her baby delighted her, but how she wished she could spare her the discomfort of her menstrual years — her little girl was meant to run, sing and be free! In the sweetness of sorrow, she felt rich and gratified.

But what of Little Jade? She was her namesake, and the true daughter of the family. Yes, she loved her too, but she was a doll, the idol of the house. Strangely, she found she could stand away from her a little. After all, Little Jade was the third child. Child rearing was already a well-trodden path.

Righteous Virtue was her friend, companion, and co-conspirator in their journey together. She savored his presence every evening. When he left for work, her mood was redolent of quiet trust and silent affection. Words were often unnecessary between them. Both understood that their only recourse was stoic acceptance. In an unspoken pact, they never mentioned the impending family separation to the rest of the family. They held on to the thread of hope that perhaps the combined power of the American fleet in Hawaii, the British fleet in the harbor, and the limited air defense force in Kaitak Airport might deter the Japanese advance.

After dinner, a gentle breeze lifted the heavy, sluggish air of September. The whole family piled into the Buick. Righteous Virtue drove slowly toward Wan Tsai Gap and the Peak. As they passed the white mansions of the British, they admired the trim, neatly manicured lawns and hedges.

"Father." Silver Bell poked her head close to the front seat. "When you wrote to us in Shanghai, you said the foreign women garden with their gloves on. How come we never see the English women gardening here?"

"The English at home are different from the colonists here, I can assure you." Her father kept his eyes on the road. "Ordinary middleclass people in England become pinnacles of society in the colony. They have to put on airs because they are not used to their good fortune."

"You mean when the women return home, they will be expected to garden again?" Purple Jade asked, feeling sorry for these elegant "madams and misses."

"Oh yes." Her husband grinned. "Not only will they have to garden, some may even have to cook and scrub their own floors!"

"Oh no!" Purple Jade recoiled in mock horror.

"Yes, the colonists are too pampered in Hong Kong — too much alcohol and too many servants." Comely Brook seldom ventured her opinion, but now she spoke with authority: "When a person is not book-fragrant — not immersed in the wisdom of our ancient scholars — it is best to keep busy, or there will be trouble."

"You have excellent common sense, Brook-*mei*." Righteous Virtue beamed. "Our cousins Yu Wei and Chou Ling are good examples of the troubles you speak of." He pointed to a fancy rock garden at a white mansion. "Here the small isolated society of white people, living their elegant lives in these palaces, are segregated from the realities of our local population. The Chinese feel humiliated, and 'white' arrogance breeds antagonism. Someday, they — and unfortunately we, too — may suffer for it."

They arrived at the Peak and took a leisurely walk on the path surrounding the major summit. The evening sun dazzled the hazy ocean in a golden sheen. Triangular dots of Chinese sail boats wobbled red and brown in the offing. The

English warships lay like toy pieces in a harbor glistening in the light. A breeze sent tufts of silky vapor scudding across the greenery and buildings beneath them.

"Virtue-*ko*." Purple Jade touched her husband's hand. "Doesn't the view remind you of Tu Fu's quatrain?" Her eyes glazed over and she recited:

Birds are whiter against the blue water,
Flowers flame brighter against the green mountain.
Spring speeds past before my eyes.
What year will I return?

"Ah, that's beautiful." Her husband nodded. Their classical learning clothed the foreign glamour of their surroundings. "Why don't we have a riddle game? Each of us describes something in verse. The rest of us must guess."

"Wonderful idea! Today is your day off, so you and Comely Brook must be our judges." Purple Jade was ever aware that Orchid was still ill equipped to participate in games of the mind. "Golden Bell, you begin."

"All right!" Golden Bell rose to the challenge at once. After thinking for a few minutes, she recited:

"A mist of silken veil crowning her head,
A sprinkling of gemstones around her skirt.
She is a Queen,
In regal repose."

"Ah, that is easy!" Silver Bell exclaimed. "It is Victoria Peak!"

"But that is excellent, Golden Bell." Her father smiled. "Now it is your turn, Silver Bell."

Silver Bell fell behind the others. She thought and thought; she scratched her head; she hopped from one foot to the other, but she couldn't come up with a single line.

Finally she ran to join the others and confessed, "Every time I start on a verse, I seem to slip into some song that I know."

Her mother came to the rescue. "Well, I'll give you a riddle then.

It does not knock;
It comes uninvited.
When we meet,
We caress, and I'm refreshed!"

Everyone walked on in silence, searching for an answer. Silver Bell became impatient with the quiet pondering. She tugged on her mother's hand and squinted into her sun-dappled face. "Is it an animal, vegetable or mineral?"

"None of the above."

"Is the judge allowed to guess?" Righteous Virtue ventured.

"Yes, yes, tell us, Father," Golden Bell chimed.

"Is it the wind, Jade?"

"Yes, my lord." Purple Jade smiled with contentment. "You are still the most familiar with my mind."

Chapter 15

BLINDED BY SUNLIGHT, Purple Jade sat transfixed in the ferry that carried her to Ling Ying Temple on Lan Tao Island. The rocky cliffs, pale silvery beaches and lush greenery — philodendrons and wild camellias— cascading down the mountainside added to her motion sickness. She turned her eyes away from the shore to face the offing. The South China Sea and the sky melded without a line of demarcation. The torrid tropical sun sent blue, green, and yellow blotches dancing before her eyes as she closed them to rest. The heaving roll of the steamboat, froth ruffling at its stern, ferried her to the temple.

The gently rocking rowboats, the rhythmic dip of oars on West Lake and the hazy sun of Hangzhou had been familiar and temperate in scale. Now the excesses of the tropics, accentuated by the rude grind and groan of the motorboat, filled Purple Jade with dread. The indifference of this vast ocean aggravated her unease. She had known natural human pains — birth, sickness, and death. She had made peace with her path in life, but how was she to cope in a world gone mad with destruction and war? Purple Jade's classical learning left her unprepared for action and the self-assertion necessary to deal with violence.

In her heart, she knew her timid soul was frightened by the Western religions that involved a wrathful God who died a gruesome death on the cross. With so much poverty and suffering around her, how was she to accept such a God? In time, she had determined that the nature of God is beyond comprehension. She was concerned only with morality, the maintenance of peace and prosperity in her home. This left her without the counsel of a Western God, who intervened in human affairs through priests.

She had never been consumed by a passion for religion, so she lacked the inner force that could bring her transformation and solace during a time of upheaval in her society. Buddhist priests prayed for the emptying of all human desire. Taoist priests taught the unity of reality and nonintervention — *wu-way*. These were the guiding lights of Purple Jade's religious faith. She did not subscribe to any institution of religion, or dogma. Nevertheless, she was aware of a power transcending human comprehension. The power was not always benevolent. In times of stress, her fate depended upon a harmonious interaction between the yin and yan forces of the universe. Her actions must honor and be compatible with this essential symmetry. She asked for guidance in her family affairs, seeking the intercession of benign spirits and gods who had transcended time, space and matter.

She now undertook this trip to the Ling Ying Temple to seek guidance. It was important that her actions be harmonious with *chi*, the life force that governed the world through the proper balance of Yin and Yan. To her, "chance" meant a future in which her *chi* might coordinate with the *chi* of the larger universe. For three days, Purple Jade fasted and cleansed herself of extraneous thoughts and worldly cares, so that she might be enlightened by the path of divine order.

The bus spewed noxious fumes and took her from the ferry to the temple. The engine rattled. Purple Jade felt faint and fanned herself, murmuring, "The superior man . . . interior peace . . . cool of the mind . . ." She took out her tiger balm ointment and applied some to her temples and underneath her nostrils. The elderly woman beside her watched and smiled, so Purple Jade offered to share her ointment.

Vendors and peddlers besieged worshipers outside the temple gates. They sold sundry items used in the veneration of spirits and gods: packets of incense, flowers, paper money, bullion made from golden foil, fruits, snacks and other ornaments. Purple Jade bought a packet of incense and a bundle of paper golden bullion. The fierce sunlight dazzled her.

Once inside the cool temple, Purple Jade was blinded by the change of light. Sunbursts of colored shadows danced before her eyes. She leaned against a red wooden beam and rested. As her eyes adjusted to the shade, her soul felt soothed by the chant emanating from the inner chambers of the temple. She knelt before the Buddha and pressed her palms together. She placed them before her forehead. She bowed and touched her hands and head to the floor.

Her initial devotion over, she burned the gold bullion in a bronze brazier. She prayed and directed the spirits of Glorious Dragon and Bright Crystal to accept the offering and procure for themselves the earthly comforts to which they were accustomed.

"Dragon-*dee*, Bright Crystal," she prayed, "lead me to the right decision."

A small procession of monks entered the side altar, chanting, jingling bells, and marking a familiar rhythm with wooden clappers. Purple Jade emptied her mind. She no longer felt the physical strain of her existence. Slowly she rose, unselfconscious and vacant, and walked toward a monk who provided fortune sticks.

Purple Jade placed her container of fortune sticks beside her and lit her incense. She bowed and prayed for guidance. Then she stuck the incense into the giant brazier filled with sand. She knelt before Kwan Yin, the Goddess of Mercy, and shook her container of sticks, concentrating on her question: "Should I send Golden Bell to America now?" She repeated the question in her mind.

"No." She shuddered. "One is an unlucky number!" One was loneliness, isolation, the absence of family and communal support! Her focus on only one question had been an outrageous oversight. Dread intruded. She stopped shaking her fortune sticks.

She rose, bought and lit more joss sticks. She bowed three times and added her scented sticks to the other incense burning in the giant brazier before the Buddha. She kneeled again and kowtowed. She asked for forgiveness and reverently rephrased her questions: "Should we send Golden Bell to America? Should we send Silver Bell as well? Should we send them right away?"

Satisfied with the three questions, she touched her head to the floor and concentrated on them. Kneeling and mumbling "*oh-me-to-fo*" all the while, she shook the fortune sticks and tilted the container toward the altar. She shook them more gently now, as some sticks began to move ahead. Carefully, she shook and asked for guidance until one stick fell out.

With fear and trepidation, Purple Jade picked up her fortune stick and took it to the medium —a stocky man dressed in a rough gray robe. His head was shaved, and two golden teeth glistened in his mouth. This sign of prosperity comforted Purple Jade, because it meant that the medium was much consulted, and therefore a good one.

The medium fanned himself and read the number written on the stick. He consulted a corresponding text and read in a laconic drawl: "Kwan Kung, the honorable hero, faithfully followed the direction of Tao, sent his two nieces to safety."

Fanning himself with a tiny flutter of his wrist, the medium looked into Purple Jade's eyes, and with the air slipping through his gold teeth, he sibilated with strange energy: "You have been virtuous and patient. You must be more patient and wait. The hand of fate will lead things to fruition. Do not interfere and rush into deeds against your heart. Your life will be outstanding."

Purple Jade received her message in stunned silence. Wringing her hands in anxiety, she stood and responded in Cantonese, "*Duo-chai*" (Many thanks).

On her return journey, her heart lightened. She had initially responded with dread to the medium's pronouncement that her life would be "outstanding." Again, that was an indication of oneness, a lone, singular existence. Yet, the first part of her message was vastly comforting: she must not act precipitously. She would not have to send her children away soon. Golden Bell would finish high school here. She would be patient and wait for the kind hand of Buddha. She felt a strange exhilaration.

Golden Bell had always dreamed of going to America to study. However, the war tempered her enthusiasm. She was happy to finish high school and stay at home for another year.

Chapter 16

ENGLISH INVOLVEMENT IN the European war made daily headlines in the Hong Kong papers. Many Chinese hoped and prayed the British would help them drive out the Japanese. But the British did not intervene in the war among the yellow people. Meanwhile, the island was at peace, living under British rule. The household on Blue Pool Road took on a new rhythm.

Over the year, Purple Jade's reputation for benevolence had spread among the boat people. Her midwifery duties often called her away in the evening. On her free days, she enjoyed the cool nights and read into the wee hours, getting up late the next morning.

Comely Brook gave birth to another daughter, Coral Bell, in May 1940. She wept and apologized for not having produced a son. To distract her, Righteous Virtue began giving his concubine driving lessons. Up at night with the new baby, Comely Brook was also late to rise. Righteous Virtue returned from the newspaper office every morning, and had breakfast with Golden and Silver Bell and Little Jade before seven. As he prepared for bed, the older girls left for school, and Winter Plum took Little Jade to the open market in Happy Valley.

The morning marketing was the highlight of Winter Plum's day. She fingered the vegetables, pinched the fruits, bargained with the peddlers, met her friends, and gossiped with the other amahs. Several months earlier, she had become acquainted with the young owner of a rice shop.

It was Little Jade who initiated the friendship. Wherever she went, Little Jade licked her chubby fingers and waved "hello" and "bye-bye." With her hair swaying and her cow eyes sparkling, she recited her greetings and farewells in Shanghainese, Cantonese, Hangzhounese and English. The fruit peddler always added an extra fruit, the vegetable peddler more greens. Thus Winter Plum became friendly with Mr. Cheng Big Fortune, the young owner of the rice shop.

In June 1941, Golden Bell matriculated with distinctions in mathematics, English and history. Her passport and student visa were ready. Purple Jade helped her daughter pack and reminded her repeatedly that she was to behave like the son of the family — she must uphold their dignity and that of her country at all times. Golden Bell left on July 30 for Syracuse University in New York.

On December 8, Righteous Virtue was more than an hour late coming home. After her breakfast, Silver Bell went to school at seven thirty. Winter Plum decided to wait no longer and left for the market.

"Where is everybody?" Righteous Virtue bellowed as he stormed into the quiet house. He woke up Purple Jade and Comely Brook.

"It's almost eight," Comely Brook said. "Winter Plum probably left for the market with Little Jade, because she doesn't like to be left with picked-over produce."

"The Japanese bombed Pearl Harbor last night!" Righteous Virtue said, his voice weighted by the new horror. "This morning they declared war on America!"

"Oh my lord, how are we to communicate with Golden Bell?" Purple Jade exclaimed.

"Worse yet," Righteous Virtue growled, "the Japanese will surely attack Hong Kong soon. The American navy for the Pacific is all destroyed!"

"Then you must flee!' Purple Jade had long contemplated this possibility. Panic reminded her of her recurring nightmare. She saw anew the devastation of her home, the fly-infested, blackened carcasses, the grunts, the screams, the smell of smoke, and the drone of . . . airplanes? bombs?

The distant detonations grew louder. Thundering roars followed as windows shook. An earthquake seemed to have been set off and its vibrations continued long after the planes droned by. Righteous Virtue pulled Purple Jade to the floor. They cowered near the sofa. Comely Brook flew upstairs to fetch Coral Bell, who was crying.

Sirens wailed, dogs barked and columns of thick black smoke curled up into the sky and darkened the morning sun. People were struck dumb, and everyone craned their necks and stared as another swarm of Japanese airplanes flew in formation, swerving past Happy Valley. One plane released, as if in an afterthought, what looked like a black egg. This last bomb was the worst. A deafening roar of flames and the sound of crashing buildings followed. Windowpanes shattered; plaster fell from the walls, and people screamed on the street.

Comely Brook ran downstairs with Coral Bell sucking on her breast. "Where did the bomb fall? Causeway Bay? Central? The market?"

"Little Jade!" cried Purple Jade in a shrill whisper. She sensed the proximity of the last bomb, and remembered Winter Plum and Little Jade were out shopping. Her regular route to the harbor was to walk through the marketplace. She staggered into the street.

Righteous Virtue stood in a tremor of sweat. Without a word and wild with terror, he forced himself out of the house, confused and uncertain of the directions of the bomb. At a half-run, he tottered toward Causeway Bay and Silver Bell's school.

As planes appeared from nowhere, Winter Plum was telling Cheng Big Fortune, "My master was still not home when we left. I wonder what kept him."

When the plane dropped its last bomb, everyone in the market was still gawking, pointing at the strange sight. They had lived with the threat of war for so many years that no one actually expected it. Then there was a loud explosion. Arms, legs, bricks, vegetables— everything — flew into the air and came tumbling down in a shower.

Winter Plum saw a flash of blood as a bright light splashed before her face. She felt a sharp pain in her gut; vomit rose in her throat, and she lost consciousness.

Righteous Virtue and Silver Bell met Comely Brook on the street outside their house — the baby still asleep on her breast.

Comely Brook wailed: "Where is Little Jade? Have you found Little Jade?"

When no one responded, she placed baby Coral Bell in Silver Bell's arms and ran toward the market. Righteous Virtue told Silver Bell to stay home. He followed his concubine.

Chaos reigned in the market. Smoke and dust choked the streets. Smoldering buildings and flickering fires lit up the dust-covered faces. Frantic people clawed at the tumbled portals, archways and cracked cement, calling out the names of friends and family members. Many were blood-drenched. Animals escaped from their cages. Squawking chickens, flapping ducks and pigeons waddled amid the rubble, pecking at the smashed tomatoes, melons, cabbages, and spilled rice. Snakes slithered in and out of the fallen bricks and crevices. Turtles waded into the bombed-out wine shop and recoiled from the streams of pungent liquor. Comely Brook elbowed her way into the turmoil screaming "Little Jade, Winter Plum, where are you?" Her voice was lost in the chaos.

Buffeted on all sides by the uproar, Righteous Virtue realized that he must remain calm. He soon caught sight of Purple Jade working feverishly to clean wounds, bind cuts, and clear spaces for the wounded. Toddling on her small feet, she was an unlikely figure of authority as she commanded an army of confused people. She had somehow stationed herself near the bombed-out pharmacy, so had a liberal supply of salves, bandages and even brand-new acupuncture needles. Righteous Virtue nudged close to her and reassured her that Silver Bell was home safe. The sight of the wounds sickened him. Inspired by his wife's fortitude, he went to help with the digging. By ten o'clock, he saw Comely Brook working beside him.

"Go home," he urged hoarsely. "I'll find them. Coral Bell needs you."

"Silver Bell is minding the baby." Comely Brook carried on the grim work without another word. She waded through a pile of vegetables and began to stack them. She pulled up an apple and found that she had grasped the fingers of another hand clutching the same fruit. The hand belonged to a severed arm. She flung it off with a loud scream and collapsed. Righteous Virtue had to carry her home.

All morning Purple Jade ministered to the wounded. She frequently stopped to question the others whether they had seen Winter Plum and Little Jade.

At noon, Purple Jade went home with a group of volunteers. On the stretcher lay Winter Plum and Little Jade. Someone had cleaned their faces, but they were cold and stained with blood.

Comely Brook began to retch and wail. Righteous Virtue nearly fainted at the sight. Purple Jade revived him by massaging his neck and rubbing him with tiger balm. When Righteous Virtue recovered, he wiped his tear-stained face with his sleeve, and went to the coffin maker.

Purple Jade trudged upstairs, and stripped a sheet from a bed to cover the bodies. She saw Silver Bell holding the new baby and rushed to hold them both.

In the living room, the neighbors stayed to commiserate and gossip.

"Kaitak Airport was bombed, and so was the center of the city."

"We can't see it in the valley, but I heard that the whole British Air Defense fleet was parked neatly in Kaitak Airport, and the Japs got every one!"

"The entire British air defense was bombed out at Kaitak?"

"Yes, the entire British air defense for the Pacific!"

"The British always seemed so efficient, but they were incompetent!"

"How is it they never expected this?"

"They don't have any intelligence from the mainland."

"We have known for months the Japanese were amassing their most seasoned troops across the border from the new territories!"

"Why didn't someone tell the British?"

"The British wouldn't believe anything the Chinese told them!"

Chapter 17

THE JAPANESE BOMBS did not destroy the ineffectual British fleet in Hon Kong Harbor. The English defended Hong Kong valiantly for eighteen days, hoping against hope that the Australian or English at home would come to their rescue. It was inconceivable to them that they would suffer defeat at the hands of a yellow race. On December 25, 1941, instead of the festivities of a Christmas dinner, the white masters of Hong Kong surrendered. White women, children, and feeble men were herded into concentration camps, while the able-bodied were conscripted into hard labor. The Japanese began a brutal reign of Hong Kong.

While the British stubbornly resisted, retreating into the western part of the island, the Japanese soldiers wreaked vengeance on the civilians of the occupied areas. Every evening, the drunken soldiers returned and raised a racket for miles up the road. Righteous Virtue and his neighbors decided to set up a patrol. The houses on Blue Pool Road backed on to a gentle hill. When a noise was heard, the patrol signaled it with two short and one long toot of their whistles. Within seconds, the whole neighborhood melted into the hill and hid among the bushes. The soldiers broke into some homes but could not find anyone. They grabbed what they could and vandalized everything.

One afternoon, Mr. Pien, a fisherman, was at the door. His wife had gone into labor. Purple Jade had monitored her pregnancy in the last eight months. Mrs. Pien was of diminutive build and had boasted of her large round belly, certain that the baby would be a big strong boy. Purple Jade had taken note of the woman's small pelvis. When the call came, she warned the family: "The labor will be long. Do not expect me home until tomorrow." Purple Jade changed into Winter Plum's baggy black pants and old blue jacket. Donning a fisherwoman's big straw hat, she trotted beside Mr. Pien. They made their way through the market and managed to reach the waterfront without incident. Mr. Pien rowed swiftly toward his houseboat and his wife.

On the evening of the following day, Righteous Virtue conferred in the living room with a few neighbors to plan for a cache of provisions in the wooded hill. Comely Brook grew apprehensive and fidgety when they still had no word from Purple Jade.

"I'm going to find out how *Tai-tai* is doing." She drew Righteous Virtue out of his conference and whispered to him in the hallway, "Silver Bell is watching the baby."

"Take the car," her husband answered in a hurry. He knew the car provided status, and could perhaps offer safety. Trusting her common sense, he did not question her. He returned to his meeting.

Comely Brook drove the Buick into the market. The fish stall owner willingly hid the car and led her to the waterfront, where another fisherman ferried her to Purple Jade.

Mrs. Pien's labor had lasted twenty-six hours. Purple Jade massaged, manipulated, cleaned, and used her needles to ease her pain. When Comely Brook arrived, Purple Jade had just delivered an eight-pound boy. The Piens were ecstatic. They would not let the women leave without first celebrating with a toast of wine and a small repast of sausages and cakes which they had saved for the occasion. It was already dark when the Huang women returned to their black car. Comely Brook drove home stealthily without turning on the headlights. They stopped in the shadows of each corner to make certain the way was clear .

As they came to the mouth of their street, they saw Japanese soldiers scrambling up the hill like spectral shadows. Screams and whimpers erupted all over the mountain.

"We must distract the enemy. Draw them down!" Purple Jade felt strangely energized, like the time Glorious Dragon took her to raid Prosperous Dream. She was a different woman then. She had gone along to watch her brother, but now she was directing the action.

Comely Brook did not answer. She turned on the headlights and floored the gas pedal. The Buick roared down the street like a streak of lightning.

The drunken soldiers gave chase immediately. They fired their rifles at random. Comely Brook swerved back and swept past them at great speed, trying not to hit anyone. The body of a soldier on their street could spell death for every man, woman, and child on Blue Pool Road. When they turned the corner, the car skidded to a stop. Comely Brook's heart thudded so violently, she could not think. She gasped as she saw in the rear-view mirror that the staggering soldiers had followed them.

"They've left our street." Purple Jade turned to look. "Duck, they're going to shoot!"

The women ducked just in time. They had seen the two dogs barking wildly at the soldiers' heels, and the drunkards raising their rifles . . . A sudden yelp and the scream of a ricochet of bullet sent them cowering to the floor. The rear window shattered as a bullet whizzed by overhead and pierced the windshield. Crouching in the front seat, and holding her sister-wife's cool hand, Comely Brook was jolted into a sudden calm.

"There is a long straight stretch of road in front of us." Purple Jade squeezed Comely Brook's hand for courage. "Let's steer the car from where we are. Drive slowly enough so they think they can reach us."

"You sit on the floor on your side, guide the steering wheel with your right hand, and push the gas pedal with your left hand," Comely Brook commanded in strange animation. She lay down on the front seat and adjusted the rear and side-view mirrors. Twisting her body like a contortionist, she worked the clutch, the brake and the stick shift. Stealing glances at the mirrors, she directed her former mistress: "Steer right. Now stay the course. More pressure on the gas . . . less now, slower, slow — slow." Together, they eased down the road, and kept the speedometer below twenty miles an hour.

Sweating, they felt the steering wheel and stick shift slip from their control. They grappled with hands, elbows, and knees and heard the frenzied curses, the whine of bullets, the spurts of cement flying off the walls of buildings, and the sudden rattle of the car as a shot found its mark. Their snug, blind ride filled them with a surreal peace. Purple Jade could not help but remember the time of idle waiting in the car when Glorious Dragon burned the opium den. Now she was an active participant. She smiled at the thought that her brother would be delighted.

"We're their sole target now," Comely Brook whispered.

A bullet shattered the window on the passenger side. Comely Brook squeezed her eyes shut, cursing, as glass hit her left arm and face. She jerked herself upright and sped the car down the road, turned another corner, waited for the soldiers to catch up and sped to another corner, leading the soldiers farther and farther away from the neighborhood. Hissing and breathing through clenched teeth, she ignored the sight of splattered blood all around her and Purple Jade cowering beside her. She grabbed the slippery, bloodied steering wheel as she readjusted her rear-view mirror. The soldiers shouted, cursed, tripped over themselves, draped themselves on lamp-posts, and crashed into road signs and buildings. The run had exhausted them; their bullets went wide of the mark. At last they drifted off to cause trouble elsewhere.

Comely Brook switched off the headlights and turned into a side street. Purple Jade's eyes blazed with satisfaction and excitement. She gave her sister-wife a quiet nod and a shy smile as they prepared to steal home. Just as they felt free and triumphant, a soldier appeared from nowhere. He tucked his wine bottle into his pocket, and flung himself in the path of the car. He raised his rifle in the pool of street light and aimed straight at them. Purple Jade froze in her seat. Panic flushed Comely Brook. The car lurched forward in a spurt of smoke. The rifle shot muffled a loud thud and the soldier's final shout as they ran him down.

Comely Brook stopped the car while Purple Jade helped her push and pull the soldier into the back seat. Purple Jade's heart pounded and her head ached, but her eyes registered the scowl on the face of the dead man. The soldier had unbuttoned his uniform and taken off his undershirt, leaving his hairy chest exposed to his waist. In the tangle and tussle of pushing the dead man, the bottle slipped out of the loose flapping jacket. The sound of shattered glass and the sudden stench of cheap alcohol rushed them to finish the task. A quiet tension enveloped them. Comely Brook crept up to the end of the street and parked the car in the shadows to steady their nerves.

"We did right." Purple Jade was the first to speak. "If we left him dead on the street, this whole neighborhood would suffer."

"We can't bring the dead body home."

"We'll dump him in the ocean. Perhaps we should dump the car with him. It'll be easier to go home on foot, now that the soldiers are looking for our car." Purple Jade was barely audible.

Comely Brook did not answer. Her head was a whirl of pain. Making sure the road was clear, they stole toward the harbor. They met no patrols; the soldiers must have gone on their separate drunken sprees. They edged close to a deserted embankment and Comely Brook let Purple Jade out in the shadows of a building. Comely Brook opened her door and raced the engine. She rolled out of the moving car and watched their beloved Buick plunge into the sea with a loud splash, carrying its deadly cargo.

There was no sense of triumph as they trudged home, hiding in the shadow of houses and buildings along the way. They whispered to each other and wondered what they might do if the soldiers returned the following evening. What if the Japanese found the car and the dead soldier in it? What if the soldier had not been dead after all, and somehow managed to get back on shore? A cold sweat drenched them. Fear enveloped them like heavy, humid air. Their cooperation, which had been so exhilarating, now evaporated.

Righteous Virtue, pacing in extreme anxiety, was waiting for them as they limped in the door looking like lacerated ghouls. With a horrible cry, he prepared hot water, as Purple Jade began picking the pieces of glass from Comely Brook's face. She ignored her own injuries and proceeded to clean and dress her sister-wife's wounds. She remembered the only other time she had touched Comely Brook's face — when she had helped Orchid apply makeup before their raid of the opium den. Oh, how they had all changed. Glorious Dragon would be so proud of them. She smiled.

"I killed a man tonight!" Comely Brook whispered in a trembling voice. "He might have been a father. He wore a wedding ring."

"Hush, Brook-*mei*, you did what you must." Purple Jade opened her medicine bag. She worked meticulously with a steady hand, and her mind raced back to the escape. "Eventually, they will find our car. My lord, they will assume you killed the soldier! You must find a way to leave for Chungking as soon as possible."

"If I'm not here, they will punish my whole family. No! I will not leave."

Purple Jade knew it was futile to argue. When Comely Brook was all bandaged, Righteous Virtue was allowed to wash and clean Purple Jade's cuts.

The next day, Purple Jade again changed into Winter Plum's clothes and stole into the market to contact the fishermen. They arranged for a fishing junk to take her husband to Hainan Island, where there still remained a small stronghold of the Nationalist army.

When Righteous Virtue learned of the plan, he still refused to go. He would only leave, he said, if his family returned to their home in Shanghai. He finally wrote a note asking for help and took it to his office, where he managed to cable Iris Kamasaki in Shanghai.

Chapter 18

THE GROVE OF green bamboo by her house across the causeway glistens in the charcoal haze.

The bamboo erupts. Flying pieces of cane ignite in a macabre display of fireworks. Plumes of black smoke suffocate the morning sun and drain the blue horizon.

"Help, help . . ."

"Little Six, where are you . . . where are you?"

"Water, someone, please, water . . ."

The cedar in the garden singes like incense sticks, filling the air with pungent smoke. Flickering fires rain on heaps of broken furniture, collapsed doors, shattered windows, and grounds littered with torn clothing and broken toys.

Purple jade shook herself to regain her composure.

Another interminable week had passed. The balmy winter days were cool and dry — perfect for picnics and walks around the Peak. Purple Jade remembered former family outings with a painful knot in her chest. The winter sun warmed her, but she no longer saw the colors. Although the Chinese New Year was approaching, she felt no need to prepare. The splendor of Hangzhou brought poignant memories of perfume, color, music and pain.

The shipping office was closed, so Righteous Virtue could not arrange passage for the women to Shanghai. Calls to his friends were fruitless. Many had suffered greater losses than they. Though it would mean the breakup of his family, he did his best to find a way to escape before the Japanese could find the car in the harbor.

They felt safe in the daytime. But at night there was never-ending vigilance. The marauding soldiers left everyone's nerves frazzled. They fumbled through the day like old people who had lived too long, bent and burdened by time.

Silver Bell seemed to have lost all her childish ways. She wept with the adults, studied hard even though she no longer attended school and attended to baby Coral Bell's needs everyday.

Righteous Virtue tried to find solace in his reading. As usual, Comely Brook did physical labor to allay her fears. The house was scrubbed clean, and no one noticed that she had fully resumed her role as a servant, cooking, cleaning and serving.

One day, Purple Jade found Comely Brook standing by Little Jade's empty bed, trembling and staring at it. Without a word, she led her sister-wife to her husband, searching for a way to calm her.

"Brook-*mei*, it was good of you to come and fetch me at the Piens. I might not have made it home otherwise."

Righteous Virtue saw the women's tear-stained faces and motioned them to sit.

"I think I wanted to kill the soldier because of Little Jade. Now the master's life is in danger!" Comely Brook sobbed.

"Brook-*mei*, we're at war with the soldier we killed." Somehow, Purple Jade felt her hatred of the enemy had been drained into hollowness. Her patriotic rhetoric sounded trite. The old saying rang true:

How rhen boo doung bing.

(A good man does not become a soldier.)

She knew she must not dwell on her old learning but find a way to distract her sister-wife.

"Did I tell you how I finally delivered the baby?"

"No." Righteous Virtue caught on immediately. "You often said Mrs. Pien would have a difficult delivery."

"That she had. Although Mr. Pien helped me massage for hours, we were unable to relax his wife's pelvic muscles. Finally, she looked so uncomfortable, and my arms were so sore, I asked her what she felt like doing. Imagine my surprise when the woman apologized and said she did not want to make demands, but she thought she would be more comfortable squatting."

"I imagine that's what she's used to doing every day on the boat: washing, cooking or eating," Righteous Virtue chimed in.

"Yes, I imagine so. We helped her onto their low dining table. When she relaxed in her squat, the baby came!"

Drawn into the narration, Comely Brook took a deep breath and wiped her face.

Purple Jade grinned at her husband and her sister-wife, much gratified. She had behaved with atavistic courage in the face of disaster. Yet whenever she was alone in her room, she stared at the vacant walls and relived her idyllic days in Hangzhou. In the midst of the family's general affliction and distraction, no one noticed her slipping into reverie.

Once, while watching Comely Brook cook, she said, "Orchid, remember to cover the silkworm baskets tonight. The chilly night winds might kill the new worms."

Comely Brook kept her own counsel. She did not wish to add to her husband's burden by informing him of Purple

Jade's mental lapses. She knew everyone was frustrated and anxious over the forced inertia.

One morning, while the family rested fitfully, a big black limousine flying the Japanese flag on its antenna drove up to the Huang residence on Blue Pool Road. Two Japanese soldiers stepped out of the car and held the door open. A uniformed officer emerged and rang the bell at the garden gate.

Righteous Virtue opened the gate and froze. Fighting an instinct to crouch and bow, he stared at a tall Japanese officer. He was certain they had come to arrest him. Time had been on the side of the enemy; they had discovered the Buick and the dead soldier.

"This house is requisitioned for the *Kempetai*!" the lieutenant shouted. He marched straight in and ordered the limousine to be driven into the garden.

When the gates closed, two soldiers stood guard outside. The limousine door opened again. Miss Tyler and Iris emerged.

The Huang women were peeping out of the windows and shivering in terror. They did not recognize Lt. Kamasaki. They ran to greet Iris and Miss Tyler immediately.

"I'm Akiro Kamasaki," the officer introduced himself to Righteous Virtue and a gaping Purple Jade. She was speechless to find the Mr. Kam she had known turning into a hated East Ocean Devil. She at once recognized the hand of fate.

Miss Tyler and Iris related their story.

Since the attack on Pearl Harbor was totally unexpected, Miss Tyler had no time to leave Hangzhou. All the British and Americans, except the small numbers of Germans and Italians, were rounded up for the concentration camps. The Hangzhou natives hid Miss Tyler in a vegetable cart, then transferred her into a boat — following the same water route that had carried Purple Jade two years before — until the American was delivered to Petain Road where Iris was looking after the Huangs' house. Once there, Lt. Kamasaki gave her Vichy French papers.

"Thank goodness the Japanese cannot tell the Caucasians apart. They thought my terrible French quite acceptable!" Miss Tyler gave a bitter laugh.

Righteous Virtue sighed. He produced Lt. Kamasaki's high school ring. All thoughts centered for a long, quiet moment on Glorious Dragon and Bright Crystal.

Silver Bell told them of the death of Little Jade Bell and Winter Plum.

Purple Jade was further devastated when she learned that Dr. Rankling had died in the concentration camp. Her true advocate and one source of edification was gone. Desolation awaited her in Shanghai. She felt she was groping in the storage room of her Hangzhou house. *Shafts of dusty light sifted through the window vents and she saw in the corner a single petal dangling on a once-blooming peony. Oh, dear Buddha,* she groaned inside, *where has the light gone? Must I stand quite so alone?*

"She might not have been willing to leave her patients in the camp anyway," Comely Brook murmured, as much to herself as to the others.

Yes, I will always have Orchid. Out loud, Purple Jade mumbled Tu-Fu's poem:

> *"Fame of a thousand years may be imperishable*
> *But it remains a small after-life affair."*

Comely Brook shuddered, knowing her mistress was trying her best to minimize her loss. She whispered, "Dr. Rankling has gone to her heavenly reward."

Purple Jade kept very still, but other lines by Tu Fu came unbidden:

If I knew where Heaven was
I would not linger here.

My home is the humble assembly of my loved ones. I'll be crushed if I lose them. Still, Orchid and baby Coral Bell came from my prideful choice. I owe them life and dignity. But my lonely boat, as ever, is moored to the heart that longs for home.

"I hope I'll meet her again in the next life," she whispered.

Purple Jade's silent thoughts seemed to have filled the air with somber anguish.

"I apologize for the crimes of my compatriots," Lt. Kamasaki spoke, lowering his eyes to the ground.

"War is never decent. All soldiers loot and burn throughout history. Oh what bitterness!" Righteous Virtue muttered. "Let's hope we can all leave this soon."

"I cannot leave. The lives of my parents and the honor of my family in Japan make me a hostage to the military objectives. But I will help you escape if you have any idea where you want to go." Lt. Kamasaki looked at the worried faces before him. "I plan to go with Iris and Miss Tyler to Saigon. From there, I'll send them on to Calcutta, where Miss Tyler can get in touch with her mission and go back to the States. My country has gone crazy. They've declared war on the world!"

"My place is by your side," said Iris. "I will remain with you in Saigon. Perhaps the Huangs will go with Miss Tyler."

"Our thanks will never repay your kindness." Righteous Virtue bowed deeply to their former maid and her husband. "We've had many hours of discussion during the last weeks. We wish to send Silver Bell to the States to join her sister."

"Yes." Miss Tyler nodded. "I can place Silver Bell in a high school near Syracuse University."

"No!" Silver Bell cried and clung to her mother. Purple Jade held her in a fierce embrace, as much to console her daughter as herself.

Righteous Virtue continued, "Comely Brook and the baby should not endure the hardships of interior China. Purple Jade has agreed to take them back to Shanghai. For myself, I cannot sit idle while the country burns. I must go inland and help the Nationalist effort in Chungking. We have already arranged a fishing junk to take me to Hainan."

"Then this shall be done," Lt. Kamasaki answered right away. "Silver Bell will leave with us for Saigon next week as Miss Tyler's servant. There will be no problem getting her papers ready. A ship leaves for Shanghai this afternoon at three. It will fly a flag identifying it as a refugee ship, so it will be safe from the Allied planes. I will wire Mrs. Chou Ling in Shanghai to meet her cousin, Comely Brook and the new baby. For yourself, Mr. Huang, I'll need a few days to find a good cover."

He paced back and forth, making jerky turns. "The South China Sea is patrolled thoroughly by the Japanese Imperial Navy, where I have no influence. You'll never pass as a fisherman." He came to an abrupt stop and extended an open palm. "Yes, I have it. I'll give you identification as a special agent of the *Kempetai* under my command."

As Righteous Virtue thanked Lt. Kamasaki, Purple Jade stood tall to fortify herself. The parting she dreaded had come. Ignoring the anguish in her heart, she commanded coldly: "Silver Bell, kneel before Miss Tyler!" She pointed an imperial finger at the floor. She straightened her shoulders and held her breath. "From now on you shall honor, obey and serve Miss Tyler as your mother!"

Miss Tyler did not move. She understood the honor conferred upon her. She would have embraced Purple Jade, but that would rob her of her dignity. When Silver Bell Kowtowed, Miss Tyler lifted her and hugged her. Silent tears streamed down her cheeks; she was unable to speak the words of reassurance surging through her mind.

Purple Jade refrained from clasping Silver Bell to her when the girl broke loose from Miss Tyler and pressed wordlessly to her mother's side. *I shall never let her go if I held her,* she thought. She gently pushed Silver Bell to Miss Tyler again.

Then she walked to the bureau and took out the passbook for Silver Bell's American savings account. She held it out to Miss Tyler with a bow.

"Thank you," she said in English, surprising everyone. She bowed again and gave her face a quick swipe. She wobbled toward the stairs as if her bound feet were again a torment.

Comely Brook knelt at the foot of the stairs, blocking her way. "*Tai-tai,* I must abide by your decision, but I know what you're doing for Coral and me." She wept so bitterly, she could not continue.

"Rise up Brook-*mei*. Come and help me pack." Purple Jade raised her. "Be strong, you are my only support now." Together, they tottered upstairs, weeping quietly in each other's arms.

When they came down, Purple Jade and Comely Brook were both dry-eyed. Purple Jade carried the three gray scarves. She bowed deeply to Righteous Virtue and gave him the large, plain piece. "My master, you've taught me decency, harmony and peace. Let this remind you of our time of grace."

Righteous Virtue accepted the silk with downcast eyes, trying to maintain his composure.

Purple Jade gave the scarf with the peony flower that she had embroidered herself to Silver Bell. The luster on the silk was gone, but the peony flower took on an ashen sheen that melded into the gray scarf. "Yes, we are the silk. We should remain supple and gracious." She gave her little heart-and-liver a brave, small grin. "This is your silk; never forget who you are."

When Silver Bell reached to grab her mother, Miss Tyler drew her to her side, and placed the silk on her shoulder.

Clutching Little Jade's scarf with the orchid, Purple Jade whispered, "We are ready to go."

Comely Brook held her head erect, imitating her mistress's stateliness. She bowed to Righteous Virtue. She allowed Silver Bell and Iris to embrace Coral Bell one last time and followed Purple Jade and Lt. Kamasaki out the door.

Purple Jade wore a blank mask of dignity and walked stiffly toward the waiting car. Fingering her silk all the while, she did not look back.

Historical Background

Like that of many other early peoples, Chinese civilization developed along river valleys. The fertile plains of the Yellow and Yangtze Rivers nurtured a sophisticated culture thousands of years before the West learned of its existence — a culture that flourished, remote and undisturbed, largely thanks to the protection of its geography.

To the north and northwest, the sere Mongolian deserts shielded China, while the Himalayan Mountains loomed to the south and southwest. Along the eastern shore, a rugged coastline ran from Siberia to the jungles of Southeast Asia. The vast Pacific Ocean was an effective obstacle against intrusion from that direction.

It was not until the thirteenth century and the famous travels of Marco Polo that the Europeans were alerted to the fabulous wealth of this empire in the inaccessible Orient. The advent of the Renaissance saw every major European sovereign launching his galleons — including those of Christopher Columbus — to find a shorter trade route to the fantastic riches of the East.

By the nineteenth century, when the industrial revolution poised the Western powers for mercantile imperialism, the Chinese were experiencing the twin ravages of deforestation and overpopulation. The Chin (Pure) Dynasty (1644-1911), a Manchu government, had ruled the majority Han race for almost three hundred years, and its vigor would soon dissipate under the control of Tz'u Hsi (1835-1908), the corrupt, capricious consort of the Hsien-feng Emperor. The Empress Dowager maneuvered herself into absolute power by allying with conservative officials and powerful court eunuchs, who helped her suppress badly needed reforms.

At a time when the West had acquired a taste for tea, silk, porcelain, and other fineries of China, the Chinese were weak, divided, and incapable of safeguarding their treasures. When the Western flotilla arrived in the nineteenth century to end China's "splendid isolation", China was introduced to the world community under the muzzle of the gun.

Supported by the British sovereign position in India and its supreme naval forces, the East India Company cultivated poppy plants in India and shipped opium to China in defiance of Chinese imperial prohibition. China went to war in October 1839, and lost. Hong Kong became a British colony. There followed one unequal treaty after another, until the major powers — Russia, Germany, Japan, France, Portugal, and Britain — all held Chinese territories as concessions in which Chinese sovereignty was waived and extraterritorial rights and privileges granted to the interlopers. Although the United States did not acquire territorial rights in China, traders participated in the opium trade alongside the British, and benefited consistently from advantages gained by the British through the unequal treaties.

The Chinese's early encounters with the unruly European sailors confirmed their opinion of foreigners as barbarians. Traditional Chinese esteem for the liberal arts and disdain for military matters further blinded them to the power of Western technology. They stubbornly refused to open the country to foreign trade. In 1860, England and France sent another expedition to Beijing to force the government to open North China and the Yangtze Valley to trade. The Chinese handled the delegates with brutality. The response was the invasion of the capital. The Emperor's favorite residence, the Summer Palace (Yuan Ming Yuan — Round Bright Garden) was burnt to the ground. England and France not only achieved their objectives, but received eight million dollars each from China for added indemnities. Russia pretended to mediate the conflict, and for its non-interference it received the confirmation of treaty advantages it had gained in Manchuria, including the Ussuri River territories. The Chinese town of Haishenwei became Vladivostok.

Japan defeated China in the war of 1894-1895. The treaty of Shimonoseki forced China to cede Taiwan and the Penghu Islands and to pay a huge indemnity, recognize Japan's hegemony over Korea and allow Japanese industries in four treaty ports.

The ignorance and corruption of the Dowager Empress's court fed upon the foreign intrusions, and engendered a hatred for foreigners that simmered, steamed, and finally boiled over into the court's fatal support for the Boxers. The Boxers claimed to hold sufficient magic in their bodies to withstand bullets and guns. The court sanctioned the massacre of missionaries in late 189l. By June 1900, the Boxers' siege of the legations brought on the punitive invasion of Beijing by twenty thousand troops representing eight foreign nations. In September 1900, the Forbidden City, the Emperor's residence, was sacked. Chinese and Manchus alike, regardless of social rank or guilt, suffered looting, rape and other atrocities. Priceless national treasures were carted off to Europe, vandalized or destroyed.

At the turn of the century, the Japanese and European scramble for territorial concessions had reached its zenith.

China was saved from dismemberment only through competition and jealousy for spoils among the invading powers.

Altogether, Chinese history in the early twentieth century was a study in national humiliation and defeat. Out of the chaos, stirred by internal strife and foreign aggression, rose Nationalism. Nationalists saw the need of a modern state to liberate China, not only from Manchu rule but also from foreign imperialism. Under the leadership of Dr. Sun Yat-sen (1866-1925), the first Republican government was born in 1911.

The Western democracies refused aid to the young revolutionary party. In the summer of 1918, the Soviet government announced that it was freely abandoning the privileges extracted under the Tsarist regime. It retained the territories in the Maritime provinces, but assisted the Chinese Nationalist party (Kuomintang) with money, training and military organization. The divisive interests of the workers and peasants on the one side, and the land-owning gentry, the businessmen, and the warlords on the other soon shattered the united purpose of the Nationalists. By 1930, the Kuomingtang, under the leadership of Chiang Kai-shek (1887-1975), had begun large-scale campaigns to extirpate the Communists.

Both Japan and China helped the Allied causes during World War I. The Paris Peace Conference of 1919, nonetheless, confirmed Japan's claims to the Shangdong Province, which it was already occupying. Massive student demonstrations broke out in Beijing and Shanghai to protest against Japan, the Allies and the inept Chinese government. This was the unifying Nationalist May fourth movement.

Japan seized Manchuria in September 1931 and established the puppet regime of Manchukuo in 1932. It soon annexed Jehol and cultivated opium in almost all its arable land. Opium became so plentiful in China that the poorest coolie could buy a day's supply for a few Chinese pennies.

Opium poisoned vital segments of Chinese society. Its government, industry, and economy were perverted by the addiction. Ambitious foreign elements wasted no opportunity to exploit the complicated struggle within the country. They played one power faction against another, supplying one warlord with arms, another with opium trade privileges, a third with ideologies. Communism, fascism, Nazism, Christianity, and democracy all claimed rival adherents.

The Communists and the Nationalists were nominally united after the Xian incident in December 1936. Faced with Japanese aggression and Communist unrest, Chiang had stated to Theodore White in an interview: "Japanese are a disease of the skin, and Communism a disease of the heart."

This novel begins in 1937, when Japan proclaimed China its exclusive protectorate. In July of the same year, Japan invaded China openly and the stage was set for World War II.

Glossary

A list of Chinese terms, idiomatic expressions and historical/political events referred to in the novel.

amahs — Female servants.

"Arise, those who not be slaves" — A patriotic song sung during the Second World War. It is now the national anthem of the People's Republic of China.

become a vinegar bottle — Become jealous.

bitter labor — A literal translation of "coolie". During the First World War, hundreds of thousands of Chinese "coolies" were sent to the European continent to dig trenches, build bunkers and clear minefields for the British and French armies.

bonsai — The Japanese term for the ancient Chinese art of penjing, or the cultivation of plants in shallow pots. These miniature trees are living sculptures.

book-fragrant — Learned.

bride price — Gifts of food, furniture, bedding, fineries and sometimes cash that the groom's family is expected to present to the bride's family. The troth is confirmed when the bride's family has accepted the gifts.

Brook-mei — It is the polite way of addressing Comely Brook as a younger-sister .

brown dwarves of East Ocean — The Japanese.

Bund — The waterfront in downtown Shanghai, located in the British concession.

bureaucracy of the Chin Empire (1644-1911) — The bureaucracy that for centuries, from one dynasty to the next, administered the Chinese government. Positions in the bureaucracy were acquired through competitive examinations. In theory, this was democratic, because the government consisted of people who have demonstrated cognitive skills and literary appreciation. In practice, however, the custom discouraged creativity and concentrated power among the rich who could afford the long years of study and cultivation of the mind.

"by cultivating oneself" — The popular quotation taken from "Ta Hsueh" (Great Learning), a chapter of the Li Chi (Book of Rites). It was attributed to Tseng Tzu, a disciple of Confucius.

catties — A standard of Chinese measurement, about 1.3 lbs.

cheongsam — A lady's straight sheath with a high mandarin collar, and a slit on each side reaching the knee to facilitate movement. The hemline of the sheath followed the fashions of the time. In the 1930s, it fell to just above the feet. Cheongsam is translated from the Cantonese dialect because it is the form popularly known in the States. In mandarin, the official dialect, it is called a chi pou.

chi — Breath, or the life-giving energy. The Chinese consider it the dominant principle of health.

Chiang Ching-kuo (1910 - 1988) — Son of Chiang Kai-shek by his first wife. Ching-kuo was sent to study in Moscow in 1925, when his father was the head of the Soviet-trained Kuomingtang army. He twice denounced his father's anti-Communist activities while in Soviet Russia. He returned to China in 1937 with a Russian wife, shortly after the Xian Incident, to help negotiate the integration of the

Chinese Communists into the Nationalists' anti-Japanese effort. In later years he claimed that he had been detained in Russia, and forced to denounce his father. He was the president of the Republic of China in Taiwan from 1975 until his death in January of 1988.

Chiang Kai-shek (1887-1975) — Ruler of China from 1928 to 1949. He remained president of the Chinese government in exile on Taiwan until his death. He was popularly referred to as the "Generalissimo.

Chou En-lai (1898-1976) — A prominent revolutionary who became a communist during the twenties while studying in France. He later served as the premier and foreign minister of the People's Republic of China.

concubine — In the old days, it was customary for Chinese men to have several wives. The first wife held a position of power while the other wives or concubines owed her services and deference. This is no longer legal in China.

cow eyes — Round eyes.

Chungking — the capital of the Republic of China during WWII.

cut off his pigtail — This act symbolized republican aspiration and rebellion against the Manchu emperor of the Chin Dynasty (1644-1911). The Manchu are a Chinese minority race that came from Manchuria. Throughout the Chin Dynasty, the majority "Han" people were required to follow Manchu custom and wear a pigtail to indicate their subjugation to the Manchus.

dim sum — Literally, "to dot" (dim) "the heart" (sum). It is an idiomatic expression referring to a meal of dumplings and small delicacies, eaten in the mornings or late evenings, before bedtime. Again, the Cantonese pronunciation is used here because it is popularly known in United States. In Mandarin, it would be pronounced "dian shin".

don't place sadness in your heart — Don't dwell on your sorrows.

double good fortune — A description of a woman who is both pregnant and has gained weight.

dragon eye — A fruit similar to a leechi nut. It is mustard colored, round and has a smooth skin.

Dragon Well tea — A green tea produced near Hangzhou. The top grade of this tea is considered the finest in aroma and flavor. Connoisseurs recommend that the tea be brewed with clear water that is several degrees below the boiling point. Steeping it for too long affects the delicate color and turns the infusion bitter.

drink vinegar —Be jealous.

dumb egg — Stupid person.

East Ocean Devils — The Japanese.

first moon — The first month of the lunar calendar, popularly used in China. In the third book, Righteous Virtue dates his letter to his wife at the end, according to Chinese custom and the lunar calendar, but in his English letter to his daughters, he writes the date at the beginning according to the Western solar calendar.

Five Classics and the Four Books — These are the books of Confucian scholarship. The five classics are the Book of Song, Book of History, Book of Change, Book of Rites and the Spring and Autumn Annals. The Four Books are the Analects of Confucius, Mencius, The Great Learning and The Doctrine of the Mean.

foreign concessions — Chinese territories held by foreign powers. In the nineteenth and early twentieth Centuries, the West acquired a taste for tea, silk, porcelain, lacquerware, and other fineries of China. Smug and unable to appreciate the advantages of Western technology, China did not want to buy anything from the Western powers. Britain shipped opium to sell in China, in defiance of Chinese imperial prohibition. China went to war in October 1839 and lost. Hong Kong became a British colony. There followed one unequal treaty after another, until the major powers — Russia, Germany, Japan, France, Portugal and Britain — all held Chinese territories as "concessions.". Colonialism gave the western nations economic advantages in trade, political and military power to protect their interests and religious opportunities to proselytize. Until Japan bombed Pearl Harbor, Japan did not consider itself at war with the Europeans. Therefore, the inhabitants in the foreign concessions enjoyed the rights of non-belligerents.

Fragrant harbor — Hong Kong.

gas car — Automobile.

go down — Warehouse.

Golden Rule of the Mean — *Chung Yung*, one of the four books of Confucian learning. In it, Confucius taught a humanism that exalted the paramount virtues of filial piety, moderation (the golden rule of the mean), compromise, patience, tolerance, pacifism, and reverence for the aged, learning, experience, and ancestors. These are considered essential traits of gentlemanly behavior.

Greater East Asia Co-prosperity sphere — A Japanese proposal set forth in 1938 to induce Chinese co-operation in creating a new economic order based upon Japanese technological know how, and Chinese labor / resources. The plan proposed to expel European influences and left no room for Chinese independence. The "co-prosperity sphere" was a well known slogan in Japanese occupied China during World War II.

Have you eaten your rice? — How are you? A popular form of greeting.

heart and liver — precious.

Hong Kong — An island south of Kwangtung Province, in southern China. It became a British crown colony in 1841, after the Chinese lost the opium war. Before the Second World War, many Chinese thought Hong Kong would be a safe haven from the Japanese.

Hwangpo — A channel of the Yangtze River, where Shanghai is situated.

I know your heart — I understand you.

I look to the east and west — I hesitate.

Jade Emperor — The chief God of heaven according to Chinese beliefs.

Jade-mei — Younger sister Purple Jade. It is civil to call one's wife, a sister.

Jei-jei — Older sister.

jen — Benevolence, the foundation of Chinese humanism. This Confucian precept is similar to the Western concept of charity. However, "jen" is focused on man as the center of universe, not God. The cornerstone of this humanism is filial piety. In Hsiao Ching, or Book of Filial Piety, Confucius said, "The Superior Man teaches filial piety in order that man may respect all those who are fathers in the world; he teaches brotherly love in the younger brother, in order that man may respect all those who are elder brothers in the world."

jump house — Hopscotch.

kang pai — dry cup. It is a toast, and a gesture of good fellowship to shout kang pai as one tosses down a drink, and then holds the cup upside down.

Kempetai — Japanese secret police.

Kwan Ying Buddha — The goddess of mercy.

Lan Tao Island — An island off the southern coast of China, about an hour's boat ride from Hong Kong.

legislative council — In the novel, it is a regional body of elders, or prominent citizens who mediate on local affairs.

Long March — The eight thousand-mile trek that Communists undertook in 1935. Upon the death of Dr. Sun Yat-sen, Chiang Kai-shek gained control of the Kuomintang. He expelled the Communists from the Nationalist party. By 1930, he began undertaking large-scale campaigns against them. In 1934, advised by General Von Seeckt of the German army, he embarked upon the fifth campaign to extirpate the Communists. To avoid total annihilation from this well organized attack, Mao Tse-tung (1893-1976) led one hundred thousand Communist troops in a withdrawal from Kiangsi. The communists trekked through five provinces, reaching the barren, northern Shensi Province a year later. Only thirty thousand survived the hazardous journey, harassed all the way by the pursuing enemy. This long march became the legend of the new People's Republic of China. Most leaders of the new republic came from the survivors of the march.

lord — Master of the house.

M-ma — Mother.

Manchukuo — The name of the puppet state established by Japan in the Chinese province of Manchuria in 1931. In 1934, Japan transformed Manchukuo into an empire by enthroning the heir to the Manchu Dynasty. It had become a staging ground for Japanese invasion of the Chinese mainland.

Manchuria — Land on the Northeastern part of China, abutting Korea and Russia. The pine forests and rich mineral deposits of the area provided an industrial basin coveted by all the neighbors. In China - A Short Cultural History, C.P. Fitzgerald writes: "The name, Manchuria, is unknown to the Chinese and Manchu languages. It is a foreign term coined by Europeans . . . . After the Manchu conquest, the three provinces of Manchuria were collectively known as 'the three eastern provinces.' Manchukuo, the name given to Manchuria during the Japanese controlled puppet regime 1931-1945, was merely a translation into Chinese of the word, 'Manchuria'.

Manchus — A Chinese minority from Manchuria. They were the ruling class of the last Chinese Dynasty (Chin 1644-1911). They adopted the Chinese form of government, and were totally assimilated into Chinese culture. Today, they're indistinguishable from other Chinese.

Mao Tse-tung (1893-1976) — The leading Chinese communist revolutionary who established the People's Republic of China.

May 4th movement of 1919 — Massive student protests in Shanghai against Western Imperialism after the Western Powers met in Paris and awarded the German possessions in Shantung Province to Japan, discounting the Chinese "bitter labor" contribution to the Allied forces during World War I.

Mei-mei — younger sister.

Mencius — A fourth century B.C. philosopher who is accepted as an orthodox interpreter of Confucianism. Mencius reaffirmed filial piety (hsiao) as the foundation of society. He taught the fundamental goodness and educability of man, and that the mandate of Heaven (tien ming) is conferred upon the ruler when he practices benevolence (jen) and righteousness (i).

meridians — Invisible channels that lie at different depths in the human body. These are the pathways of chi used in acupuncture. The meridians do not correspond to the nervous system, and they have no anatomical structure. Modern investigations seem to indicate that the flow pattern of the meridian is similar to the patient's description of pain sensations. The acupuncture points are located along the length of the main meridians in carefully defined places. By inserting a needle into the appropriate points and twirling it, the blockage in the channel is cleared and the free flow of chi restored.

Middle Kingdom — China. The term conveys the understanding that China was the cultural center of the civilized world.

Monkey King — A rebellious monkey from a sixteenth century Chinese novel, Journey To The West. The Monkey King upset the order of heaven and earth to assert his independence. He is well loved by Chinese children.

moongate — A circular opening in a wall. It is often lined with tiles or lacquered wood, usually without a door.

Mme. Chiang Kai-shek (Soong Mei-ling 1897-2003) — One of the famous Soong sisters. The first sister, Soong Ai-ling married H.H.Kung, a direct descendant of Confucius. Kung later became the finance minister of the Nationalist government. The second sister Soong Chin-ling married the father of the Chinese revolution, Dr. Sun Yat-sen. Mei-ling introduced Chiang Kai-shek to Western culture and Christianity. She was educated at Wellesley College, and was a spokeswoman for China during World War II. She moved to New York after her husband's death in 1975 and died in 2003 at age 105.

my heart and liver — My precious darling.

Nanking — The capital of a united China during the Republican era 1928-1937. At the end of World War II from 1946-1949, Nanking resumed its status as capital of Chiang Kai-shek's Nationalist government.

new territories — A portion of Kowloon peninsula bordering the Kwangtung province in southern China. It was leased from China in 1898 for 99 years.

New Year's goodie boxes — The box or bag containing foods that symbolize all the good wishes for the new year. Apples — peace, lotus seed — blessings, olives — long life, kumquats, tangerines, dried lychees and dragon eyes — wealth.

New Year's money — Money bestowed on children and servants on the Chinese (lunar) New Year. The money is handed out in red envelopes . Everyone celebrated his or her birthday at New Year's.

Nine Rivulets and Eighteen Gullies — A famous tourist attraction in the West Lake region of Hangzhou, where many small causeways are joined by tea gardens and stone bridges. Willows droop over the water 's edge along the walks. Marco Polo considered Hangzhou one of the most civilized and idyllic places on earth.

"Oh-me-to-fo" — A Buddhist chant to the Goddess of Mercy.

old turtle — A dense and obstinate person.

one-foot kick — A servant who does everything: cooking, cleaning, washing etc.

open your heart — Relax.

pedicab — A tricycle pedaled up front by its driver, with a hooded passenger carriage in the back.

personal maid — "mui-tse" in Cantonese. It translates literally to mean "little sister". Poor families often sold their daughters into rich homes to serve as housemaids or personal maids to the mistresses of the house. These maids did not receive a salary but were given money, clothes and personal items during the holidays. In some unethical families, the maids were exploited. In general, except in dire circumstances, the maids were never re-sold. They were married off with dowries when they reached marriageable age. Since the maids' fortunes closely followed those of their mistresses', they often became the mistresses' confidantes and closest allies in the large, multi-generational homes. This "mui tse" system persisted well into the twentieth Century.

pillow book — A sex manual.

place it in the heart — Dwell on it.

Po-po — An old woman or mother's mother.

reaching the clouds and rain — Reaching orgasm.

red-eyed monster — Jealousy.

rousing heat — A fete of fun and festivities.

scholar — A person belonging to the highest class in the traditional, Confucian society. It is the scholar who enters official life, and governs the country according to the tenets of Confucian humanism. John King Fairbank in his The United States and China observed: "As a code of personal conduct Confucianism tried to make each individual a moral being, ready to act on ideal grounds, to uphold virtue against human error, especially against evil rulers. There were many Confucian scholars of moral grandeur, uncompromising foes of tyranny. But their reforming zeal, the dynamics of their creed, aimed to reaffirm and conserve the traditional polity, not to change its fundamental premises." The scholar may be poor and live the life of an ascetic, but the merchant and the gentry most often court him for his wisdom and prestige.

second koo-ma — father's second younger sister.

self-coming water — Water from a faucet.

shai shai — thank you.

Shih ba-ba — A polite form to address an elder. "Ba-ba" indicates he is the father's older brother even though he may not be related by blood.

silkworms and mulberry leaves — Silkworms feed on mulberry leaves. Therefore, the hatching of their eggs must coincide with the growth of mulberry trees. Silk production is a centuries-old industry in China. The adult female silkworm moth lays between 300 and 500 eggs on sheets of paper provided by the breeders. The larvae (silkworms) that hatch from the eggs look like tiny ants initially, and then turn pale and worm like reaching a maximum length of about three inches in forty-five days. The worms weave cocoons of a continuous silken thread. The cocoons are most often white in color, but occasionally, yellow, pink or light green. Usually the thread is unwound intact for commercial use after killing the pupa in steam or hot water. Many Chinese children cultivate the worms as a hobby or care for them like pets.

Sing Song girls — Girls of ill repute who make their living by entertaining men.

skywell — A small courtyard attached to the front or back of a house. It is surrounded by high walls on all sides and looks like a well from the sky.

sleeping with willows and lying with flowers — Being on intimate terms with women of ill repute.

soaked in vinegar — Very jealous.

Soong, T.V.(1894-1971) — A brother of Mme. Chiang Kai-shek. Soong was educated at Harvard, and at various points served as the minister of finance and the minister of defense in the Republic of China.

sour meat — Lewd.

spirit screen wall — In a Chinese traditional house, a free standing wall is built facing the front gate. The wall was supposed to prevent evil spirits from entering the house.

spread what is not — Gossip.

sprouted good fortune — Gained weight.

steel organ — Piano.

stir up what is not — Cause trouble.

Sun Yat-sen Dr. (1866-1925) — Leader of the Chinese Revolution who established a republican government in 1911. The Chinese honor him as the George Washington of China.

Sun Yat-sen suit — The present day 'Mao suit'. Instead of the traditional Chinese robe that some men found comfortable but inconvenient, some Chinese wore this suit to indicate modern Nationalism.

swallowing bitterness — Suffer.

swatting a fly on a tiger's head — Doing a very dangerous thing.

Tai-tai — Mistress or Mrs.

Taihu rocks — Rocks that are most prized for garden designs. They are limestone boulders found on the bottom of Lake Tai, west of Suzhou. The rocks were eroded by the water and sand of the lake giving them the look of miniature mountains, or natural sculptures of birds, animals or gods.

Tang poets — Poets of the golden age of poetry in China during the three centuries of the Tang Dynasty (618-907).

Tang-ko — "Tang" indicates a paternal relationship, and "ko" means older brother.

Tao Te Ching — The best known classic of Taoism. The true authorship of Tao Te Ching is unknown, although it is popularly attributed to Lao Tzu (circa 590 B.C.) In China, a Short Cultural History, C.P. Fitzgerald wrote, "The Taoist represented a revolt from the trammels of a decadent society. They preached a renunciation of the world, a return to primitive simplicity . . . . The sage should himself find the Tao (the Way), and then by his passive example lead men to follow him. . . . Only the sage could find the Tao. It was aristocratic and necessarily exclusive."

third day ceremony — According to ancient customs, the formal announcement of birth and the first bath are performed on the third day.

Three Character Book — A beginner reader in the Chinese classics for children. All verses are composed of rhyming couplets of three characters.

Tiger-Run Spring — A spring located on the grounds of a monastery close to the city of Hangzhou. The clear water from the spring is renowned as a perfect mate for the superb Lung Ching (Dragon's Well) tea.

to lose face — To lose the good regards of society.

T'ung Ming Hui — An alliance, mostly of young people, which was formed under the leadership of Dr. Sun Yat-sen. It was dedicated to the Republican cause, and the overthrowing of the Manchu Dynasty. Later, the T'ung Ming Hui was amalgamated into the Kuomingtang, which is still the dominant political party in Taiwan.

wasting mouth water —Talking too much.

Western ocean barbarians — Westerners.

Wind-and-water men — Geomancers, people who practice divination according to the lines of land, water and winds. They are consulted for important events such as marriages and building houses and graves. Westerners know it as fung-shui, the Cantonese pronunciation for Wing and Water.

wind organ — Organ.

wood shaving water — A viscous liquid obtained by soaking wood shavings. It was used to make hair shiny and manageable.

Xian incident — See "Zhang Hsueh-liang". Chiang Kai-shek referred to the Xian incident as the beginning of Communist victory. Most Westerners find Marshal Zhang's behavior quixotic and inexplicable. Yet, Marshal

Zhang was behaving in the most inspired Confucian tradition of the scholar official who braves torture and death to inveigh the Emperor on his misrule, and lead him on to a course of virtue.

yin and yan — The male and female principles of the universe. Yin stands for the feminine, dampness and the dark side of things. Yan stands for the masculine, the sunny and bright side of things. The balance of yin and yan, and the cyclical nature of the universe is basic to Chinese belief.

Zhang Hsueh-liang (1901—2001) — Zhang is the ping ying spelling for Chang. He was the son of the Manchurian warlord Chang Tso-lin. The elder Chang was assassinated by the Japanese in 1928. The young Marshal brought his Manchurian troops under the Chinese Nationalist flag after the Xian incident, and he was recognized as the leader of the Northeastern (Manchurian) forces. When the Generalissimo came to Xian to ensure the Northeastern (Manchurian) forces' role in his sixth campaign to exterminate the Communists. Zhang Hueh-liang kidnapped Chiang Kai-shek, and forced him to join with the Chinese Communists in a united effort to drive the Japanese invaders out of Manchuria. On December 1936, the Generalissimo agreed to form a coalition. In classic Confucian tradition, the young marshal returned to Nanking with Chang Kai-shek to give the Generalissimo face and to ensure the success of the coalition. The marshal had been kept under house arrest by the Nationalist government until both Chiang Kai-shek and his son Chiang Ching-kuo were dead. He visited the United States in 1991. On June 14, Harrison Salisbury reported "Young Marshal Zhang Xueliang has embarked on a new crusade — to bring Beijing and Taiwan into a unified China."

Amy S. Kwei — A graduate of St. John's University (BA) and Vassar College (MA). She is retired from teaching in Bennett College and Dutchess Community College. She has twice won the Talespinner Competition sponsored by the Poughkeepsie Journal. One of the judges, Michael Korda, commented: "Has a very strong cultural appeal, and gives the reader a quick, instant understanding of Chinese values, and how they differ from our own. As well, it is simply written, perhaps the best written of all the stories here."

Her young adult novel *Intrigue in the House of Wong* was published in 2009. Her short stories and essays have appeared in Prima Materia, Short Story International, CAAC Inflight magazine, Westchester Family, Dutchess Magazine, The Country, and Dutchess Mature Life. Andover Green published one of her children's stories in Six Inches to England.

Amy is working on *Under the Red Moon*— a sequel to *A Concubine for the Family*. An excerpt from the book was published as a short story in the Skollie magazine of the Aspen Writers Foundation.

For more copies of the book, please order from the following venues:

Your neighborhood bookstore

Amazon.com

Kindle. iPad, Nook, and other digital readers

CPSIA information can be obtained at www.ICGtesting.com
Printed in the USA
LVOW041447231012

304091LV00001B/52/P

9 780981 5499